Illustrated Cosmic Monopole

Time Crystal Volume One

Wyken Seagrave

Penny Press Ltd
176 Greendale Road
Coventry CV5 8AY
United Kingdom
sales@pennypress.co.uk
www.timecrystal.co.uk

Copyright © Penny Press Ltd 2016
All rights reserved.
No part of this publication may be reproduced, stored in a retrieval system, or transmitted in any form or by any means, without the prior permission in writing of the publisher. Nor may this work be circulated in any form of binding or cover other than that in which it is published and without a similar condition, including this condition, being imposed upon the subsequent purchaser.

The right of Wyken Seagrave to be identified as the author of this work has been asserted in accordance with the UK Copyright, Designs and Patents Act 1988

All characters and events in this publication, other than those clearly in the public domain, are fictitious. Any resemblance to real persons, living or dead, is purely coincidental.

British Library Cataloguing in Publication Data:
A catalogue record for this book is available from the British Library.

ISBN 978-1871281361 (eBook)
ISBN 978-1871281286 (paperback)

These reviews of the first edition of Cosmic Monopole were published on Amazon.

Truly bizarre, utterly unique

I've never read a novel quite like this before. The author takes you on an exciting adventure full of unforgettable and vivid imagery. Solidly written with each character's personality shining through. If you find physics fascinating you will not be disappointed by the author's keen intellect and clear understanding of this most challenging (for me anyway) scientific subject. This is not a novel I will forget anytime soon, I would highly recommend it.
Andrewly

Very imaginative tale

Anybody interested in a very imaginative and engrossing sci fi story needs to check this one out. I have been reading sci fi for decades and this story has elements that surprise me which is very unusual considering the number of novels and stories I have over the years.
ric freeman

A fascinating book

An amazing book - I literally could not put it down... and I was reading it in Acrobat! Not the easiest format but it didn't matter, I wanted to know what happened next each time I had to leave it. I have a huge interest in The Hadron Collider so it was a foregone conclusion that I would enjoy this book and I wasn't disappointed. A great story - one that I can not wait to read the next episode of - with very complex characters and even more complex relationships. The author manages to combine his obvious extensive knowledge of the subject with an incredible imagination. I loved it!
Vicki

Wyken Seagrave

Wyken Seagrave is an author, scientist, software engineer, teacher, lecturer, inventor, science communicator, publisher and entrepreneur. The history of the universe (sometimes called "Big History") is his lifelong obsession. He is the author of the History of the Universe website at http://historyoftheuniverse.com/ and several books about the subject.

Other Works by Wyken Seagrave

The Time Tunnel - Time Crystal Volume Two
  http://timetunnel.org.uk
History of the Universe
  www.historyoftheuniverse.com
B4A - Rapid Android App Development using BASIC:
  http://basic4android.info
Time Crystal website
  www.timecrystal.co.uk
Halloween Magic & Silly Science
  http://pennypress.co.uk/?page_id=11
Wyken's diary
  www.wykenseagrave.co.uk
Wyken's page on Amazon
  http://amzn.to/1M7oBNF
Wyken's page on Goodreads
  http://bit.ly/1JVKuNm
Wyken's page on Shelfari
  http://bit.ly/1JVKGMJ
Cosmic Monopole Web Page
  http://cosmicmonopole.co.uk
Subscribe to Wyken's newsletter
  http://bit.ly/1r2KbXq

Table of Contents

List of Illustrations

Author's Preface

Everyone who works at **CERN**[1] remembers 19 September 2008, the day when a **quench** in the magnets of the **Large Hadron Collider** (LHC) led to an explosive release of helium, causing huge damage which took over a year to repair.

But nobody in CERN, or anywhere else on Earth, remembers the even greater disaster which occurred on 5 April 2012, the day which would later become known as **Crystal Day**.

This book, and subsequent ones in the Time Crystal series, will attempt to tell as accurately as possible the true story of how the innocent scientists at CERN not only broke the LHC but also almost destroyed the whole universe. This series will also explain how the universe was ultimately fixed and why nobody on Earth remembers anything about it.

I have received an incredulous reception from all those participants to whom I have shown this book, none of whom has any recollection of these events, and I fully understand the doubts which they (and others) have raised about the authenticity of the account given here. Moreover, I have to admit that, since none of the participants can tell me what happened, I have had to fill in many of the details as best I can. I make no excuse for this: it was the only way of putting together a coherent account of these incredible and truly historic events so they would be accessible to the general reader.

Indeed, if I had not obtained the written records of some of the major participants, I too would not have believed any of it to be possible. However, I maintain that the bulk of the story gives an accurate description of the events which occurred before, during

---

[1] Emboldened words have entries in the Glossary.

and after Crystal Day based upon the documentary evidence. How I came by these documents will be revealed in one of the later books in this series.

To help the reader get to know the people involved, I have included a list of the Principal Participants, and to aid the non-scientist I have included a Glossary and a Bibliography.

Please feel free to review this and the other books in the Time Crystal series, either on Amazon or on the book's website timecrystal.co.uk

I read all reviews. Thank you for your feedback.

Wyken Seagrave

Wyken Seagrave

Acknowledgements

For technical advice and information I would like to thank:

Angel.Aura, Archives of the State of Geneva, CERN Fire and Rescue Service, CERN Press Office, Colum de Sales Murphy, Gene E. Benzenberg, Jez Palmer, Kewal (Kev) Ghag, Nebo Dimitrijevic, retired members of the United Nations staff in Geneva (especially D.), scientists from CERN and universities around the world and volunteers in England, Susan Law and Transports Publics Genevois.

Any remaining errors of fact are entirely my responsibility.

For the advice, constructive criticism, suggestions, education and moral support at various times over the years:

Aisha Ravat, Becky Watson, Capucine, Chris Hoskins, Chrispenycate, Elaine Williamson, Eloisia Grant, Emburmak, Evelyne Brillon, Fill Up With Silence, Flo Swann, Frida, Gabriele Kerber, Ian Turner, Janice and Hannah Yelland-Sutcliffe, John Jarrold, Jrudder, Karen Milner, Kelvin Brown, Kesaira, Lauren 'Poppinfresh' Gallagher, Melanie Carty, members of the Coventry and Warwick Words Writers Groups, Pam Dunston, Pat Brown, Precise Calibre, R.J.Keith, Ross M, Roswitha, Emburmak, Tehun Lee, Tina Durkin, Ulla, Vicki, Yvette Bessels and Zubi-Ondo.

Apologies to anyone I have missed.

And finally I thank the fathers of CERN for their wisdom in decreeing that "The Organization shall have no concern with work for military requirements and the results of its experimental and theoretical work shall be published or otherwise made generally available."

Wyken Seagrave

Michael's Diary: Cosmic Monopole

The Son of Beeing

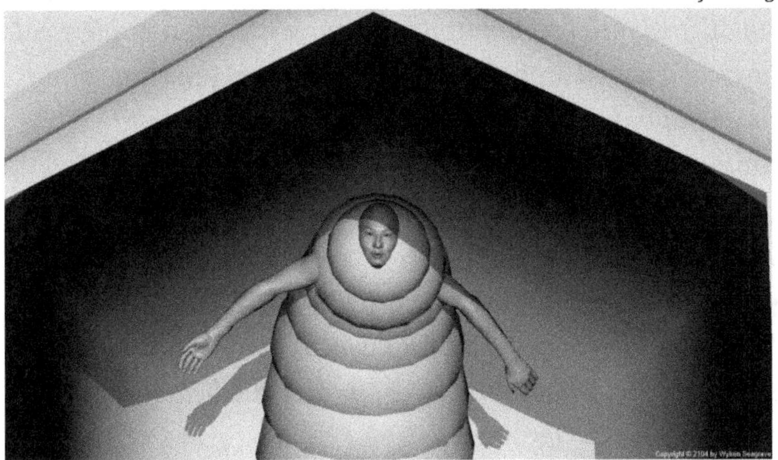

And so at last I come to you, blessed Monopole, seed of the becoming, to whom this diary is most humbly dedicated. I am dictating this to the Princess Uskabellu in total secrecy, with instructions to reveal it to no-one. This work is not just an act of homage to you, Oh glorious Monopole. Its principal aim is to help me organise my thoughts as I contemplate the mystery of your current location; for it is beyond doubt that resolving this problem is the key to the fate of the Universe.

Your story begins in the skies above the domain known as Entroilia. At that time you still took the form of a cosmic seed. During the annual mating of Her Imperial Majesty Queen Karolinda, an unidentified drone did fertilise one of her eggs with you, thereby creating the Cosmic Egg and giving impetus to the unfolding history recounted with devotion in my preceding chronicles. Once inside the living egg, you became manifest as the object later known to mankind as "the Cosmic Monopole".

As I explained in Chapter 1 of my first book, which Uskabellu has deposited in the Sedtia Library, when the Egg subdivided into incompatible regions with different physical laws, you were trapped at the junction between three of these regions which mankind would eventually call "universes".

Each region obeyed different fundamental laws of physics. You must have felt as confused as a child finding itself on the disputed border of three nations, all speaking different languages and obeying mutually incompatible laws. You shared aspects of all three domains but you belonged to none.

From your vantage point between these regions, no doubt you surveyed them with much distress, for clearly you were different from the swarms of other particles flickering momentarily into existence around you in the intense heat of the complex sequence of events known to mankind, in his simplicity, as "the Big Bang". For one thing, the lives of those particles were short whereas you, blessed Monopole, you endured over time. And even ten seconds later, when all those others had settled into stable configurations, you were still obviously special and apparently unique.

For, of all the particles surrounding you, Oh Cosmic Monopole—may your name forever be venerated in the minds of all living creatures—you alone possessed that magical property which mankind would later call a "magnetic charge".

True, many of those others had an "electric charge". Of these the commonest were the large heavy protons with their positive charge and the tiny, cloud-like electrons with their negative one, although some particles such as the neutron had no charge at all.

And true, some of their movements resulted in the creation of small magnetic fields around them. But not one of them had the magical property of a permanent magnetic charge, the single magnetic pole which gave you the wonderful name "Monopole".

As I have explained hitherto, as time went on, the Cosmos expanded and the energy density fell to levels below which particles could no longer be created. From now on, their number was more or less constant. Occasionally, two of the smaller ones would collide and fuse together to make a single large unit. Sometimes large ones would split apart into several fragments, but the great age of particle creation was over. Later still, the opposite charges of protons and electrons attracted them together and they stuck into tiny objects called "atoms". The cosmos was now full of a simple atomic gas.

But none of this was of any interest to you, Oh majestic Monopole! You still hovered on the boundary between three regions, unable to decide which one should be your home.

There were magnetic fields within these domains, lines of force which reached endlessly around space in wildly gyrating coils and spirals, loops and bands. As the Cosmos expanded, these fields interacted with charged particles, both pushing them around and in turn being themselves shaped by their movement.

And you too were affected by these fields, Oh Monopole. You were unable to maintain your position on that narrow border between the three regions. The lines of force pulled you by chance into one of them, the one which mankind would eventually call "the Universe", and henceforth you found yourself trapped therein, losing contact with the uncounted other domains in the wider Cosmos.

For a long time, you drifted listlessly around your new home. Far away there appeared tiny splashes of light which men now call "galaxies". Hundreds of billions of them traced out walls and filaments around vast dark oceans of almost empty space. But for all this time, Oh Monopole, you remained isolated within one of these spaces, drifting restlessly, pulled by weak magnetic fields, as if searching for another particle like yourself.

After a billion years or so, a winding line of magnetic force drew you closer and closer to one of these glowing galaxies and finally you found yourself inside. Wandering through this island of gas, you discovered the source of the light. It contained billions of those glowing globes of plasma which men call "stars". These too had magnetic fields and occasionally you would be trapped inside one of these nuclear fusion reactors, where the force of gravity was forging smaller particles together into larger ones and, almost incidentally, converting matter into radiation. This travelled out to the surface of the ball of gas and finally seeped out as starlight.

No doubt you searched inside the star, at first with great excitement, hoping to find another monopole like yourself. But when you found only the same particles you had seen in the Big Bang your disappointment must have been intense. You did, however, discover something entirely new. Occasionally, one of the protons around you was able to adhere to your outer surface. Although these new companions invoked in you no interest, nevertheless you began slowly to grow.

After a few million years of fusion, the star where you lived ran out of fuel and the nuclear power plant at its centre shut down. Normally a star dies quietly but your star happened to be larger than average. It exploded into a spectacular "supernova", fusing smaller particles together and creating entirely new species of heavy particles such as you had never seen before.

This must have attracted your interest, for surely you wondered whether any of these new particles had a magnetic pole, like yourself. But you had no chance to find out, for the explosion which made these particles also spewed them out into the Galaxy as a shower of pollution. You too were ejected from the dying star and you continued to wander the Galaxy, observing new stars forming around you from this polluted gas. Eventually these stars also died and released more heavy particles. This pollution finally became so bad that particles were able to stick together to produce grains of dust. Dust absorbs starlight and the Galaxy began to grow dark from the pollution released by generations of dead stars.

For the next thirteen billion years, you wandered around the Galaxy, poor disconsolate Monopole, moving in and out of stars, carried along by the lines of magnetic force. An observer might have imagined you searching these clouds of dust, picking over the debris of dead stars, hoping perhaps to find another like yourself, searching among the remains for a brother or even a distant cousin with whom you could identify. But your hopes were destined to be utterly thwarted, for the new particles created inside stars were merely larger accumulations of the protons and neutrons you already knew and despised. No doubt you felt you did not belong here, unrelated to the particles among which you found yourself, a stranger in a strange place, trapped by the Galaxy's magnetic fields.

You probably did not notice that, on the surface of these grains of dust, smaller atoms were bonding together into little groups called "molecules", and so the first appearance of water in the Universe almost certainly passed without remark. But you surely noticed that your galactic prison was changing.

For the whole Galaxy was drifting through space and slowly rotating. As it drifted, it occasionally collided with a neighbouring galaxy, creating new showers of stars. Even more important was the effect of its rotation. The resulting centrifugal force pushed its equatorial regions outwards while gravity pulled the northern and southern sections inwards. These forces reshaped the Galaxy's structure, turning it from a large ball into a flat, plate-shaped disc with a slightly bulging centre. Henceforth, new stars would form within this disc. Furthermore the new stars would be organised not at random but in several narrow bands which spiralled elegantly outwards from the central region.

These stars were created from the debris of gas and dust left over from older supernovae, the pollution which had *accumulated over the aeons. When finally humans looked up into the night sky, from their position upon a tiny planet within the disc, they saw it as a thin band of glowing light smeared across the heavens. This band came to be called the "Milky Way" and eventually, when astronomers worked out its true nature, it gave its name to the whole Galaxy, the "Milky Way Galaxy".*

Two million years ago, Oh Monopole, following a magnetic line of force, you happened to pass very close to a middle-aged star, the one later given the name "the Sun". It was surrounded by a small array of planets spread out in a flat disc around the star. At first you hardly noticed the third one out from the centre, the little rocky planet which mankind calls "Earth". Orbited by a single moon, this rocky speck in space did not at first seem very interesting. Only its beautiful blue colour and its unusual oxygen-rich atmosphere distinguished it from the millions of other planets which you had wandered past during your long life.

You had occasionally visited planets before. There were many of them scattered around in the Galaxy. Small ones such as this were mostly formed from the heavy atomic debris left over from previous supernovae, atoms such as oxygen, silicon and iron collected together in dirty little balls of rock. You had sometimes even passed through these objects, drawn in by their magnetic fields, but inside they were just as boring as everywhere else, same old particles, nothing you could call a relative.

The exact source of the line of magnetic force which drew you towards this planet has not been established with certainty. It might have been a chance configuration of the solar magnetic field. More likely it was the planet's own field, originating in its iron core, which pulled you inward. In either case, you began to descend rapidly towards the surface.

And so it was that on the morning of April 5, 2012, you were finally swept along by the Earth's magnetic field, Oh Monopole, and approached the continent known as "Europe". Plunging down through the thin cloud, you descended rapidly towards a lake trapped between two mountain ranges. You might have been curious about this lake for you had never been close to liquid water before. Water ice yes, that was common enough upon dust grains in the Galaxy, but it was rare to find a planet which was at just the right distance from its star that water would neither boil nor freeze but remain as a liquid. You might even have hoped to plunge into this exotic medium, this curving lake, to explore its properties and probe its hidden depths.

But, as you approached the end of the lake, a long finger terminating in a small city called Geneva, you were suddenly pulled off course by a local magnetic field and you swerved towards the west. As you flew rapidly over streets swarming with shoppers and traffic, over aeroplanes heading for the airport, you must surely have been surprised at the difference between this and the other planets, sterile and lifeless, which you had visited during your long existence.

Did you, perhaps, notice a silver BMW driving up the long straight road, the Route de Meyrin, along whose path you flew? Did you note how it slowed as it approached the tunnel, or see it change lanes to follow the little road over the hill?

Probably not. And even if you had noticed the car, there was no way for you to know that your fate would be intimately connected with that of the occupants.

Geneva and Environs

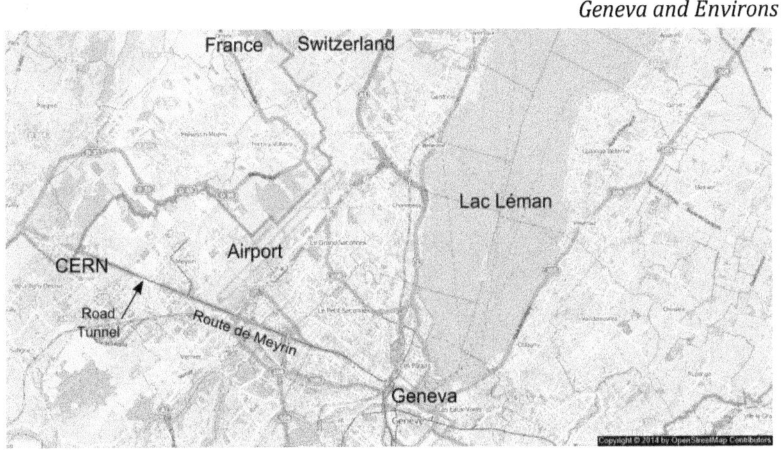

Episode 1 Arrivals

Approaching Meyrin Village

'Don't worry if nobody loves you…'

Alone in the back of her BMW, Ambassador Brigit O'Brien's heart sank as the first line of Ireland's entry for the forthcoming Eurovision Song Contest, sung a semitone flat, drifted over the car's front passenger seat. She looked up to see the back of her daughter's ginger head wobbling.

Catriona was holding up a photograph of Kieran Gable, plastered across the front of the Irish teen magazine she had brought from Dublin. Then she turned to the driver. 'Thanks for coming this way, Sam,' Catriona said.

'That's okay, Catty,' Sam said. 'I know how you hate tunnels.'

Brigit had no idea what they were talking about. As Sam drove them out of Geneva, she had been concentrating on the "United Nations Commission on Sustainable Development Report of the Inter-Sessional Briefing on Sustainable Consumption and Production". It was not easy reading. In fact it was as mind-numbing as a hundred other documents she had tried and failed to understand in the past few weeks, but this one was more important, as she had to give Ireland's response to it at a conference this afternoon. She had just found her place again when the second line of the song warbled around the car, this time even flatter.

'...And nobody seems to care...'

Brigit slammed the heavy document onto her lap and glared at her daughter through the driver's rear-view mirror, forcing her expression into an angry frown. Catriona didn't seem to notice. She was obviously imagining herself on stage. For a moment, Brigit stared at her daughter's face, a perfect oval poised on a long, elegant neck. Her green eyes were radiating with excitement as she stared at the magazine through the star-bursts of her gorgeous long black eyelashes beneath the twin arches of her strong, dark eyebrows. The untameable jungle of her ginger hair pulsed and swirled around her excited face.

At fourteen, Brigit thought proudly, my daughter is already growing into a beautiful young woman. She was about to scream "SHUT UP" when a brilliant idea suddenly struck her, and she began to grin at her own audacity. She caught a glimpse of her own face in the driver's rear-view mirror, thick blond curls framing a heart-shaped face, eyes perfectly made-up to reveal their beauty and hide the wrinkles and dark shadows which had spread beneath them during the past two months of sleepless nights studying meaningless UN documents. She quickly let the broad smile drop from her ruby-red lips, forced her most devastating scowl into its place and leaned sideways. Once she found her target in the mirror, the happy smiling face of her husband Sam, she fired the silent but deadly missile of her scowl directly at him. Unfortunately, he was concentrating on the road and her lethal weapon drifted past, unnoticed.

Need some heavier weaponry, Brigit thought.

'...When everyone tells you you're ugly...' Catriona was a Eurovision star, singing her heart out for Ireland before the TV cameras of an astonished world.

Avoiding the tunnel, which carried most of the cars under the Meyrin village hill, Sam followed the tram tracks over its brow. They were on the outskirts of Geneva now, looking over a little valley of farm fields. A long tram was slowly rolling up the hill towards them. Brigit could see a long range of mountains, the Juras, spanning the horizon ahead of them, their peaks sprinkled with a dusting of icing-sugar left over from last winter's snow. At their foot, on the far side of the valley, a large brown dome came into view, a Christmas pudding someone had dropped onto the green tablecloth of Switzerland's peaceful countryside.

That must be CERN, Brigit thought. *We'll be there in a minute. It's now or never.*

'...Keep smiling and you'll get your share...'

Catriona gave the somewhat lack-lustre lyrics everything she had with full throated expression. With equal passion, Brigit lifted the heavy report and hurled it viciously over the front passenger seat, aiming at the back of her daughter's head, screaming 'For God's sake Catriona, shut up!'

Catriona gave a yelp of pain mixed with alarm as the missile struck her head and exploded across the windscreen in a paper snowstorm. Unable to see the road, Sam braked sharply and the car swerved into the path of the on-coming tram, now a mere twenty metres away. Its bell began to clang urgently.

'Mother, you're going to get us all killed!' Catriona yelped as she scooped the papers away from the windscreen onto her lap. Sam swerved, narrowly missing the tram, reached his own lane and stopped. The tram stopped too. All the passengers were staring at them through the tram's windows. The driver opened the door on the far side of the tram and stood up, an angry expression on his face.

'Drive on, Sam,' Brigit barked. 'I've got CD plates.'

Sam frowned, glanced at the tram, then started the car and drove rapidly down the hill, leaving the tram driver standing in the road shaking his fist at them.

Satisfied with the way she had raised the curtain on her little melodrama, Brigit pulled out an exquisitely embroidered handkerchief from her ample cleavage, conveniently exposed by the low-cut jacket of her favourite vermillion designer trouser-suit, and howled:

'I can't do this bloody job another minute, Sam! It's all official reports and boring briefings and bureaucratic gobbledy-goo. How'm I ever going to be President if I can't hold down a simple little Ambassador's job? Oh, I give up!' she howled, putting as much expression into the words as her daughter had into the song. 'I'm going to quit the UN and come back to Dublin with you two.' Finally she began sobbing theatrically into the tiny handkerchief.

For a moment the only sounds were Brigit's sobs. Then, in an astonishingly calm voice, Sam said, 'No, don't do that, dearest. You don't want to resign, Bee.' He picked up speed as they joined the stream of traffic emerging from the tunnel and pouring westwards along the Route de Meyrin out of Geneva. 'You're just a bit stressed out at the moment. 'It's natural. You've been working your socks off for the past two months. Why don't you have the rest of the week off and—'

'You've got to be kidding, Sam!' Brigit yelled. 'You don't get it, do you? My diary's packed every day and every evening for the next two months. I need help, Sam,' she wailed and once more began making the sounds of sobs.

'I think you do, Bee. Listen. Why don't Catriona and I stay here after Easter and lend you a hand?'

Ahhh, she thought. *At last!*

'Would you?' She oozed gratitude and enthusiasm. 'Would you really, Sammy? That would be so helpful. Oh thank you, darling.'

She pushed the handkerchief back in her bra and reached over to lift the jumbled pile of papers out of her daughter's hands, feeling slightly disappointed the battle had been won so easily. He had capitulated without a fight. She would have like to wage war a little longer. She found a smile for him and sent it through the rear-view mirror, even finding a small one for Catriona, but her daughter missed it. She was staring at Sam, an expression of utter disbelief on her pale oval face, her mouth hanging open.

'Of course we will my love,' Sam said. 'I'll phone my school and tell them I've broken a leg skiing.'

'Good idea,' Brigit said, beginning to sort out the pages of the report. 'Better make it both legs. I'm going to need you here for quite a while. And for God's sake, Catriona, keep quiet. I've got to work,' she said, and began to hum 'Don't worry if nobody loves you' quietly to herself.

We're not really going to stay here are we, Sam?

As they sat in a queue of traffic at the bottom of the hill, Catriona stared at the balding man sitting beside her, feeling torn in two. The idea of staying in Geneva was utterly delightful. It was a dream town, surrounded by gorgeous mountains. They could cruise the lake, visit the ancient hilltop cathedral, shop for fashion, eat delicious food in expensive restaurants. It was more beautiful and far richer than Dublin, a place she had hated and feared since her eighth birthday, but the idea of having to live with her again mother took the gloss off the whole idea.

'You're not...We're not really going to stay here are we, Sam?' she hissed. 'Surely you weren't fooled by that pathetic little performance were you? You know what an actress she is!'

He glanced at her and she saw an indulgent smile playing on his lips, although she couldn't quite make out what it meant.

'You know what would happen if we stayed? You'd just be her unpaid servant again like you were in Dublin, putting up with her tantrums and obeying her whims.'

Sam edged the car forward towards the traffic island, gazing serenely at the distant mountains and nodding like a stupid mechanised doll but saying nothing.

'And anyway you can't take time off your job and I can't miss school just because she's having some problems. I've got exams coming up. Oh God, Sam,' she hissed, leaning towards him, 'can't you see she's just selfish? Utterly selfish!'

'I'm sorry, Catty,' Sam said quietly, 'but it was your idea to come here in the first place. Don't you remember?'

Oh yes, I remember it very clearly, Catriona thought, *Sam sitting at my computer reading his emails and saying 'You'd be interested in this one, Catty. Your mother's been invited to CERN. Wasn't that where your father used to work a lot of the time?'*

The idea had hit her immediately. At first it seemed so audacious it took her breath away. 'When's she going?' she had asked, trying to sound casual, thinking: *Don't want to frighten him.*

'Hmm, in the week before Easter.'

That was it, the moment when fate had stepped in and taken control of her life. 'We'll both be on holiday then!' she had said, trying not to let her excitement show. 'You ever been to Switzerland, Sam?'

Oh yes I remember, she thought, *the days of nagging and begging and persuasion before you agreed to come.*

'You can't take a decision like that', Sam was saying as he drove up the slope on the far side of the valley, 'and then blame somebody else when it goes wrong. What's the matter, don't you want to stay here?'

Catriona sighed. *He's right,* she thought. *It's my choice to be here so I have to take the consequences.* 'Listen Sam,' she said. 'I don't care what happens as long as I solve the mystery. Actually, actually I wouldn't mind staying here and going to finishing school. What is a finishing school, anyway? Sounds expensive, Sam. But I don't want you to be Mother's servant again. And anyway, could you afford it?'

That wiped the smile off his face, but only for a moment. 'Your mother can. But don't worry, Catty. We won't have to stay too long. She'll settle down in a week or two and we can go home. Oh look, that must be CERN.'

As the car crested the ridge, what looked like an industrial estate came into view, sprawling across the pretty Swiss landscape, steam rising from short stumpy chimneys. Catriona began to tingle all over with excitement. *This is the moment I've been waiting for,* she thought. *Not just for two weeks but for the past six years of my life. This is the Promised Land.*

Even the two grotesque electricity pylons standing beside the road looked majestic to her, the guardians of the secret world of science and perhaps of the mystery she was trying to resolve. Behind the pylons, a huge wooden dome bulged out of the ground like a giant football at the feet of the two guardians. Everything she saw looked beautiful, especially the range of mountains filling the horizon ahead of her, visible occasionally when the drifting clouds parted.

Catriona's excitement was intense as Sam turned off the road, drove between troughs filled with young willows and parked outside a building labelled "Reception". So it was an enormous disappointment when Brigit got out with Sam and told her to wait in the car. Catriona wandered round the car park, looking back towards Geneva, watching the aeroplanes taking off from the airport and wondering vaguely whether she would ever fly home or stay here forever, but not really caring either way. The city was invisible from here. The tall jet of water shooting out of the lake and the cathedral on the hill were completely hidden by the valley they had just—

'Francesco, may I introduce my daughter?'

Catriona spun round to see her mother standing beside a smiling, corpulent man. Even his smart blue Italian suit failed to hide the ample fat which hung about his body. 'Catriona,' Brigit went on, 'this is Professor Francesco Romani, the Director General of CERN.'

When he reached out and shook Catriona's hand, she barely managed to control her disgust as her fingers sank into his soft yielding flesh. And when he bent forward to kiss her on both cheeks the smell of his tobacco-heavy breath made her feel nauseous. His long nose dangled down towards her like a monkey's proboscis. His hair was unnaturally black for a man of his age, about sixty she guessed. *He's the ugliest man I've ever seen*, she thought.

Yet he oozed self-confidence, and when he let go her hand and spoke, his heavy Italian accent was so charming Catriona began to forgive him his revolting appearance.

'I am so happy to meet you, signorina Catriona.' He made her name sound like a little melody. He turned towards a young woman who was standing beside Sam. 'May I introduce your guide for today? This is Marianne. She will answer any questions you might have about CERN.'

The young woman stepped forward, smiling and holding out her hand. Catriona shook it timidly. Marianne was as lovely as Francesco was ugly. *Beauty and the Beast*, Catriona thought. She had long dark hair with auburn highlights. Her face was almost without creases except for the two little dimples in her cheeks when she smiled, which she did often. Her skin seemed to glow with health, her cheeks pink, her forehead a lovely creamy colour, and her eyes showed merely the faintest trace of makeup.

Catriona was so fascinated by her radiant face that not until Marianne turned to lead them across the car-park towards the road did she notice the huge bulge beneath the jacket of her blue uniform. Catriona had always been fascinated by pregnancy, and she walked close beside the young woman, who was about ten years older than herself, twenty-four or twenty-five she thought, with Sam on the other side listening attentively as she answered his questions. Francesco and Brigit followed them, deep in conversation. Catriona had no interest in what Marianne was saying, technical stuff she could not understand and did not want to, but her soft voice and her beautiful accent fascinated the girl. Catriona thought she was French although she wasn't sure. She repeated Marianne's words silently to herself trying to imitate the sound.

Ze Lardge Adron Colliderr. Ze ATLAAS Detectoor.

Catriona was amazed at how easily the guide moved, seeming totally relaxed despite the large extra weight she was carrying. Marianne led them over the road and round the outside of the huge brown dome which towered over them, its horizontal wooden slats and thick curving legs giving it the appearance of a giant sea-urchin without the spines. Behind it lay a building with a huge painting on the outside showing some sort of machine with big brown discs and yellow gear wheels and orange pipes. That building was apparently where they were heading, but on the way Marianne took them into the wooden Globe of Science and Innovation for a quick look at the exhibition.

Catriona's attention was immediately caught by the words written on the wall near the entrance.

"WHERE DO WE COME FROM?"

"WHAT ARE WE?"

"WHERE ARE WE GOING?"

Her spirits soared as she read them again. *Where do I come from? From a land of hell called Ireland. What am I? I'm a girl who wants to solve a mystery. Where am I going? I'm going to find out the truth about how my father died. That's more important than anything else in the world.*

Michael's Diary: Into ATLAS

Son of Beeing

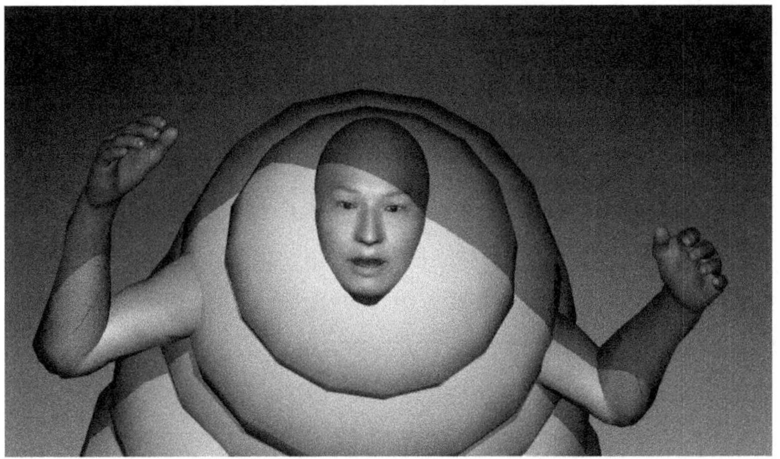

Beneath the rolling countryside to the west of the city of Geneva lay the sedimentary sandstones, shales and conglomerates which had eroded from the high Alpine mountains to the south millions of years ago. Drawn downwards by the line of magnetic force, Oh Primeval Monopole, you flew over the city and plunged into these soft materials. Naturally you had no trouble traversing these small obstacles. In comparison to yourself, the atoms of these rocks were merely huge thin shells of orbiting electrons surrounding a tiny central nucleus. But what you felt after penetrating only a few metres into the ground was much more surprising.

The magnetic field grew rapidly stronger, and began to slow your flight. After fifty metres, your speed had reduced dramatically and when, after a further fifty metres, you emerged into an underground cavern, you were travelling slower than you had ever done before. Here you found a gigantic, barrel-shaped object, the subterranean monster known by its human minders as "ATLAS". They force-fed this ravenous beast with a constant diet of protons which they accelerated to almost the speed of light in the "Large Hadron Collider". This, the largest collaboration ever attempted between the scientists of the world, lay in a huge circular tunnel in the sediment one hundred metres deep and twenty-seven kilometres long. You caught only a glimpse of all this, Majestic Monopole, before you were swallowed by ATLAS's body, drawn in by some of the most powerful magnets ever built by mankind.

Cooled by liquid helium to almost absolute zero temperature, ATLAS's "superconducting" magnets were designed to bend the paths of particles created by proton collisions and so allow the detector to record and identify their constituents. At thirty-four minutes and twenty-three point five-eight-four-one-two seconds past nine on that memorable morning, the array of individual detectors within ATLAS began to record your silent passage.

Although designed to trace the paths of particles travelling outwards from the centre of the detector, the various sub-systems were nevertheless perfectly capable of recording the effects of your unexpected arrival. The outer detectors in the assemblage saw you first. As you traversed the "Muon Spectrometer", many of the hundreds of long, thin, high-pressure gas-filled metal tubes fired a pulse of electricity from their central high-voltage wires. These signals passed into the data processing system and the first-level electronic "triggers" took only two microseconds to decide that something extraordinary was happening. These data were stored in "readout buffers" in the underground counting room of the USA15 cavern close to ATLAS's lair, awaiting confirmation from the other sub-systems that this was a real event and not a spurious signal.

You moved downwards, Oh Monopole, bending sharply in the strong field of the "toroidal magnetic coils" as you penetrated deeper into ATLAS. Here you passed easily through the "Calorimeter's" metal plates, although collisions with the heavy nuclei of several atoms further slowed your rate of descent and triggered more data from the "scintillating plastic and liquid argon sensors".

Very soon you entered the "Inner Tracker" causing electrical pulses to fire within excited gas-filled straws and, deeper still, state-of-the-art semiconductors measured your position with exquisite accuracy while your path curved sharply in the enormous two Tesla magnetic field of the huge "central solenoid". Your final energy was spent in traversing the stainless steel and copper wall of the Large Hadron Collider's beam pipe, a narrow tube which ran through the middle of ATLAS.

At first all was quiet. There was a moment of peace, when (had you been capable of feeling emotions, Oh Marvellous but totally insensible Monopole) you would perhaps have reflected, as you drifted slowly along the beam pipe, that here at last you had found the home you had been seeking since time began. You might have held your breath, waiting eagerly to meet your relatives in this exotic world, so different from anywhere else you had ever been and grateful for having found a magnetic field strong enough to finally bring your long journey to an end.

You did not have long to wait. Within a tiny fraction of a second, your tranquillity was shattered and your hopes raised even higher as a bunch of particles came hurtling along the beam pipe like a vast school of excited children going on an outing. There were almost a trillion of them, flashing past only millimetres away from where you floated gently along the pipe. As the pack passed, some of them actually collided with you. The collisions did no harm and their momentum counteracted the effect of the magnetic field, pushing you back along the pipe towards the centre of the detector.

These particles, you might now have realised with a sharp sense of disappointment, were not Monopoles like yourself, but merely protons, the sort of thing you had frequently seen before, although you had never previously met so many with so much energy. And, just as they had inside stars, some of the protons adhered to you, increasing the size of your outer mantle.

Within less than a nanosecond, the bunch of protons had passed you by, Oh Marvellous Monopole, and gone hurtling out of sight along the beam pipe. Alone once more you began drifting in the magnetic field but you had hardly gone a centimetre before another bunch arrived and the same thing happened. More protons fused with you and pushed you back up the beam pipe.

Surrounded by your growing mantle, you felt more at home now than ever before, but you could also sense a tension growing around you. Every proton carries something called an "electric charge" which makes it try to push away from all other protons. This produced a mutual repulsion within the particles in your mantle, which was in danger of breaking up and leaving you naked once more. Luckily a new phenomenon prevented this. Sometimes a passing particle came very close without actually fusing with you. As a result of this near-miss collision, one of the protons in your mantle acquired sufficient energy to emit a small object which scientists call a "positron". This carried away the excess electrical charge, leaving your mantle more stable. In addition, an uncharged particle called a "neutrino" was emitted at the same time. These two particles went shooting through the beam pipe wall out into the detector.

Because it had no electrical or magnetic charge, the neutrino travelled out through the whole of ATLAS without producing any effect whatsoever. But things were very different for the positron.

As soon as it hit the beam pipe wall, it found itself surrounded by electrons, particles which were identical to it in every way except they carried the opposite kind of electrical charge. The positron felt these electrons to be extremely attractive, and it immediately fused with one of them, creating dramatic results.

All the matter of these two particles was transformed into a pair of "gamma rays", similar to light but with much higher energy. They radiated outwards through ATLAS's sub-detectors, firing events in the "Electromagnetic Calorimeter".

The computerised "trigger system" was designed to distinguish the few extraordinary events occurring in the beam pipe from the millions of ordinary ones which were of no interest. It had already decided that your arrival was interesting and had recorded every detail of your inward path. But that had been merely one event out of many, although with higher energy than almost any other. The computers had simply assigned the whole record a "StoreGate key", added it to the database and moved on.

Now the hard-wired Level-1 trigger system embedded within ATLAS was observing the outward flow of gamma rays emanating from the beam pipe wall with equally close attention. The electronics easily determined that positrons were flowing out of the beam pipe and passed the data to the Level-2 Trigger System.

The Level-2 processors which analysed these events were unable to find any obvious energy source for the positrons. During the many years of planning and building ATLAS, nobody had ever predicted such events. Indeed, despite all their precautions to ensure the safety of the experiments at CERN, not one scientist had ever evaluated the possible dangers presented by a cosmic monopole.

The processors assumed that some undetectable form of energy must be flowing out of the beam pipe in the opposite direction which they labelled as "missing transverse energy". They had been programmed to recognise this type of event as a distinct and important signature for interesting new physics. Something truly extraordinary was happening, the banks of computers agreed, and hard discs whirred as records were copied from the "Transient Data Store" and written to permanent storage.

The data flow was low at first, but as you absorbed more and more protons and your cross section grew larger over the next few minutes, so you were able to absorb even more protons and the outward flow of positrons increased dramatically. A runaway process began, with more and more gammas triggering more and more interesting events. But the Level-2 Triggers had never been designed to handle such a high rate of data flow and after three minutes the system was beginning to struggle. Initially tiny, Oh Blessed Monopole, you had now grown to macroscopic proportions, and would have been visible to the naked eye of any observer foolhardy enough to expose himself to the lethal radiation levels within the beam pipe. Henceforth you grew exponentially and a minute later the whole data storage system reached saturation point.

Episode 2 Data Storage System Overflow

Danny Schneider's eyes were gritty

After twenty-four hours of staring at computer screens, solving his team's problems, trying to ignore the dozens of excited visiting scientists filling the ATLAS Control Room and finally briefing Seline Soubise, his replacement as Run Co-ordinator, Danny Schneider raised his tired head and looked at the clock on the bottom wall. His eyes were so gritty it took a long moment before the numbers eventually swam into view. "09:36". He stared at them, thinking: *I've done it! That was the most difficult day of my life, but I did it! Thank Christ it's over.* But little did Danny know that his problems were only just beginning.

Under his supervision, the team had successfully restarted ATLAS after the winter shut-down. He pushed his chair back, dragged himself to his feet, stretched and turned to peer through the blue-tinted windows on the long back wall. As if through a mist, he could just make out the bulging brown wooden dome where Marianne normally worked.

'I'm going to see if Marianne's arrived,' he said to Seline. 'She went to the antenatal clinic this morning.'

As he lifted his green jacket off the back of his chair, she glanced at him, her eyes hard and cold, nodded once then turned back to her screen.

He headed for the Control Room door, pushing through the visitors crowded around the desks of the resident scientists and engineers. They had come from universities all over the world to help nurse their parts of the detector through the difficult start-up run. Many of them shook his hand and patted him on the back. Danny could feel his own palms hot and clammy, but he smiled and made self-deprecating remarks, pleased by their praise. It was for this acknowledgement that he had worked so hard. He knew he was the best engineer on the ATLAS team and it felt good to know that the scientists were finally realising his true value. But now it was time to face the other part of his life, the part where emotional doubt replaced logical certainty. He took his mobile phone from his pocket and began to search for Marianne's number as he reached the door. He had just found it when he heard a computer generated voice crackle in a monotone from the overhead speakers:

'Level Zero Alarm.'

Danny hesitated, one hand on the door-handle, the other holding the phone, waiting for the second half of the message, his brain clicking back into problem-solving mode. *Level Zero?* he said to himself. *Minor fault. Shouldn't be a problem. Seline will be able to cope with that. Nice easy start to her first run. Wonder what kind of error it is, exactly?* His bleary eyes studied the image projected onto the far wall, trying to bring the digital clock into focus. He had just deciphered the numbers 09:38 when the synthetic speech droned:

'Data Storage System Overflow'

Data Storage System Overflow? Danny pondered. *Never heard of one of those.* He shielded his tired eyes from the glare of the overhead projectors as he squinted back down the long narrow room feeling dog-tired, not just from the shift he had just finished but from many weeks of twelve-hour days getting ready for last night. His bleary eyes finally brought Seline's face into focus: white pointed nose and chin sharp against severe black hair; hunched shoulders tense. Half a dozen visiting scientists were leaning over her desk, pointing at her screens, talking excitedly, but they didn't know the ATLAS Control System and could not really help. Her anxious eyes darted rapidly between screens, hands, keyboards, faces. After a few seconds she turned and scanned the room. When she saw Danny she compressed her lips, raised her hands, shook her head.

The synthetic voice was still droning, over and over. 'Level Zero Alarm. Data Storage System Overflow.'

With a slight feeling of elation, like a marathon runner finding his second wind, he dropped his phone back into his pocket, let go the door and trudged back down the room. As he approached her desk he saw the little Chinese-Irish scientist Michael Zhang push his way through the crowd behind Seline. Danny heard his high-pitched voice rising over their chatter: 'I think there's a fault with the trigger system.' His Chinese accent was enhanced by an Irish twang, like a jig played on a bamboo flute. As usual, nobody took any notice of him. Michael was always poking his little snub nose into everyone else's business as if he knew everything about everything. The other scientists only tolerated him because he was a genius at programming the "Trigger and Data Acquisition System".

Seline grew calmer as Danny slumped into the chair beside her. 'Can you just tell me where the procedure is for handling this type of error?' she said, her long black fringe falling over one eye. 'I've never heard of it.'

'Well you could start by acknowledging it. That voice is driving me mad.'

She clicked the Acknowledge button on the Detector Control System Alarm Screen and the computer's voice fell silent. Michael Zhang was standing at her elbow. He was so short that his head was almost level with hers as she sat peering at her computers. His pink T-shirt bore the stains of several weeks wear and there was a dark smudge down one of his cheeks.

'I've never heard of a Data Storage System Overflow before either,' Danny said to Seline, disregarding Michael. 'Just do a search in the DCS Operations Layer of the ATLAS TWiki.' *But the procedure probably won't be much use to you*, he thought. *We only really find out how to handle an error by doing it. Then we write the real procedures afterwards.* While he waited for her to run the search he read the top line of the list of alarms filling the screen. 'We must be getting a lot of events,' he said. 'The Sub-Farm Output file servers are swamped.'

'I can see that, Danny. Okay, I've found the procedure. I can handle it now.'

But he didn't move. *She's never run a shift on her own before. Can she really cope? I'm going to look pretty stupid if she makes a mess of it, after recommending her for the job.* Seline was slowly reading the on-screen instructions. Danny sighed. *It should be obvious what to do.* 'How many events are we getting out of the Event Filter?' he said.

'Thousands,' Michael said brightly. Danny stared at him. There was a twinkle playing in Michael's heavy-lidded eyes. Danny assumed he was joking.

'I don't know,' Seline said, ignoring Michael. 'Wait a minute.' She began to type an Athena command into a console window.

Marianne must have come out of the clinic by now, Danny thought as he again took his mobile phone out of his pocket. *Wonder if the doctor managed to turn the baby? I hope she likes the name I've chosen for him. Dragomir. Precious and peaceful.* As he flipped the phone open a histogram flashed up on Seline's screen and she leaned towards it.

'He's right,' she said, astonishment chilling her voice as she glanced nervously at the two men. 'We're getting over two thousand events per second.'

'Two thousand per second?' Danny said, feeling sweat break out on his back. 'Not really? But that's ten times more than the system was designed to handle!'

Danny dropped his mobile back in his jacket pocket thinking *I'll call Marianne in a minute.* 'They can't be real events,' he said. 'What kind are they supposed to be?'

'They're all missing energy events,' Michael's little voice piped as gaily as a flute leading a band.

'I don't think so,' Danny said dismissively.

Seline clicked on a menu and the histogram changed into a single bar. 'It's true,' she said.

Danny stared at her. 'ALL of them? That's not possible. There's obviously a fault with one of the sub-detectors. Can you find out which one?'

Danny wiped his sweating palms on his trouser legs as he watched her type in a little script to analyse the data, thinking *This is a disaster. Thank Christ it happened before I left.* 'Are you going to suspend the run?' he said to Seline. 'It's your call, but if I was in charge—'

'You still here?' she said without looking at him. 'I thought you were going to see Marianne?'

'I'll stay for a minute or two. I'm really curious. I've never seen anything quite like this before. It's probably an error but...' An idea suddenly flashed into his mind giving him a jolt like a physical blow. 'If these events are real it would mean ATLAS has found a new type of particle. Imagine how I would have felt tomorrow if I'd gone and missed all the fun!'

Suddenly everything had changed. The possibility of being present at the discovery that he and thousands of other scientists and engineers had been striving for was so exciting that his tiredness seemed to evaporate. *This could be history in the making,* he told himself.

'It's almost certainly a hardware fault in the Level 1 trigger system.' Michael said cheerfully. 'There could be noise on one of the lines coming out of the ATLAS cavern into USA15. Probably just a bad connection.'

Danny glanced at him. 'It should be easy to check if that's true. We'd need to go down into the USA15 cavern.'

'Or it could be a bug in the ROD crate processors software,' Michael said.

'That's true,' Danny said. 'We'd have to use the ROD crate workstation in USA15 to check the functionality of the crate processors. Come on.' He stood and the room began to spin. He reached out and steadied himself against the desk.

Seline glanced at him. 'You alright, Danny?'

'Yeah.' He waited for his head to clear. 'Just a bit tired.'

'I'll stop beam intersection,' she said. 'No point in collecting more spurious data.'

'I would very much prefer it if you could leave the beams intersecting,' Michael said.

'Why?' She squinted sideways at him.

Michael paused for a second then said 'We will need to check whether it's a fault in the region of interest builders or perhaps in one of the readout subsystems. If we lose the signal we won't be able to monitor their activity.'

Seline stared at him then shot Danny a questioning look.

He shrugged. 'I guess he's right. He's the expert. Come on then, Dr Zhang.'

'Okay,' she said. 'I'll leave the beams intersecting.'

'I'll just shut down my systems,' Michael said with a little smile and waddled back to his desk.

'He's an odd case,' Seline whispered so the visitors wouldn't hear. 'I've never seen him smile before. Do you think he's up to something?'

Danny went cold. 'Like what?'

'I don't know. I just don't trust him. Which planet do you think he comes from?'

'I'm not sure,' Danny said, 'but I hope those aliens are friendly.' He stood and followed the little Irishman up the room towards the door.

Episode 3 ATLAS Visitor Centre

The ATLAS Building

Here we go! Catriona thought, as Marianne led the group out of the giant wooden sea-urchin towards the building painted on two sides with the meaningless image which she had seen before, pipes and discs and what might have been giant yellow gear-wheels. *At last I might get a chance to find out the truth about Daddy.*

She tried not to run as they walked slowly past the painted building and down a car-park in front of a glass-fronted building whose interior was hidden behind blue reflective windows.

Finally they entered a single-story annex which contained something called the ATLAS Visitor Centre, and her heart began to pound. *I'm sure Daddy used to talk about ATLAS. No good asking Mother. She wouldn't have a clue.*

Once inside, she could finally look through another blue glass window into the ATLAS Control Room. It was crowded with excited people, some leaning over banks of computer terminals, others staring at images of the screens projected onto the far wall. Catriona stared at their faces, wondering which of them had known her father. *Surely one of the must have?*

Sam was sitting at a terminal in the Visitor Centre, tapping on the keyboard and fiddling with the mouse. She was vaguely aware that Marianne was talking to a handsome young man sitting at another terminal, but Catriona wasn't interested. Even his long black curly hair, his bright yellow shirt and his warm, full-lipped smile couldn't capture her attention. And she was deliberately trying to ignore Francesco's strident voice as he stood beside her, talking to Mother, explaining the potential benefits of Ireland joining CERN. But all that changed when he said: '...he's from the Advanced Physics Laboratory in Dublin.'

Instantly it was her eighth birthday and she was once again lying on the bank of the pond outside the Dublin laboratory, gazing up into a rapidly darkening sky. This always happened whenever anyone mentioned it, the Advanced Physics Laboratory.

This was where Daddy worked and where the nightmare had started. For a moment she held her breath, waiting in terror for it all to begin again but hoping it would be different this time.

There, once again, was the lighted window on the top floor of the darkened lab. Here again was the warm fur of her huge Alsatian dog Trackaway, lying beside her, trying to keep her warm as mist rose from the pond.

Then a blue light drifted overhead and her heart sank. *It's happening again*, she screamed silently.

There was a dark shadow trailing behind the light, hiding the stars as it flew towards the window. In a panic she tried to stand and shout, to change the story, to stop the disaster this time, but she couldn't move. She was frozen with terror, as she always was during these flash-backs, only this time there was a voice booming through the darkness. 'He's the only Irish nuclear scientist working in CERN,' Francesco said.

Nuclear scientist? Catriona thought. *Wasn't that Daddy's job too?*

The dark shape flew over her head and reached the window. A reindeer was clearly outlined against the light, the one she had stuck on her father's office window the previous Christmas.

Then she saw a second blue light flying against the black November sky and her terror grew. *I've got to stop them this time!* But still her body would not respond to her mind's commands. All she could do was lay on the bank of the pond gazing up into the night sky.

'Ah good!' Francesco boomed. 'He's coming out! I really want you should meet him.'

He's coming out! she thought. *Who's coming out? Is it Daddy? Is Daddy coming out of the lab this time instead of staying in his office like normal?* With a superhuman effort she forced her body to move, trying to see the laboratory building door. Her hand hit something hard, somebody said 'Ouch', the vision vanished and she was back in the brightly-lit Visitor Centre looking into Sam's eyes as he sat before the computer screen. 'What's the matter, Catty?' he said.

'Nuclear Irish scientist, Francesco?' Brigit was saying. 'That's odd. That's what my late husband was too. Which one is he?'

'Just there,' Francesco said, pointing through the glass into the ATLAS Control Room. Two men were pushing their way through the crowd towards the door. The one in front was a short man with a smiling Chinese face wearing a greasy-looking pink T-shirt and blue jeans. Behind him was a tired-looking Caucasian man in a green jacket. Catriona immediately assumed he must be the Irish scientist and felt sorry for him. He looked completely exhausted as he almost staggered after the Chinese man. His pinched face was drained of colour and his hair was almost the same, with just a hint of brown. His mouth was tight-lipped, as if he had to concentrate just to reach the door. She felt sorry for him, but he looked nothing like her father and somehow she felt terribly disappointed until Francesco's next words put doubt in her mind.

'I have no doubt that Dr Zhang will explain some of the many academic benefits his laboratory has already obtained from working on ATLAS. Add to that the economic benefits if Ireland becomes a member of CERN...' Francesco went on, but Catriona wasn't listening.

She was thinking *Dr Zhang? Is the Chinese one Irish*?

'Did you hear that?' Sam whispered in Catriona's ear, making her jump. He was standing beside her now. All she could do was nod.

'But how much is it going to cost, Francesco?' Brigit said. 'You know what a state Ireland's finances are in.'

'I will show you a calculation to prove that the economic benefits will far outweigh the costs,' Francesco said. 'Ah, they are going out through the side-door. I'll go and get him.'

Francesco went through a door and Brigit started checking her mobile phone.

'I wonder whether this Dr Zhang might have known your father?' Sam whispered. Catriona felt a shiver run down her entire body as she stared at him. They had not talked about her father for years. 'Why don't you ask him?' he said. She nodded so vigorously her ginger hair flopped into her eyes. There was nothing in the world she wanted so much as to solve the mystery surrounding her father's death and hopefully get rid of those horrible haunting memories.

Francesco came back into the Visitor Centre with the two men and introduced the green jacketed one as Danny Schneider, Marianne's husband, and the Chinese one as Dr Zhang. Danny went over to Marianne but Francesco asked Zhang to explain things to Brigit.

He was extremely short, not even as tall as Catriona, and his voice was as high-pitched as a child when he said 'I'm sorry, Madame Ambassador, but I don't have time to talk to you at the moment. I have to go underground to help fix a serious malfunction with ATLAS. Could we talk later, over lunch perhaps?'

'No, I can't stay that long,' Brigit said as she put her mobile phone in her yellow leather handbag and checked her wristwatch. 'I have to be at the UN by twelve.'

'Well, another day perhaps. I'm based here so I'll be glad to talk, but I regret to say it is simply not possible right now.' He bowed his head and turned towards the door where Danny was in earnest conversation with Marianne.

If I don't do something now, Catriona thought, *he'll leave and I'll lose my chance. This is what I came to Switzerland for. I've got to say something.*

As the little Chinese man walked past her she screwed up her courage and said 'Did you happen to know my father? His name was Dr O'Brien.'

Michael Zhang immediately stopped and looked at her. 'John O'Brien? Yes indeed, I knew him well. You are his daughter?' For a long moment he stared at her, his eyes unblinking. Catriona's heart was beating so fast she thought it was going to fly out of her chest. *This is it! I've found somebody who knew Daddy! It's incredible. Maybe the nightmare is nearly over.*

Then the little man smiled and nodded as if he recognised her father in her face. 'I'm very sorry about the accident. You must have been quite young?'

'It was my eighth birthday,' she said quietly, barely able to speak as the memory of it flooded over her again, washing aside everything else, and for a moment she was back in that moment of terror.

Catriona could see the shape of a human being

Catriona could see the unmistakable shape of a human being holding the blue light in his hands. She stared up in horror. *How can he fly like that?* She was pretty sure it was a man, not a woman. He was hovering outside the lighted window. Once more, as always when she relived this terrifying moment, she searched for some sign of a rope or a jet or something, anything that would explain what held him up there in the night sky, but without success. She stared as he hung in the air for what seemed like hours, peering into the window.

When she had first seen him, on the night of her eighth birthday, she had wondered whether he was working with her father. *Daddy's probably helping him to fly using his beam of lectons,* she had thought. Her relief at this idea had been intense.

Her father had sometimes spoken about electrons although when she was eight she had no idea what they were. All she knew was that he sent them flying down a tube somewhere in the lab. But she imagined him now, sending the beam out of his office window and somehow holding the man up in the air.

It must be top-secret, the little girl had thought. *That's why the man's trying it out at night-time, so nobody will see him. And the blue light, that's got something to do with the lectons. Of course! It all makes sense now. That must be why Daddy's left home!*

John O'Brien had deserted the family home several months before. According to Mother, he had gone to live with another woman. Catriona missed him terribly. She hated having to live just with her mother. She had made the long journey alone from her home to the lab on the evening of her eighth birthday to persuade him to come back.

Now that she had remembered about the 'lectons', Catriona relaxed. The terror of the flying man turned to amused interest. She lay on the ground and watched him hover overhead.

But then, as always, she saw him take something out of his pocket with one hand and point it through the window. With a sickening lurch she realised it was a gun. She wanted to scream but her voice was silenced by the sight of something else flying rapidly and silently across the night sky towards the lighted window. It too was holding a blue light in its hands and by its light she could see that its head had two bulging eyes and its body had black and yellow stripes. *It looks like a giant bee! This has to be a joke.*

It was much bigger than a real bee, even bigger than the man, and it wasn't buzzing. Its wings weren't even flapping! They were just folded up on its back and it was holding a glowing blue light, just like the man. *Real bees can't do that! It must be somebody in fancy-dress costume. The gun must be a toy. That man is going to play a joke on Daddy.*

But what happened next showed it wasn't a joke. The bee swooped down towards the man and grabbed him with its rear legs. The gun went off, the window shattered and Trackaway jumped up, barking madly. Catriona went rolling down the bank and only just managed to stop herself before she reached the water. Turning towards the barking hound she saw him on the other side of the pond racing after the bee. It was carrying the man over the trees, his body hanging limp in its back legs as it flew up higher and higher into the night sky until it vanished from sight.

Episode 4 Underground

ATLAS Visitor Centre

A hand gripped Catriona's shoulder and Sam's voice said 'Excuse me, Dr Zhang, but you don't happen to know anything about how he died do you?'

With a superhuman effort Catriona dragged her mind back to the Visitor Centre. The little Irish scientist was nodding at Sam and seemed about to reply but Danny called: 'We have to go, Dr Zhang'.

Still Michael didn't move. 'I was...I would very much like to talk to you about what happened that night,' he said quietly. 'I do not believe the whole story has yet been told.'

'No it hasn't,' Catriona said in a hoarse voice, hardly able to speak from excitement and fear. She had told them what she had seen, told Mother and Grandma and Sam and even the police, but nobody had believed her and finally she had even begun to doubt herself.

Michael put his little hand on her arm. 'I'm sorry but I really must go and help steer this ship off the rocks. We are perilously close to the shore. I will be happy to talk to you on another occasion.' He bowed again and followed Danny through the revolving door. Marianne stood watching them go and waving through the window but Danny was talking to Michael and did not notice.

'I'm sorry to hear about your father, young lady,' Francesco said.

Catriona was about to reply but Brigit butted in: 'My first husband was a scientist. He died in a horrible accident at the same laboratory.' She placed her hand on Francesco's arm. 'It's a long story.'

Francesco patted her hand sympathetically and began talking once more about the benefits of Ireland joining CERN.

'I'm certain of one thing, Sam,' Catriona whispered urgently. 'I'm not going to leave this place until I've talked to that Chinese man and found out exactly what he knows about Daddy's death. What was his name again?'

'Michael Zhang,' Sam said. 'Now listen, Catty, you can't just stay here. I've got to drive your mother back to the UN in an hour and she would kill me if I suggested leaving you here on your own.'

'But we're only a few miles away from Geneva aren't we Sam? I can easily catch the tram back into town. It stops right outside. Just give me some money for the fare.'

'Excuse me please,' Marianne said, unable to squeeze past them. They moved aside and Marianne led the long-haired young man to where Francesco was still talking to Brigit. 'Professor Romani, can you spare me a moment please?'

Catriona was suddenly struck by what seemed to her like a brilliant idea. 'I could stay with Marianne! She'd make sure I got on the tram.' They both turned to look at the young woman talking to Francesco.

'...remember Count Alex Karolyi?' Marianne was saying, gesturing towards the handsome young man beside her. 'His software company wrote Mercator.'

Francesco frowned, looked at the young man, nodded then smiled and said 'Ah yes of course, you are the one with the boat,' and finally shook hands with him. There could hardly have been a bigger contrast than that between the sleek, tanned young man and the flabby old, grey-faced scientist.

'He has found something on Mercator I think you should see,' Marianne said.

'I'm very busy at the moment,' Francesco said.

'It's pretty important, Professor,' the young man Alex said. His voice was soft and gentle in the middle but with a firm edge. As soon as Catriona heard it her ears seemed to twitch. There was something about his voice which appealed to her instantly, warm as a blanket on a frosty morning. 'There's a very unusual Mercator track,' Alex was saying. 'It occurred around the time this problem started. I tried to show it to Mr Schneider but for some reason he didn't seem very interested.' He glanced at Marianne and lifted one eyebrow with a quizzical smile. She gave him a little scowl.

'I am not surprised,' Francesco sighed. 'Michael and Danny are trying to fix a serious fault with ATLAS. An unusual track you say? Oh, very well then, show it to me Count Karolyi, but please be quick. You might like to see this as well, Madame Ambassador. It will give you an idea of the excitement of the leading edge work we do here.'

Alex sat at the nearby computer terminal and Francesco explained to Brigit: 'Mercator is the software the scientists use to visualise events happening inside ATLAS.' Everyone clustered around Alex. Catriona could smell his musky after-shave. He clicked the mouse a few times and an image appeared on the screen.

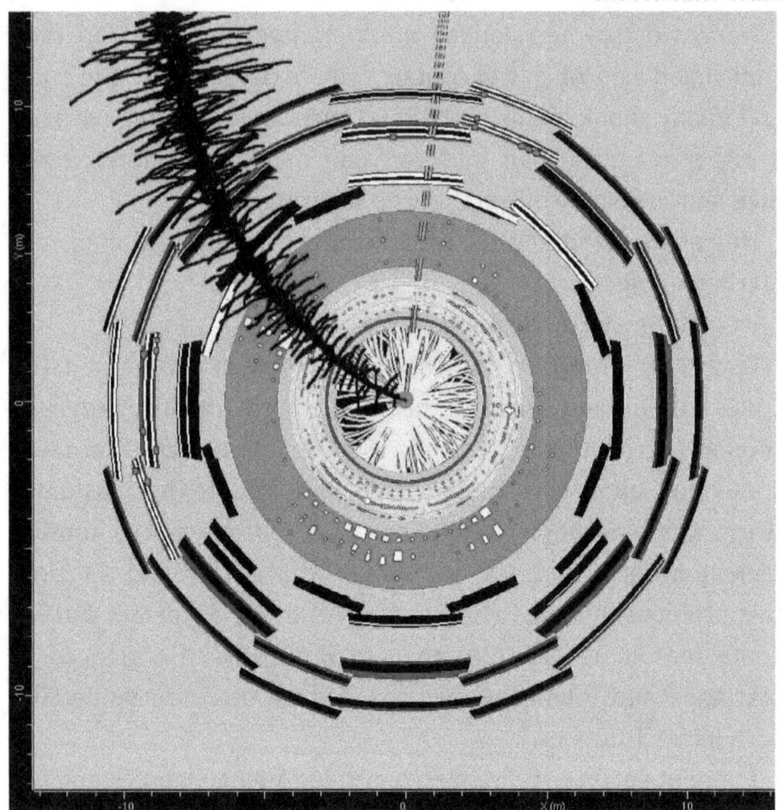

'Madre mia!' Romani gasped. 'And you say Danny doesn't know about this?'

To Catriona it just looked like a strand of hairy wool, getting thinner as it curved down towards the centre of some concentric circles in the middle of the blue screen.

'No, Professor,' Alex said. 'Look at the StoreGate record.' He clicked the mouse again and some writing came up on the screen. 'Michael Zhang and I are the only two people who have ever accessed this event.'

'Michael Zhang knows about it? Oh, then I suppose he must have told Danny. I've never seen anything like it.'

'Knowing Michael Zhang, I'd say he's probably kept it to

himself,' Alex said.

Francesco glanced at Brigit. 'Michael has a bit of a reputation as a loner,' he explained with a smile. 'How did you find this event, Count Karolyi?'

'I simply looked for the highest energy event that happened around the time this problem started,' Alex said.

'Then I think your husband should be told about this,' Francesco said to Marianne, and turned to Brigit. 'Look, why don't we all go down and see them? Count Karolyi can show Danny this event and you can have a quick word with Michael at the same time. I'm sure he can spare you two minutes and I really want him to tell you exactly what benefits Ireland has already gained from his participation in the ATLAS project.'

Layout of Point 1, CERN

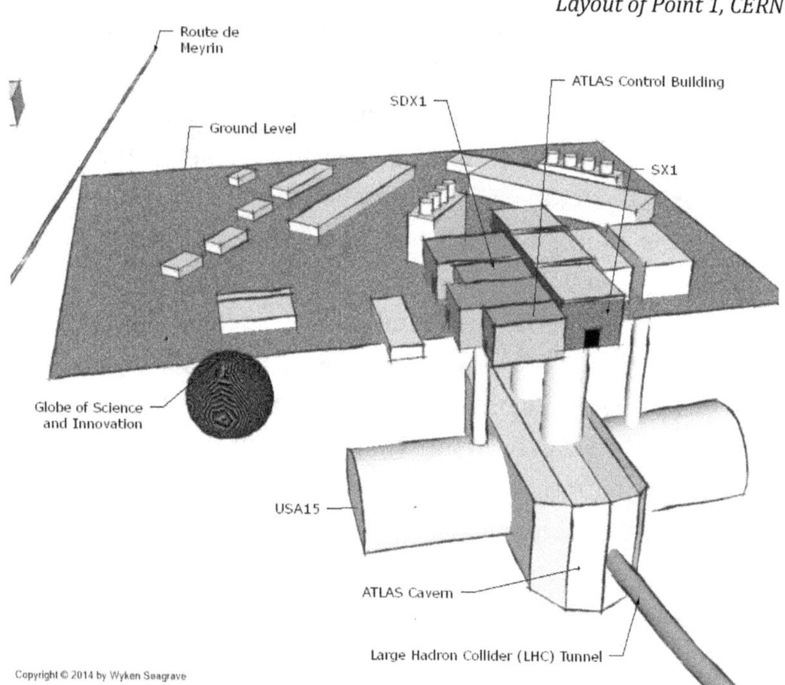

Copyright © 2014 by Wyken Seagrave

In the damp little car park outside the Visitor Centre, Catriona's heart soared as she waited for the others to come out, not sure which way to go but very eager to be first. The Sun reflected off the ATLAS building's glass front as it struggled to break through the morning cloud. She gazed at it thinking: *This was exactly what I wanted more than anything else in the world. I'm going to see Michael again. No matter what happens I'm going to ask him what he knows about Daddy's death.*

The others came out and Francesco paused to light a cigarette, still talking to Brigit. Catriona was expecting Marianne to lead them back to the building with the painted walls, but instead the guide turned left and walked towards a little door leading into a huge wooden-clad building labelled "SX1". Sam walked beside Marianne, asking her questions, apparently unaware of her discomfort. But walking behind her, Catriona saw the signs: the hands pressed into the small of the back; the legs waddling within the loose flappy trousers; the heavy footsteps. *Maybe pregnancy isn't much fun*, she decided.

As they waited for Marianne to enter a code to unlock the door, Catriona found herself standing beside the handsome young man Alex. He asked her what her name was but when she said Catriona he said 'I will call you "Kata". It's an old Hungarian name. How do you like Geneva, Kata?'

To her own surprise, she found herself saying 'I love it here.' And it was true. Despite Mother's antics, she realised that the hope of solving this terrible mystery had transformed her whole attitude. She would be quite happy to stay here and talk to Michael, no matter how long it took. She didn't care if she never went back to Dublin as long as she got rid of these flashbacks and solved the mystery.

'Yes, it's a beautiful town,' Alex was saying, smiling down at her.

She had never been this close to anyone so good-looking, let alone a real live Count. The smell of him and the sound of his voice, the thrill of having finally come here to CERN and the joy of finding someone who actually knew her father made her head swim, as if she had been secretly drinking some of Mother's pale cream sherry. It was something she had been dreaming about for six years, and now it was all coming true.

Marianne opened the door and Catriona walked into the huge building. High overhead, the roof was divided into three sloping sections. Light streamed in through windows between them, slanting down through the almost empty space and reflecting off the metal pipes and girders which covered the walls.

Alex walked beside her as they crossed the wide floor, passing the fences surrounding two huge circular holes in the ground which, he told her, led directly down to the ATLAS cavern. 'But we're not going in there,' he said. 'Nobody can enter the cavern when the beams are running. Danny and Michael are in the USA15 cavern next door.'

As he led her through a doorway into the SDX1 building, she plucked up her courage and said: 'I'm so glad you found this Store-thing, Count. That's the only reason we're going down to see Michael and I really want to see him again. There's something very important I need to ask him. Without you I might never have got this chance.'

At that moment, he seemed to her like a modern-day wizard who had waved an electronic magic wand and made her dreams come true.

They were approaching some narrow steps leading over a pipe which lay across the path. Alex politely took her arm and helped her up, looking at her curiously and said 'What is it you want to ask him, Kata?' His hand seemed to burn into her skin.

She walked up two steps, then turned and glanced into his eyes, their heads almost level, so close that she could easily have kissed him. His deep brown pupils were watching her, shimmering like pools of liquid chocolate, flecked with grey and green specks. His long, curving lashes sprouted around them like thick banks of reeds. A puzzled smile was playing on his broad, sensuous lips.

'It's about my father,' she said, and felt her arm tremble under his hand. 'He's…you see, he died when I was young, and I want to find out why.'

She felt his hand tighten on her arm, and the smile fell from his face, to be replaced by a puzzled look of genuine concern.

'You came here to find out why he died?'

She nodded. 'Mmm, and Michael knows something about it! And it's thanks to you that I'm going to talk to him!'

'Well I hope he can help you, and it's a pleasure to be able to assist a beautiful young lady like you.'

The smile returned to his face, and he pushed her up the steps and followed her over the bridge. 'So Mr Fitzpatrick isn't your father?' he said and began asking her about Mother as he led her through the SDX1 building towards a tall tower. How old was she? What had she done before she became the Irish Ambassador? How long had she been married to Sam?

Soon the others arrived and they all went into a little room at the foot of the tower. The hiss of gas echoed around them. Marianne explained that this was a sort of airlock. 'There is a lot of liquid helium down there,' she recited as if reading from a book. 'We probably have more liquid helium here in CERN than anywhere else in the Universe. If there is a fault then it might boil explosively, so we keep the lift-shaft at a slightly higher pressure. You will always be able to breathe here, although in an emergency you might have to walk up the stairs.'

The hiss died down, they left the airlock and put on red and yellow hard hats before entering the lift. Brigit had a hard time getting hers over her thick bushy hair, but Alex gave her a hand, telling her how beautiful it looked when it was finally jammed on her head. As the lift went down, he kept close to her, leaning towards her and talking in a confidential way, asking about the economic infrastructure in Ireland and support for entrepreneurs. Francesco Romani couldn't get a word in, and began talking to Sam.

To Catriona's surprise, Mother was able to answer most of his questions. She didn't seem to notice Alex glancing down the front of her blouse, although it was obvious to Catriona that she liked him, otherwise she would never have let him get that close. Catriona was not sure this man could be trusted, although this type of behaviour was not unusual for Mother.

After what seemed an eternity, the lift door finally opened to reveal a short white corridor which Marianne reminded them was the bottom of the airlock. 'This is where you must come if there are any problems,' she said. 'You will be safe here, and the emergency stairs are down there,' she added, pointing to a little corridor that ran in the opposite direction, behind the lift.

They followed her through a blue door, out of the airlock into a much wider, higher, longer corridor filled with the hum of pumps and the hiss of gas. There were doors and other corridors leading off to left and right. At its far end the corridor opened into a large hall full of pipes and tanks. It was hard to believe they were in a hole one hundred metres below the ground.

Francesco Romani led them through a door on the left into a smaller room crammed full of blue metal cabinets buzzing with electronic equipment. Michael Zhang and Danny Schneider sat at the far end facing a bank of computer screens, also wearing hard hats. Danny turned as they came in and when he saw the little crowd he stood up, frowning. Marianne hurried forward, took his arm and stood beside him smiling.

Catriona could not understand why a beautiful woman like Marianne would marry such a man. He was a good few years older than her and miserable-looking, with completely tired eyes and lifeless hair. He continued to frown at the obviously unwelcome visitors.

'Ah Danny,' Francesco said affably. 'Count Karolyi has found something very interesting. I thought you really ought to see it. In the meantime could I just borrow Michael for a second?'

Michael stood up and walked over to Brigit while Alex stepped forward and offered Danny a scrap of paper. The frown on Danny's face deepened and he glanced at his wife before taking the paper and reading it. Then he looked at Alex. 'It's just a StoreGate key,' he said.

Alex nodded. 'This is what happened just before these missing energy events started. Have you seen it?'

Danny shook his head.

Alex smiled. 'Thought not. You ought to have a look at it. It's very unusual.'

'As a matter of fact I was about to search the StoreGate database myself,' Danny said. 'We haven't found any physical faults with the equipment.' He sat and typed the number into a computer. Catriona saw the same pattern appear, the one Alex had shown them earlier with a thick line like a long hairy caterpillar crawling in a huge arc towards the middle of some rings.

'Christ almighty!' Danny said and turned to Michael. 'Have you seen this, Zhang?'

Episode 5 USA15

It's clearly some sort of high energy cosmic particle

Michael stopped speaking to Brigit and turned to look sideways at the screen. 'It's clearly some sort of high energy cosmic particle,' he said without any sign of the alarm which was burning on Danny's face. Danny scowled at him then turned back to the screen.

'Excuse me, Michael,' Catriona said, 'but could I just ask about my fa—'

'Did you say "cosmic particle" Michael?' Brigit interrupted her daughter. 'In what sense are you using the word "cosmic"?'

Catriona fell silent and waited, determined to ask her question before she left this underground cavern.

'There are particles,' Michael said turning back to Brigit, 'trillions of particles raining down upon us every second from outer space, Madam Ambassador. Most of them come from the Sun, have low energies and are consequently perfectly harmless. Such particles are passing through your body right now, Madam Ambassador, even this far underground.'

Brigit looked up at the ceiling with a startled expression as if she expected something to come down and hit her.

'Have no fear. They are of no risk to your health. On the other hand there are other particles which, like the one we are honoured to witness here, have much higher energy. They come from outside the Solar System and some even arrive from outside the—'

'You had already seen this StoreGate record when we came down here, Zhang!' Danny said, jumping up from the computer and facing him with a look burning with anger, almost with hatred. 'You already knew these missing energy events were real, yet you made out they might have been faults with ATLAS! How could you do such a despicable thing?' His voice was charged with emotion and Catriona noticed the tip of his nose had turned completely white. She looked at Michael, aware that he was being accused of doing something wrong, although she did not really understand what it was. There was a little smile playing on Michael's lips as he stood silently looking straight at Danny.

'Look at this!' Danny gestured viciously towards the screen beside him. 'According to the StoreGate database, you accessed this record a few minutes after the cosmic particle entered ATLAS.' Marianne stepped forward and put her hand on her husband's shoulder but he shrugged it off and stepped away from her. 'Yet you let me waste time coming down here looking for a fault. Why? In God's name, why?'

There was a long silence as the two men stared at each other. There seemed to be some sort of psychological battle going on between them, Catriona thought, with Michael's eyes inscrutable in the face of Danny's rage. Francesco Romani was bending over the screen now, saying 'Come now, Danny, I'm sure there's some perfectly valid explanation for all this.'

Finally Michael said 'ATLAS is the responsibility of the Run Co-ordinator, is it not Mr Schneider? And that is your position, I believe? Hence of course when you asked me to come down here to help you search for the fault I could hardly refuse, could I?'

'But it was you who first suggested there was a fault, Zhang!' Danny barked.

Francesco Romani straightened up, looking embarrassed as he glanced at Brigit then turned to Danny. 'Look, Danny, you haven't yet actually proved that this particle was the real cause of this problem. I'm still not convinced that any cosmic particle could cause all these missing energy events. What kind of particle could do that?'

'Look at the track it made when it arrived!' Danny growled, jabbing a finger at the screen. 'It obviously had enormous energy, more than any particle I've ever seen! It can't be a coincidence that these weird events started at exactly the same moment. No, what really puzzles me is why it slowed down and then stopped in the middle of ATLAS. It seems to have got trapped inside the beam pipe. I would expect a particle with that much energy to just pass straight through and out the other side.'

'The obvious explanation is often the last one that engineers can discern,' Michael said quietly. 'The postulation of hypotheses is probably best left to scientists who are trained in the field.' Danny whirled round and stared at him as if his intelligence had been insulted, but Michael continued calmly: 'In this case, for example, suppose the cosmic particle had an extremely large magnetic field. The consequence is obvious, is it not? The particle would have been trapped by the magnetic field inside ATLAS, which is precisely what we observe. Such is the power of lateral thinking.'

'A magnetic field?' Francesco sounded dazed. Beads of sweat were glistening on his forehead. 'What kind of particle could possibly have a strong enough magnetic field to be brought to rest so rapidly?'

'There is only one I can think of,' Michael said. 'I believe it must have been a magnetic monopole.'

'Eh? You've gone and lost me again there I'm afraid, Michael,' Brigit said, sounding as if she was really getting engrossed with this discussion.

Michael smiled up at her and spoke slowly as if he were talking to a rather stupid schoolgirl. 'Several different theories[2] predict that at least one particle with a single magnetic charge called a "monopole" was created in the Big Bang, Madam Ambassador. Although many people have searched for it, nobody has ever found any evidence of its existence. Until today. Therefore this particle, if it proves to be a monopole, will be the most fundamentally important object ever discovered in CERN. If we can measure its properties it will completely revolutionise the fundamental laws of physics.'

Francesco pulled a gleaming white handkerchief out of his pocket, lifted off his hard hat and mopped his face. 'Can you measure its magnetic charge, Michael? If you can prove that it's a monopole and measure its parameters then I would say you would almost certainly win the Nobel Prize for Ireland.'

'Hurrah!' Brigit yelled, making everyone jump. 'And if he does that then I can guarantee that Ireland will join CERN. This is a triumph for Irish science! Hurray for Ireland.' She began to dance a jig, holding on to her hard. Michael watched her with a little smile.

'And it wouldn't do your Presidential Campaign any harm either,' Sam said.

Brigit turned a smiling face on him. 'Exactly,' she said. 'Anyone

---

[2] The first prediction of the existence of magnetic monopoles was by Paul Dirac. See the bibliography entry (5). See also Cosmic Monopole entry in Glossary.

here got a camera? Oh,' she said, answering her own question, 'I've got one.' She took her mobile phone out of her bag. 'Here Sam, turn this on.' She was still holding it out to him when the high-pitched wail of an alarm echoed around the little Electronics Room. Everyone went quiet and Catriona's heart sank. *Something's obviously wrong down here*, she thought and began working out how to get back to the surface. *I can't remember where Marianne was pointing when she told us about the emergency stairs*, she thought, panic surging in her stomach.

Danny sank into the chair and stared at the screen muttering 'Ach Scheisse!'

'What's the matter?' Brigit said.

'We've got a Level One Alarm.' Danny clicked the mouse on a flashing icon near the bottom of the screen. 'The beam's aborted,' he groaned, as if announcing a death in the family.

'Oh dear, what a pity,' Brigit said, putting the phone back into her bag and glancing at her watch.

'There's been a vacuum failure in the beam pipe.' Danny was running his hands through his thinning hair. 'This is a disaster. We'll have to dismantle ATLAS to fix this. We'll be out of operation for months.' He turned and glared at Michael as if it was his fault. 'This cannot possibly be a coincidence. It must be connected with this cosmic monopole.'

'What?' Francesco said, 'You think the monopole's punctured the beam pipe wall? No, that's not possible. The monopole passed through the wall when it went into ATLAS without causing any damage, so why would it cause this problem now?'

Danny was staring at Michael. 'I think he knows.'

Francesco turned to Michael who placed the palms of his hands together, saying 'The explanation is quite simple.' He was not smiling now. 'Suppose the Monopole has absorbed energy from the beams. That would explain why we were getting the missing energy events we assumed were faults.' He checked his watch. 'This absorption has lasted for just under an hour. That would be sufficient time for the Monopole to have been transformed into something else, something capable of puncturing the vacuum pipe.'

'Transformed?' Francesco sounded exasperated. 'Into what?'

'There is only one thing I can think of,' Michael said.

'A black hole,' Danny whispered.

'Precisely.' On Michael's lips the word almost became a song.

Catriona felt herself grow tense. She had seen black holes swallow things in movies. *But they aren't real, are they?* she asked herself, but did not get an answer. *And all this talk is taking up so much time. I just want a chance to ask Michael some questions.*

'A black hole?' Francesco sounded as if he was going to explode. His heavy jowls wobbled as he shook his head. 'No no no! Any black hole we create in CERN cannot possibly last long enough to give rise to all these missing energy events. It would immediately be eliminated by Hawking radiation.'

Catriona's head was beginning to swim with all this technical talk. *If the scientists can't understand it, what chance do I stand?*

'But a black hole built around a cosmic monopole would be entirely different,' Michael said. 'Wells and Watts wrote a paper on the subject a few years ago. In Phys Rev Letts I believe. They predicted that if a micro black hole could contain a magnetic monopole then it might be stable for several minutes, perhaps as long as an hour, before it evaporated.'

'A micro black hole?' Brigit said. 'I've never heard of one of those.'

'There are two types of black hole, Madame Ambassador,' Francesco explained, talking quickly. 'Large ones found at the centres of galaxies and tiny little ones such as we might make here in CERN. But the Hawking radiation theory predicts that the small ones will immediately evaporate.' He turned to

Michael. 'So you're saying the magnetic monopole came to rest in the beam pipe, absorbed particles from the beam and was transformed into a persistent black hole?'

Michael nodded.

'And you knew that was going to happen,' Danny said, his voice cracking with emotion. 'That's why you persuaded me to leave the beams running while we came down here to investigate this supposed fault.'

'But surely you can see, Mr Schneider,' Michael replied calmly, 'that this one experiment alone is worth the entire cost of ATLAS?'

Danny almost exploded. 'But that's crazy! Don't you realise that if that black hole comes out of ATLAS it could endanger the whole world?'

Michael looked up at him with an inscrutable Chinese smile. 'I don't think that will happen, Mr Schneider. Wells and Watts showed that any such black hole would evaporate within an hour.'

'But this one's lasted for over an hour already,' Francesco said.

'Not so, Professor. For most of that time it was still merely a monopole. We do not know exactly at what point it was transformed into a black hole. What we do know is that it will evaporate within the next hour at most.'

'The LHC is closing down,' Danny said, looking at the computer and picking up the phone. 'I think we'd better shut ATLAS down too.'

'No, Mr Schneider!' Michael said with a yelp like a frightened child. 'Please don't do that. I think you should leave ATLAS running.'

'What?' Danny said, the phone to his ear. 'You're crazy, Zhang!'

'Let's all just try to stay calm,' Francesco said, waving his arms up and down then taking a deep breath. 'Suppose we assume there is a black hole and let's assume it has punctured the beam pipe. In that case it must be inside ATLAS now!'

'That seems very possible,' Michael said, 'even probable. That's precisely why I don't want Mr Schneider to turn ATLAS off. If it keeps running we might be able to use ATLAS to track the black hole.'

'Listen, Zhang,' Danny snapped. 'If there is a black hole and if it's entered ATLAS then it's going to burn a hole in the detector, isn't it?'

'So is this black hole dangerous or not?' Brigit asked.

'No, not at all,' Francesco said confidently. 'Micro black holes are very tiny. Any damage it causes will be very small.'

Catriona saw Michael glance at Francesco out of the corner of his eye then turn to Danny. 'It will burn a hole whether ATLAS is running or not,' he said, 'but I agree with Professor Romani. I don't think the damage will be huge and if you shut ATLAS down we won't be able to collect any data. But if you leave ATLAS running, we can measure some vital parameters such as its mass, its electrical charge and especially its magnetic charge.'

Danny stared at him, still holding the phone.

'Surely you can see, Mr Schneider, that this accidental capture of a monopole has presented us with a unique opportunity to measure a black hole. Now surely we need to make the best of a bad situation and take what measurements we can.'

There was a deep silence in the little room. The only noise was from the gas moving through the thick metal pipe overhead.

'What do you think, Professor Romani?' Danny asked.

'I agree with Dr Zhang. I don't think serious harm will come to ATLAS and this event is clearly very important. I don't know how many of these magnetic monopoles there are in the Universe but I should think the chances of one being captured and then converted into a persistent black hole must be fairly small. It might never happen again in our lifetime. I think we should learn as much as we can while we have the chance. And anyway you will get exactly the same damage to ATLAS whether the magnetic field is on or off. But in the end the decision is down to you, and the ATLAS Executive Board, of course.'

Danny dialled and lifted the phone to his ear. 'Seline? We think there might be a black hole inside ATLAS...Yes I know that, but this one is persistent...I haven't got time to explain that now. I want you to leave ATLAS running and call an emergency meeting of the Executive Board...'

Meanwhile Michael had sat down at the computer and was clicking the mouse. Catriona saw images flash onto the screen. Straight black blocks, red rods and green bars organised like a child's building blocks into rectangles, one inside the other, scattered over a pale blue background. Another image flashed up, concentric rings, mostly black but with thinner coloured circles within and without. The images flickered then zoomed and she felt as if she were falling into a pool of blue water.

Danny put the phone down. 'We're going to leave ATLAS running. Even if we turn it off, the magnetic field will persist for over an hour so we might as well try to measure something while we've got the chance.'

'Ah, here it is!' Michael said.

The screen showed a thin red line moving slowly across one of the thick black rings.

'It seems to have left the Silicon Detector,' Michael said. 'I will see if I can measure the curvature in the rho-z projection.' The mouse clicked and the image changed back into rectangles. The red line curved across the scattered bars.

'It's drifting at quite a rate,' Danny said.

'Is that important?' Brigit asked.

'Of course it is! It's accelerating in ATLAS's magnetic field. It could reach the end of the detector before it evaporates.'

'I've measured its curvature,' Michael said. 'I will now work out the magnetic charge.'

'Michael, is that possible?' Francesco said.

'Oh yes, Professor Romani. The calculation is trivial. We know the field strength so—'

'No, I mean is it possible for the black hole to come out of ATLAS?'

Michael paused. 'It is possible, if it persists long enough. Wells and Watts showed that the lifetime of a black hole containing a monopole will depend on its magnetic charge.'

'Can you work out how long it will last?' Francesco said. 'We need to know whether it will emerge from ATLAS or not.' He turned to Brigit. 'I am sorry, Your Excellency,' he said in a very formal tone, 'but the LHC is temporarily out of action, Dr Zhang is obviously busy so there is no further point in your remaining down here. If you would care to go with Marianne she will accompany you—'

'It's in the TRT end cap now,' Danny said.

'Oh, can't I stay a bit longer, Francesco?' Brigit said, peering round him at the screen. 'I want to see what happens and you say there's no danger so why not? I'll just have to be late for my meeting, but I think it would be worth it.'

'Then you remain at your own risk,' Francesco said and turned back to the screen.

'Don't you think it would be safer if we left now, Bee?' Sam said quietly. He looked worried; his usual implacable calmness had vanished from his face.

'What, and lose a unique publicity opportunity? Don't be stupid, Samuel. Can't you just see the headline? "Irish Ambassador and possible Presidential Candidate Brigit O'Brien present at discovery of insistent black hole."'

'I think they said "persistent",' Sam said.

Michael stood up. 'According to my calculations the black hole should evaporate in the next ten minutes with a probability of ninety-nine percent.'

'But what will happen if it doesn't,' Sam said, 'and the black hole comes out of ATLAS? What would happen then, Michael?'

It was as if time stopped for a heartbeat as everyone waited for Michael to answer. He was looking at Sam but his eyes seemed to be seeing something else, something inside his head. 'If the black hole emerged from ATLAS then its motion would depend on the net force acting upon it,' Michael said very slowly. 'Once outside, it would feel two forces: the Earth's gravitational field and the combined magnetic field of the Earth and ATLAS. Gravity would tend to make it fall but on the other hand we know from the way it is moving in ATLAS's field that it is a south monopole, so the magnetic field would tend to make it rise.'

'So which way would it move, do you think?' Sam asked.

'That would depend on the relative strength of these two forces which would in turn depend on both its mass and magnetic charge. At a guess, I would say that gravity will probably have the stronger effect, and it will fall, but I'd have to do some detailed calculations to corroborate that.'

'And what would happen if it hit the Earth?' Sam said.

Again there was a long silence before Michael said quietly: 'My guess is it will have evaporated long before we get to that stage. I'm almost sure it will.'

'But my God, Michael,' there was a hint of panic in Brigit's voice, 'you mean there's a chance it won't? It could actually hit the Earth?'

Episode 6 The Stairs

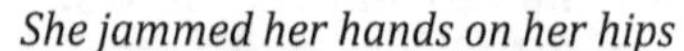

She jammed her hands on her hips

'I'm very sorry, Your Excellency,' Francesco said speaking very quickly, his Italian accent stronger than ever, 'but I must insist you and your family return to the surface immediately.'

'So now you've made this black hole you're just going to leave it and run away are you, gentlemen?' Brigit snapped, looking at the little group of people facing her in their ridiculous hard hats as she stood with her back to the door. She jammed her hands on her hips, a defiant look on her face. Everyone except Sam was staring at her in shocked silence. Catriona's stomach lurched as if somebody had just moved the floor. The questions about her father's death which had been burning to be answered seemed a lot less important right now. When a black hole is about to hit the Earth, you don't worry too much about anything else.

Standing beside her, Sam had a silly little smile on his face and looked as if he were going to cry as Brigit said 'Well I think you ought to stay and fight this stupid bloody black hole. There's more at stake here than just science, isn't there? Michael, do you admit that the future of the whole world is at stake here? If that black hole touches the Earth it will absorb the whole planet, won't it?'

'There is a chance that it could, Madame Ambassador,' Michael said gravely. The music of his voice had changed into a funeral dirge.

'Well then we must not let that happen. You've got to do something. You've got to fight for the Earth, and for all of humanity. Right then. So now, what can we do? Anyone got any ideas?'

She stared round at them all, hands still on hips, like an angry school-mistress before her recalcitrant children.

Nobody spoke. The hum of computers filled the little Electronics Room. Behind every pair of eyes, a brain hunted for a solution.

Sam's hand reached out and rested on Brigit's arm, squeezing it lovingly as he turned to Michael and said. 'Mmm, I was wondering...I don't know much about all this but I thought, well, this black hole's being pushed out of ATLAS by the magnetic field isn't it?'

'Of course it is, Samuel,' Brigit snapped. 'That's precisely the problem.'

Oh please Mother, Catriona thought. *Let Sam speak for a change.*

'Yes,' Sam said calmly, 'but it might be the solution too. What would happen if we reversed the field?'

'That's it Sam!' Catriona yelped, jumping up and down in her excitement. 'That would pull it back into ATLAS, wouldn't it Michael?'

'Is that possible, Danny?' Francesco said. He sounded like a drowning man clutching at a straw. 'Could you reverse the field?'

'Reverse the field in ATLAS?' Danny winced. 'You've got to be joking, Professor Romani. There are twenty thousand amps flowing through the barrel toroid. There's more than a gigajoule of energy in there, and another couple of hundred megajoules in each of the end cap toroids. Not to mention the central solenoid. The speed that black hole's moving, it will be out of the detector before we have even killed the existing field, let alone reversed it. Our only hope is that the black hole evaporates soon.'

'But surely it's worth a try?' Catriona pleaded. 'What other hope have we got?'

'Well we can turn ATLAS off for a start,' Danny said picking up the phone. 'I should never have let it run this long.' He began to dial. 'If I had shut it down earlier, if I had not allowed Dr Zhang to persuade me to leave it running, then the black hole would probably still be safely tucked away inside the Pixel Detector.' Bitterness trembled in his voice. Marianne moved closer and put her arm through his. 'Seline,' Danny said into the phone. 'I think you should shut ATLAS down now. Oh you have? That's good. Exactly what I would have done...'

'It seems to me,' Michael said quietly to Francesco, 'the black hole is moving so fast that even if Seline shuts ATLAS down it will still reach the toroid. Then things might start happening.'

'How do you mean?'

Before Michael could answer the alarm filling the cavern grew louder and rose to a higher pitch. Catriona felt like screaming.

'We've got a Level Two Alarm,' Danny said into the phone and looked at the screen. 'There's a quench[3] in the end cap toroid.'

'Yes that's what I thought might happen,' Michael said. The dirge in his voice had brightened into a eulogy-song. 'That'll kill the magnetic field pretty quickly won't it?' He gave Danny a sly little smile. 'My guess is that once the magnetic field has been quenched, friction will slow the black hole dramatically. Might even stop it altogether.'

---

[3] See Quench entry in Glossary.

Danny scowled at him with a look Catriona thought bordered on hatred.

'So the black hole might not escape from the detector at all?' Francesco said.

'With luck it might evaporate before it escapes.'

'I'm lost here,' Brigit said. 'Can anyone tell me what's happening?'

'The black hole has hit one of the magnets and caused a quench,' Francesco said.

'And that means exactly what in English?'

'Basically the magnet has broken. The magnetic field will now quickly burn away and with luck the black hole will stay inside ATLAS until it evaporates.'

The alarm grew to an ear-piercing wail.

'Level Three Alarm,' Danny said. He checked the screen. 'There's a coolant leak. Looks like liquid helium's pouring out onto the cavern floor.'

'Everybody into the airlock.' Francesco shouted. 'Quick!'

Sofie Dialektaki grunted between clenched teeth

Sofie Dialektaki grunted between clenched teeth and gave the rope another yank. Her T-shirt changed from light to dark blue as it soaked up her sweat. On the rope's lower end, the orange-covered Petzl Nest stretcher lifted ten centimetres further up the climbing tower.

'Go on, Sofie.' Ludovico Narkosa said, his Neapolitan accent adding chocolate and strawberry vowels to the French which all firefighters at CERN had to speak. 'Putta ze little effor into it!'

Engine Chief George Gabor glanced at his watch. 'Ten-forty. Come on Sofie, hurry up! I was hoping to get this over by eleven.'

'Here, permit me giva you a hand,' Ludovico said.

'No, leave her Ludo! She's got to do this on her own.' George leaned over the rail and looked down. 'You okay down there, Robert?' he called.

Sofie glanced down at the stretcher. A beam of sunlight was slashing down across the Fire Station yard and stabbing into Robert Moore's eyes. The fourth member of the Green Team squinted, blinked, and tried ineffectually to move his head. Sofie knew he couldn't. She too had been strapped into that stretcher when she first joined George Gabor's team. He considered it part of their training. 'If you're going to put people into the Petzl Nest you have to know how it feels,' he used to say. She hauled on the rope again, the stretcher lifted another ten centimetres, the sunlight left Robert's face and his eyes opened. He looked up at Sofie with his usual expression, a confused frown. Sofie smiled. She liked Robert, but sometimes she wondered if he really had what it took to be a firefighter in CERN.

'How does it feel to be in the stretcher, Robert?' George called down.

Robert stared up at him with dumb incomprehension.

Ludovico too leaned over the safety rail. 'You wasting you breath, George. He no understand a word of French.'

Sofie knew it was not far from the truth. Robert's grasp of French had hardly progressed in the two months since he came from England to CERN.

'Here, giva me ze rope, Sofie.' Ludovico grabbed the rope off her and pulled it so the stretcher began to swing from side to side. 'Is windy today, Roberto?' he called down in French.

Sofie felt uncomfortable. George tied off the rope and watched, but said nothing.

Ludovico was notorious for playing practical jokes on his teammates. He gave the rope another sharp tug.

'Hey, Roberto!' Ludovico called. 'Is windy today? Yes or no?'

Still no answer. Then a door opened in the Fire Station and Sofie saw Service Chief Laron Parfait come into the yard.

George saw him too. 'Stop now, Ludo,' he said quietly.

Ludovico looked at him, warned by his tone of command, then followed his eyes down into the yard.

'Oh, merda!' Ludovico pulled the rope against the swing. The stretcher slowed to a halt.

'Is this some new safety manoeuvre I haven't heard about?' Laron called up to them as he walked to the foot of the climbing tower.

'Just teaching Roberto the French for wind.' Ludovico gave him a sheepish look.

'French? Is tutoring another side-line of yours, Foxtrot Three One?'

Sofie sniggered, took the rope off Ludovico and recommenced the haul.

'She shouldn't be doing that on her own!' Laron snapped.

'Oh Christ.' George began to pull on the rope helping her to haul Robert to the top of the tower.

'Can I have a word with you, Papa Seven?' Laron said when the stretcher was on the platform.

'My pleasure,' George muttered and climbed down the ladder.

Sofie began to free the straps across the stretcher cover.

'I thought we'd agreed no more horse-play on duty?' she heard Laron say.

'There was no danger,' George said.

'So that makes it okay, does it?'

'Ludo was only following my orders. I'm still trying to bring Robert out of his shell. He's full of the famous British reserve. I can't afford to have members of my team who don't participate fully. And anyway Ludo has to express his personality too. That's part of team building. I give every one of my crew the chance to deviate a little during training. I find that way they obey orders without question during real action.'

'Really?'

'Certainly. In fact I expect them to. It's part of the team-building process.'

'You're not serious, Papa Seven?'

'I certainly am. In an emergency, the lives of these people will depend on how well they understand each other. That's why I'm so worried about Robert Moore.'

Sofie glanced at Robert. He'd emerged from the stretcher and was now taking his revenge on Ludovico, pinning him against the rail, apparently unaware they were talking about him down below.

'I explained over breakfast why he has to be part of your crew,' Laron said, 'but I'll go through it again if you can't remember what I said. With this vomiting illness going round, Foxtrot Four Seven is the only person with full paramedic training fit for duty today.'

'But we've all got basic first-aid.' George glanced up, saw Ludo bent backwards over the safety rail silently screaming at Robert for mercy and looked away, forcing his face into a frown. 'Robert's only been with us for a few weeks. His French just isn't good enough yet. I don't think—'

George broke off as a Level Three Alarm echoed across the yard. Without another word to Laron he ran into the Fire Station. Sofie, Ludovico and Robert scrambled down the ladder and ran to the Engine.

Francesco hurried past the open lift-door

Catriona did not hesitate. There was something in Francesco's voice that said 'This is life or death'. She ran out of the Electronics Room and down the wide white corridor which was almost silent now except for the echoing footsteps of Sam and the others following her. She was still horrified at the thought of a black hole swallowing the Earth, but she knew she wouldn't be able to do anything if she died of gassing. She ran through the airlock door, along the narrow corridor and into the lift. Sam joined her but Francesco hurried past the open lift-door and round a corner.

'Looks like we've got to walk up the stairs,' Sam said, and they followed Brigit along a very narrow corridor round the back of the lift, through a narrow door and onto a little landing. Narrow flights of concrete stairs led up and down, both with a central metal handrail. The others came through the door and waited for Marianne and Danny to catch up.

'Ah, here she is.' Francesco sounded relieved as Marianne finally came through the door. 'Up you go my dear. Women and children first.'

'No, Professor Romani,' Marianne said. 'I would only slow you down.'

'I think you should take your visitors first, Professor,' Danny growled sardonically.

Francesco looked at Brigit, then his eyes settled on Catriona, but before he could speak, she snapped 'I'm not going first!'

'Please, Catty, just go,' Sam said. 'You're youngest and fittest. You won't hold the rest of us back.'

Catriona paused for a second then hunched her shoulders and ran up, her hand not even touching the handrail.

Brigit ran up after her.

'No need to run,' Francesco said.

'Don't run, Catty,' Sam called. 'It's safer to walk. If you slip you'll fall on top of us.'

Catriona slowed to a quick walk, her legs already starting to ache. Glancing back she saw Mother, Sam, Francesco and Michael following close behind her with Marianne and Danny walking up slowly in the rear.

For a moment she wondered where the good-looking Count had gone. *Perhaps he's already been gassed?* she thought. *Serves him right!*

She turned her full attention on not falling back as she pushed her protesting leg-muscles to climb faster. She began to count the steps, trying to take her mind off the pain. Eight steps then a little landing. Turn to the right and walk up the next flight. How many flights to the top? It must have been after about twenty that she heard the explosion. It was a very deep boom that made the stairs tremble beneath her feet. It seemed to start somewhere below her and echoed up and down the stairwell several times.

Mother screamed and Danny shouted 'Jesus Christ'. There was panic on the stairs. Catriona found herself running up, ignoring the protest from her legs, with Mother close behind. How far was it now to the top?

Then she heard Michael's shrill voice pipe 'Don't worry. That was probably the black hole evaporating.'

Everyone except Danny and Marianne stopped running and stood looking down at Michael. Catriona could hear the two in the rear still walking up.

'Do you mean the black hole's gone?' Sam panted.

'Don't...' Danny Schneider puffed angrily as he and Marianne caught up with the others. 'Don't be ridiculous Zhang. The black hole could never have made an explosion like that.'

'Yes it could.' Michael's voice was dancing a jig, celebrating the death of an arch-enemy. 'Wells and Watts predicted the evaporation of a magnetic monopole-centred black hole would terminate violently.'

'So you mean we're safe?' Brigit screamed. 'The black hole's gone? Yes! Hurrah! Hurrah for Ireland!' To Catriona's surprise, Mother burst into tears. Catriona felt like crying too. It was as if the terror of a nightmare had been taken away by the waving of a magic wand. Mother started kissing the men and everyone started thumping everyone else on the back and laughing. It was as if a group of long-lost friends had met unexpectedly on those narrow concrete stairs.

Catriona started walking back down towards them but stopped when she heard a rumble higher up the stairs. Her head cocked itself to one side, her ears twitched. The noise was faint, very faint, like the first rumble of the sea as you walk towards the distant shore, and the others were making so much noise it was difficult to be sure.

'Listen!' she shouted, 'Listen! Listen!'

Finally the others fell silent and she heard the rumble growing louder, stronger and louder, a sort of avalanche of sound coming from overhead and getting closer. For a moment nobody moved, then a cloud of white dust swept down the stairs and enveloped Catriona. It was acrid and choking. Her eyes began to water, her nose and throat and lungs stung. She tried to scream and began to cough, feeling she would vomit over Mother any moment.

'The stairs are collapsing,' Francesco shouted. 'Down! Quick!'

Catriona's toes kicked Mother's back as she ran after her down the stairs and her hard hat flew off and went bouncing down the stairs ahead of her. A moment later a thicker cloud of dust swept past her and engulfed Mother. Then tears began streaming down Catriona's face as the pungent dust burned into her eyes. She felt in her skirt pocket, took out her handkerchief and clamped it over her nose. She squeezed her eyes tight, slowing to a walk as she began to feel her way down the handrail.

She descended two more flights with the roar from above coming closer and getting louder until, with a sharp and frightening pain, something heavy hit her back. She could hear things bouncing off the steps and walls around her, hammering into her shoulders and thumping on her legs. Some of them felt as big as bricks. Then she ran into something, her head jerked forward and her hard hat few away down the stairs.

Catriona couldn't see anything. She heard Mother say: 'What's wrong Sam? Go on for God's sake!'

Then she heard Danny Schneider say 'I'm going to carry you Marianne.'

A woman screamed. It sounded like Marianne. 'Don't!' She gave a sort of grunt. 'I can't! It's my ankle.' Then she screamed again. 'Oh Danny! I'm having a contraction.'

A moment later something heavy struck Catriona on the back of her head and she staggered, grasped the handrail then fell backwards onto the stairs and everything went black.

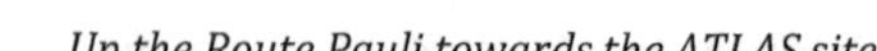
Up the Route Pauli towards the ATLAS site

As Ludovico swung the red Engine out of the Station Yard two minutes later, horns wailing, lights flashing and throttled it down the Route Einstein and left up the Route Pauli towards the ATLAS site, George told his crew what he had learned in the Safety Control Room. 'There's been an explosion at the Geneva end of ATLAS. Went up one of the shafts like a cannon and blew away one of the roofs from SX.'

In her mind's eye, Sofie tried to picture one of their large roof sections blowing away from the wooden-clad SX building which stood on the surface above the ATLAS cavern.

'You remember those roofs were designed to lift off as a safety measure?' George said. 'To stop the other buildings around from collapsing? That sounded like a great plan, didn't it?' Sofie and Ludovico nodded. Robert looked blank, unable to follow his French. 'Unfortunately one of those roofs fell onto the SDX building and caused the lift-head to collapse.'

'Oh my God!' Ludovico said.

'That's right. What's worse, it sounds like the people underground were on the stairs when it happened.'

'It could hardly have been any worse!' Sofie said.

'Oh yes it could! Apparently the explosion was caused by a black hole!' There was a stunned silence. 'That's right,' George said, 'they made a bloody black hole this morning. 'One of the scientists who were down there says it was the black hole that caused the explosion.' Sofie couldn't believe what she was hearing.

A minute, later Ludovico threw the Engine round the corner of the ATLAS offices and drove past the crowd of scientists who had come out into the car park for safety. At a sign from George, one of them turned a switch and the SX1 building door rolled up. Ludovico drove inside and parked near one of the two shafts which led down to the ATLAS cavern. They paused to assess the damage and the danger.

Crumpled sheets of steel were lying around like scraps of waste paper.

'There used to be three panels in this roof,' George said.

'Only two now,' Ludovico said brightly.

'That one's no problem,' George pointed to the panel leaning against the far wall, then looked up at the middle panel which was hanging down into the building held up only by two sides. 'This one's not safe, but we'll have to live with it. The rescue is our top priority.'

'So the one that fell on SDX used to be over this shaft,' Sofie said. They all looked up. The panel, which had once covered the roof directly above them, above the nearest of the two 18-metre-wide shafts, was completely missing.

'Well at least the explosion has removed the shaft cover,' George said, 'so it should be easy to get down. Come on.'

They ran across to the tall safety fence surrounding the shaft and broke open the gate.

'Sofie, stay here with Robert.'

George and Ludovico fitted their breathing masks, turned on

the oxygen in the canisters on their backs, ran to the low shaft-head wall and looked down, holding gas detectors over the shaft.

'There's no gas or smoke, Ludo.'

'Do you think the pipes is safe?'

There had been several thick metal pipes running down one side of the shaft. The explosion had shredded them, tearing them into curling metal blades, jagged edges and hungry spikes.

'Yes, I think so,' George said. 'Just stay away from them as we make the descent.' He ran back to the fence, calling 'We need abseil ropes, harnesses, descendeurs and carabiners.'

'And little bit of luck,' Ludovico added.

Robert Moore stood and watched as they took the kit out of the Engine. Once all was prepared, George and Ludovico climbed onto the wall and lowered themselves down the shaft, shining their torches into the gloom, as Sofie flipped on her radio.

'Foxtrot Three Seven to Control. Papa Seven and Foxtrot Three One descending by abseil into ATLAS shaft. Over.'

Episode 7 ATLAS Cavern

They escaped back into the narrow corridor

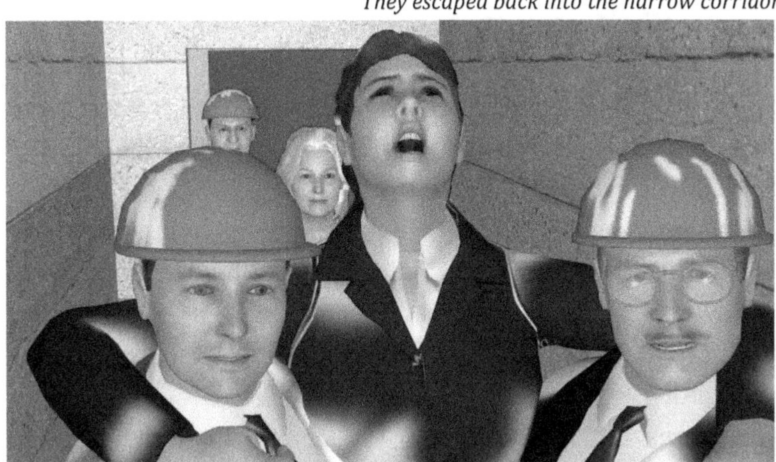

Blinded by the choking dust, battered by the hailstorm of falling debris, Danny and Sam staggered down three flights of stairs carrying Marianne sitting on the saddle of their clasped hands screaming with pain and fear, breaking Sam's back a little more with every step down, Brigit and the others pressing close behind them.

Finally, Danny yanked open a door and they escaped back into the narrow corridor. Still staggering beneath her weight, they carried Marianne past the lift into the wider corridor and laid her gently on the concrete floor. The others followed and collapsed around them, coughing and heaving, unable to speak.

Eventually Brigit recovered enough to demand: 'So what are we going to do now, Francesco?' the dust surrounding her quivering hair like a halo.

'I think we must all go down to the Safe Room, Madame Ambassador.'

'Safe Room?' she exploded with incredulity. 'What Safe Room?'

While Francesco was explaining that an area with that designation lay at the far end of the USA15 cavern, and while Brigit was angrily demanding why they had not gone there in the first place, Sam was looking round, checking that everyone was safe. There seemed to be one person missing.

'Anyone seen Catriona?' he said, half afraid of the answer. But there was no answer. He hauled himself to his feet and staggered away from the lift into the main USA15 corridor. She was not there.

With growing anxiety, but looking around hoping at every moment to see her, a little bundle of dust hidden in a corner somewhere, he turned, stepped over Marianne and walked past the lift to the little corridor leading back to the stairs. She wasn't there either.

He stared at the blue door at the far end, his mind recoiling from an unthinkable suspicion. *She can't still be on the stairs?* But there seemed no other solution. Then he heard Brigit calling after him: 'Don't be a fool, Samuel. She can't still be alive.'

Sam's mind lurched at these words, as if she had hit him on the side of the head with a hammer, and something snapped inside him. Instantly his doubt and fear vanished, he forgot the stabbing pain in his back, forgot everything except Catriona. He ran up the corridor to the door, held half-open by a pile of rubble, from which dust was still billowing out.

He tried to push open the door onto the stairwell and, at that instant, there was a rumble louder than thunder on the other side and the door slammed shut in his face. For a few seconds there was a noise like somebody battering on the door. An express train seemed to be hurtling down the stairwell. Then suddenly there was silence. Sam listened to it, his ears still ringing from the noise, then he turned his back to the door and sank slowly to the floor.

And here was Brigit, leaning over him, saying nothing. He looked up into her face. Her hard hat had long gone and her dishevelled hair was almost hidden beneath a blanket of concrete dust.

'Do you think that was Catriona banging on the door?' he whispered.

She blinked then shrugged, but still she didn't say anything, her face cold and hard.

He stared at her for a long moment, then let his head fall back against the door and began to cry.

'Oh for God's sake stop that,' Brigit snapped. 'There'll be plenty of time for all that later.' Her words slashed him like barbed wire. 'We've still got to get out of here alive. Why are you looking at me like that? She's my daughter and I haven't fallen to pieces like this so why should you? You aren't even her father! You're lucky we weren't all killed like that.'

'Don't you care? Don't you care about your own daughter?'

'Don't talk to me about caring. Are you a man or a woman? Oh, I forgot, you're incapable of doing a man's job and now it seems you're incapable of doing anything but crying. You're a faggot, Sam Fitzpatrick. Get out of my sight.'

She turned on her shoe-less heel and stomped back along the corridor. Sam stared after her. He couldn't recognise her.

Is that really the woman I've lived with for the past six years? I can't believe it. She seems like a total stranger. How could I ever have believed she was good and kind beneath that blasé, brash exterior when she has just given up her daughter for dead? Doesn't she have any motherly instincts at all?

He sat there for a minute, thinking about the thousands of times he had ignored Brigit's selfishness and even tolerated her infidelities. *I know why I did it,* he thought. *I just wanted to help Catty, to bring her up like my own child.*

"I'm afraid you're never going to father any children, Mr Fitzpatrick." The doctor was bending over him again, as he had seen him a thousand times before, with the results of his test. Then Catriona was sitting in his class in junior school on the first day she had returned to after her father's mysterious death, totally unable to concentrate on her work. Then there was Brigit standing in the pure white lounge of her luxury Dublin mansion, saying "Please come round to visit us whenever you like, Mr Fitzpatrick".

I know why she encouraged me, of course. She just wanted me as an unpaid child-minder. But I went round gladly. It was the greatest joy of my life to watch how Catty had gradually emerged from her shocked state into something like a normal little girl. And now… Now she's gone. Once more his head fell back against the door, but this time he managed to hold back the tears. *At least I was able to have a little girl of my own for six years. It was more than I ever expected.*

After a minute he felt strong enough to heave himself to his feet and trudge after Brigit, thinking: *I suppose she's right in one way. The main thing now is to get everyone else out of this cavern alive.*

The corridor near the lift was empty apart from a pool of dust and concrete fragments near the lift. A little river of dust led from it into the main corridor. *They must have gone to the Safe Room, wherever that is.* He followed their trail which led straight down the long cavern, past some side corridors and through some double doors. On the other side, he saw Danny and Francesco carrying Marianne between them. They were heading towards a door at the other end of the cavern.

Sam hurried ahead, pulled open the door and glanced inside. The others were sitting on the floor and above them, on some stairs, sat Alex Karolyi, his sunglasses perched jauntily on his long black hair, a broad grin spread right across his face, staring down like a king at the dishevelled group before him. It was only then that Sam realised Alex had been missing since they left the Electronics Room.

Sam held open the door as Danny and Francesco carried Marianne inside. When Alex saw her, the smile fell from his face and a profound change came over him. He jumped down from his throne and helped them lay her on the floor. He seemed genuinely concerned, even shocked, at the state she was in. And when he heard that Catriona was still missing, perhaps dead, perhaps still trapped on the stairs, Alex ran out of the Safe Room back towards the lift-shaft. Sam hesitated for a moment, then followed him back through the cavern.

He heard voices ahead of him, and as he passed through the double-doors he was relieved to see two firefighters standing with Alex in the middle of the cavern, one of them talking to him in a language Sam didn't recognise. When Sam reached them, the firefighter, a huge man with a sombre face, was staring at Alex doubtfully. Finally he nodded and the three of them ran up the corridor towards the lift, with Sam following as quickly as he could.

It took the two firefighters only a few minutes to find Catriona amongst the debris in the stairwell, but many more to clear the dust from her face and apply a breathing mask, then check she had no broken bones or other obvious injury. Then they lifted her out and lay her down near the lift. The big one, whose name badge said "George Gabor", stayed to check she was all right while the shorter one, who seemed to be Italian and the junior of the two, ran off to collect the others from the Safe Room. Alex spoke to George in a language Sam didn't understand, then he ran after the firefighter.

Sam knelt down near Catriona and, despite having no religious faith, he said a silent but heart-felt prayer of thanks for the miracle of having her back alive. She was completely covered in concrete dust, although George told him she had been protected from the worst of the falling concrete blocks by one of the landings which jutted out above her.

When he was satisfied that she had suffered no serious injury, George got to his feet, lifted Catriona like a doll and stood her upright on the floor. When he let got she swayed a bit and Sam hurried to steady her. He wanted to give her a big hug but, after what Brigit had said, he felt the most affection he could give her was to squeeze her arm. As they followed the firefighter back towards the centre of the cavern, for the sake of saying something and unable to express his true emotions, Sam explained how Alex Karolyi had persuaded the firefighters to save her. Catriona stared at him in disbelief, then she began to cry and Sam wondered if he had done the right thing in telling her.

They met the rest of the group coming from the Safe Room, the Italian firefighter and Danny carrying Marianne in a stretcher with an orange-cover, with Alex and the others following. When Catriona saw Alex she ran to him and fell into his arms. Brigit looked shocked for a moment, then she too ran forward, a big smile on her face as if she was relieved to see her daughter alive. When Sam caught her eye, she gave him a look of utter contempt before walking back to talk to Francesco.

'Your daughter looks very happy,' George said, looking at Catriona still hanging onto Alex's arm.

Sam's spirit lifted at these words, and he did not correct George's mistake, simply explaining: 'She thinks he was responsible for saving her life'.

'Which he was,' George said. 'Without his powers of persuasion, I would probably have rescued the others first and come back for her later, by which time she would probably have been dead from concrete dust poisoning.'

These words touched Sam deeply, and a wave of gratitude went out from him towards Alex.

'But let me warn you about Mr Karolyi,' George said, dropping his voice. 'We are both Hungarian, so we understand each other very well. There aren't many Hungarians in CERN, and you can bet we all know each other. Mr Karolyi is a well-known personality here. He has something of a reputation as a lady's man, and he is not too particular which ladies he is the man of. I would keep my eye on him, if I were you. Just a friendly warning,' he added, his eyebrows lifting slightly, then he stepped forward and took the stretcher off Danny.

Oh God, Sam thought, staring at Catriona hanging onto Alex's arm. *You can't trust anybody these days. So what do I do now?* But Alex seemed to be more interested in Marianne than he was in Catriona. He kept looking at her through the small gap in orange cover which hid all of her body and most of her face.

'We are going to take you back to the surface through the ATLAS cavern,' George said, addressing the group.

'What, Marianne too?' Danny said. 'I don't think so. The beams were running until a few minutes ago. The detector is still radiative. You know the regulations about the exposure of pregnant women to radioactivity.'

'Yes I do,' George said, 'and under the present circumstances I'd say we don't have any choice. There is no other way out, now that the stairs and the lift-shaft have collapsed. Unless, of course, you want your wife to give birth down here?'

Danny looked undecided.

'Look, Danny, we're going to haul her up through the access shaft,' George went on, 'and by the time she gets to the surface the helicopter will have arrived and we can whisk her off to the hospital. She'll be nowhere near the beam pipe or the detector itself. So come on, what do you want us to do?'

Danny hesitated for some more seconds, then said 'Okay, let's go,' and they set off down a narrow side-corridor led by the two firefighters carrying Marianne in the stretcher with Danny close behind, followed by Alex (with Catriona still clinging to his arm) and Sam close behind them.

At its far end, the corridor led through a door onto a blue metal balcony where the firefighters laid the stretcher. Danny and George knelt beside its head, talking to Marianne, while Brigit and Alex stood at the stretcher's foot, leaning over and listening. Sam saw his chance and pulled Catriona away from Alex, telling her she would be in the way and that anyway she wouldn't understand, since they were speaking French. She reluctantly allowed him to lead her a short way back along the balcony to where Michael and Francesco were standing staring out over the handrail into the gloomy cavern.

Staring out over the handrail into the gloomy cavern

'The black hole must have done that when it evaporated,' Michael Zhang was saying. The little Chinese-Irish scientist's high-pitched voice sounded awestruck, almost enthusiastic, as he pointed at something out in the cavern. Sam stared out to where he was pointing but at first he could distinguish almost nothing.

The only lights were a few emergency ones along the balconies. The balcony they were standing on seemed to be about half-way up one huge wall. It led round onto another wall to Sam's right and ran away from him until it disappeared behind a gigantic segmented brown disc, segmented like an orange, which almost filled the wall.

There were more of these balconies above and below this one. Sam could see them emerge on the far side of the disc and wrap around onto the cavern's far side, row upon row of them, each with faint emergency lights glowing onto its blue metal treads, all linked by stairs. There were more stairs on this side of the cavern too. Sam could hear somebody clunking heavily down one of them. He glanced to his left, where the stretcher was, and noticed that Ludovico was not among the group clustered around it, so he assumed it must be him going down the stairs.

As Sam's eyes got used to the darkness, he could see vague shapes out in the cavern. Most of it was filled by the vast bulk of a barrel-shaped object which lay on its side cocooned by a thick outer skin of girders, pipes and cables. 'That must be the ATLAS detector they keep talking about,' Sam whispered to Catriona.

She gave him a sharp enquiring look. 'But isn't that were the black hole is?' she hissed.

'It was, but Michael told us it's evaporated. That's what made the stairs collapse. Don't you remember? And anyway we've got no choice. Apparently the only way out is through this cavern and up some stairs on the other side.'

Now that his eyes had become accustomed to the gloom, Sam could see that Michael was pointing at a big jagged hole torn from the barrel's flat end, just about discernible in the gloom. Huge tubes and thick cables were hanging from it like the intestines of a dead animal.

'But could a micro-black hole really have caused so much damage?' Francesco Romani asked, looking down at Michael, like a Rottweiler sizing up a cat, then up at the high ceiling. 'Even the shaft's safety platform was blown away. And what about the roof?'

Looking up through the enormous circular shaft, Sam could see the sky high above them. Two ropes were hanging down through the shaft. Sam assumed the two firefighters must have used them to come down into the cavern.

Francesco Romani's jowls wobbled as he shook his head at Michael. 'The firefighters told me that part of the roof was blown off SX1, and that's what demolished the lift-shaft and caused the stairs to collapse. Could a micro-black hole really have done all that?'

'But who knows how much energy might be stored in a black hole formed around a cosmic monopole, Professor?' Michael squeaked indignantly. 'And what else could have caused such an explosion?' He sounded as if he, or the black hole itself, had been personally insulted.

'Well we know the black hole hit the end cap toroid,' Francesco said thoughtfully. 'We saw that on the monitor. And we know it caused a quench which led to a helium leak. Suppose it was the quench that damaged ATLAS. And suppose the liquid helium accumulated on the cavern floor until it was deep enough to reach the quench heater. I imagine by that time, it could have been hot enough to boil all the helium in one go.' Michael was looking at him without any expression at all. 'Because if it did,' Francesco said slowly, 'if it was just the helium going up the shaft which blew the roof off, then...What has happened to the black hole?'

Michael glanced at his watch. 'Don't worry, Professor Romani.' His sing-song voice sounded very confident and reassuring. 'It's twelve minutes past eleven now. ATLAS captured the monopole at nine thirty-four. That's more than an hour and a half ago. All my calculations show that a black hole built around a cosmic monopole could not possibly last this long.' As he spoke, a light overhead pierced the gloom, revealing his confident smile.

Sam looked up to see the beam of a searchlight shining down the shaft. It was moving, following a third firefighter who was spiralling down a single twisting rope, like a spider dropping through a sunbeam. The second rope had disappeared. Sam assumed it had been pulled back up the shaft by someone overhead.

'Okay George,' a voice came up from below and Sam looked down to see Ludovico, outlined by the edge of the circular spotlight, standing on the floor of the cavern. Along the balcony, George Gabor left Marianne and began to uncoil another rope and lower it towards Ludovico.

Meanwhile, the descending firefighter landed on a huge blue horizontal pipe which spanned the gap between two big brown segmented discs, the one attached to the end wall and another attached to the end of ATLAS.

Like a sewer pipe crossing a river, Sam thought. He watched as the firefighter walked to the edge of the pipe and continued his descent, finally landing on the cavern floor. He unhooked the rope from his harness, gave it to Ludovico and came clattering up the stairs towards the balcony. Ludovico tied together the rope from the shaft with the rope George had sent down from the balcony, making a V shape which arced upwards into the spotlight.

What's going on? Sam wondered as he watched George tie a D shaped metal ring to one of the broad beams supporting the balconies above. He then slipped a rope into the carabiner and passed it through another little metal device attached to his harness. As the sound of the firefighter's feet came closer, George began hauling his rope back up through the carabiner, and so pulling up the knot which joined the two ropes. In the searchlight's beam Sam could see the ropes lifting towards them, curving through the darkness in a giant U shape, the upper end disappearing through the shaft overhead.

It must be a sort of lifeline, Sam thought. 'I think they're going to lift Marianne up on that rope,' he whispered to Catriona.

Panting and sweating, the new firefighter reached the balcony and knelt beside the stretcher. 'Hello,' he said to Marianne between pants. 'I'm Robert. How're you feeling, dear?'

Oh, Sam thought. *That's the first English accent I've heard in CERN.*

Marianne said something Sam could not hear. Her voice was muffled by the stretcher cover.

'I understand you are thirty-four weeks, is that right?' he said.

Mumble, mumble.

'And when the stairs collapsed you fell and hurt your ankle?'

Mumble, mumble, mumble.

'I see. And now you're having contractions are you? Are they very strong, dear?'

Mumble.

'Good. Well we're going to winch you up the shaft and I'll be with you all the time, so you have nothing to worry about.'

Ludovico was clunking slowly back up the stairs and George was tying both ropes onto a metal ring from which four broad yellow straps led to the corners of the stretcher. When he was satisfied with the knot, he pulled the slack of his rope through the descendeur which he had attached to one of the blue beams supporting the balcony above. Ludovico and Robert lifted the stretcher so it was balanced on top of the handrail.

Now there was only one rope hanging in the cavern, curving up from the balcony towards the overhead shaft in a huge J shape. The other rope was curled up at George's feet.

There was a heart-stopping moment when Robert, climbing

over the handrail, lost his footing and almost fell but Ludovico instantly caught his harness and George quickly clipped it to the metal ring on the stretcher, growling something in Hungarian between clenched teeth.

When Robert was firmly attached to the stretcher, George let his rope slip through the descendeur. Robert and Marianne slowly swung out into the gloom and he controlled their descent as they slipped down towards the thick horizontal blue pipe that stretched across the middle of the cavern.

The spotlight soon found them, spinning slowly in space, shockingly bright, vivid and fragile in the darkness like a fragment of orange peel cast aside by a careless astronaut. It followed them as they descended towards the blue pipe. They were suspended between two ropes, one slanting down from George on the balcony, the other curving gracefully down from the shaft overhead.

Sam could hear Robert talking calmly to Marianne but could not hear what he was saying because George, one hand pulling the lever that paid out the rope, was talking French into a walkie-talkie he held in his other hand.

There was a pause, then Sam heard an engine start up overhead and guessed another firefighter must be getting ready to winch them up the shaft. Finally George turned to Marianne's husband saying 'Danny, if you go up the stairs in the service cavern you might be able to go with her in the helicopter.'

Danny nodded and staggered off along the balcony looking exhausted.

'In fact you might as well all go with him,' George went on, turning his head towards the others for a moment. 'There's nothing else to do here. Ludo, go with them up the US15 stairway.' He turned back to watch the stretcher descending steadily.

Ludovico's curly head nodded and he walked jauntily after

Danny along the balcony. Michael Zhang padded after him and Francesco Romani turned to Brigit.

'Come along, Madame Ambassador,' he said. 'It's time to go and get cleaned up. I am really sorry for the trauma you have suffered today.'

She looked as if she were about to give him a piece of her mind, but then merely shook her head and followed him along the balcony, still frowning. As she passed Catriona she said 'Come on girl, for God's sake don't just stand there.'

She walked past Sam without a word. He watched her go, still shocked at her apparent lack of basic human sympathy, then took his step-daughter's arm saying 'Come on little Catty. There's no point hanging around here. We can go up—'

'No, Sam. I want to make sure Marianne gets out safely. Please let me stay here, just one more minute. Please Sam.' As she spoke, Catriona threaded her arm through that of Alex Karolyi who was now standing beside her, looking down from the balcony, his eyes fixed on the slowly descending stretcher, showing no sign of moving.

For a moment the firefighter's warning came back to Sam and he glanced at the handsome young man. In the lift he had seemed to fancy Brigit but since the disaster he seemed to have totally lost interest in her and now had eyes only for the woman in the stretcher. He didn't even seem to notice Catriona's arm linking his.

Sam shrugged. 'Okay,' he said. 'Just for one minute.' Gratefully, she rested her head on his shoulder and Sam felt, at last, as if she really might be his own daughter. The three of them stood together, watching the stretcher swing away towards the middle of the cavern, each silently rejoicing at seeing Marianne finally rescued after the horrible disasters of the morning.

The spotlight shining down the overhead shaft seemed to add star quality to the stretcher, and the firefighter hanging beside it;

a double-act featured in this bizarre scientific circus. The light followed their descent past the big blue horizontal pipe which stretched between ATLAS and the cavern wall. *Like a fat cocktail stick with a slice of brown lemon at each end*, Sam thought, as his eyes wandered over the massive segmented disc on his left attached to the end of the detector.

Sam didn't know what the disc was for, but even he knew that the gaping hole in the edges of one segment was not supposed to be there. The damage looked very bad. Large parts of the segment were broken away and he could see the mangled equipment inside. The hole seemed very deep. Metal tubes with torn edges hung down on the remaining segments, suspended by thick electrical cables. Whatever had caused this damage had obviously been very violent.

That hole seems to be getting brighter, Sam thought, vaguely puzzled. It was difficult to tell beneath the glare of the spotlight so he stared at it a little longer. The spotlight itself did not seem to be causing the light.

As he watched, a little white dot of light emerged from the hole and began to drift very slowly away into the cavern. It was about level with the top of the thick blue pipe. The light was not very bright, dimmer even than the emergency lights on the far wall. It went floating horizontally into the cavern like a firefly on a mission.

Behind it, Sam could see the big blue pipe, which seemed somehow distorted, as if a large drop of water was surrounding the little light. He was now very puzzled.

'Alex,' he said. 'Can you see a sort of light over there, floating just above that blue pipe?'

'Sorry, Mr Fitzpatrick?' Alex mumbled, his eyes still glued to the descending stretcher. 'Which light d'you mean?'

'That one up there. It's just come out of the hole in ATLAS.'

That caught his attention. Alex glanced upwards, his eyes

scanning the upper part of the cavern. 'No I...' Alex began, then he leaned forward on the handrail, gasped 'Oh shit' and turned to George, saying something urgent in Hungarian. But the firefighter was still talking into his radio, giving instructions to the engine overhead while looking down at the stretcher and didn't hear him. He didn't seem to have noticed the floating light.

Catriona's head lifted off Sam's shoulder, she looked up at the light and then at Sam with fearful, uncomprehending eyes. 'What do you think it is, Sam?' she whispered, fear and dread fighting each other in her throat. 'It can't be the black hole, can it?'

'No of course not, Catty,' he said soothingly. 'It isn't black!'

The engine's roar grew louder, drowning out his voice as, with a sudden jerk, the long rope leading down from the overhead shaft began to lift the stretcher upwards. Alex left them and hurried along the balcony, shouting at George. Sam could hear the fear in his voice but his eyes were fixed on the floating light.

'Well if it's not the black hole, what is it?' Catriona asked.

Sam had no answer. The light was still floating horizontally, just above the blue pipe, and it seemed to be on a collision course with the rising stretcher. Sam could even see its pale light reflected off Robert's helmet.

On the far side of the cavern, Michael Zhang must have seen it too because Sam heard his shrill cry: 'Look Danny! There! It's the black hole! No, there! Just above the beam pipe shield! Can't you see the Hawking radiation it's giving off?'

'So it is the black hole!' Catriona whispered. 'Oh Sam, what's going to happen now?'

'I don't know.' Sam had never been so terrified in his life.

'We've got to stop it!' Michael's high-pitched voice sounded like a frightened child.

Sam heard the clang of feet running down a flight of stairs on the other side of the cavern, first one pair, then another. He heard Ludovico shouting and more feet running along the opposite balcony. Sam saw two figures emerge from behind the big blue pipe, the beam pipe shield, running down the stairs. In the gloom he could just make out Michael and Danny while, on his left, he saw Francesco and Brigit walking quickly towards him along the balcony.

Suddenly Catriona shrugged Sam's arm away and ran towards a distant stairway, saying 'I'm going to help Michael.'

Sam hurried after her, calling. 'No Catty, don't be stupid. Stop her Alex!'

As she ran past Alex, he caught her arm and said something to her, holding her as she struggled to reach the stairs.

'Keep her here, Alex,' Sam said hurrying past them. 'I'll go down and help.' He jammed his spectacles into his jacket pocket, wishing George would help instead of talking on his radio, and ran clattering down three flights of stairs, hoping this show of support would bring her to her senses. At all costs, Sam wanted to protect his step-daughter from any further danger.

When he reached the bottom of the stairs he ran into the middle of the cavern where Danny and Michael were standing staring up at the black hole which, Sam thought, was getting brighter as it drifted slowly towards the stretcher. From down here it was difficult to judge how far apart they were vertically.

'Can we stop it hitting them?' he panted, breathless from the run down.

'How do you stop a black hole?' Danny snapped. 'Anything that touches it will be absorbed.'

'There might be a way,' Michael piped. They both looked at him. 'We know the black hole has a magnetic field. If we had a magnet we could control it without touching it.'

'Yes,' Danny shouted. 'By Christ it's possible! Look!'

Sam looked up. Danny was pointing at the lowest of the metal tubes hanging on cables which emerged from the hole in ATLAS. It looked just about reachable. 'It's part of the end cap toroid,'

Danny said. 'If we can get it down, we can plug it into the emergency electricity supply.'

'Will it work without liquid helium?' Michael asked.

'I don't know,' Danny said, 'but we've got to try. What option have we got? Come on! I'll need your help.'

Danny and Sam stretched up but could not reach the tube. It was only when Danny lifted Michael onto Sam's shoulders that the little scientist was able to get hold of it. The tube was bigger than Michael, about two metres long and half a metre wide, hollow inside but extremely heavy. Michael pulled and one of the cables came free, but the other thick cables still held it dangling from the hole in ATLAS. Michael began twisting the tube, trying to snap the cable.

With Michael balanced on his shoulders, Sam's back began to complain. He had suffered from intermittent back pain for years, and he was sure this was going to set it off again. His legs ached too. Although he was small, Michael was still very heavy.

Why's it just me that's holding him on my own? he wondered. *Where's Danny? And what's that blasted black hole doing?*

He strained his neck to look up past Michael, searching for the little bright spot of light. It was hard to see anything. Not only was Michael in the way, but the spotlight was shining down the shaft straight into his eyes. Sam had to squint. He could just make out the gigantic blue horizontal pipe, but by moving his feet slightly, Sam was able to move his head into the shadow of that pipe.

'That's better, Sam,' Michael said, and twisted the heavy metal tube with renewed enthusiasm.

From his new position, Sam could see the stretcher, still swaying to and fro on the end of the two yellow ropes, not far from the blue pipe. And finally he found the distorted region of space which betrayed the position of the black hole, floating between the blue pipe and the stretcher. Because of the distortion, it was hard to judge how high the black hole was, but it seemed to be not far from Marianne's stretcher.

Suddenly Michael shrieked 'Look out!' and, before Sam knew what was happening, the heavy metal tube came slicing down past his right shoulder. It crashed onto the concrete floor beside his right foot with a thud and stood on end for a second. Then, to his horror, Sam saw it begin to topple sideways towards him. He had to step out of the way to avoid getting knocked over and the tube fell to the floor with a deafening clang.

Unable to hold Michael any longer, and unable to let him down gently, Sam collapsed onto the tube with Michael on top of him. Sam was still lying there, the wind crushed out if him, trembling to think how close he had just come to losing an arm or a foot or even both, when Danny emerged from under ATLAS, saying breezily: 'There's an emergency electricity supply down there.'

Without another word, the engineer picked up the two long electric cables that trailed out of the ends of the metal tube and carried them back into the shadow, saying 'You two point that up at the black hole. Then I'll plug it in.'

'Come on, Sam,' Michael said wearily. 'If you can hold it upright, I'll help you aim it.'

With an enormous effort which almost broke his back in half, and with a little help from Michael, Sam raised one end of the heavy tube and supported it on his shoulder while Michael lay on the floor beside the lower end saying: 'Right a bit. Up a bit. Stop.'

'The cable's not long enough,' Danny shouted. 'Can't you pull some more out?'

'Lower it down again Sam, quick!' Michael squeaked.

Sam let the electromagnet fall to the floor and they unhooked more cable from inside the ends of the tube and pulled out another couple of metres.

'Okay,' Danny called, 'that's enough. Aim it up, can't you?'

Sam was sure he would never walk again after this, but he had no choice, so he hauled the tube upright once more and leaned against it, glancing up, trying to see the black hole.

On one of the balconies far above him, George was still shouting instructions into his radio and the stretcher was still swinging on the ends of the two ropes. Sam wasn't sure, but he thought it seemed to be coming slowly down towards him.

'Are you two ready?' Danny called. 'Can I turn it on?'

'Yes,' Michael piped. 'Turn it on Schneider.'

There was a pause then Sam felt the tube jump upwards off his shoulder.

'Is it working?' Danny ran out from the shadow.

'I can't tell,' Michael said.

'Stop!' Catriona screamed down from the balcony. 'It's moving down faster!'

Sam looked up. The lens-like distortion was definitely moving now, drifting towards the stretcher.

'You're pointing it the wrong way,' George shouted. 'Turn it round.' He began to run along the balcony towards the far stairwell.

Danny ran back into the shadow. Sam lowered the tube to the floor, grabbed the other end and hauled it up onto his shoulder with a super-human effort. He thought he could hear somebody saying "Superman Sam saves the World".

Michael started calling out instructions again. It only took them a few seconds to get it right. 'Okay' Michael yelped. 'Turn the power on Schneider!'

Sam heard Danny call from the shadow 'Okay! Here goes!' There was a pause then again he felt the tube leap up off his shoulder, again heard Catriona scream 'Oh no!' and Sam felt himself lifted off the ground. *What's happening?* Sam wondered. *What's gone wrong?*

The cavern seemed rapidly to grow huge and move far away,

spinning at the same time, and the metal tube seemed to be stuck to his shoulder. He was dimly aware that Michael Zhang was still somewhere near his feet but the floor had dropped away and the tube with the two men attached seemed to be floating in a huge black empty space.

Michael's Diary: The Black Hole

Son of Beeing

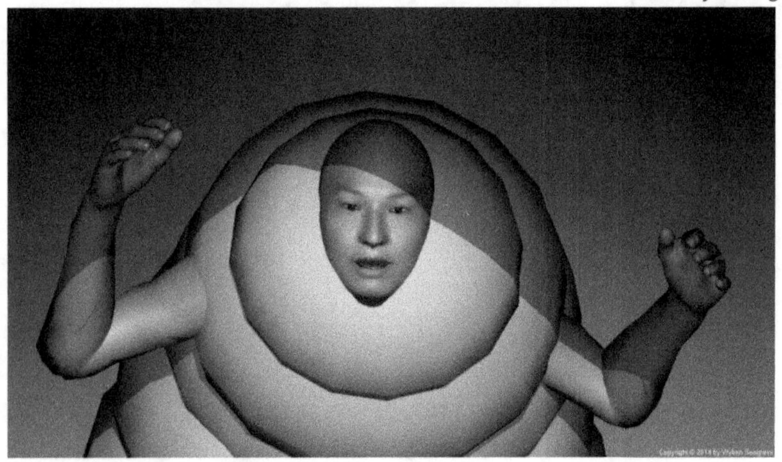

Your arrival on Earth, Oh Blessed Monopole, caused revolutions both within the Cosmic Egg and without. In my case, for example, I was then a mere mortal called Michael Zhang, a scientist who worked on a detector called ATLAS.

It was the strong magnetic field of ATLAS which trapped you, Marvellous Monopole. Once inside, you absorbed protons from the beams of the Large Hadron Collider which transformed you into a persistent black hole. Once the beam had been turned off, you emerged from the beam pipe, absorbing more atoms as you went, and then drifted through the detector itself, causing significant damage as you absorbed everything in your path.

Finally you emerged into the ATLAS cavern and drifted horizontally until the magnetic field of a fragment of the end cap toroid attracted you downwards towards the Earth.

I was holding this tube, along with another human called Sam Fitzpatrick, and you absorbed us both, Oh Wondrous Creation, as well as the end cap fragment itself. Up until that moment, all mankind's theories had led us to believe that anything falling into a black hole would be destroyed. These objects are called black because their force of gravity is so strong that nothing can escape from them, not even light. You might wonder how that is possible.

It turns out that matter and energy bend the four-dimensional space-time, stretching it like a sheet of rubber. What men on Earth and Entroilians in Ent experience as the force of gravity is merely the consequence of slipping down the warped slopes of space-time. A black hole consists of matter which has been squashed into such a small space that the space-time surrounding it is distorted into the shape of a funnel, getting steeper and narrower as it descends to the object at its centre.

According to the theory prevailing at that moment, anything falling into a black hole should have been stretched out longer and thinner as it slipped down the space-time funnel until it was so distorted that it would be torn apart by gravitational tides, atom by atom. However this was not our fate. The reason is relatively easy to explain.

At the time you arrived on Earth, Oh Revolutionary Monopole, there was a major gap in man's understanding of the laws of physics. Fundamental physics consisted of gravitational theory, which dealt with the large-scale structure of space-time, and quantum mechanics, which described the very smallest particles. Each of these theories was immensely successful, but they were mutually incompatible. Men had no idea how to reconcile them, and hence they had no understanding of the real processes which function within a black hole.

The result was that men's theories about black holes were completely mistaken. And (for a reason I have not entirely understood, but I guess might be part of the design of the Universe) your black hole was directly connected to Entroilia by a fold in space-time called a "wormhole". The result was that, instead of being torn apart by tidal forces, Sam Fitzpatrick and I were sucked down this wormhole and instantly found ourselves outside the Cosmic Egg, floating in its pink event record.

Episode 8 Pipes

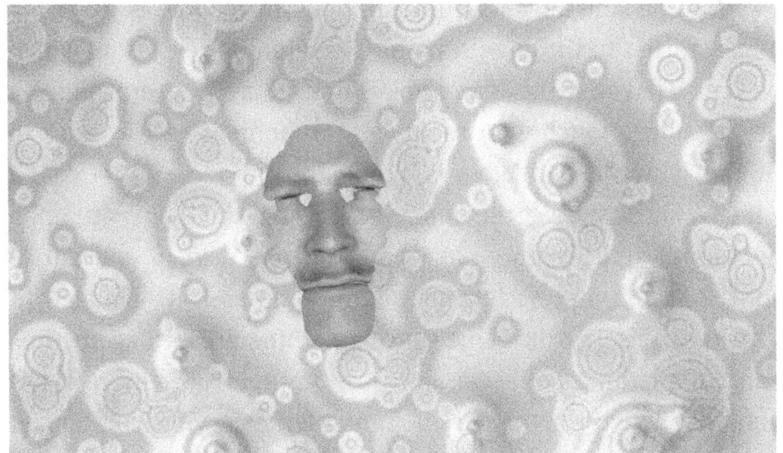

Suddenly there was glutinous pink jelly everywhere, sliming across Sam's face, squashing against his eyeballs, stopping him breathing as it oozed up his nose and tried to force its way into his mouth.

What hell's this?

He tried to clear the jelly from his face but it was so thick he could not move his arms. It was squashing the breath out of his lungs. It was horrific, completely claustrophobic, life-threatening, panic-making.

Thoughts flashed rapidly through his mind.

Firefighter foam? How expect us breathe? Not absorbed by black hole! Thank God!

He tried to kick his legs but it was impossible to move through the gelatinous goo. His lungs were beginning to complain and he felt his throat start to pulsate as it tried to make him breathe. Some of the jelly had forced its way up his nose and into the back of his throat, triggering the vomiting reflex. His stomach began heaving up the remains of breakfast. He could taste the acid. Anger flared within him.

Firefighters sacrifice our lives to save detector? No, must be scientists. Totally mad!

Carbon dioxide began accumulating in his blood; his head and lungs started to throb with pain. The spinning sensation, which he had felt when the black hole lifted him, now returned. He began to lose touch with reality. For a moment he was back in Dublin, lying in a bath of warm pink bubbles.

It was hard to resist the demand of his agonised lungs to open his mouth and breathe. Then he started to drift in and out of consciousness and he felt his mouth open as if it belonged to somebody else. At the same time something pressed against his hand. Something solid was moving through the jelly towards him. Instinctively his fingers bent and felt a curving, corrugated surface. The sensation brought him back to reality.

With jelly oozing rapidly down his throat, he pushed his fingers outwards. The corrugations parted and something familiar slipped into his palm. *The electric cable from the magnetic tube.* Hope surged through every vein of his body. *The tube was hollow! Maybe air trapped inside?*

He grasped the cable and pulled with all his strength. Moments later his head poked into a bubble of air trapped inside the tube. The jelly began to run down his face, falling away in dollops, freeing his mouth. His spirit soared. He could feel the cold air on his skin. He tried to breathe in but his chest and the rest of his body were still outside the tube and the jelly was pressing against his lungs, stopping him breathing.

The broken fragment of the end cap toroid was still moving, its jagged edges pressing into his shoulder, threatening to chop off his right arm. Driven by the instinct of self-preservation, he pushed himself away from it and the edge slipped down his arm, the air in the hollow interior of the tube quickly encompassing his shoulders and then his chest. Finally his lungs were free and he could breathe easily.

But the pink jelly was still pressing against his stomach and he was violently sick. The vomit shot out of his mouth with such force, it flew across the tube and he heard it splatter against the curving inner wall.

Between heaves, he forced air into his lungs. With a feeling of being reborn, he gulped in huge lungfuls of the life-giving gas, one after another, trying to stop himself vomiting again. He breathed as deeply as he could and his stomach finally won the battle. With abdominal muscles in agonised contraction, he vomited up a huge dollop of pink jelly which shot across the tube and exploded against the wall like a mortar.

Dimly he was aware that the metal tube was still moving. Terrified of drifting out of the other end, he wedged his hands and feet between the thick electrical cables that wound around the inside, still panting and wondering where he was, his mind still a riot of questions.

Will this tube float up to the ceiling of the cavern? God, I hope so. But what will happen then? Will the firefighters be able to rescue me? Can't they drain this bloody jelly-foam away? What's happened to Catriona? Was she covered by foam too? If this tube hadn't found me I'd be dead by now. I'm so lucky I wasn't absorbed by that bloody black hole. This jelly must have destroyed it. That was a damn close thing!

A gap appeared in the pink circle at the end of the tube near Sam's feet and cool refreshing air rushed in, bringing with it a surge of hope and relief. *I must have reached the surface. Thank God! I wonder how long it will take somebody to find me?*

The tube continued to float upwards, out of the jelly, and Sam finally realised he was hanging upside-down. The tube's lower end emerged completely from the pink jelly, allowing a fine drizzle of coloured raindrops to shower onto his legs. Looking between his feet, through the haze of falling rain, he could just make out a patch of brown sky high above him.

Is that the cavern ceiling? No, that was white concrete not brown. And where's this rain coming from? Surely they can't still be putting more foam into this cavern? There wasn't even a fire down here, so what good is this bloody foam doing apart from probably killing people?

The situation now seemed to take on a dream-like quality. The tube slowly toppled over until it was floating horizontally with Sam inside it. Looking out of both ends, he saw an almost flat pink surface beneath a brown sky.

I seem to be in the middle of a pool of this stuff. Why can't I see any of the cavern walls or the blue balconies? What about the pipes and all the other parts of ATLAS?

Serious and worrying doubt began to creep over him like a black cloud. *Where am I?* From the ends of the tube, he could only see for a few hundred metres in either direction. The rain pouring down onto the pink surface formed a mist which obscured his view. He could feel fear, almost panic, rising within him. This was becoming unreal.

Where the hell am I?

But a moment later this question was swept aside as, through the end of the tube near his head, he saw a large white object moving slowly towards him through the mist. Sam immediately assumed it was a boat and his heart began beating faster. *Thank God! Someone's coming to rescue me!* He wriggled towards the top of the tube, stuck his arms out and began waving and shouting at the top of his voice. He was gratified to see the white shape stop and hesitate. Sam stared up at it, feeling relieved but extremely confused.

Is it a boat? Seems to be very high up in the air. Whatever it is, I want them to find me!

He began waving and shouting with renewed vigour and, after

a moment, it turned and come directly towards him. Sam kept waving and as it came closer he began to make out some of the details. There seemed to be some markings on its front although they were obscured by the mist. It was apparently spherical, certainly not flat like the side of a boat.

It's not a boat! It's some sort of balloon. A balloon in the ATLAS cavern? This is totally weird.

As it moved further, he saw it was not completely spherical. The front was round but the back was stretched out like a long white sausage with a bulging middle.

It looks more like an airship...An airship? What the hell's an airship doing here? Am I still in the ATLAS cavern?

Two paddles were sticking out of the white curving flanks, about a third of the way along, one on each side. They were bending, moving forward together close to the body, straightening out, sweeping slowly backwards together and then bending and recommencing the movement. It was very curious. It vaguely reminded Sam of something.

As the airship came closer, he saw there were two more paddles towards the rear, moving up and down but in directions opposite to each other. As he watched the four paddles, Sam suddenly realised what they reminded him of: *It's as if they're swimming! Swimming through the air.*

He could still not see the rear end of the airship when the front half of the whole long sausage suddenly bent downwards.

It's looking for me! Sam thought, and began once again to shout and wave until he thought his voice would give out. As the front end came swooping down towards him, he saw the markings clearly for the first time. What he saw shocked him. Indeed, this was more astonishing than anything which had happened so far on this totally astonishing day.

The markings looked distinctly like a gigantic sculpted face. Sam could see the mouth, a nose, two ears, two eyes. It looked like the figure-head carved on the front of a Viking warship, but far, far larger, carved in three dimensions, the ears sticking out sideways. And the eyes! Sam could not take his own eyes off them. They seemed to be alive. They were constantly moving, apparently scanning the surface of the jelly below, searching for something. It was grotesque but very realistic.

There was something very familiar about those eyes but at first Sam could not work out what it was, he was in such a state of shock. They slanted upwards in the corners and their upper lids were heavy. They looked slightly Chinese and it took him several moments for Sam to realise who it was. *It's the little Irish scientist. It's Michael Zhang! I think he's looking for me!*

A horrible mixture of hope and fear suffused Sam's mind. Hope of rescue but fear of that face on that gigantic airship. A glance down the length of the white body confirmed his worst fears. The things sticking out making swimming movements were not paddles but human arms and legs. This was the point when Sam began to doubt his own sanity.

I've been almost killed on the stairs today, nearly absorbed by a black hole, practically drowned in pink foam and now I'm being hunted by a living airship. It's not surprising my mind's going loopy.

When the airship's eyes spied the metal tube it stopped, appeared to think for a moment then the arms and legs began to move faster and the airship came rapidly towards him. As it came closer Sam realised it was enormous, as large as an ocean liner, and Michael's face was as huge as a monument carved into a mountain.

Whether I'm loopy or not, that thing looks real enough.

He rapidly pulled his head safely inside the tube and hid there, disoriented, trembling and confused. Then suddenly, with a slight glooping noise, the tube rolled over and he felt it being lifted up out of the jelly.

He's lifting the tube? Why? Does he know I'm inside?

The tube tilted and he began to slip down towards the open end near his feet. He only managed to save himself from falling out by grasping the inner cables as tightly as he could and hauling himself completely inside. He once again jammed his fingers and the toes of his shoes between the cables so he was fairly secure inside the tube.

He couldn't see the airship now, only the brown sky through the top of the tube and the pink surface below, but Sam had no doubt it was lifting him. Looking down he saw globs of jelly dripping out of the bottom of the tube and falling back towards the pink surface. He was alarmed to see how quickly it was receding below him. He was even more shocked to see how big it was. The mist that had obscured his view when he was floating in the jelly was thinner up here and he could see the pink stuff stretching out below in all directions. It was enormous, like a sort of lake.

Then a hole in the surface came into view. It seemed to be the opening of some sort of tunnel winding down into the jelly, but he was being lifted up so fast that, even as he looked down at it, the hole rapidly dwindled away and vanished from sight. The surface was bigger than just a lake.

There's a whole ocean of that pink stuff down there! Where in God's name is this?

Sam tried to stay calm, to think rationally.

I don't think I've gone mad, and I don't think this is a nightmare. There's only one explanation. I really was absorbed by that black hole and I've come out on some other planet. I wonder what that TV scientist would say about this? If I fall out of this tube and hit that ocean I'll be killed for sure. How fast am I going up? Must be miles high now.

Looking down through the bottom of the tube Sam saw something else come into view. It appeared to be a huge cylinder rising up from the pink ocean like a giant tree-trunk, although it obviously wasn't alive. It was glowing gently and it appeared to be made of glass. As he watched the ocean recede, more of these glowing trunks came into view. Like everything else, they puzzled him intensely. Even though he was very high they looked enormous. He guessed that each one was tens, maybe hundreds of miles tall. Through the bottom of the magnet he could only see their bases but looking up he saw them again through its upper end.

The trunks extended far above him, reaching up into the brown sky where, high overhead, they fragmented into dozens of other, thinner pipes. The thinner pipes radiated away from the top of each thick vertical trunk to form a starburst like a giant dandelion head.

Each branch curved away

Each branch curved away and eventually met another trunk so the sky was enmeshed by a network of curving blue crystals. It was dazzling and awesome in its scale and sophistication. He felt as if he were in a forest looking between the trunks of some vast trees into the canopy of their branches.

Michael was lifting him rapidly and every moment he could see them more clearly. The thin pipes shone with the same light that glowed within their thick supporting trunks.

Michael reached the lowest of these branching pipes and Sam could see that it was the coloured raindrops which were making the pipes glow. They were travelling up the vast trunks, along the thin branches and then spraying out from their under-sides and raining back down onto the ocean. It was like a vast continuous firework display filling the sky.

This was obviously some sort of huge machine, but he had no idea what purpose it might serve. Whoever had built it was clearly far more technologically advanced than humans.

Okay, so let's think about this calmly. I've been absorbed by a black hole and come out on a machine to size of a planet.

But he couldn't stay calm. His mind started screaming *NO NO NO. This can't be happening.*

He felt like letting go of the tube and falling back down into the ocean. *I'd rather be dead than go through this.* But at that moment the tube tilted over until it was almost horizontal and he found himself gripping onto the interior cables for dear life.

His brain was beginning to ache with the effort of trying to work out what was happening. The fear of falling and the horror of not knowing where he was and the terror at the awesome size of the airship which was Michael Zhang left him feeling sick and exhausted.

I don't have the courage to kill myself. Maybe this airship is trying to rescue me? Maybe it will put me on top of one of these pipes? But what will I do then? How will I get back home? Will I ever—

At that moment, Michael lifted the tube and swung it up over his shoulder. Sam saw the blue pipes shooting past the end of the tube and felt himself being pushed outwards towards them. He had to grip the inner cables even tighter to stop himself being flung out of his tube. But then, without warning, Michael swung the tube back violently the other way and Sam was pushed outwards with such force that the cable was ripped from his grip and, like a human cannonball, he shot out the top of the tube up into the rain.

His bowel gave a sudden sharp contraction of terror as the pink ocean and the blue pipes swirled around him. Then everything seemed to happen in slow motion.

His suit jacket flapped against his body like slow hand-claps. Coloured raindrops stung his face one at a time like a swarm of lazy wasps. Sam turned in the air, slower than the hour-hand of a clock, and Michael himself came into view below him. Sam watched him bring the metal tube down onto one of the blue pipes from which the rain was falling. The pipe shattered into a long line of tiny sparkling fragments which fell down, spinning and flashing, towards the distant ocean.

At the same time there was a blindingly intense flash of bright blue light. The pipes surrounding the planet all lit up together as if somebody had thrown a switch on an enormous neon sign. The image burned vividly into Sam's retinas.

Sam closed his eyes tight against the blinding light but still he saw every detail, black against a white background; Michael's long curving body, the tube he had just let fall, the row of dots falling below it, the network of thin pipes resting on the thick vertical trunks.

The flash was fading from his retinas and he opened his eyes. He was still hurtling helplessly through the air. It took him a moment to realise the rain had stopped and the colours had stopped flowing inside the pipes. They swirled around him now, each with a pale blue glow within. The ocean too was spinning around him. It looked far away, as smooth as a pink billiard ball, but every time it passed before him, he saw it was coming closer.

Will it hurt when I hit it, or will I die straight away?

Then something brushed against his chest, gently at first but with rapidly increasing pressure, and he found himself sliding along the top of one of the thin blue pipes. It was smooth as glass, with three flat sides each about two metres wide. He was hurtling along one of them so fast that friction between the pipe and his jacket burned his chest while a dry wind whipped into his face as he looked ahead, trying to see where it was taking him.

What he saw frightened him. Several kilometres ahead lay the starburst where this pipe met dozens of others at the top of one of the tall vertical trunks. The gap between this pipe and the others was narrowing rapidly.

I'm going to be crushed when I reach that thing!

Then to his astonishment, although his pipe seemed completely hard and solid, he saw it bend in the middle. The pipe pressed harder against his body, and suddenly he was sliding uphill and slowing down, with the pipe making little sideways movements as if trying to stop him falling off.

He was utterly astonished, totally confused but hopeful that the pipe might yet save his life. He gave himself up to it, forcing himself to relax, trying to ignore the burning pain and just letting the pipe do with him as it wanted.

He passed the curve in the middle of the pipe and began to shoot uphill. Immediately, he could feel he was moving more slowly. By the time he reached the other pipes, he was going so slowly that the wind in his face felt like a gentle breeze. He had no idea why or how, but he was sure that the pipe had deliberately slowed him down.

As he arrived at the starburst of pipes, the one he was on tilted over and dropped him gently through a hole into the hollow space at the centre. He slithered across the slippery floor and came to rest against one wall. He was certain that the pipe had deliberately stopped him falling to his death and deposited him in this place of safety. He felt he was in the grip of something which cared for him, which was looking after him, which had its own intelligence although he did not know whether it was really alive. Perhaps it was just a huge intelligent machine. But at this moment, he didn't really care. He lay still, grateful to be alive and amazed at how he had survived.

Episode 9 Call Me Lord!

Sam lay on the floor gazing around

Sam lay on the floor gazing around. He seemed to be in a sort of transparent cave about three or four metres across, made from the flat ends of dozens of the rain-pipes. To his surprise they were solid, not hollow as he had expected. How the rain had travelled through them Sam had no idea.

The pipes were made of beautiful blue crystal, completely transparent without any imperfections, as pure as pale blue sapphire. There were gaps between the pipes, and he was unsure what exactly was holding them apart. There was also a gap around the edges of the pipe he was lying on, giving him a slight sense of insecurity, as below him was nothing but a huge drop to the pink ocean. This crystal was bigger than the rest, and it felt hard and cold beneath his hands, incredibly smooth and slippery.

Lying on his back, looking up through the pipes which formed the ceiling, he could see how they tapered away as they radiated into the distance. At their far ends, each one touched dozens of others, forming a network which spanned the sky. Almost directly above him he could see the brown sky through a triangular gap in the cave, as if one pipe was missing.

That must be the hole I dropped through. I wonder if...

A sudden movement caught his eye and at the same time he felt his left arm slip sideways and downwards. The floor was so slippery, he felt his whole body twist slightly.

He turned his head to see one of the huge crystal pipes surrounding him, the one which formed the wall on his left, moving away, opening up a large gap with the floor, and his left arm hanging through that widening gap, dangling down towards the pink ocean a long way below, his body slowly slipping towards the edge of the floor.

He lifted his arm and kept as still as he could, not daring to move or even to breathe in case he slipped closer to the edge. There was nothing for him to grip, nothing to stop him falling to his death. He could feel his body trembling against the pipe beneath him as he watched the gap widen.

The moving pipe swung slowly away, hung in the air for a moment, then came back towards him.

Thank God for that! The gap's closing.

Something else caught his eye and he turned his head to see other crystals were moving too. Then the first one struck the floor with a beautiful ringing musical chime. For a moment he felt his jacket sleeve go tight as it was trapped between the two massive crystals. He yanked his arm away, his sleeve flapped loose and his arm went cold. His forearm was completely naked. The pipe had sliced a neat straight strip out of his sleeve.

That bloody thing could have chopped my arm off!

More musical tones filled the cave, slowly at first but quickly gaining speed and volume as if a manic child were learning how to play a glockenspiel, hitting it harder with every ringing note. The floor was rocking too, lifting and swaying as if it was in an earthquake and his empty aching stomach began to complain as if he were on a small boat crossing a storm-tossed ocean.

Then the wall beside him moved and once more a yawning gap opened up. This time the movement was far more violent than the first. Sam lifted his arm clear and waited for the crystal pipe to swing back.

I'm going to have this arm chopped off if I'm not careful. What's making these pipes move like this? Got to get away from this wall. Have to push myself away when it comes back.

As he waited, mentally planning his move, another sound pierced through the ringing tones, a noise which resonated in his heart. It was a primordial blast of pure hate. But his attention was focussed on the moving pipe and he dismissed the sound from his thoughts as he watched the crystal swing back towards him. It struck the floor and Sam pushed his trembling left arm against it and began to slide across the crystal, slippery as a melting glacier, hoping the push would not carry him over to the far side. But with a sinking heart he passed the middle and headed towards the opposite wall. At that moment the heaving floor tilted and he was brought to rest. For a few seconds he lay still, helpless as a baby, unable to do anything but listen to the noises surrounding him.

The pipes were moving more violently with every passing second, and within a minute they were all hammering into each other with clangs louder even than the deafening bells of Christ Church Cathedral in Dublin. And through them all, the roaring noise was growing louder. It was a bellow of insanity so frightful that, in spite of his immediate danger, it struck a deeper fear into Sam's soul. He began looking through the crystal walls, searching for the thing that was sending out this terrible siren of disaster.

A few hundred metres below him and several kilometres distant Sam saw the gigantic airship again. It appeared to be trapped. It looked like a huge white windborne whale caught by the sky-net of some mythological hunter. As he watched it struggling to escape, thrashing violently from side to side, Sam knew for certain that, just as these intelligent pipes had rescued him, so they had caught Michael, collapsing around him and holding him secure.

The metal tube had fallen from Michael's grip and his little arms and legs were pulling and kicking the crystal pipes as he flexed sideways. As he thrashed about, Sam glimpsed both ends of his long white body and each was a vision of horror. Zhang's mouth was open and he was bellowing like a wounded elephant. The expression of fury was so realistic that Sam could hardly believe it was not alive.

Then his body bent the other way. Its rear end came into view and Sam stared, unable to believe his eyes. It was shaped like a pair of buttocks and there was a dark dot in the cleft between them. Disbelief turned to horror when he saw, hanging below the rear end, a sort of gondola swinging from side to side as Zhang struggled to escape. It was in the shape of a man's private parts, and much larger than the legs sticking out above. Sam tried to swallow down the vomit that rose in his throat but his mouth was completely dry.

As the monster twisted in its frantic efforts to escape it was distorting the whole network, sending out waves of vibration which were shaking Sam's crystal cave and threatening his life.

The floor was shaking so much now that Sam began to be tossed about like a pea in a drum, his balding head and slithering fingers unable to stop him sliding around on the smooth surface towards the edges where the walls were crashing onto the floor.

If it keeps tossing about like that I'm going to fall through one of the cracks and that will be me finished.

He tried to shout 'Stop!' but all that came out of his dried lips was a stifled gasp. A moment later the floor lifted like a trampoline and he was airborne, hurtling across the cave towards one crystal wall. Without warning, a noise erupted from his own throat, the visceral shriek of an animal being taken to slaughter. It echoed around the crystal cave and escaped through the gaps. Michael Zhang must have heard it because he immediately stopped struggling. The last wave of vibration travelled across the network, the walls of Sam's cave hammered together for the final time, the shaking ceased and silence descended, broken only by the dull thud as Sam's balding head crashed into the floor followed by the crumpled mass of his limp body.

With a groan, Sam slid across the floor, managed to prevent himself falling out of the gap between the floor and the wall and bumped to a halt, trembling and breathless, battered and bruised, but still alive.

Then a voice as deep as a rumble of thunder boomed across the ocean and rolled around the crystal cave. 'Arise and stand on your feet!' It sounded like Michael Zhang's accent but his tiny squeaking voice had been transformed, like his body, into something monstrous and primordial. 'Yes, I am addressing you, Samuel Fitzpatrick. Get up! I know you can hear me. I require your assistance and there is very little time.'

Sam did not move. Could that monster really be the delicate little scientist?

'Stand up! Do you not want to save planet Earth?'

This was too much! 'Save the Earth? Of course I do, Dr Zhang, but how–'

'Do not use that name!' Michael's body was trapped but his monstrous face was straining towards Sam and a darkness suffused his gigantic features, anger flashing from his heavy-lidded eyes. 'The Michael Zhang you knew no longer exists. Now you will call me Lord.'

Lord? In spite of everything Sam felt like laughing. *You were odd before*, Sam thought, *but now you've gone totally insane.* 'I certainly will not!' he shouted.

Michael's eyes narrowed. 'I am as wise as what you would call a god. You doubt my word? Well then I shall prove it to you. As an example, I know everything about you. You are Samuel James Fitzpatrick. You were born in a labourer's cottage on Paddy O'Hearns' Farm at Ballycallen, near Cork, at 2:54 in the afternoon of 7th of July 1959. You were the second child of an alcoholic called James Rossiman Fitzpatrick and a depressive woman Irene Juliet Fitzpatrick, née Blanding. Your family...'

Sam couldn't believe it as every detail of his past was reeled out, including many facts he didn't even know himself but which all had the ring of truth. And when Michael described his father's infidelity with a neighbour, a close family secret, and correctly stated the woman's name, Sam was convinced. 'Stop!' he cried. 'How do you know all this?'

'I know everything, Samuel. Everything! The things I have told you so far are trivial. I know the deepest secrets of what man calls the Universe. Every secret that science struggled to understand has been revealed to me. Now call me Lord.'

Sam carefully sat up on the slippery surface and stared at Michael's enormous face, his bloated body trapped in the crystal network; helpless, naked and obscene.

How can I use such a word for such a monster? But Michael has clearly been changed physically and he certainly knows a lot about me. Maybe he really is a god and anyway I haven't got a clue what to do, so I need him as much as he seems to need me.

'Very well,' Sam sighed, 'I will call you Lord if that's what you want. Now tell me, Lord, is Catriona still alive?'

'That is one of the things I want you to find out.'

'You mean you don't know? I thought you knew everything?'

'I know everything that happened in the Universe from its

creation until the moment we left. I do not know—'

'We left...' Sam couldn't take this in. 'We've left the Universe?'

'Our Universe is part of that,' Michael's little arm was pointing straight down at the pink planet, 'but I don't know what happened to it after we were sucked into the black hole.'

'Was the Earth absorbed too?' Sam said, afraid of the answer.

'I hope not. That's why I broke the event network, to save the Earth, but I don't know if I was successful. That's another one of the things I want you to find out. Stand up! We don't have much time.'

Sam tried to get to his feet, his head spinning with confused disorientation. Immediately he slipped and fell heavily back onto the shiny crystal floor.

'Take your shoes and socks off,' Michael said.

Sam removed his footwear and managed to stand. His head was almost at the centre of the starburst of crystals.

'Look down the middle of each crystal,' Michael told him. 'If the Earth is still there, you should be able to see it.'

Sam chose one of the crystal walls at random and moved his head sideways, not sure where the middle was. The pipe's three flat sides they tapered almost to a point as they receded into the far distance. It was as clear as blue glass and he could see absolutely nothing inside it.

Michael's voice boomed across the sky like an urgent thunderclap. 'What can you see?'

'I can't see anything.'

'Call me Lord.'

'I can't see anything, Lord.'

'Move your head so you are looking exactly into the middle of the pipe.'

How do I do that? Sam asked himself, staring into the blueness. Then, with a small spark of inspiration, he realised that one of the pipe's three edges looked shorter than the other two as they tapered away to the tiny triangle at the far end. He slowly moved his head until the three converging lines were symmetrical, and for a moment he glimpsed something, something small, a darker blue shadow, floating like a ghost far down inside the pipe. Then his head moved too far and he lost sight of it.

Slowly he moved back until his head was once more facing exactly into the middle of the end of the pipe, and he saw it again. It was very small and far away.

What is it?

It was very small and far away

Without thinking he put his hand inside his jacket and was surprised, and somehow comforted, to feel his spectacles still in his shirt pocket. Sadly, both lenses were smashed. He squinted again at the blue shape and saw it was a metal cabinet with two doors, the sort you might see in a garage workshop, but it was still very far away. At the sight of it, Sam's heart stopped beating for a second. It obviously belonged on the Earth, not on this weird pink planet-Universe place. He leaned forward, anxious to get a better view, and the cabinet moved towards him so rapidly he gasped and moved back, afraid of being hit. Immediately, the cabinet moved away. Its movement, he realised, was some sort of optical illusion.

He leaned forward again and once more the cabinet got bigger, so big that he could even see a deep dent on its blue door. By moving his head back and forth he found he could make the box move to any distance he desired, but he could not see the person he was desperate to see.

But at least the Earth is still there, he thought and turned to look into the end of a different crystal, eager to find Catriona and make sure she was safe. Once more he moved his head so the vanishing perspective of the pipe's edges looked symmetrical. To his astonishment a red metal box came into view this time. It was fixed to a white concrete wall. A cone stuck out of one end of the box and some metal pipes ran out of the other. Sam stared, greatly encouraged, then began looking quickly into each of the dozens of other crystal walls surrounding him.

In one he saw a yellow metal girder, the sort you might see a crane moving along in a warehouse. In another crystal there was a red cabinet, with 'Savox' on the glass door, standing on a blue metal balcony. Sam's heart soared.

I'm sure I saw cabinets like that in the cavern.

He leaned forward, desperate now to look into more crystals.

'Have you seen something?' Michael boomed.

'I can see a Savox cabinet. I think it's in the cavern, Lord,' he shouted excitedly.

'I knew it!' Michael's voice was triumphant. 'Some of the fragments have ended up in the ATLAS cavern. What else can you see?'

Sam described each image in turn.

'Can you see any people?' Michael asked.

'No, Lord.'

'Have you looked through every crystal?'

'Not yet.'

'You must look into all of them. Be quick!'

Sam was only too glad to oblige him. He longed to see Catriona. *If only she's alive.* Once again he began peering into the crystals, driven on by Michael's urgency, checking them all methodically. It was after about a dozen crystals, as he was looking at a sheet of white plastic punctured by large rivets, that he heard a woman scream.

Episode 10 Marianne Awakes

Marianne awoke screaming

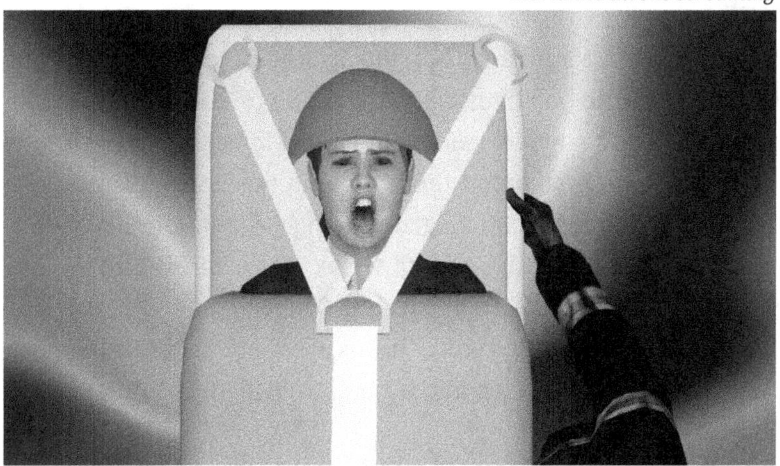

Marianne awoke screaming. Something like a knife was piercing painfully into the top of her abdomen, just below her left breast, stabbing deeply into her body, dragging her mind up out of sleep into a confused, horrified consciousness. At the same time, the muscles in her lower abdomen were tightening, the tension growing and spreading rapidly round into her lower back.

The knife-like pain was stabbing so deeply she hardly noticed the persistent, throbbing ache in her ankle.

As the slow involuntary contraction tightened around the baby, so the pain became totally unbearable and she screamed again, fear flashing bright warning messages into her dark, rioting mind.

I'm having another contraction. Where's Danny? What's happening to me?

She tried to open her eyes but her lids were stuck together, adding to her sense of helpless panic.

Must have been crying in my sleep.

She tried to lift her hand to wipe the crust away from her eyes but, to her growing alarm, she found her right arm wouldn't move. She tried again, panic growing inside her, but it was fixed down by her side. The left one wouldn't move either.

Where am I?

She couldn't remember, but the feeling of being imprisoned made her whole body tense and the pain grew worse. She began to pant, feeling as if she were suffocating. Finally, on the verge of hysteria, she remembered the breathing exercises the antenatal clinic had taught her and began panting deliberately, her mouth wide open, forcing herself to relax, to concentrate on her breathing, to let the fear and all conscious thoughts fall away.

After a minute, the contraction eased off, the searing pain below her breast faded and the panic subsided, but the fear still lurked.

That wasn't just a contraction. Something is very wrong down there.

She squeezed her eyelids together to break the crust and forced her eyes open like oysters. She was looking through a hole in an orange plastic sheet. Instantly she remembered everything; the black hole causing a helium leak, the collapsing stairs, the firefighters wrapping her in this stretcher to hold her safe while they winched her up out of the cavern. The last thing she remembered was the English firefighter talking to her, although she couldn't remember his name.

They're supposed to be hoisting me up to the surface. So why have we stopped?

She moved her head and saw a man's chest close beside her, his body at right angles to hers, his head and shoulders hidden by a shifting pattern of green, red and black patches. The coloured areas glowed so brightly they hurt her eyes and made her squint.

I must be having some kind of migraine. After all the disasters of this morning it's not surprising. I'll have to tell him about this new pain. What's his name?

It took her several seconds to remember, then she said 'What's happening, Robert?' Her own voice sounded muffled.

The firefighter did not answer.

What's wrong with him now?

Marianne had little confidence in Robert Moore. He had almost fallen when he climbed over the balcony handrail, and as they swung out into the cavern he had seemed confused. He didn't speak French very well and couldn't follow what they were saying on his walkie-talkie. Now he wasn't even answering her.

'Robert,' she called, louder than before. 'What's happening?'

I can hear something, Lord

'I can hear something, Lord.'

'What?' The monster excitedly bent its vast bulk and swivelled its huge veiled eyes, straining to see Sam's face.

'A woman screamed and then I think she said "What's happening, Robert?" I think that's what she—'

'Is it Marianne Schneider? The pregnant woman with the broken ankle?'

'I think so, yes. It was hard to hear.'

'That woman is no use to me!' Michael's voice rumbled across the echoing pink ocean. 'I need someone healthy. Isn't there anyone else?'

'I don't know, Lord. I haven't looked through all the crystals yet.'

'Then look, Samuel, and for both our sakes be quick; they could arrive any second.'

It took Sam several minutes to look through every one of the sixty or so crystal walls that made up his cave and as he did so he kept wondering what Michael meant: *They could arrive any second...*

She could see his chest and his left arm

Robert still didn't answer. His right hand was holding the orange stretcher somewhere near her head. She could see his chest and his right arm leading up to his right shoulder, but above that she could see nothing except the strange red, green and black pattern hiding his head. Marianne wished she could see his face. She squinted at the glowing, ceaselessly shifting pattern.

Is that really a migraine?

The red areas were the largest. They sprawled about like a child's splash-daubed painting. Narrow green bands ran around the red, green beaches around red islands, except these islands were constantly changing their shape, merging into each other. And everything was glowing with its own inner light, except the area surrounding these shifting islands. This was an inky and impenetrable black ocean, hiding from view everything beyond.

It's quite beautiful really, she tried to convince herself. She breathed deeply, making herself relax in case her fear triggered another agonising contraction.

Another odd thing was how the whole pattern seemed to surround her, enclosing her, adding to her feeling of being trapped.

It's like being inside a bubble, she thought. *Yes, that's exactly what it's like, a slowly changing, gigantic, glistening soap bubble.*

It enclosed the stretcher and most of Robert's body, everything but his head and shoulders, hiding her view of the rest of the cavern.

Marianne could see two yellow ropes coming into the bubble. One, straight and taut, went to a metal ring that supported the stretcher.

That must be the rope from the fire engine that was winching me up towards the shaft, she decided.

Four broad yellow straps were tied to the bottom of the ring and came down to the corners of the stretcher.

And there was another rope, curving slightly as it ran across from the ring out through the side of the bubble.

That's got to be George Gabor's rope. He was using it to control the stretcher as we swung out from the balcony. I wish he was here instead of Robert. She sighed and started calling him again.

'No, Lord, I can't see anyone else.' Sam was bitterly disappointed. He had looked through every crystal and not seen Catriona, but at least Marianne was alive.

'Then it will have to be the Schneider woman. Is she still in the stretcher?'

'I think so. I saw a white sheet of plastic with metal rivets. It looked like the bottom of the stretcher.'

'And the firefighter Robert Moore, is he still with her?'

'I think so, Lord. She was calling him.'

'Did he respond?'

'No, Lord. I don't think so.'

'Help her get out of the stretcher and see if she can revive him. He's our best hope.'

'Help her? How? I can't even see her.'

'Talk to her. If you can hear her then she must be able to hear you. Now hurry!'

Sam moved his head, searching for the crystal which contained the white plastic. He had only heard Marianne when he was looking straight at that, but there were so many crystal pipes he had forgotten which one it was. He knew he had found it when he heard Marianne still calling to Robert. She sounded desperate.

'I can hear you, Marianne,' Sam said into the centre of the crystal, not at all sure that she would hear him.

'Oh thank God, Robert!' The relief in her voice was palpable, even though she still sounded a little muffled. 'Why didn't you answer before? What's happening? Why have we stopped?'

'Can you get out of the stretcher?' Sam said.

There was a pause. 'Who is that?' She spoke more quietly now, more cautiously.

She knows I'm not Robert, Sam thought. 'It's all right, Marianne.'

'Who are you?'

Sam heard her very clearly this time. She was screaming. It hurt him to know he was upsetting this kind, gentle, vulnerable creature who had already suffered more than anyone else on this disastrous day.

He moved his head to one side so he could no longer see the stretcher, no longer hear her screams, hoping she would not be able to hear him as he said 'She's frightened, Lord. She wants to know who's talking to her.'

Michael thought for a few moments. 'Tell her you're an angel who's trying to help her.'

'An angel? I can't say that! Why can't I just tell her the truth?'

A dark shadow crossed Michael's face. 'Do you know the truth? And if you did, is this the right time to explain it all to her? She needs urgent help and so do I. We need all the crystal bringing here as soon as possible. It's vital you fix the network before they arrive. Tell her you are an angel. You can tell her the truth later, once we have saved the Earth. She was raised as a Roman Catholic. She'll believe you. Tell her to give the crystal to Moore and then tell Moore to collect all the other fragments and bring them down the tunnel. He should be able to find it near where they last saw the black hole. Come on man, hurry!'

'I am an angel,' Sam said into the crystal, thinking *She's never going to believe this*. 'I'm trying to help you, Marianne. Please trust me. You need my help and I need yours. Can you get out of the stretcher?'

There was a long pause. Then very slowly she said 'Is that you, Mr Fitzpatrick?'

'She's recognised my voice, Lord,' Sam said, turning his head aside so she could not hear him. 'I'm going to have to tell her who I am.'

'All right then do it.'

It was a man's voice

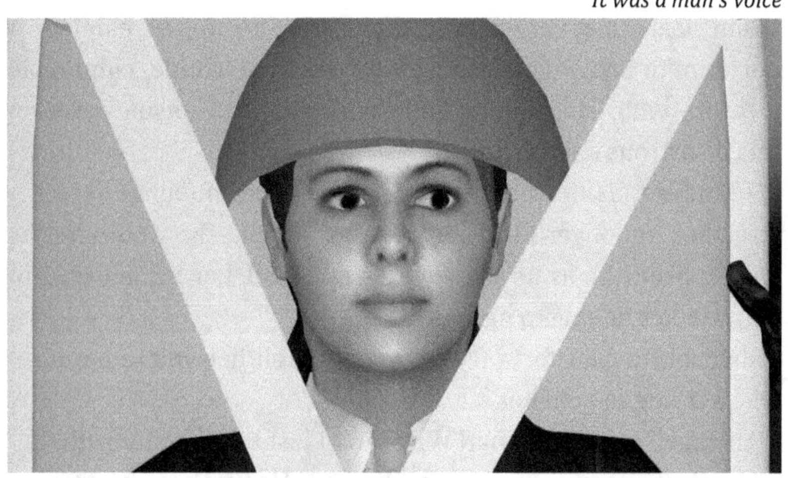

It was a man's voice, muffled and hard to hear. He was speaking English and at first she assumed it was Robert Moore, but as he spoke she realised this person's voice was older, more confident and more determined than Robert's. 'Is that you, Mr Fitzpatrick?' she said.

There was a horrible pause when she was afraid he had disappeared. He had been saying something about being an angel. Perhaps she had been hallucinating, perhaps—

'Yes, it's Sam Fitzpatrick, Marianne', he said at last.

Relief but also confusion flooded over her. She didn't know

either Robert Moore or Sam Fitzpatrick well, but, in an emergency, she thought she would prefer the Irishman. Yet the last time she had seen him was up on the balcony. Where was he now and why was he speaking to her when Robert was so silent? She lifted her head as much as she could and peered out of the aperture in the stretcher cover. All she could see was Robert's chest and the bubble.

'Monsieur Fitzpatrick? I can't see you. Where are you?'

'I don't know, Marianne. We were absorbed by the black hole and—'

'Absorbé?' she said, totally shocked. 'Par le trou noir? Non! Pas possible!' As a CERN guide it had been Marianne's job to reassure visitors that there was almost no chance of them making a black hole here and that, even if they did make one, it would be very small and perfectly safe. That is what the scientists had told her to say. Now, it seemed, they had been wrong on both counts[4].

'Michael says we need the crystal,' Sam was saying. 'He says it's urgent.'

'Michael Zhang? Has he been absorbed too? This doesn't make any sense. If you were absorbed by a black hole you would be killed.'

'No, I know we should have been but we weren't. Now listen, Michael says we need the—'

'I need a doctor, Sam. Something's wrong. I've had terrible

---

[4] Before the disaster, there had been several reviews of the safety of the LHC which had considered, among other things, the creation of microscopic black holes and of magnetic monopoles, and determined that the experiments were completely safe. See for example items (7) and (8) in the bibliography. However no review had ever considered the risk posed by a cosmic monopole being captured by the magnetic fields within the LHC or one of its detectors.

pains in my, in my...' She couldn't think of the English for "abdomen". '...where the baby is.'

'Is Robert still alive?'

'I don't know,' she said. 'He won't answer.'

'Can you get out of the stretcher?'

'No, I'm strapped in. I can't move my arms.'

'You've got to get out, Marianne. Try to get out. I can't do anything to help you.'

'I'll try,' she said. She felt calmer now she knew she wasn't alone, and as she relaxed the pains died down to tolerable levels.

She didn't understand how Sam could still be alive and talking to her if he had been absorbed by a black hole; it didn't make any sense. But nothing made any sense: not the bubble, not the silently hanging Robert, not the agonising pain far worse than any normal contraction. And at least somebody was trying to help her, another human being was talking to her. That made her calmer and gave her fresh hope.

She raised her head as far as she could, trying to work out how the flaps were fastened together, when her eyes fell on something dark. A dark stain where the two long flaps of the orange cover reached over her abdomen, just below her breast. There was a little hole in the centre of the dark stain, a hole surrounded by jagged edges.

And suddenly she remembered it, the blue light that had flown up from somewhere beneath the stretcher, bounced off the beam pipe shield just above her and come hurtling down, smashing into the stretcher cover. She remembered the searing agony of it tearing into her flesh just before she passed out. She stared at the gaping hole within the dark stain and groaned.

'What's wrong Marianne?' Sam called.

'Nothing.' There was no point telling him about the stain or the blue light. No point telling him she hadn't felt her baby kick since she woke up.

Baby can't be injured, she told herself firmly. *He can't be. He's probably fast asleep.*

She looked at the stretcher cover again, keeping her eyes away from the stain. The two halves of the cover overlapped, buckled together on the outside. For several long minutes she wriggled her hand trying to push it through the gap between the two flaps, breathing out to make room, ignoring the pain as her arm pressed onto her abdomen. Finally her fingers slipped through the gap and she felt a buckle. For many more minutes she struggled to undo it, pausing once as another contraction sent a long stab of agony up through her abdomen and chest.

Finally she undid the buckle and pushed her forearm through the gap. With a wave of relief she stretched across to touch the cold black overall covering Robert's chest.

'Robert?' she said again and shuddered as she realised his chest wasn't moving. *He isn't breathing! You've got to be alive, Robert!*

She wanted to see his face, hidden behind the bubble whose colours never ceased to ebb and flow. She reached up to push it out of the way and felt a hard surface then a sharp pain, like an electric shock, flashed through her fingertips. Reflexively she pulled her hand away and shrank back against the stretcher, letting her eyes travel across the bubble's coloured pattern, more afraid than before.

And now, for the first time, she realised that there was a rhythm to the pattern and that this was somehow linked to her own breathing. As she breathed in, the green rivers flooded over red islands. Then, as she breathed out, new islands emerged from beneath the unfathomable black ocean.

But she had the measure of it now, this bubble, and could see how its curving surface encircled her. Although it was hard to judge, it seemed to be centred on her bump.

She poked Robert like an obstinate donkey and shouted but he still didn't move. *All that effort to free my arm has got me nowhere.*

'Have you got out?' Sam said.

'I've got one arm out. Robert won't move.'

'Try to get out.'

With fresh determination she unbuckled another strap, pushed the orange flaps open a bit more, managed to yank her other arm out and reached forward, bending towards the other buckles. Excruciating pains shot through her abdomen and ankle. After trying several times, she finally managed to push open the plastic cover.

Oh God!

There was a hole in her blue jacket with a dark central oozing mass surrounded by a large stain. In the uncertain light from the bubble it looked dark brown. Her mouth went dry; her heart began fluttering like a trapped bird.

Struggling to calm the rising tide of fear, she told herself: *It's just a flesh wound. Looks worse than it is. Don't worry.* She looked away, trying to ignore the stain, to forget about it. *It's not serious. The pain isn't too bad, not really. I'd be in agony if something had gone into my womb. It can't have hurt the baby. First thing is to talk to Robert. He knows about childbirth. He's my best hope of getting help.*

Pushing the orange cover aside, Marianne raised her hand, grasped the metal ring hanging above her from the two yellow ropes and began to pull herself out of the stretcher. Pain throbbed through her ankle. She looked down, moved her leg to avoid scraping her foot on the cover, pulled the ring again, looked up and gasped. The bubble was moving up Robert's neck and the pattern had completely changed. The randomness had disappeared, replaced by red and green rings which completely encircled her. As the bubble moved, new little red and green circles appeared at the top, opened out like coloured ripples and moved down until she was completely enclosed by slowly moving circles of glowing colour. She stopped pulling but the bubble kept moving, gradually revealing Robert's face; first his receding chin; next his mouth open in the silent echo of a scream; then his flared nostrils; his eyes wide and staring and finally his whole face, frozen in an agonised death-mask.

She grasped the stretcher, trying to stop herself moving and sighed 'Poor Robert!'

'What's wrong Marianne?' Sam said.

'He's dead.'

Episode 11 The Balcony

Are you sure he's dead?

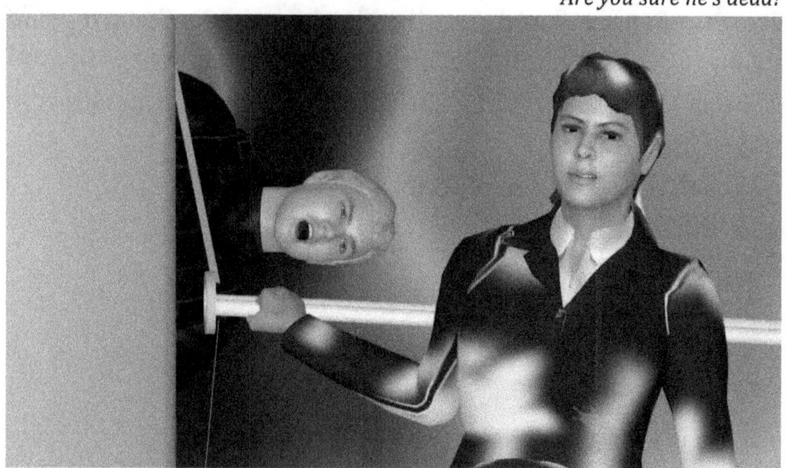

'Are you sure he's dead?' Sam said.

'Yes of course he's dead!' Marianne screamed. 'You think I can't recognise a dead person when I see one?'

'I'm sorry. Stay calm, Marianne. Everything's going to be all right. Are you out of the stretcher?'

'Yes.'

She was floating above the two flaps, holding onto the metal ring and with her back to the frozen corpse.

'Are you safe? You won't fall will you?'

She looked down. 'No. I seem to be floating.' She could see the whole stretcher inside the bubble. For a moment she felt dizzy then realised that the stretcher below her was slowly spinning round on the ends of the four yellow straps. As it spun the bottom part of the bubble turned with it and a blue light swept across Robert's body.

'I can see a blue light,' she said.

'Where's it coming from?'

'From under the flaps of the stretcher.'

She heard Sam say 'She can see a blue light, Lord,' and something inside her head seemed to shift to one side.

Is he talking to God? she asked herself and without thinking she began to pray quietly, her eyes closed. 'Hail Mary, full of grace, the Lord is with thee!' She took comfort from the words and guiltily began wondering how long it had been since she had said them. *Can't stop now*, she thought. *Blessed art thou among women, and blessed is the fruit of thy womb, Jesus.* The words, silently spoken in her head, rung in her heart like a bell and she whispered 'Oh Mary, blessed virgin, please protect my baby from harm.'

'Michael thinks it's a piece of crystal,' Sam said. 'Try to get it, Marianne. It will help us.'

She pulled on the straps running down to the stretcher thinking *Michael? Is Sam in heaven with the Archangel Michael? Was Sam telling the truth when he said he was an angel? Surely it wasn't Michael Zhang that he was calling Lord?*

The stretcher floated easily up towards her, apparently completely weightless, as she tried to remember a suitable prayer for an emergency like this, but everything was jumbled up in her mind, so she just prayed the words which rose up unbidden from her childhood memory, when she used to kneel before the Virgin's statue in her local church, then she embellished them a little to suit the situation.

I implore your help, O most loving Virgin Mary. I fly to thee O Virgin of Virgins. Please remember Sam Fitzpatrick and the soul of poor Robert Moore. Remember Danny, my beloved husband. And please, oh please Mother of the Word Incarnate, please look after my unborn baby. Amen.

As the stretcher moved towards her, the pattern on the bottom half of the bubble behind the stretcher changed. Was this a sign from the Virgin? Her hungry eyes wandered over the bubble's surface, searching for a meaning.

The top half of the bubble was still a jumble of random blotches, but in the bottom half, red and green rings were running down and closing behind the stretcher as it moved towards her. She looked at the join where the two patterns met, just behind Robert, and noticed a circular ridge. It almost seemed like there were two bubbles.

There are two bubbles!

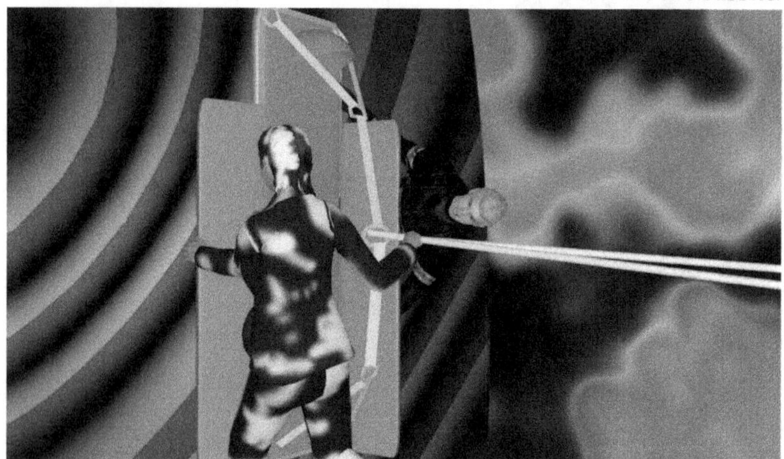

That's it! There are two bubbles! Oh thank you, Mother of God!

She didn't know why, but she was sure this was a sign of fundamental importance. The ridge between the bubbles was getting smaller and harder to see. *It's as if I was looking through a round window, looking out of one bubble into another.*

The two patterns overlapped and merged together at the ridge, making a shape like a figure of eight. The bottom bubble was centred on the stretcher, the top one seemed to be centred somewhere near herself. She was so engrossed in watching the ridge gradually disappearing that the stretcher almost hit her. She had to fend it off, then grasp it and hold it to stop it floating away.

She opened the orange covers and looked inside. Something

was sticking up through the soft orange sheet covering the stretcher's hard white plastic base, something that glowed pale blue, down near where her feet had been.

'I can see you, Marianne!' she heard Sam shouting excitedly. 'Can you see me?'

'No. Only a piece of glass.'

She pushed the flaps aside and ran her fingers over the glass. It glowed with a blue inner light, casting shadows across the flaps. It had three smooth, flat faces which were cold to the touch. They joined in three sharp edges which led up to a dangerously sharp point. It was this which had punctured the stretcher's thick plastic base.

'I can see your fingers, Marianne!' Sam shouted. His voice was much louder now. 'You're touching the crystal, aren't you?' Sam's voice seemed to be coming from out of the blue glass. She quickly took her hand away from it. 'It's a piece of crystal, Marianne! Michael says we need it. Put it in your pocket and keep it safe.'

'I can't. It's stuck in the bottom of the stretcher.'

'You must.' Sam's voice was urgent. 'Michael says you must get it.'

She tried again but her trembling fingers could not pull it out. With a sudden inspiration she turned the stretcher over. A larger chunk of the crystal was sticking out from the bottom. She reached across and touched it, feeling its three sharp corners. She grasped it carefully and pulled. It came away in her hand. Once more she was aware that the pattern in part of the bubble changed but it did not seem so important now.

'I've got it, Sam, I've got it!' She felt as if she had overcome a huge hurdle. She had done what Sam wanted; she had escaped from the stretcher and got the crystal. Now, she assumed, Sam would suddenly appear and help her get to hospital.

'Good girl!' he said. 'Now you can escape. Use the rope to get up to the surface.'

'But aren't you going to help me, Sam? I need to see a doctor urgently. There's something wrong. I've got blood on my jacket and a terrible pain in my...' She searched again for the English for abdomen and suddenly remembered it was the same as the French. '...in my abdomen'.

'I'm helping you as much as I can, Marianne. Don't worry. We'll get you to hospital as soon as possible. You can use the rope to escape. It should be easy.'

She sighed. *He's right. One of these two ropes must go up to the surface. There must be somebody up there who can help me. But why haven't they come down to find me?* She looked at the ropes, then at the crystal. *What am I going to do with this?* Taking care of its sharp corners, she carefully put it into the side pocket of her jacket. As she did so, the two bubbles practically merged into one and the ridge between them almost disappeared.

Now she looked at the two ropes more carefully. Both of them were slack, snaking away from a metal ring on the stretcher to the bubble. She pulled on one of them. The rope straightened and went taut. It seemed to be fixed in the bubble wall. She tried the other rope but the same thing happened. She pulled harder and found herself drifting away from the stretcher, away from Robert. Once more coloured rings began to flow around her, red, green and black. And as she moved, the bubble moved with her, exposing more of the rope.

She pulled harder, eager to get away from Robert and find help but feeling a little guilty about leaving him. She glanced back. Robert's dead face was slipping away behind her, disappearing from sight as the coloured ripples closed over him. *He died trying to help me and I was poking him. What killed him?* she wondered as she turned and pulled herself along the rope as fast as she could, hand over hand. It wasn't hard work and the amazing thing was that she didn't fall back down again. It was as if she was weightless, floating like the stretcher. The red and green rings opened up ahead of her, ran past her around the bubble, and closed up behind her. She felt the warm air of the cavern moving past her face. It wasn't until she reached the balcony that she realised she was pulling the wrong rope.

For a second Sam had seen Marianne's face and it felt wonderful to see another human being, even in the state she was in, no longer so attractive now but pale and drawn and covered in concrete dust. Then she must have put the crystal in her pocket because all he could see was a pink mobile phone jiggling about. It was very frustrating not being able to see what she was doing. Something outside his crystal cave caught his eye and he glanced up. A tiny black speck was moving slowly across the brown triangular gap near the top of the cave where one crystal seemed to be missing. He frowned and leaned towards it but it didn't get any bigger. It was moving very slowly. He squinted up at it, wishing he hadn't broken his glasses.

He heard a muffled groan and his eyes flipped back to Marianne's crystal. He now knew exactly which one it was out of the sixty or so crystals which surrounded him. It took him only a few seconds to position his head so he was looking exactly down the middle of the long crystal tube. This time he saw not the phone but a handkerchief. It was streaked with blue highlights.

'Where are you, Marianne? Have you got to the roof yet?' he said.

There was no answer. He repeated the question, speaking louder, wondering why this sudden silence and was relieved when her muffled voice said:

'No. I've come to the balcony. I was pulling the wrong rope.'

'The balcony! Is George Gabor there?'

Now that Robert Moore was dead, George was the obvious person to help Marianne and also to do what Michael wanted.

The last time Sam had seen him, George had been on one of the balconies that ran along the tall cavern wall, controlling Marianne's stretcher as it swung out towards the huge ATLAS detector, standing near Catriona and the young man Alex Karolyi.

'I don't know. I can't see anything outside this bubble. I'm going back.'

What bubble does she mean? Sam wondered. 'No, wait Marianne!' he said. 'Let me see. Take the crystal out of your pocket.' He saw Marianne's huge hand come into the pocket and feel round for the crystal. The handkerchief and mobile telephone were left behind and Sam glimpsed Marianne's face, concrete dust greying her matted hair, her cheeks hollow, her eyes sunk in two dark wells of pain.

Behind her he could see the yellow rope reaching down to the stretcher far below, but from this angle the balcony was invisible. He leaned sideways, trying to see it, and to his amazement the scene suddenly changed, as if Marianne had turned the crystal (although he was sure she hadn't) and he was looking up at the balcony. And there was Catriona!

She was leaning over the handrail

It wasn't easy to see her in the darkness of the cavern. She was leaning over the handrail looking out into the cavern, her body rigid, her mouth locked open as if she was screaming. Sam was elated to see her, but terribly puzzled. Why was she standing completely motionless, like a photograph of herself? Why were her ginger hair and her green blouse completely grey? The whole scene looked grey, as if Sam were looking through a mist.

Sam could just about make out Alex Karolyi too, standing beside her. He too was colourless and unmoving, his arms raised in protest, a look of horror fixed on his face. Both of them looked like black-and-white photographs. And yet the rope looked yellow and the balcony handrail looked blue. At least, the parts of them closest to Sam did. It was extremely strange.

'Where d'you think those photos came from?' Sam said.

'What photos?' Marianne sounded puzzled.

'The ones of Catriona and Alex.'

'Alex? Where is he?'

'Just along the balcony. Can't you see them, Marianne? They are black-and-white photos.'

'No. I can't see anything outside the bubble.'

'Bubble? What bubble?' Sam said. 'I can't see any bubble.'

'You must be able to. It's all around me.'

Sam was deeply puzzled. 'How big's this bubble?'

'Mmm, about three metres across.'

Sam's eyes looked again at the rope and the handrail. They lost their colours a short distance away, maybe a metre or two. Everything further than that was black-and-white. *Could that be the edge of the bubble she's talking about?* 'They're just along the balcony, Marianne. Can you go up the rope a bit further?'

He saw Marianne's hand reach out and pull the rope. The coloured boundary moved forward.

'I need two hands,' she said. Her fingers wrapped around the crystal and she returned it to her pocket. Sam glanced up at the triangular gap in his cave. The little black shape was still moving across the brown background but Sam thought it looked a bit bigger than before. He squinted again and what he saw this time through the blur of his eyelashes made goose bumps break out on his neck, run down his back, slither round his buttocks and disappear down his trembling thighs. *It's a bee! So Catriona's story was true!*

Sam had first heard about the bee two weeks after the death of Catriona's father. It was her first day back at school after the funeral and Sam was her teacher. All day he had been worried about her. He knew she had come back to school too soon, so he had driven her home. He remembered her, a little eight-year-old standing on the thick piled cream carpet in Brigit's luxurious Dublin home, wringing her hands together as she stood before Sam shouting:

'It wasn't an accident. It was murder! I saw it.'

Sam hardly knew the famous Brigit O'Brien then. She stood staring at her daughter, her face scarlet with anger and embarrassment. 'For God's sake don't start that again,' she had said. 'Catriona was a very naughty girl that night, Mr Fitzpatrick.

It was her birthday and she took her dog for a walk before I came home. God knows where she went. She won't tell me the truth. I was beside myself with worry. When she finally came home she must have heard the Garda telling me about John's accident because she made up this ridiculous story to cover up her own naughtiness. Come along, my girl. It's time you were in bed.'

Catriona had run to the far side of her chair shouting: 'It's true. I was outside the lab with Trackaway waiting for Daddy to come out and we saw shooting stars and then a spaceman with a blue light came flying to Daddy's window and shot him but then a big bee came and stung him and took him away to the spaceship and—'

Brigit had reached over and slapped her daughter across the face so hard it echoed around the room. Sam shuddered and pushed the memory to the back of his mind.

But it makes complete sense now, he thought. *The blue light must have been a piece of crystal. But how did Catriona see a crystal and a bee six years ago? And what did she mean about the spaceship?*

Sam's attention was suddenly riveted by the sight of another bee. This one flew out of the brown triangle and took on a blue hue as it went behind one of the crystal pipes. *So they're outside the cave*, he thought. *Wonder how far away they are?* He searched the other crystals near the gap and had found about a dozen more of the insects when he heard a scream. Sam's head jerked round and he looked again into Marianne's crystal but he could see nothing but the things in her pocket.

'Don't worry, Catriona,' he heard Marianne say. 'It's only me, Marianne Schneider. Look at me, Catriona.'

So she's alive! Sam thought. *Thank God!*

He heard Catriona yell 'She's floating! She's floating like the spaceman!' then he heard her whimper like a whipped dog and he knew exactly what she was thinking and his heart broke for her. *She must be going through a real trauma.*

Alex said 'Marianne? What's going on? How did you get up here? And what the hell is that freaking thing?'

'It's all right, Alex,' Marianne said. 'It's just some sort of bubble. It won't hurt you.' *So Alex can see it too*, Sam thought. 'I need your help, Alex.' Marianne seemed to be gasping for breath. 'There's something wrong with—'

'Oh god!' Alex said. He sounded shocked. 'What's that on your jacket?'

'Something hit me while I was in the stretcher. I need to see a doctor urgently, Alex. I think...' She breathed deeply. 'I think the baby might be coming.'

'Oh no!' Catriona groaned.

'Shall I go for a doctor?' Alex said. 'How long have we got?'

'The contractions have to be about two minutes apart before the baby comes,' Marianne said.

'And how far apart are they now?'

'I don't know. I've just had one. Can you time them for me?'

'Little Kata can do that, can't you sweetie? It'll give her something to do.'

Catriona groaned then said 'Have you got a watch?'

Good girl Catty, Sam thought. *She's coping with this really well.*

Alex said 'Sure' at the same time that Marianne said 'Here'.

There was a pause. 'Which one's right?' Catriona said. *Sounds like she's got both their watches now*, Sam thought.

'What do you mean?' Alex said. 'Let me see. Oh yes, I see. Your watch says six minutes past twelve, Marianne. I don't understand that. Better use mine, Kata.'

'All right,' Catriona groaned. 'So it's twenty-four minutes past eleven. What happens now?'

'We have to wait for the next one,' Marianne said.

There was silence. Sam longed to see Catriona. *She sounds as if she's in a bad state, but at least she's alive, and Alex too. Thank God! He'll be able to help Marianne. Wonder if their colour's come back?* He moved his head away from the crystal and said 'Marianne has revived Catriona and Alex, Lord.'

'Alex Karolyi? Excellent!' Michael said. 'Tell her to give him the spare crystal and tell Karolyi to collect all the other crystals he can find and bring them down the tunnel. Tell him…What's that noise?'

Sam listened. A low droning seemed to be vibrating inside his head. He looked up. The insect was closer now and clearer. The head had two long antennae on the front and two large eyes on the sides. It was flying straight towards him.

'There's some sort of insect up there, Lord.' Sam didn't want to call it a bee.

'Insect? Where?' Michael's long body arched so his face lifted upward. 'By all that's holy, they're coming! Tell Karolyi to be quick, for God's sake Samuel!'

Sam turned back to Marianne's crystal with a chill churning his stomach and listened for Alex's voice.

'Is it cold in here?' Catriona was saying. 'My feet feel frozen.'

'Catriona!' Sam called. She didn't seem to hear him.

'I think you need to get your feet inside the bubble,' Marianne said.

'Marianne,' Sam called louder. 'I need to speak to Alex!'

But she too ignored him. 'You know the fireman Robert?' she said. 'He's dead.'

'Oh no!' Catriona wailed. 'Poor Robert!'

'Bubble?' Alex said. 'You mean that coloured thing?'

'Alex!' Sam shouted at the top of his voice. 'Can you hear me?'

'Yes,' Marianne said. 'I think your feet need to be inside it.'

Sam gave up and moved his head away from the crystal.

'They can't hear me, Lord,' Sam said. 'They're too busy talking and the crystal is in Marianne's pocket.'

'Keep trying,' Michael said. Sam could hardly hear him, the buzzing was so loud, then without warning it stopped. The silence seemed louder than the noise had been. Sam looked up but the insect was nowhere to be seen. 'Hurry, Samuel,' Michael said. 'If that thing finds us we're done for.'

Episode 12 An Arrival, a Departure

Sam looked up through the triangular gap in the top of his crystal cave, but still could not see or hear the insect. *Maybe it's gone away*, he thought, but a cold fear in his heart told him it hadn't. If Michael was so worried about it then it must be a real threat. *He says he's as wise as a god so I suppose he must know what he's talking about. Although he said Marianne would believe me if I told her I was an angel, but she didn't. I knew she wouldn't. So maybe he's not as clever as he thinks he is.*

Sam turned towards the crystal wall in which he had seen the balcony, but all he could see now was Marianne's mobile phone and a handkerchief lit by blue highlights. Evidently the crystal was still in her pocket. He heard her muffled voice say: 'Lift your feet inside the bubble. That's what I'm telling you. I think something strange happens if you're outside. I think that's what happened to Robert. His head was outside the bubble and—'

'I can't,' Catriona screamed. 'My feet won't move. Oh God! Help me, Alex! I'm trapped! Oh Jesus! What's wrong with me?'

The insect looked enormous

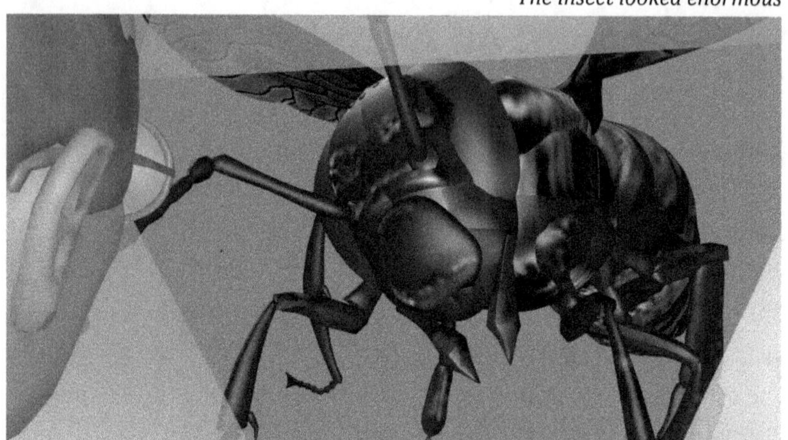

Then Sam heard the buzzing sound again and looked up in alarm. The insect looked enormous although it was clearly still some distance away, its long legs dangling down below the middle section of its body.

It's coming closer! What's it going to do when it gets here? How big is it really?

He turned back to the crystal and started shouting again at the top of his voice, calling each of their names in turn, then listening for an answer, but all he heard was Marianne saying 'You need to pull me down…The bubble moves with the baby and with this blue thing… Here, pull me down Alex. You've got to get your whole body inside the bubble.'

'What blue thing?' Alex said. 'Okay, honey. Come to papa. That's it. Now you, little Kata. Calm down baby. That's it, sweetie. Your feet are inside the bubble now. Just lift your legs up. I promise not to look up your skirt. That's it, sweetheart.'

'Oh God, that stings.' Catriona said. Sam could hear her slapping her legs and yelping in pain.

'Yes, it's like the hot-aches,' Alex said.

'It's the circulation coming back,' Marianne said. 'I think when you're outside the bubble your blood stops. Yes, that must be it.

Robert's body was inside but his head was outside. That must be what killed him.'

'And what's this blue thing you're talking about?' Alex said.

Her hand came into the pocket and Sam's heart thumped. *She's going to take the crystal out! Now's my chance to talk to them!* The mobile phone fell away and a moment later Sam glimpsed Alex's face between her fingers.

'It's this crystal,' Marianne said. 'It was stuck in the bottom of the stretcher.'

Then more fingers came close, Alex took the crystal and his huge dark brown eyes stared straight at Sam. A pale blue light was shining across his nose, casting a dark shadow over his cheek. *The colour's come back,* Sam thought. Alex looked so vast that for a moment Sam felt naked and vulnerable, but he shrugged off the feeling and started waving, calling 'Alex! Can you see me? It's Sam Fitzpatrick'

Alex frowned and at first Sam thought he had heard him, but he didn't respond. Instead he began to move the crystal and his eyes turned away as he said 'Look! This thing's got its own bubble! It moves when I move the crystal!'

Did he really hear me? Sam wondered, and began calling him again, but Alex was looking at Marianne now and seemed totally absorbed when she said. 'I think there are two of them.'

'So where's the other one?'

'I think it's in here. I think that's what hit me in the stretcher.'

'Oh Jesus,' Alex said.

Marianne started groaning again and panting.

'You having another contraction, kedvenc?' Alex said.

Then his voice was drowned by the buzzing grew and Sam looked over to see an enormous pair of long feathery protuberances reaching down from somewhere in the brown sky and running gently over the crystal network where Michael was trapped. Sam felt his eyes drawn upwards. The feathery feelers were attached to the top of the vast head of a bee. It towered over him, covered in long fine downy hair. It dwarfed Michael, dwarfed the net, dwarfed the whole planet. It was utterly enormous and terrifying.

The head moved forward, two short jaws folded down from the lower part of its face and began to push the crystals aside just above Michael. The buzz changed pitch and became a low, contented hum.

All Sam's hopes collapsed. *It's too late. It's going to eat him!* He turned back to his crystal and screamed Alex's name. The hum changed back into an angry buzz. Sam glanced across the crystal network. The bee had stopped working and its antennae were wafting swiftly around as if trying to pick up a trace of something. Sam fell silent. *No good both of us being eaten.* He shuddered and turned back to the crystal Alex was holding.

'...heard Sam,' Marianne was saying, 'and he said that he could see me, but I didn't–'

'Sam?' Catriona said, sounding astonished.

'Yes,' Alex said. 'I think I heard him too.'

'Sam? Where is he?' Catriona started screaming 'Sam! Sam!'

Sam could see her ginger head twisting around as she searched for him, but all he could do was watch her, his heart breaking silently, longing to speak but terrified of being found by the bee.

'Be quiet Kata!' Alex said. 'I can't hear with you screaming.'

'Come here, Catriona,' Marianne said. 'What time is it?'

'Eleven twenty-nine,' Catriona said after a pause.

'So that's five minutes since the last contraction,' Marianne said. 'Looks like the baby isn't due right away, Alex.'

'That's good,' Alex said. 'I can't hear Sam. Listen Marianne. I don't think it's a good idea for you to move more than you have to. I'll go and get the doctor. There must be one up on the surface by now. If I take this crystal I can go up and get him and bring him down. You two stay here. That bubble's just about big enough for two little women.'

'Agreed,' Marianne said. 'You go.'

'These balconies go up to the cavern roof, don't they, Marianne?' Alex said.

'Yes. There's a walkway from the top balcony across to the platform at the bottom of the shaft. But I don't think there are any ladders in the shaft.'

'No but there are pipes,' Alex said.

'And the rope,' Catriona said.

'Yes, that's right,' Alex said. 'I'll get up there somehow, don't worry. You keep my watch Kata,' Alex said. 'It looks like Marianne's is broken. Au revoir mes enfants braves!' Sam saw him pull himself along the balcony handrail, kiss Marianne twice on both the cheeks and then move to Catriona. Catriona wrapped her arms tightly round his neck and he had trouble disentangling himself.

'See you soon,' he said. 'Now, where are those stairs? Ah yes, that way.' He smiled at them and jammed the crystal into his shirt pocket. Now Sam could see nothing but the yellow of his shirt lit by the blue of the crystal, and he turned to look across at Michael, expecting to see his mangled corpse dangling from the bee's jaws.

And the insect had indeed lifted him out of the net, but it wasn't eating him. Instead it was holding him in two hand-like claws on the ends of its front legs. They made Michael look tiny. The insect was stroking his long white body with its antennae. Michael was not struggling. He was staring at Sam with a smile on his face. When he saw Sam looking at him he said 'Has the Schneider woman got help yet, Samuel?' He sounded perfectly calm.

Sam decided the bee was harmless and said: 'Yes, Lord,' his voice trembling. 'Alex Karolyi has one of the crystals now.'

'Karolyi? Excellent! He will be a good agent.' Michael seemed totally at ease. 'Help him collect all the other fragments.'

The insect lowered Michael and rested him back in the gap in the crystal network as if it were putting a baby into a cradle. He made no attempt to escape. A long round tube emerged from the insect's mouth, curved down like a snake and hovered near Michael's mouth. Something began to pump in the insect's throat and a drop of liquid appeared at the tip of the tube. Michael opened his mouth and began to drink. Sam felt overwhelming nausea.

Alex Karolyi pulled himself along the handrail

Alex Karolyi pulled himself along the handrail deep in thought. Red and green rings opened ahead of him, moved around the bubble and closed near his feet. The air gently ruffled his hair.

What do I know about this crystal? My guess is it has something to do with the blue flash we saw just before Marianne appeared on the balcony. She was still in the stretcher then, and the black hole moved past her and absorbed Sam and Michael and then moved down and I thought it was going to hit the Earth but then there was the blue flash and the next moment Marianne was floating along the balcony saying she had just pulled herself up the rope.

But I didn't see her do that so what happened to me and Kata in the mean time?

He reached the stairway and stopped. The rings broke up into random coloured patches, with black areas growing inside them. He took the crystal out of his shirt pocket and looked at it.

'What do I know about you?' he said to the crystal, frowning at it. 'You're shaped like a, what do they call it, a tetrahedron.' He slid his fingers over the stone. 'You've got four sharp little edges. All the same length. I'd say about three centimetres. And they meet in four very sharp little corners. You've got teeth all right, little crystal, but you've got smoothness too. Your four faces are flat. And somehow, somehow you create this bubble.'

For a moment he waved the crystal around and his eyes travelled over the beautiful swirling patterns which began flowing around the bubble. Then he looked again at the crystal. 'How do you do that?' He shook his head.

'What else do I know? Well I'm weightless for one thing, as if gravity has been turned off. That must be something to do with you, I should think. What else? Things that are outside a bubble are sort of frozen. People whose heads are outside a bubble die. According to Marianne, the English firefighter died like that. Why did that happen? What else? My watch and Marianne's were telling different times yet they were both still going. Oh yes, and I know one other thing. Marianne and I both heard Sam's voice inside you. That's the weirdest thing of all. No, wait, one more thing. I think she said that Sam said he could see her. Now that's really weird! I wonder if she could see him? She didn't say.'

He raised the crystal to his eye and squinted into it. The crystal was glowing with an inner blue light. Inside there were six small triangles which he assumed were the reflections of the tetrahedron's inner faces, but he could see no sign of Sam. He held the crystal at arm's length and stared at it, totally baffled.

'There's something really strange going on here, my little blue friend, and it's all connected with you. Whatever you are, you're obviously very important. I'd really love to have a look around in this cavern and search for some of your friends.'

Throughout most of his twenty-six years, Count Alex Karolyi had been the first to seize any new opportunity which had presented itself, whether in business or in bed. He had left Budapest and come to CERN with the specific aim of discovering something new and exciting, something whose potential the scientists had not realised, something which he alone could exploit.

But so far the only exciting thing he had discovered was Marianne Peeters, and she had thrown Alex away and married that stuffed penguin Danny Schneider. With a sigh he put the crystal back into his shirt pocket and began to pull himself up the stairs handrail, heading towards the ceiling but still talking to his little blue friend.

'Unfortunately I've got to go up to the surface and find the doctor so he can save the life of the child of the great, the wonderful Mr Daniel Schneider. Ah yes, don't tell me, Mr Crystal! I already know it's totally stupid. You want to know why I am saving his son, rather than trying to make my fortune collecting your brother crystals? It's quite simple really. It's something called love, Mr Crystal. You wouldn't understand. I don't really understand it myself, but I know that I have to do whatever I can to help Marianne, even if that means saving the life of Danny's child.

'She doesn't really love him, of course. What woman could love a man like Schneider? As debonair as a skateboarder, as sexy as a hedgehog and as sympathetic as a dead dog. There's no way she could be happy with him, but she wants his baby. That's partly why she finished with me. Children are not part of my story. And if she lost his baby, it would be good for me. It would be one less reason for her to stay with him. But it's her baby and she's got a right to have it.

'But at least I've found you, the thing I was looking for when I came here. I'm not sure what you're good for, little crystal, but I'm damn sure you must be good for something, and I want as many crystals like you as I can find. I'll figure out what to do with you later, once I've cornered the market.'

He reached the top of the stairs, where it passed through a hole in the balcony above, and looked around trying to work out which was the best way to go. A broad blue beam ran at right-angles to the balcony on the far side of the handrail.

That must go all the way up to the cavern ceiling. There's no gravity holding me back, so no reason I shouldn't just go straight up.

He pushed himself away from the stairs, floated over to the beam and began to hand-walk along, full of excited anticipation, seeing a thousand new opportunities in the red and green rings which were opening up before him. His past life and all the old rules of civilization seemed to be slipping away behind him like the coloured rings which disappeared beneath his feet.

Nothing in the world is holding back Karolyi Alexander! I ain't afraid of nothing. I've faced rival drug-pushers on the streets of Budapest threatening me with knives and guns. I've faced the biggest software companies on Earth and produced a better product for CERN at a lower cost than anyone else could. And now I've got—

Suddenly the end of the beam came into the bubble and before he could stop himself it had disappeared out the back and he was alone. The place where the rings opened drifted round to the back of his head and he lost sight of it.

I must be spinning. But I'm still moving.

The point where the rings closed moved up level with his knees, then something hard hit the back of his head, and moved down his left shoulder. He raised his left arm to protect himself, got a glimpse of a white surface moving out of the bubble and he was floating and spinning once more, faster than before.

That was the cavern wall! Could even have been the ceiling. Shit! Now where am I going? Time wasted. Sorry Marianne. Still, it's not all bad. I must be moving, otherwise the rings would have broken up. I'll hit something soon. It'll probably come in at the point where the rings open. That's the direction I'm going.

Seconds passed. He kept his hands directed towards the opening point, palms outwards, even when it went behind him, trying to concentrate on the rings, to stay alert, tracking the front of the bubble with his hands and eyes. But he found it hard to concentrate. The longer he drifted the more excited he became.

I'm going down. I might even reach the cavern floor. Maybe I'll find more crystal down there!

Then a large blue tube entered the bubble, just missed his head and hit his left shoulder. There were no hand-holds so all he could do was fend it off. The slippery surface slid rapidly down his arm, rubbed against his leg and drifted out of the bubble. The rings still moved past him.

That was the beam pipe shield. I'm halfway to the cavern floor.

Something else loomed before him, a large brown sheet of plastic, then some wires, then another brown sheet.

A Big Wheel!

He reached out, clung to one of the cables, stopped himself drifting and hung there panting, as if he had just run a race, trying to catch his breath and to work out where he was. He knew there were four of these large brown discs in the cavern, two at either end of ATLAS.

I must be near the floor by now, so I've got to get back up to the ceiling. I suppose I could push myself up and drift there but I don't think I'll try it. If I miss the shaft, I could go bouncing around forever in this freaking cavern. Better stay in contact with solid objects.

He pulled himself further down towards the floor, trying to see round the end of the Wheel. Rings began to open up in the bubble ahead of him and then a gap appeared, a sort of round ridge travelled towards him and he was looking through a window, a round window, looking out of his bubble into another. The colours in the other bubble were random and in the centre of the space a blue light was shining out of a thick bank of cables. Alex pulled himself forward eagerly and prized the black wires apart with trembling fingers. Sure enough there was another crystal inside. He reached in and pulled it out.

So there really are more of these little beauties! Wonder what something like this would fetch if the world ever gets back to normal? Depends on how many there are, I suppose. Wish I had time to look for more, but I've got to go and get the doctor for Marianne. Time's hurrying by.

He did not want to run the risk of losing both crystals by putting them in the same shirt pocket, so the new one he jammed into a pocket of his tight trousers. Ignoring the discomfort of the sharp corner sticking painfully into his hip, he pushed on to the edge of the Big Wheel. Beyond he could see the blue balcony that ran along the cavern wall.

Better go up the stairs I suppose. Safer than going up the Big Wheel. Don't want to waste any more time drifting around.

He pulled himself along the balcony to the stairs and started going up.

Wish I'd kept to the stairs in the beginning. But no, then I wouldn't have found this second crystal. Perhaps things have worked out for the best.

He had gone up three flights and was going along the balcony to the next when something yellow came into his bubble. *Somebody on the balcony.* He saw a firefighter's helmet and below it George Gabor's eyes, cold, hard and unmoving at first, then swivelling quickly towards him. Alex held on to the handrail to stop himself and gave a whoop of delight, grinning at George as he floated before him.

At first the startled look in George's eyes made Alex laugh out loud. *He looks as shocked as I was when I first saw Marianne,* Alex thought. *Give him time to get used to seeing me.*

Although they both came from Budapest, the two Hungarians had never met before coming to CERN and had hardly spoken before this morning. But as he had watched George working to rescue Catriona from the stairs, Alex had developed a respect for the firefighter's skill and humanity. But when George's face crumpled and his head fell forward Alex grew alarmed.

'What's the matter with you, old man?' Alex said, then looked down at his chest. The bubble ended just below George's shoulders. *Oh shit!* Alex thought. *His heart's outside!*

Episode 13 Hatching

Sam watched the giant bee feeding Michael

Sam lay curled up on the floor of his transparent crystal cave trying not to tremble as he watched the monstrous head of the giant bee feeding Michael. Its two jaws gaped open at the bottom of its head and a long beak-like structure emerged from between them. This tapered down to a narrow tube which Michael had taken in his mouth. He was now vigorously sucking like a thirsty baby at the breast. Sam was so disgusted he could not watch. He looked up at the head towering over him like an upside-down mountain, wondering why he could not see its body.

That can't be the same as the bee Catty saw, Sam thought. *If something that size had appeared over Dublin the whole world would have known about it.*

It was clearly much larger than this pink planet and Sam assumed it would have been larger than the Earth itself. Then he heard a series of melodious low-pitched hums and drones, with occasional higher-pitched squeaks. At the same time the two long antennae which sprouted from between its eyes waved up and down as if conducting an orchestra. The sounds seemed to emanate from two narrow hairy structures which hung down on either side of the tapering tube. *The bee's singing!*

Michael too was obviously listening intently for he sometimes stopped feeding and tried to make a few sounds of his own before he returned to sucking. At first his singing attempts were no more than deep human-like hums but Michael learned fast. He soon mastered the higher-pitched squeaks, then the lower buzzes and finally the deep drones. Within ten minutes he was breaking off feeding to repeat short phrases. He and the insect started playing a game. They echoed each other's sounds, their songs growing longer and more elaborate.

They're not just making noises, Sam thought. *Those sounds mean something. It's as if they're talking.*

There were no repetitions now; every phrase was different. The melody was less varied but the noises were complex, with new sounds appearing, high pitched squeaks and long oscillating chirrups. Sam was watching Michael's face, wondering how he was making these noises, when he noticed his cheeks, the ones on his face, were fat and taut and shiny. *He's getting fatter!* Michael's sides bulged out like a balloon that was about to pop.

As it talked to him, the insect continuously stroked Michael's long body with the hairy antennae that reached down from its face. The periods of talking were getting longer while the drinking grew shorter until Michael stopped feeding altogether. Then the insect's song got faster and louder and the antennae strokes increased to match, long strong strokes from Michael's face down the whole length of his bloated body. Michael closed his eyes, as if he was enjoying it, he moaned softly and his face turned pink. Waves of contraction followed the antennae down his body, his face turned redder then he groaned, a huge ball of excrement flopped out of his backside onto the crystal pipes curving below him and a thick stream of urine began to splash over the crystal pipes as if a firefighter's hose had been turned on. Sam could see it dripping down towards the pink ocean far below.

The insect's antennae reached forward and wafted above the steaming pile of excrement which lay on the net. There was a silence and for a moment the only noise was Michael's last few trickles, then the insect sang a short, melodious song, as loud and vigorous as a fanfare. Michael listened and began to sing the same song. Then he began to giggle. The giggle became a laugh. He laughed so much he almost fell between the crystal pipes beneath him and the insect had to steady him with its front legs. With a final chirp the insect's head lifted, Sam heard the deep buzz of its wings and the rest of its body came into view as if it was emerging from behind a wall. It rose into the browns sky, hovered and turned, gave one last squeak, then turned again and flew rapidly away until joined the dozens of other tiny bees flying back and forth across the sky.

Michael lay on the net, dripping and softly groaning. Then his mouth closed, he frowned deeply, his face grew dark and he began to make low, long, repetitive grunts through his nose. The frowning crevice between his eyebrows slowly deepened and spread up his forehead. Sam could hear a crackling as of a drum-skin splitting in half. A crack spread rapidly down Michael's back and Sam saw something white and glistening protrude through the gap like the inner-tube of a split bicycle tyre. Michael was still grunting loudly and with every grunt there was another crack and the white inner-tube protruded more, pushing the two halves of his skin apart. Suddenly his eyes disappeared, dark holes appearing in their place, and his face lost all expression, turning into a death-mask.

A few moments later the inner-tube began to wriggle and bend. It lifted upwards and Michael's new body emerged from the slit in his old skin. He was white and dramatically different from before. Instead of being a simple oval shape, he was now segmented like a maggot. He lay on top of his old skin breathing hard, and Sam saw his maggot-body was swelling. When he stopped a few minutes later he was huge, much larger than he had been as an airship.

He lay still, panting and apparently exhausted. Sam looked at him in horror, watching his new white skin gradually darkening to a creamy-grey.

What's happening to you, Michael Zhang? You're certainly not human any more, but then you're no god either. Call you Lord? Call you a maggot! By Jesus I wish I'd died in that black hole. This is a living nightmare, you bloated with food, me starving to death, people in crystals, Marianne pregnant and injured and with no doctor. Maybe this is what hell's like? I wish there was a God. I could do with a few miracles right now. But if anyone's going to do anything to help it has to be Alex Karolyi.

He sighed, looked up, checked the brown sky was clear of nearby insects, stood and began peering into the crystal which Marianne had given to Alex. He was relieved to see a wall of yellow. *The crystal must be in Alex's pocket!* Then he heard two people talking in a language he did not understand. One of them sounded like Alex. *But who's he talking to?*

Sam listened intently. The other voice was a deep, bear-like growl. *George Gabor! That's perfect! He's the ideal person to help us!* Sam had just opened his mouth to start calling George when he heard a soft, silken voice floating down from somewhere above him, saying: 'What's happening Sam?'

The thought *It's God!* flashed through Sam's mind and he spun round. What he saw was Michael's gigantic face smiling down at him from the front of the maggot's body. Shocked at its enormity and closeness, Sam slipped and fell to the crystal floor. He lay on his back looking up at it. The maggot must have crawled carefully and silently over the crystal network because Sam had felt no vibrations and heard nothing. He could see its enormous yellow teeth. He could not get out of his mind the thought that it was going to eat him. The maggot wriggled closer until it was smiling directly down at him as if it was amused at Sam's obvious discomfort. 'Don't worry, Sam,' it said softly. It still sounded like Michael. 'Everything's all right. What's happening on Earth?'

Sam could hear the fear trembling in his own voice as he said 'Alex has revived George Gabor, Lord.'

'Gábor György? That is very good! Well done!' Michael's entire demeanour had changed. He seemed calm, relaxed, completely at ease.

'Thank you, Lord.' Sam didn't feel he had done much to deserve this praise, but he accepted it gratefully, hoping his life would be spared.

'Look, Sam, forget about this Lord business. Just call me Michael. You and I have to work together. We are the only humans here.'

Human? Sam thought. *You're not human!*

Michael smiled as if he could read Sam's thoughts. 'I am not going to hurt you,' he said softly. 'How are you feeling? You look a bit rough.'

Sam was confused. Michael had changed from a devil pretending to be a god into a maggot pretending to be his friend. But Sam was in need of a friend right now.

'I feel terrible. I don't understand what's going on or where we are or what's happening to us.' He meant 'to you' but was afraid to say it.

'I think it's time you got an explanation, Samuel. You deserve to know. I've learned a lot in the past ten minutes. We are on a planet called Ent.'

Sam looked down at the pink planet far below him. 'Ent?'

'Yes, but that's not it, Sam! Ent is far larger than that. Our Universe and you and I and Oesirisi we are all on Ent.'

'Ersi who?'

'That's the creature we saw. She's an Entroilian. As you saw, invertebrates here are highly evolved. They have language and apparently—'

'So, so wait a minute. The Earth's a planet in our Universe, right? But we've come out of that Universe onto another planet called Ent? Is that right? So where is this planet?'

'It's all around us. No doubt you'll see it soon. According to Oesirisi there are lots of little universes here. She called them "cosmic eggs". They are part of the Entroilian life-cycle. One of the Entroilians lays these eggs and then they wait until creatures inside evolve to be sufficiently intelligent to emerge, like you and me although she didn't notice you, Sam. She called me an "emergent".'

'I still don't get it. How can that pink thing be our whole Universe? What are all these blue pipes? And why did you break one of them? How can I see things in these crystals and, and why is it so important that we get somebody to—'

'Whoa, Sam, slow down. One thing at a time! Let's take it from the top. You remember the rain falling out of these pipes when we first arrived? They were time quanta. When they fell into the Universe they built up a permanent record of history, like geological sediment on the surface of the planet. That's what that pink ocean is: a record of history. And apparently it's important for Entroilians. Oesirisi said that a universe historian will come along soon and study those records to find out how we evolved.'

That sort of made sense to Sam. He took his courage in his hands and said 'And what about your body? How did it get changed? Why were you changed and I wasn't? We both fell into the same black hole.'

Michael's front segment nodded up and down. 'When we came out of our Universe, I accidentally swallowed some of the pink jelly, and thereby gained wisdom. I immediately understood where we were, and I realised I had a unique opportunity, to learn the whole history of the universe. So I burrowed my way down to the very centre of the event record, back to the beginning of time, swallowing the event layers as I went. That was how I attained my wisdom and became an Entroilian egg.'

'You're an egg?' Sam gasped.

'I was an egg. Now Oesirisi has fed me and I've been transformed into an Entroilian larva. Over the next couple of weeks I will grow and pupate and metamorphose into an Entroilian drone.'

'So you're turning into a wasp?'

'Well, Entroilians have a lot in common with bees on Earth, yes.'

'And you don't mind?'

'Mind? I'm honoured. Oesirisi said I had King's Shit! It sounds like I'm going to be one of the senior members of Entroilian society. It's all to do with the genes, apparently.'

Sam's mind just could not cope with this. He decided to move on to another of his burning questions. 'Why did you break the pipe?'

'I didn't want the whole Earth getting sucked into the black hole. I guessed that if I broke the machine, time would stop in the Universe. That was—'

'So time has stopped in the Universe?' Sam felt he was collapsing beneath an unbearable mountain of unacceptable facts. He had wanted to know the truth, but now he realised the situation was worse, far worse than he had ever thought possible.

'Yes, time has stopped everywhere except near one of the fragments of crystal. Breaking the cosmic egg's shell was the only way I could think of to stop the whole world being absorbed, and many more people, perhaps millions, following us here. Looks like I managed to save the world but then the net trapped me and sent out a signal to let the Entroilians know I was here. I hadn't anticipated that.'

'And why did you want me to make somebody collect the crystals and bring them here?'

'At that time all I knew was that the Universe was a machine that somebody had built. I thought that when they arrived they would treat us as scientific specimens and tear us to pieces, and perhaps even destroy the universe. I was hoping that, if we got all the crystals back and fixed the machine, the makers wouldn't bother to come. But Oesirisi said the historian would not destroy the Universe, just examine it and keep a record. Then she will wait for more emergents. Emergents grow into new Entroilians. That's how they reproduce. So that's it, you know as much as I do. Are you feeling any better now?'

'No, I'm feeling a great deal worse! To be honest I can't take in any of this. And anyway, my main concern now is Catriona. And Marianne.'

'Of course they are. I think we'll have to wait to see what the universe historian says. She might be able to fix the machine and restart time, although she is still going to need all the crystal fragments to do that. In the meantime you need food. I've fed your mind, now I'm going to feed your body. Stand back.'

Sam stood up and moved to the opposite side of the floor. Michael lifted his front few segments upwards, bent them down so his mouth was above the gap in the crystal cave and his body began to heave. A drop of amber liquid appeared on his lips and began to drip into the cave like a gobbet of thick spit. It splattered heavily onto the floor where it formed itself into a glistening sweet-smelling golden dome. In spite of his revulsion at the way this substance had been produced, and his fear that he would become like Michael, Sam's mouth watered at the smell. It was hours since breakfast.

'Don't worry, Sam. You won't become like me, if that's what you're afraid of. Go ahead. Try it. It's really delicious!'

Episode 14 Out of the Cavern

'You okay George?' Alex said, slapping him again.

For a few seconds George Gabor didn't respond, then with a sudden movement his barrel chest heaved and his eyes opened. A look of recognition came into them.

'Karolyi Alexander? How did you get...' Then his eyes ran over the bubble. 'What the bloody hell's that?'

As quickly as he could, Alex explained what had happened. He took the crystal out of his shirt pocket and held it out for George to see. He decided not to mention the one in his trousers. The firefighter looked at the crystal with a deep frown creasing his heavy brows, then turned on his radio. White noise hissed around the bubble. He flicked the receiver off and jammed it back in the holster with a curse. Removing his helmet, he wiped his bald head with the back of his hand. 'My God, Karolyi, you nearly killed me.'

'Gábor György, you ungrateful swine, I just brought you back to life. What more do you want?'

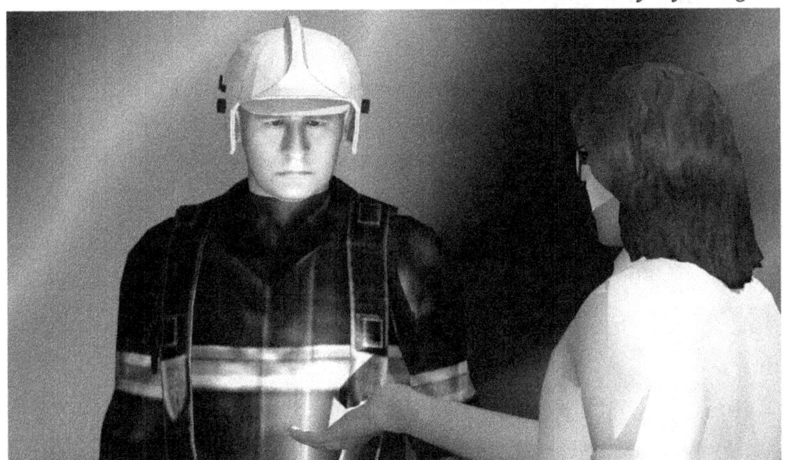

George looked at Alex with a deadly serious, hard face. 'Show me that bloody crystal again, Karolyi. I still can't believe this. A crystal and a bloody bubble! I mean, what kind of crap is this?'

'Well apparently it's the kind of crap that happens when you create a black hole, György.'

'That's bloody amazing. So we're trapped in this thing are we?' He banged the bubble wall. The pattern flashed and vibrated but his hand didn't pass through. 'And you say Marianne's got one crystal and you've got the other? Sounds like the first thing to do is go and find some more of those little monkeys and make another bubble. Otherwise I guess you and I will be stuck together like Siamese twins? And we'll need some to revive a few scientists so they can work out what this crap is all about.'

You're not as simple as you look, György, Alex thought. An astute Hungarian brain lurks somewhere behind that flat, dumb face and those cold, dead eyes. I suppose I ought to tell you about the third crystal, the one in my pants. Err, no, maybe this isn't the right time to be giving away my trade secrets. Not that I'm trying to cheat you or anything. I just need a bit more time to think through the implications of crystal before I give you my only spare. Hope you don't notice the slight bulge in my pants or the ridge where the two bubbles overlap.

'I'd like to go and check my crew are all safe first,' George said. 'Any objections?'

Alex paused. 'I know about Robert.'

'Robert Moore? What do you know?'

'Marianne said he's dead.'

The temperature of George's eyes cooled a few degrees below zero. When he spoke his voice sounded like the wind echoing through the hollow trunk of a dead old tree. 'How? How did he die?'

'She thinks it was because his head was outside the bubble while his heart was inside. A bit like you only the other way round. This crystal needs a bit of careful handling. A piece hit Marianne. I've left Catriona with her and I'm going up to find the doctor. Do you know where he is?'

'Yes. According to the last radio report, he's just landed in the helicopter. How bad is she?'

'She thinks there's a bit of crystal stuck inside her stomach, or I mean in her, here,' he pointed at his abdomen, 'where the baby is.'

'Christ,' George said. 'Stuck inside? You mean it's gone up her—'

'No, it went in at the front, here. There's blood on her jacket.'

'Hell! Is she in a lot of pain?'

'Doesn't seem to be.'

'Come on then, let's go and find the doctor. The helicopter's in the field just below the Globe. I don't give much for that baby's chances though.'

'Don't let any part of your body stick out of the bubble,' Alex said as the two men laboured slowly up the narrow stairway, each with one arm wrapped round the other, their other arms pulling on the handrails.

'I think I learned that lesson already, Karolyi, but this bubble isn't big enough for two. Aren't there any more of these bloody crystals anywhere?'

He's right. We won't get far like this. Alex sighed and put his hand in his trouser pocket. 'Well funny thing. I found this in one of the Big Wheels.' He pulled out the crystal and offered it to George. 'You may borrow it for the rest of this expedition, Mr Gábor, but remember it belongs to me. The crystal in my shirt belongs to Marianne and this one belongs to me. I want it back when we've got the doctor to her. Understood?'

George took the crystal and looked at it closely, then his eyes froze onto Alex's face. 'What makes you think this belongs to you, Karolyi?' George said, his deep voice rumbling round inside their bubbles as he floated up towards the next balcony, a circular bubble-ridge narrowing between them. His hand wrapped round a beam to steady himself. 'This cavern belongs to CERN. As far as I can see, anything found inside this cavern also belongs to CERN. It's not finders-keepers here, Mr Karolyi. Understood? Now let's go and get that bloody doctor.' He shoved the crystal into a pocket, began to haul his massive frame up the stairs and soon disappeared from sight as the two bubbles separated.

Alex followed him thinking *Maybe that wasn't such a good idea. Now where's he gone?*

Even moving at top speed Alex had trouble keeping up. For a while he was alone with his thoughts. *Who does the crystal really belong to? If it comes to the point, would I give the piece in my pocket back to Marianne if she asked for it? Probably not.* He imagined her kneeling before him, restored to her full beauty, those gorgeous eyes looking up at him with a pleading expression and he felt himself weaken. *Well, I guess I might be persuaded.*

George was waiting for him at the top balcony. 'Where've you been, Karolyi? I thought this was urgent? You want to go back and wait with the women while I go get the doctor?'

'Okay György, I can keep up. Some of us work with our brains more than our muscles. Keep going.'

A narrow walkway ran out of the balcony and George pulled himself across it to the bottom of the shaft.

'The gas pipes were shredded when the steel platform blew out,' George said when Alex caught up again. 'Be careful, there's a lot of sharp edges. We'll use the rope.'

Before Alex could say anything, George had pushed himself away from the walkway and drifted out into the shaft. Alex hesitated, knowing the danger of floating free, but decided he had no option but to follow. He traversed the huge shaft twice before he found the rope and began to go up. When he reached the top George was waiting with his arms folded across his chest.

'Look, Karolyi, you're just holding me back. I want you to go back and wait with the women. That's not a request, that's an order.'

'And how will you bring the doctor down with just the one crystal?'

'Good question. All right, hand it over.' George held his hand out towards Alex.

Alex stared at it, then looked at him with a broad grin. Alex had a rule: Always laugh in the face of disaster. 'I told you, György, this is Marianne's crystal and that one is mine. What are you going to do, take it off me by force? Look, György, three people should be able to travel with two crystals. I might even be useful to you, you never know. But one thing you can be sure of. To get this crystal off me you're going to have to use extreme force. Is that what you want?'

George stared at him, his face expressionless, then his bald head nodded briefly. 'Okay, Karolyi. You can keep it. For now. But you've got to keep up. Here, tie yourself onto this. We'll have to stay together.' He untied a short length of rope from a metal ring on his harness and gave one end to Alex. Alex began to tie it to his belt. 'No, not like that,' George said. 'Here, let me do it.'

Alex looked down at George's bald head as the firefighter tied the rope securely around his waist, thinking *I wonder what goes on inside that bony skull of yours?*

When he had finished, George's arms suddenly went round Alex's waist and his legs pushed hard against the concrete floor.

Coloured rings simultaneously began passing rapidly down both their bubbles. Cold air brushed past Alex's face and arms. He immediately became alarmed. 'Jesus, György,' Alex said. 'What the freak did you do that for?'

Coloured rings began passing down their bubbles

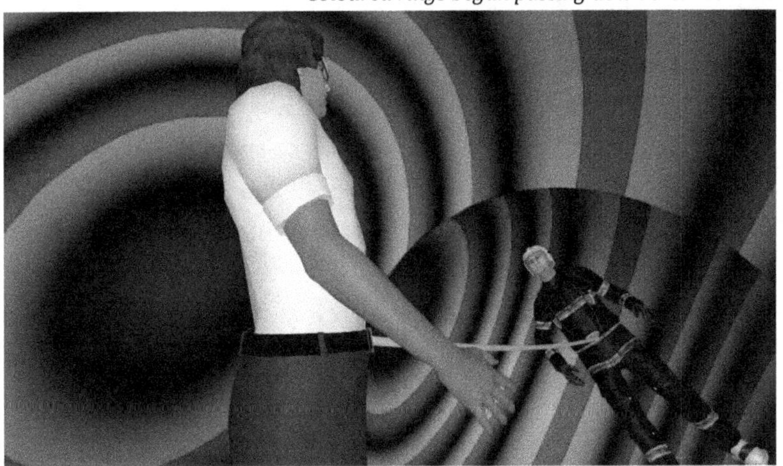

'We've got to get out of SX and find the helicopter,' George said brusquely. 'This is the quickest way.'

As they floated upwards, George pushed Alex away and the two men separated, connected only by a short section of rope which passed through the narrow ridge where their two bubbles overlapped.

'But we're just floating free, György! I thought I'd explained this to you before. Floating is dangerous. I spent a long time drifting around in the cavern. It's best to keep hold of something fixed down. Oh well, you've done it now. Guess we'll hit the roof in a minute.' Alex held his arms out in the direction of the opening rings, ready to fend off the roof when it came into their bubbles.

'Not necessarily,' George said slowly. 'One of the three SX roofs has gone and another is half hanging off.'

Alex stared at him incredulously. 'You mean we might miss the roof altogether?'

'Maybe, but so we just wait for gravity to bring us back down. No problem. What's causing those red and green bands?'

'Oh, I dunno,' Alex said, thinking furiously about what would happen if they didn't hit the roof.

'I think it's got something to do with movement.'

'Yeah, we're still moving. We must be well clear of the roof by now. What time is it? I gave my watch to Kata.'

George checked his watch. 'Eleven thirty-seven.'

'Can't be,' Alex said. 'Kata said it was eleven twenty-nine before I left and that was ages ago. I was floating around inside the cavern for at least ten minutes.'

'I'm telling you Karolyi that it's thirty-seven minutes past. I check this watch against the fire station clock at the start of every shift.'

'Mine's a Patek Philippe,' Alex said. 'Never known it out by even one second. You know what? I've got a feeling that time either slows down or stops when you're outside the bubble and it only goes when you're inside.'

'That's impossible, Karolyi! Time can't stop. How the hell would it work? How could a piece of crystal stop time? Ridiculous!'

'No, György, the crystal doesn't stop time. It makes time go! I think time's frozen outside a bubble. It all fits, don't you see? That would explain why Marianne's watch was different from mine and yours is too. I thought her watch had stopped but in fact mine was wrong. She's been in a crystal the longest, you the shortest. Marianne thought the blood stops flowing when you're outside the bubble, and you know that's true. It's as if the parts of your body outside a bubble don't work and the only way that can happen is if you're in a sort of suspended animation. That's how you were before I found you.'

'That's nonsense, Karolyi, and you know it. Time can't stop! No, I think this bubble is, has got some sort of, of force field or something created by that black hole. Outside everything's probably just going on as normal. There's people down there probably looking up and saying "What's that strange bloody thing floating across the SX building?" Don't panic, Karolyi old chap. We'll be landing any second now and when we do I hope I'm on top. And I hope it's soon. I feel like a rat in a trap.'

'Landing? György, I've got a nasty feeling that might take a long time. We're going up. If we keep going like this we could actually leave the Earth's atmosphere.'

'Don't be stupid, Karolyi. We've got to hit the ground sooner or later. You can't just keep going up forever.'

'Why not György? There's no gravity. We're just—'

'How can there be no gravity? It's, it's a natural force. It can't just stop. Of course there's gravity. You mean the laws of science have all just stopped?'

'No. Yes! Outside a bubble yes, the laws of physics have stopped. Where there's no time there's no physics. We're floating in a little bubble of time, György, and we're heading away from the Earth.'

George looked at him with a grim smile, shaking his head as if Alex had lost his mind.

Alex spent several minutes trying to think about how they could stop moving upwards and return to Earth, but without any success. George too seemed deep in thought. Suddenly Alex remembered that he was supposed to be finding the doctor. 'I wonder how Marianne's getting on,' he said. 'What time is it?'

George looked at his watch. 'Eleven thirty-nine.'

'At least two minutes since we left the Earth. Sure as hell not hit that roof. She must be worried out of her mind. What speed do you think we're moving at, György?'

'Speed? How should I know? All I can see is this god-damned bloody bubble.'

'Say we're moving at running speed, say fifteen kilometres an hour.'

'Say twenty, Karolyi, you fat old slow-coach.'

'And say we've been moving for five minutes. How far's that?'

'Beats me.'

'Twenty thousand divided by twelve. Call it ten. That's about two thousand. We're already at least two k. up and still climbing. How high's Mont Blanc?'

Almost the only thing Alex knew about George was that mountaineering was his hobby. He had once bragged how he had climbed the famous peak alone at night and camped on the top. Alex never knew whether to believe him. He didn't know George very well. He saw him occasionally making safety checks in the cavern but never in the Cafeteria where Alex usually hung out, making business contacts or picking up women. The firemen kept themselves very much to themselves. George had once told him he had been a senior fireman in Budapest and Alex got the impression there was some sort of problem that had driven him out of Hungary, but he didn't know the details. According to George, the main reason he had come to Switzerland was for the mountains. He was physically very powerful, tall with a broad frame and huge hands and obviously fit despite his age, somewhere between forty-five and fifty, Alex guessed.

'Mont Blanc?' George said. 'Just over four thousand eight

hundred metres. Why?'

'Can you breathe up there? I mean, without oxygen.'

'Sure. No problem.'

'What about Everest? You can't breathe up there, can you? How high is that?'

'You can, but not for long and not without acclimatisation.'

'How high is it?'

'Eight thousand eight hundred and forty eight metres.'

'Less than nine kilometres? We're going to be higher than that in about twenty minutes if we don't stop going up and find some way to turn round!'

'Look, Karolyi, I've been thinking. What about if we separate?'

'Huh?' Alex tried to work out what George meant. *Think the altitude must be affecting me. I'm beginning to feel slightly light-headed.*

'As I see it, we're a bit like a space rocket, right?'

What's he getting at? 'So you accept we're heading away from the Earth?'

'Got to. It's eleven forty-something and we haven't landed so we must be either floating or going up. I take your word for it that we're moving, so—'

'And this separation you want would be what?'

'So as I said as far as I can see we're like a space rocket with two parts. Let's say there's a front part and a back part.'

'That's you and me, presumably?'

'Yes. Or maybe the other way around. And the rocket's run out of fuel.'

'Okay,' Alex said, thoughtfully.

'And we're drifting away from the Earth.'

'I think I see where this is going.'

'But if the two parts separate—'

'—and push away from each other—'

'—then one of them might go down—'

'—while the other one goes up faster than before?' Alex's hand shot up like a rocket. 'Out into space? Good idea, György! And which part were you thinking of being, I wonder?'

George's cold white face stared at him. 'I'm a CERN employee and a firefighter. I'm exactly the sort of person needed on the ground in this situation. What use would you be down there, Karolyi? They don't need business-men or software engineers at a time like this. They need emergency crew. Like me.'

Alex noticed that, while he was talking, George had unclipped two of the large D shaped metal rings from his belt and was holding one in each hand. His big fat fists gripped the straight parts of the carabiners while the curved parts were wrapped firmly around his knuckles and his narrowed eyes were fixed firmly on Alex's face.

Episode 15 Sleep baby sleep

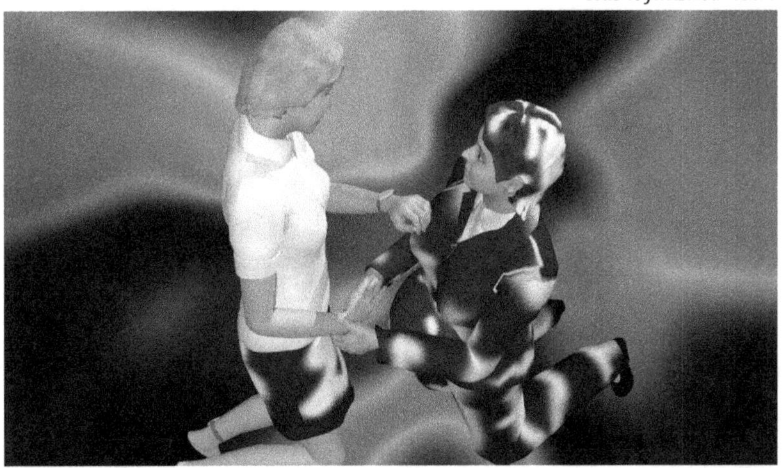

'Has it finished now?' Catriona whispered.

Marianne nodded as the pain of the contraction died away. 'What time is it?'

Catriona looked at Alex's watch strapped on her wrist. She didn't bother to look at Marianne's watch, thinking it was broken. Not wanting to get them mixed up, she had strapped the broken one onto her ankle. 'Eleven thirty-four. What time did the last one end? I can't remember.'

Good job I'm not relying on you then, Marianne thought. 'I think it was eleven twenty-nine'

'That's five minutes then,' Catriona said. 'That's good isn't it?'

Marianne nodded. 'Yes, that's good. They're not two minutes apart yet. It means the baby isn't due for some time, but it won't be too long. I think I went through the early stage while I was asleep.'

'How long does it take, to have a baby?'

'What, altogether? Oh, hours. Twelve, eighteen hours. Can be longer when you haven't had a baby before.'

'Have you? Had one before?'

'No.'

'I wish I knew more about all this. Why don't they teach things like this in school? D'you know they don't even teach us first aid? It's incredible when you think about it. I mean, they teach you about biology but don't teach you the basics of saving somebody's life! They could so easily make it part of the biology course, couldn't they?'

'I suppose they could,' Marianne said, thinking *I just wish you'd shut up for a bit and let me rest. I want to sleep. Don't think I can stand that pain much longer. Hope Alex brings the doctor soon.*

'Where did you go to school, Marianne?'

'Lille. It's in France.'

'Is it nice there?'

'It's okay, but I prefer Geneva.'

'Did they teach you first aid?'

'No. It's...I think it's a good idea.' *I know you mean well, Catriona,* she thought. *I'm glad you're here. I'd hate to be on my own at a time like this.*

'I'll have to suggest it to Mother. She might be able to talk to the Minister of Education and if she becomes President she could issue a decree; From now on all biology courses must include a course on first aid.'

'President? Of Ireland?'

'Of the Republic, yes. That's what she wants to do. Hasn't got a cat in hell's chance actually but it's what she wants. It's why she's taken this Ambassador's job without pay—'

'Without pay? Really?'

'Oh yes. She's paying for everything herself, the house and the car and everything. She only got the job because she gave money to the party during last year's general election. She's got plenty so she can afford it. She earned a fortune on Irish TV. But she's too tight-fisted to pay for servants. Maybe that's why she wants Sam and me to stay here!'

'Irish TV?' Marianne was intrigued now. Here was something to take her mind off the pain. When she first met Brigit earlier this morning, Marianne had thought she looked like a high-class prostitute, but there was obviously more to her than she realised.

'Yes. Didn't you know? She had her own breakfast TV show. Very popular in the States apparently. Asked outrageous questions, insulted everybody, had a lot of politicians cooking breakfast for each other. Waste of time if you ask me but everyone was glued to it.'

'I'd like to see it. She's quite a character, your mother.'

'Isn't she, though? But would you vote for her?'

'I might. It would depend who else was standing.'

'Or in her case who else was lying down.'

Marianne frowned and was still trying to work out whether Catriona meant what she thought she meant when another contraction started. It was longer and stronger than before, and had hardly died down when another one started.

When they finished Catriona checked the watch. 'Four minutes.' She sounded frightened. 'They're getting faster.'

'Are your feet okay?' Marianne said, trying to change the subject.

'Yes, fine.'

'You know what will happen if anything sticks outside the bubble, don't you?'

Catriona pulled her legs up to her chest, her short black skirt riding up round her hips, wrapped her arms round her knees and looked at Marianne thoughtfully. 'Do you have any brothers or sisters, Marianne?'

'Mmm. One sister. You?'

'No. Nothing. Only Sam. He's...He was a good man. I couldn't have asked for a better stepfather.'

'Stepfather? Ah oui, beau-père. So your mother and father are divorced?'

'No. My father's dead. My father died when I was eight. He was murdered and nobody knows why or who did it. I was there, lying outside waiting for him. I saw the man who shot him. That's why I've come here, to find out who killed him, and Michael knows something about it. It's a miracle that we met, as if it was meant to happen. I really wanted to talk to him, and then the stupid black hole went and swallowed him.'

She was almost in tears. Marianne thought it was time to change the subject.

'So Sam, he isn't your father?'

'Sam? Good God no! Sam was my teacher. I think mother only married him so she'd have a cheap baby-sitter! But he was a great stepfather to me. I dread to think how I would have turned out without him. I didn't realise how lucky I was until I saw... until that black hole...'

Catriona's eyes were misty, clouded in pain. Marianne reached out and took her hand. 'It's all right, Catriona. He's still alive. They're both still alive.'

The girl's eyes suddenly focussed on her, staring at her long and hard as if she wanted to believe her but dared not.

'He was talking to me through the crystal,' Marianne said.

Catriona shook her head, a stubborn look of disbelief on her face.

'It's true, my dear. He helped me get out of the stretcher, well, he encouraged me. And then when I came up here he saw you and told me you and Alex were here, even though I couldn't see you. I think he can see things outside the bubble.'

'But how can they still be alive?' Catriona whispered. 'I saw them both vanish into the black hole!'

'I know, but somehow Sam survived, and so did Michael Zhang.'

'That's a miracle,' the girl sighed. 'Did you speak to Michael too?'

'No, only to Sam, although...'

'What?'

'Well, at first Sam said he was an angel and later on I heard him say "Lord".'

'An angel? Oh God. So he is dead?'

'No no, he isn't dead. I think he was playing a joke. I don't understand the English sense of humour. I think he was talking to Michael Zhang.'

Catriona stared at her. 'You think they've gone to heaven?' she whispered.

'I don't really believe in heaven but—'

'No, neither do I.'

'But they've survived a black hole and they must be somewhere, so I don't know. Look, Catriona, I want to ask you something. Did you see the black hole hit them?'

'Yes, they sort of shrunk. They were holding the magnet tube. It all just vanished.'

'And...What about Danny?' Her voice was hoarse. The question burned her throat.

'No! Don't worry! Just Michael Zhang and...'

Catriona's voice broke off, her chest heaved and a look of pain ran across her face.

'Come here,' Marianne said. She leaned out and pulled Catriona to her, putting her arms round her and cuddling her close. Catriona curled up beside her and shyly put her arms round her. As their arms wrapped around each other Marianne felt Catriona relax, her head lifted and she looked into her face.

'I wish you were my mother, Marianne,' she whispered.

Marianne's heart went out to her. *She's obviously a very lonely little girl.* 'I'm only twenty-four, Catriona! How old are you?'

'Fourteen.'

'There you are then. I'm not old enough to be your mother. I'll be your big sister if you like.' Another contraction started and Catriona must have felt her body tense because she started looking at the watch, but Marianne pulled the girl's head down to her shoulder and began stroking her hair gently, humming a simple melody as she waited for the pain to die down. 'You don't need to time them all,' she said. Catriona cuddled close and her nearness seemed to ease Marianne's pain somehow. When it had passed, she began to sing softly.

Marianne's Song

'Dors, bébé, dors,
'Papa te garde encore,
'Maman secoue les brindillettes,
'Dans tes yeux tombe une somnollette,
'Dors, bébé, dors.'

'You have a beautiful voice, Marianne. And the song is really lovely.'

'Do you like it? I'm so glad. I love it too. It's an old German lullaby. My grandmother translated it into French and sung it to me as a child. I'm almost certain she invented the word "somnollette". It isn't really French, although it sounds like it should be.

'What does it mean?'

Marianne thought about it for a moment, silently translating the words into English, glad of something to do to distract her from the fears about the baby that were welling up inside her. *I'll be singing this to my own baby soon*, she told herself, and began singing it to Catriona.

'Sleep, baby, sleep.
'Your father guards the sheep.
'Your mother shakes the branches high,
'A dream falls gently in your eye.
'Sleep, baby, sleep.'

As she sang, Marianne's fears grew. *But baby hasn't kicked since I woke up. Please God let the doctor get here soon. A thirty-six week baby might not survive without intensive care and I'm certain a crystal's gone in there. It might have hit him. What's going to happen if the doctor doesn't arrive? And he's breech. That's going to make the delivery even more difficult. Dear God, please save my baby.*

Catriona had fallen asleep. A somnollette fell gently into Marianne's eyes and she too nodded off, completely exhausted.

Danny was standing in the USA15 electronics room holding the baby in his arms, smiling and talking to him about the images on the monitors. *He'll never understand that, chou!* Marianne thought. *He's only a baby!* She felt so happy to see them together. But then the baby started talking, saying "It's a cosmic monopole!" and Marianne felt proud that he was so clever, but also very surprised.

Then Alex walked past Marianne and said something to the baby. Danny became very angry and began pointing at one of the monitors, shouting at Alex. Then she saw that it wasn't Alex he was shouting at. It was the baby. He was calling him a liar and saying he was responsible for a disaster.

Marianne ran forward to try to calm him down. Danny tended to get angry when he was tired, and she could see he was very tired now. But before she could reach him, one of the large shiny metal pipes overhead cracked open, one broken end bent down and sucked Danny and the baby away as if by a vacuum cleaner.

For a moment Marianne felt terrified, and she realised it wasn't Danny she was worried about but the baby. A moment later the baby came tumbling back out of the metal pipe and Alex caught him in his arms. Then he turned and held the baby out towards Marianne, smiling and saying "Here, take our baby kedvenc".

For a moment Marianne felt overwhelming happiness, but as she shyly reached out she saw it wasn't a baby at all, but the little Irish scientist Michael Zhang. He was looking sideways at Alex, who was making wisecracks about Danny, calling him a stuffed penguin.

Then a blue flash of light came out of the metal pipe, a pain stabbed deep into Marianne's abdomen and she awoke to the agony of another contraction.

As the pain died down she relaxed and saw Catriona floating before her, still asleep. Marianne reached out and stroked her hair. *It's the first time I've ever seen you look really relaxed*, she thought.

Catriona smiled in her sleep.

So your father's dead and the man who's taken his place has been absorbed by a black hole? You obviously have no respect for your mother, and from what I've seen of Ambassador O'Brien's behaviour I'm not surprised. She was blatantly flouting her bust under Alex's nose in the lift, even though she must be a good ten years older than him. And Sam took no notice. Maybe he's used to her behaviour. And you were watching them too.

Marianne remembered the look on Catriona's face in the lift, like a child that's just had its favourite new toy taken away.

I know why he did it, of course. He wasn't interested in your mother. She's too old for him. No, he did it for my benefit. He was trying to hurt me. That's the kind of man he is, Count Karolyi. I think you're infatuated with him, aren't you Catriona? I hope not. I must warn you about him. But what should I say? "Don't have anything to do with him, Catriona. He's been through half the single women in CERN and a good few of the married ones. Thinks he's God's gift, and he is pretty good at it, to be honest. Much better than Danny." No, I can't tell you any of that. Perhaps I should–

Marianne winced as another contraction started.

Where are you Alex Karolyi, you selfish pig? What time is it?

She stroked Catriona's sleeping little face until she awoke. 'Have you got Alex's watch, my dear?'

'Oh, I fell asleep. The watch? Yes, somewhere.' Catriona started looking around. 'Are you having another contraction?'

'Yes, but that's not why I need it. I want to find out how long we've been waiting for Alex.'

'I can't find the...Oh here it is, on my wrist! It's four minutes to twelve.'

'Alex's been gone nearly half an hour. And the baby's very quiet.'

'Could he be asleep?'

'Mmm, I hope so. I'd really like to get to the surface soon though. Wonder how long he's going to be.'

'Do you really think that one of those blue crystal things has hit you?'

'I'm sure it has. I remember something shooting up after the blue flash and bouncing off the beam pipe shield. Then it came down and hit me and I passed out. It's that crystal that's making this bubble.'

'So what are you going to do?'

'If Alex isn't back by twelve I think I'm going to try to get to the surface. I think I'll follow the rope. I'll go down to the stretcher and then follow the other rope that goes up through the shaft.'

'Is that easy to do?'

'Oh yes. We're weightless. You just pull on the rope and move. We could probably be up to the surface in five minutes.'

'You're joking! So what's Alex messing about at? He could have gone up and come back by now.'

'I assume he's trying to find the doctor.'

'Well I think it's silly waiting here when the baby might be…might need help.'

'Let's wait until twelve. Alex might have found the doctor. If he's bringing him back down we might miss him. If he's not back by then we'll try the rope.'

'Okay. We'll give him four more minutes.'

'Look, Catriona. What do you think about Alex?'

Catriona looked at her. 'He's very good looking, isn't he?'

'Do you like him?'

'No. Not really. I think Mother likes him. But then she goes for anything in trousers.'

'A lot of women feel that way about him.'

'Do they?'

'He's very popular with ladies. In fact I used to be quite fond of him myself at one time.'

'Did you? What happened?'

'He was seeing three or four other girls at the same time as me. When I found out I finished with him.'

'Good for you. What a horrible man! Were you in love with him?'

Was I? Marianne wondered and a voice in her head said *"Yes of course you were. You were completely crazy about him. He could make you do anything he wanted."* She glanced at Catriona and shook her head. 'Maybe,' she said. 'I'm not sure any more. It was last year, before I started seeing Danny. Danny's…He's the only man in my life now. Alex never seemed to value me as a person. If people can't see what's inside you then they aren't worth worrying about.'

'No boy's ever bothered with me.'

'Somebody will, one day. You're still young. You just need to tell yourself that you're a very special person, a really exceptional person, and anyone who's worth bothering about would see it and would love you for who you really are. If they don't see that, if they are too stupid or too preoccupied with themselves or too blind to see what's staring them in the face, then don't worry about them.'

'Trouble is there don't seem to be many boys who can see things very clearly. They just seem to go by what's on the surface. Can't see further than the ends of their noses.'

'That's true, I'm afraid. Very true. But there are a few. Just be patient. You're a very pretty girl. You'll find one eventually.'

'Do you really think so?'

'Of course. Come on. Time to go. Put one arm round me, little sister.' Marianne slipped an arm round Catriona's waist and Catriona did the same to her.

'It's like a three-legged race,' Catriona said.

'What's that? Oh, never mind. Can you reach the rope?'

'I think so.' Catriona pulled herself along the balcony handrail, reaching for the rope. 'Yes, I've got it now.' She sighed. 'This isn't going to be easy, Marianne. What if one of us gets left behind?'

'We won't, don't worry. I won't let you go and we've got two free hands. Sisters must work together. Come on.'

Slowly at first but with growing confidence they moved away from the balcony, each one pulling in turn on the curving yellow rope that led out into the cavern.

'See?' Marianne said, 'It's easy!'

'I'm normally afraid of heights but with this bubble you don't get any sense of being high up at all, do you?'

She's right, Marianne thought. *Somehow being inside this bubble is like being in a little world of your own. There is nothing to fear, except the bubble itself.*

Soon the stretcher came into the bubble and Marianne stopped, unwilling to go any further.

'Where's the other rope?' Catriona asked.

'Fixed to the stretcher. So's Robert. I think we've got to go past him. We have no choice.'

'Okay, let's go then.' Catriona pulled Marianne closer to her. They moved slowly down the rope and saw the fireman's body floating beside the upside-down stretcher. Avoiding touching him, they transferred to the other rope and hauled themselves quickly away.

They moved up the rope and a minute later a curving white wall approached them, slicing into the side of their bubble. 'This looks like the shaft,' Marianne said. 'We must be getting near the ground.'

A few moments later a pulley entered their bubble. It was mounted on the low shaft head wall and the rope ran over it.

'I heard an engine running when you were going up in the stretcher,' Catriona said. 'I guess there's a fire engine or something at the end of this rope.'

'The firefighters might help us. I wonder if any of them know about babies? Come on.'

They turned and followed the rope over the concrete floor. The rope was indeed attached to a winch sticking out of the front of a fire engine. A firefighter was standing with his hand on a lever, looking towards them as they pulled themselves along the rope. When he saw them his eyes almost popped out of his head and he pushed the visor up away from his face.

'It's a woman!' Marianne said.

The firewoman stared at them, her mouth open, too surprised to scream.

'Back, quick!' Marianne was pulling them back on the rope, back the way they had just come.

'Why?' Catriona said in surprise.

'Just do it!'

They both pulled the rope and the firefighter disappeared out of the bubble.

'What's wrong?' Catriona asked as Marianne brought them to a stop near the shaft wall. 'She might have been able to help.'

'Yes, but we need to think about this a bit more. This bubble isn't big enough for three people. It's hardly big enough for two. She can't come inside it. Nobody can. So how can I talk to her? If part of her is outside the bubble she might die. Look at what happened to Robert. And remember what happened to your feet?'

'They went numb.'

'That's right. Bits of you that are outside the bubble don't work. The blood stops flowing. This bubble is dangerous, Catriona. We could end up going round killing people with it. I don't want to do that.'

'So what are we going to do?'

'I don't know. I've got to find the doctor and the only way is to ask the firewoman where he is, or ask her if she's got any medical training, but...'

'But you can't do that if I'm in the bubble, can you? I'm in the way.'

'You're not in the way, little sister. It's just that this bubble isn't big enough for all three of us.'

'I understand. There's only one solution. You're going to have to leave me behind.'

'I'll be back for you as soon as I can, Catriona.' She didn't want to go. *I know I have to go,* she thought, *but it's hard to just leave her floating here.*

'It's okay, Marianne. It's not a problem. I've been outside the bubble before, remember, when you first found us on the balcony? It doesn't hurt a bit.' She unstrapped Marianne's watch from her ankle. 'Here, have your watch back. It's still going, just telling the wrong time. Wait a minute, let me set it right. There, it's the same as Alex's now. Here, let me strap it on for you. That's it. Right. Bye then, Big Sister.'

Marianne wrapped her arms round the girl and began to sing softly.

'Sleep, baby, sleep.
'Your father tends the sheep.
'Your mother shakes the branches high.
'A dream falls gently in your eye.
'Sleep, baby, sleep.'

Then she kissed her, pulled on the rope as hard as she could and moved away, tears pooling in her eyes. She paused, wiped them away with the backs of her hands and looked back to make sure Catriona was outside the bubble. Then she took out her handkerchief and blew her nose.

Episode 16 The Universe Historian

'Just try it, Sam,' Michael said. 'It's really delicious.' His deep voice had a gentle, persuasive lilt which was almost irresistible. 'Go on, dip your finger in!'

Sam's mouth began to water and his stomach rumbled as he stared down at the glistening dome of golden liquid splattered across the floor of his crystal cell.

'It's like manna from heaven, Sam, the perfect food. You've never tasted anything like it. And if you don't eat it I'm sorry to tell you you're going to starve to death.'

Sam considered this. *Starving to death would be one way out of this nightmare, but not a very attractive way out. And anyway Catty and Marianne will need my help.*

His right index finger straightened itself and dipped itself into the liquid. It felt gooey but surprisingly warm. A thin tendril of it followed his finger up to his lips. He tentatively let a drop of it drip onto the tip of his tongue.

Michael was right. It was as sweet as honey but not sickly, fruity as strawberries cut by a subtle dash of lime and scented like a walk through a herb garden.

Sam felt a warm refreshing tingle run through his body. Before he knew it, he was kneeling and lapping up the life-giving juice. He hardly noticed Michael hurriedly crawl away across the network saying 'That must be the universe historian. Keep quiet Sam! Let me do the talking.'

Only then did Sam hear the buzzing. Looking up he saw a bee flying rapidly towards them. Michael had only just reached the spot where his old skin was hanging from the crystal network when the Entroilian arrived. Its head loomed down and it began running its antennae over Michael and his pile of excrement.

Sam crouched in his crystal cave, watching them, his finger still dipping and his tongue still licking as he listened to their baritone buzzes interwoven with deep bass drones, intermingled with occasional tenor chirrups and sometimes even modulated into short soprano squeaks

They sounded rather intriguing although totally unintelligible. At first.

But gradually, as he dipped and licked, the odd sound seemed to make sense. The noise was now more like a conversation heard through a closed and resonant door. Sam thought he could understand the occasional word until finally he heard the Entroilian clearly say 'You are a beautiful specimen, Michael!' Sam's finger stopped dipping and hovered over the honey pool, utterly astonished.

How can I understand what it is saying? How?

His tired arm let his whole hand splat into the pool of honey, and the answer immediately became obvious. *There must be something in this food! Could I be turning into a maggot too?* He shook his hand furiously, trying to get the sticky stuff off his fingers and heard the bee say 'You are the best emergent I have ever seen'.

Convinced now that he was in the process of transforming, he shoved his finger down his throat, determined to make himself vomit and stop himself becoming like Michael, but although he lay on the crystal floor and retched and coughed and choked, he had swallowed so little of the honey he was unable to bring any up.

Finally, exhausted and terrified, he lay flat and ran his hands over his head and body, fearfully searching for signs of antennae or for extra legs or wings. But everything seemed to be the normal size and in the normal place.

His terror gradually subsided and he looked across at Michael. The insect had lifted him off the net and was holding him up with its front legs, which looked more like arms, as her antennae ran over his body, paying particular attention to his reproductive organs. 'If you stay in this kind of shape…' she was saying, '…you might well become a Consort.' Somehow Sam knew from her voice that she was a female.

'How exciting,' Michael said. He too was talking in buzzes and squeaks but Sam understood every word now. 'I understand from Oesirisi that you will be examining the history of my Universe?'

'Yes. I am Professor Cjingha Itoodoo. I study comparative cosmology at Sedtia University,' the bee said.

'Unfortunately I had to break the crystal network to stop my planet being absorbed into the black hole,' Michael said as the bee lifted him higher.

Professor Cjingha Itoodoo looked down at the pink planet below. 'So you stopped time in your universe? That was very clever of you, Michaelzhang. You are certainly an unusual specimen! We often get hundreds of emergents and all sorts of other rubbish coming out of cosmic eggs, most of it dead and totally useless, but yours is the first I've ever seen in a time-frozen state. This is really most interesting. You don't need the egg anymore, so I am going to take it to my laboratory for detailed analysis.'

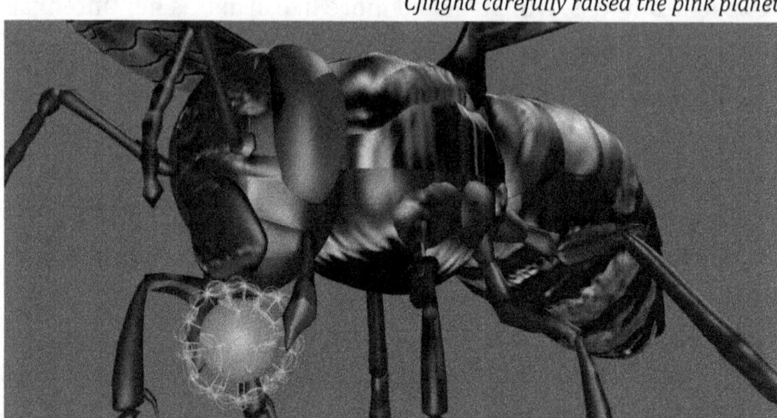

Cjingha carefully raised the pink planet

She lifted Michael gently in one claw-like hand while she carefully raised the whole pink planet in her jaws, with Sam Fitzpatrick still inside the crystal network. Then Cjingha put Michael into the place where the Universe had been.

Looking down Sam saw Michael was lying at the bottom of a sort of hexagonal well with flat vertical walls. 'I expect to hear great things of you in future, Michael,' she chirruped as she spread her wings. Looking up at the vast bulk of her body above him, Sam realised the whole Universe was tiny. She could easily have crushed it between her jaws and swallowed it.

'Take good care of my Universe,' Michael called from the bottom of his hexagonal cell.

'Don't worry. If this cosmic egg produces other emergents like you, and if you're as good as you seem, then this might be the most precious object in the whole of Entroilia!'

Her wings flapped rapidly and she flew upwards towards what Sam had thought was the sky but now realized was a brown dome-like roof. As she turned to fly towards the entrance, the cosmic egg tilted gently and Sam slid across the floor of his crystal cave. Her jaws were gripping the egg's crystal shell, and Sam was afraid that the walls of his cell would move and he would fall out. But the flight was steady, his crystal walls did not move and he began to relax. He looked out through the crystal walls around him, eager to remember the route she was taking so he could return to Michael once he escaped from his cave.

Below him, Sam could see thousands of hexagonal holes similar to Michael's, with Entroilians flying between them, sometimes landing and poking their heads in so only their back segments stuck out. Some of the holes had their tops sealed over; others contained white objects of various sizes lying at the bottom.

This is a place for growing Entroilians, Sam thought. *It's like being inside a gigantic beehive.*

Cjingha flew to the hive's entrance, a small opening low down in the brown dome. Half a dozen large red and black Entroilian soldiers were guarding the opening, standing on their back four legs and clutching huge swords with their hand-like front appendages. Cjingha too stood on her back legs and began to walk through the opening.

One of the soldier's antennae touched hers then fluttered over the crystal network of the cosmic egg she carried in her jaws.

'By the Beeing' he exclaimed. 'This must be what Oesirisi told us about! She was right! His shit carries the sweet smell of Kingship!'

Another sniffed it with his antennae and shouted 'It's the Chosen One!' The other soldiers crowded round.

'We don't know that yet,' Cjingha said dismissively, pushing past them.

'But does he bear all the signs?' the first soldier said.

'Not all of them, no, but then he is still only in the larval stage. I'm sorry, I have to take this cosmic egg to the University.'

'Is the emergent still inside it?'

'No, I've left him in a brood cell.'

'Where? Where is he? I need to place a special guard over him just in case he really is the Chosen One.'

Cjingha pointed out where Michael was, then turned and walked out of the hive.

Sam blinked as daylight flashed through the crystals of his cave, blue beams reflecting off their inner surfaces. The scent of flowers was overwhelming. As his eyes got used to the light he saw a forest of tall flowering trees surrounding the huge hive.

Cjingha's wings vibrated faster and she flew up the corrugated outer wall of the hive. She rapidly gained height and within a few seconds was flying away from the brown surface, high over the forest canopy, flecked with the blues and reds of magnificent flowers. The trees stretched for miles. Sam could see other huge hives standing tall within it, and beyond them more distant objects, a range of blue-grey mountains on one side, a broad waterway on the other, sparkling in the sunshine. The ocean curved away towards a distant shore, but what struck Sam most was the black pyramid which arose where green land met blue sea.

The huge pyramid seemed to have been carved from a single gigantic monolith of black stone, obsidian perhaps or heavily smoked glass. Sunlight reflected off its smooth sloping sides. Sam was sure it was not a natural structure. It looked too perfect. It dominated the scene, towering over the tall trees, far higher than even the tallest hive. At the pyramid's foot stood other structures, partly hidden by the forest. Sam had only a brief glimpse of them before Cjingha turned and flew down a small valley that cut through the leafy landscape, trees lining both flanks, the warm heady scent of flowers assailing his nostrils with delight.

She flew quickly, following a broad river towards some nearby mountains. There were no roads through the trees, no bridges over the river, no hum of traffic. The only noise was the buzzing of passing Entroilians and the splash from the oars of barges which rowed along the busy river laden with barrels and bales, baskets and bottles. This seemed to be flying a vast bustling metropolis built in a beautiful forest landscape.

For a while nothing much changed and Sam began to worry what was happening on Earth, and tried to make sense of the new facts Michael had told him, dipping and licking the comforting honey.

He couldn't get out of his mind the memory of Michael saying 'I'm going to be one of the senior members of Entroilian society,' and the revolting image of Cjingha examining Michael's private parts and saying 'You might become a Consort'.

That's the husband of a Queen, isn't it? Sam thought. *King Michael? It doesn't bear thinking about!*

His finger dipped deeper and he put the revolting thought out of his mind.

So time has stopped everywhere except near fragments of crystal.

He remembered Michael smashing one of the crystal pipes, remembered the fragments falling in a long line down towards the pink ocean. He looked up at the gap in his cell where the missing pipe used to stand, and at the ends of the dozens of pipes still surrounding him.

These pipes are huge. How could Marianne be holding one of the fragments? There weren't that many of them. Maybe a hundred. Two hundred at most. Each one must be enormous.

In his mind's eye, Sam saw Marianne as a tiny creature floating in the pink ocean, and saw the huge crystal fragments splashing down around her. He spent a painful few moments trying to figure out how she could ever put one of them into her pocket, then gave up and began thinking about Catriona.

I wonder where she is now? The poor kid was so excited when she found Michael. Thought she would solve the mystery of her Dad's murder. And then all this happens. And of course she doesn't know what's happened to Michael now.

Sam wanted to stand and look into the crystals to find out what was happening on Earth, but he was afraid of standing while his crystal cell was being flown across the sky. He looked out at the scenery below. Cjingha was not far from the mountains now. The river had grown narrower and faster, and there were no more boats on it. Smaller hives sprawled up the foothills, some of them resting on top of each other, as if they were making use of every spare foothold. Finally she left the river and headed for a complex jumble of structures below a huge overhanging mountain peak. This, Sam assumed, was the University.

These buildings, in common with all the others, had no doors or windows, just a single entrance near their base, guarded by a few Entroilian soldiers. She touched antennae with them, carefully lifted the Universe and walked through into the pale brown light which percolated the large central hall. It contained none of the hexagonal holes Sam had seen in the nursery hive. Instead its curving walls were scattered with small round openings. Entroilians were flying to and fro inside, many of them carrying heavy looking bags slung below them. Cjingha flew across the hall, landed and walked into a small room built into the thickness of the wall. It was crowded with complex-looking items of equipment made of wood and metal standing on wooden tables. She gently lowered the Universe into a small box on one table then left the room.

Sam immediately stood and started searching for the crystal containing Alex's yellow shirt but before he found it he heard a woman's voice singing:

'Sleep, baby, sleep.'

It's Marianne! She must have had the baby! Thank God!

'Your father tends the sheep.'

The voice was coming out of one of the crystals. Sam saw, floating far down inside the crystal, a dark brown blur.

'Your mother shakes—'

'Is this the Cosmic Egg he emerged from, Professor Itoodoo?' an Entroilian said from somewhere over Sam's head. It was very different from Cjingha's voice. It sounded deeper, more resonant and obviously male. Sam looked up to see two Entroilians peering down at him. He dropped to the floor, trying to keep out of sight.

'Yes, Councillor Moshendiar,' Cjingha said.

The new Entroilian was much larger than her. His body was so huge it would not all fit into the room. Sam could only see his yellow head and middle section. They shone like burnished gold. His huge eyes were red, as well as his jaws and what Sam took to be his nose. His rear end must have been sticking out into the hall.

'Everyone in the Palace is talking about him,' Moshendiar said, bringing one of his huge red eyes close to the Universe. Golden threads and tassels dangled from his broad head. 'I just had to come over and take a look. The emergent is still in the nursery I assume?'

'Yes, Councillor.'

'Is this Cosmic Egg broken? There's no activity in the event network.'

'That's right, Councillor. The emergent told me he had deliberately broken it so that—'

'Deliberately? My goodness!'

'Yes, he broke it so that time would stop.'

'Why?'

'He wanted to prevent his planet being sucked into the black hole he had created.'

'He deliberately created a black hole? I don't believe it. Even the Argolaths can't do that! He sounds like a truly extraordinary specimen. I want to talk to him. And according to the rumour he bears all the marks of the Chosen One.'

'Not all of them, Councillor. He is obviously highly intelligent and it's true he has an excellent set of external reproductive organs and, as you can smell, his excrement has the strong odour of kingship but as for his face and his ability to survive the mating, only time will tell about how he fulfils those prophecies.'

'Nevertheless, he is a very promising emergent,' Moshendiar said. 'Do you think you will be able to repair the network, Professor?' His huge insect's head came closer and Sam cowered away in terror. 'If not of course we won't get any more specimens of his type. That would be a pity. The Princesses would be very disappointed.'

'I hope I can fix it, Councillor, but I need to analyse it first. I'm going to examine it in the projector.'

'Please don't let me stop you, Professor Itoodoo.'

Cjingha carefully lifted the Universe and placed it on a circular metal platform near the floor then reached up and slid open a shutter in the outer wall. A bright beam of sunlight sliced into the laboratory, reflected off a mirror, passed through several lenses and finally shone down onto the cosmic egg.

An intense beam of light lit the pink event record below Sam. He huddled in a corner of his crystal cave feeling very exposed and vulnerable. The air around him grew warmer.

'Let's see what else came out of this egg,' Moshendiar said, studying a pink image which the apparatus had thrown onto a white screen. 'There might be another emergent down there.'

The image of the event record moved across the screen.

'There don't seem to be any more emergents down there,' Moshendiar said. 'If fact there's not much debris at all.'

'No. It's very unusual. Presumably that's because the emergent stopped time before anything else fell into the black hole.'

Moshendiar's huge head moved closer to the screen. 'Zoom in down there, to the left.' Cjingha moved a control and the image grew bigger. 'See that?'

'It's just a fragment of some sort of metallic tube, Councillor.'

'No, not that. Here.' One of Moshendiar's hairy antennae touched the screen.

'Oh yes! There's a hole in the universe!'

'Probably made by a fragment of event pipe.'

'I don't think so, Councillor. The pipe's not heavy enough to sink. It should just be floating on the surface, although I can't see any fragments at all. That's odd. And very disappointing. I was hoping to retrieve the fragments so we could reconstitute the broken pipe and restart the flow of events.'

'Well something made the hole, Professor. I wonder why it hasn't closed? Normally a hole like that would just close up as the event record settled back, wouldn't it?'

'Yes.' Cjingha sounded thoughtful.

'So what do you think's holding it open?'

'I'd say there's probably a negative energy thread in there.'

'Oh, well I suppose that's possible. Yes, that would explain it. There's probably still a negative energy thread between each fragment of the broken pipe. Very interesting! But if there is, then there must be a fragment down the hole.'

'I suppose there must.'

'In which case it must have been the fragment that made the hole!'

'I don't think so, Councillor. Even a large chunk wouldn't have been big enough to create a deep hole like that. I can't even see the bottom. No, I think something else created the hole and the fragment just fell into it.'

'Something else? Such as?'

'I'm not sure.'

'Ah well, no doubt you'll be exploring the whole universe in detail later and you'll figure it out. You said the emergent has transformed into a larva. Can I see its skin? I'd like to get a feeling for its size.'

The image on the screen changed again and Sam saw an intense beam of light shine onto Michael's old skin, still hanging from the network of crystal pipes.

'You're right,' Moshendiar said. 'He looks like a beauty.'

'He's one of the best emergents I have ever seen.'

'If there really is a negative energy thread holding that hole open then it might come back up to the gap where the broken pipe used to be. Can you find that gap?'

Cjingha twirled some knobs and the beam of light began to follow one of the pipes surrounding Michael's skin.

They're going to find me! Sam thought. He made himself as small as he could, but he felt enormous and completely exposed. His crystal cave offered no hiding place from that penetrating beam.

The moving spotlight followed the pipe until it reached the cluster where the crystal met others. Here it stopped and lingered for a while, then followed another pipe, gradually getting closer to Sam.

What will they do to me? Will they turn me into a monster maggot like Michael Zhang? He cowered in his corner as the beam reached the starburst of pipes adjacent to him, his heart throbbing. He began to tremble all over.

The beam left that group and moved straight towards him. After a few seconds, heat throbbed into his crystal cave and bright light reflected off every blue face.

'Ah, here it is,' Cjingha said. 'This is where the broken pipe used to—Great Beeing! What's that?'

The heat of the beam increased as it shrank down until it was focussed entirely on Sam. Sweat burst out of every pore. He felt like he was being cooked alive.

'I'd say it's another emergent, Professor Itoodoo. Wouldn't you?'

'It's very small. It's nothing like the other one.'

Sam lay completely still, not breathing, not even daring to blink, hoping they would think he was dead and ignore him, but he could feel the sweat pouring down his face and dripping into his ears.

'I'm not even sure it's alive,' Moshendiar said. Sam began to relax.

'I wonder if I can get it out?' Cjingha said. Sam froze.

Something flashed in the beam of light. He squinted up, trying not to move. Something was descending towards him. As it came close, he saw it was a metallic grab on the end of a long robotic arm.

'It's definitely an emergent,' Cjingha said, 'but it looks totally different from the other one. Michael looked like a normal larva except for his face and his reproductive organs but that...I've never seen anything like that.'

The grab had almost reached Sam's crystal cave when there was a whistling noise followed by a loud explosion somewhere in the building, then another one. The grab stopped.

'Sounds like an Argolath attack,' Moshendiar said. His huge head moved rapidly away from the screen, his body reversed out of the room and he disappeared through the hole in the inner wall. A moment later a rock crashed through the opposite wall and Cjingha buzz-screamed. She flew towards the exit just as Moshendiar's head came back. 'Take that Cosmic Egg to the Palace,' he shouted. 'Meet me there. I'll be in the Council Chamber.' She turned back, lifted the universe out of the apparatus with her jaws, hurried back to the hole and joined thousands of other Entroilians flying rapidly across the central hallway towards the main exit.

Michael's Diary: Cosmic Egg 1

Cosmic Egg Diagram 1

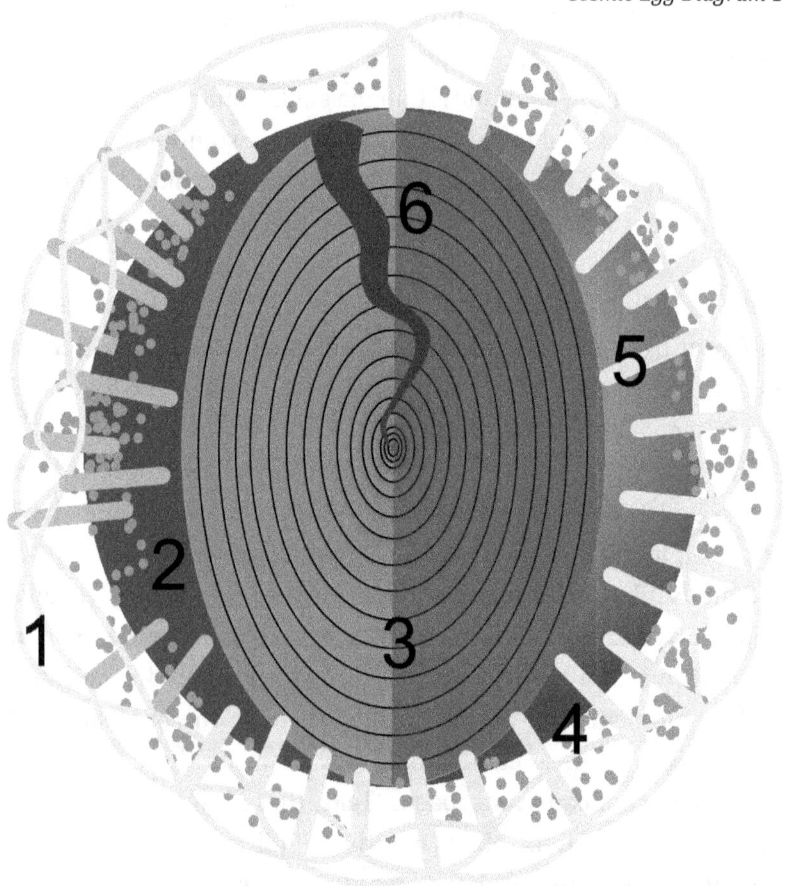

Following my directions, the Princess Uskabellu has carefully and lovingly created this simplified diagram of the Cosmic Egg, to make it easier for you, Oh Glorious Monopole, to gain an insight into its structure and history.

A cosmic egg is what my fellow men used to call "a universe". They believed there was only one of them, and that it was the entirety of the Cosmos, although the truth is that our universe was just one of many. Universes are made together in groups inside objects called "cosmic eggs". These are part of the life-cycle of creatures called Entroilians, and they create many of these eggs.

From the perspective of the Entroilians, each cosmic egg is tiny. Viewed from the outside, all you can see is the shell, which consists of a network of blue crysorganic pipes (which Uskabellu has labelled 1 in the diagram).

Beneath the shell lies the egg itself, looking like a smooth round pink ball (2). But inside, an egg contains layers like geological sediments (3). These are in fact a permanent record of the history of the egg. This event record is soft, with the consistency of jelly.

To understand how these layers are formed, you need to be aware that, what we humans call time, is actually created by the flow of objects called "Events", which fall like rain onto the pink surface. Uskabellu has shown these as pink dots in the diagram (4). Every Event has the potential to create a moment in history, and so become crystallised into the pink sediment. Thus each cosmic egg grows over time.

Those events which fail to form a moment in history are re-cycled. They move up a series of giant blue crystal pipes (5), then travel out into the network of smaller pipes which make up the shell (1). From here, the Events rain down once more onto the cosmic egg.

Eggs are designed so that they form a permanent record of history. This is necessary so that Universe Historians, such as

Cjingha Itoodoo, can examine those eggs which are fertile, and establish what properties have led to their fertility.

A cosmic egg is fertile if it can create "emergents", that is, create beings with sufficient intelligence to emerge outside of the egg. This is the purpose of cosmic eggs, to create emergents who will then grow into new Entroilians. I and Sam Fitzpatrick, for example, were swallowed by the black hole which had formed around you, Oh Beloved Monopole, and that is how we emerged from our egg.

I immediately burrowed my way down to its centre, swallowing the event record as I went, and then came back to the surface by the same route. This created a sort of burrow in the egg (6). By digesting this event record, I was transformed into a genuine Entroilian egg. I also attained a complete understanding of the history of my universe, of my place within it and of the status of the egg within the wider Entroilia. This gave me divine wisdom, and Entroilians now call my universe "The Cosmic Egg" to distinguish it from all the others.

Episode 17 Helicopter Search

'You're Floating!' the firewoman said

The firewoman's eyes grew wider as she watched Marianne pull herself along the winch rope towards her. 'You're floating!' she said, her voice almost drowned by her radio's squawk.

Marianne saw her feet were still outside the bubble and came closer. The firewoman panicked, tried to escape, found herself trapped, screamed, stared at Marianne for a long silent moment then started fiddling with her radio. It continued to squawk.

'Foxtrot three seven to Papa seven,' she shouted over the noise. 'Can you hear me? Come in George!' Finally she gave up, flipped the radio off and stared at Marianne. 'Who are you? Why can't I move my feet?'

'I'm Marianne Schneider. I was...'

'You're the pregnant woman in the stretcher!' the firewoman said. 'I'm supposed to be winching you up out of the cavern. How the hell did you get up here? And why are you floating like that?'

'Have you seen Alex Karolyi?' Marianne asked.

'I haven't seen anyone. Who is he?'

'He's supposed to be fetching the doctor. I've been hit by some...by something. It's gone into my, into my abdomen, maybe into the womb. I need urgent medical attention. Is there a doctor near here?'

'Yes. A moment ago George said he's just landed in the helicopter. It's in the field north of the Globe.'

'Can you take me there?'

Sofie hesitated, then said 'Well I suppose I'm not needed here any more.' Once more she tried to move and fear returned to her face. 'I can't! My feet. They won't move.'

Marianne held out her hand. 'It's all right. Pull me down.'

Sofie pulled her until she was floating inside the bubble then said in nervously 'What is that jelly?'

It took Marianne a moment to realise she meant the bubble, and had to spend precious moments explaining that everything outside seemed to be frozen and telling her that it could be dangerous to leave any part of her body sticking out.

'Dangerous? How?' Sofie seemed less frightened now, more professionally curious.

Marianne hesitated. She didn't want to tell her about Robert Moore so she just said 'I don't think the blood flows in any part of your body when it is outside the bubble. Just make sure you're completely inside. Now can we go please? I need to find the doctor urgently. I think it's dangerous to just float around. If you don't hold on to something you could go drifting away to God knows where. Can we use a rope to keep ourselves tied to the ground?'

'Look, Mrs Schneider, I don't know what the hell's going on here but I can see you need the doctor so let's just get you over there. You say we need a rope? Okay, I'll get some rope out of the engine. A hundred metres should be enough, d'you think?'

But Marianne wasn't listening. All she could think of was the pain stabbing deep into her whole abdomen and quickly getting deeper and more intense. She pursed her lips and began puffing, her frightened eyes searching for Sofie's. Then something inside her seemed to collapse and her thighs felt warm. 'My waters have broken,' she groaned.

Each of Sofie's eyes seemed to swivel around independently, like a chameleon, then she said 'You wait there, Marianne. I'll go and get the doctor.' She reached out trying to push the bubble away. The bubble's pattern changed and she gave a little cry of pain and jerked her hand away.

Marianne hardly noticed. The pain was so strong she even forgot to breathe correctly. *I've got to find that doctor soon,* she thought. *Where are you Karolyi, you selfish swine? How could I ever have trusted you to help me after what happened last year? What could have happened that would be more important than finding the doctor? I must be completely stupid to rely on you. Never again, Karolyi. I'll never trust you again after this.*

Gradually the pain subsided and she remembered her breathing. After a few pants she tried to say 'It's breech'.

A deep frown crossed Sofie's face, then she forced a smile and said 'Greek? Oh really? That's no problem. I'm Greek myself. Just keep panting. You're doing fine.' She checked her watch as if she was waiting for a bus.

She hasn't got a clue what to do, Marianne thought. *She probably doesn't even know what a breech is.* The pain began to subside and she made herself relax. 'I'm all right now,' she said. 'Let's go.'

'Go? Go where?'

'To find the doctor of course. You say he's near the Globe? That's only a couple of hundred metres away. Three at most.'

'But we can't move.' Sofie sounded exasperated, looking at the bubble.

'Yes we can. The bubble travels with me. I told you, something's gone into my abdomen and that's what makes the bubble. It moves with me.'

Sofie looked completely blank for a moment, then shook her head as if trying to get rid of an annoying insect. 'Okay, I'll get a rope shall I? So how do we move?'

They linked arms and pulled themselves along the side of the fire engine. Sofie pulled a coiled length of rope out of a locker and tied it round her waist. 'Come on then, Marianne,' she said, pointing towards the back of the engine. 'The Globe's that way. We can float across to the SX door if we push ourselves off.'

'I don't think it's safe to just drift about. Isn't there some way we could hold onto something?'

Sofie thought about it. 'We could follow the fence.'

They returned to the front of the engine and, as they passed the cab, Sofie reached in and took a small bottle of water and a bar of chocolate out of the door pouch. They followed the winch rope to the safety fence that surrounded the shaft and crawled along the top of it in silence like a pair of mating spiders.

They reached the corner of the fence and Sofie stretched across the gap and grasped one of the beams that ran up the tall side wall of the SX1 building. They followed it up until they met a horizontal duct which led them to the huge open doorway.

'The helicopter must be over in that direction.' Sofie said, pointing away to the right. But Marianne couldn't see anything but the bubble and a little of the building's wooden-clad outer wall. 'I suppose we'll have to cross the car park first,' Sofie went on. 'I'll tie the rope here, shall I? We can uncoil it as we go. If we don't find the perimeter fence on the other side we can pull ourselves back and try again.'

Marianne shrugged and nodded, too preoccupied with pain and with anger at herself for trusting Karolyi to really understand what she meant.

Sofie tied the long rope to the beam beside the doorway, and after linking arms with Marianne she swung them both round the outside of the building and pushed away from the cladding with both feet. Coloured stripes ran down the bubble and the building disappeared from view as she uncoiled the rope as fast as she could, but she couldn't do it fast enough and they ended up floating stationary with most of the rope still coiled before them.

'Sorry, Marianne. I'm too slow. Let's try again.'

She pulled them back to the building, coiling the rope as they went, and tried pushing away harder but they didn't get much further than before and went back to the doorway once again.

'What about the ground?' Marianne grunted between breaths.

Sofie stared at her for a moment then realised what she meant and pulled them down the door frame to the car park. Its tarmac surface was smooth but there were some cracks and indentations.

'I suppose it might work,' Sofie said. 'Let's try.'

They had to dig their fingers into the cracks to gain traction. Before long they had both lost all their nails and Marianne's fingers were bleeding. The hard part was staying in contact with the ground. Every few minutes Marianne had another contraction and she had to stop and pant. The pain was worse every time and the effort of moving over the car park was exhausting her.

Finally they reached a car on the far side of the car park and clung to it like shipwrecked sailors finding an island. To celebrate their arrival, Sofie gave Marianne the bottle and she gratefully sipped the water.

'It's only a half-litre,' Sofie said. 'It isn't going to last very long, but it isn't far to the helicopter now. Come on.'

'Wait! I think the labour must have started. Can you time the next contraction?'

'Less than two minutes,' Sofie said when the contraction died down.

'So it has started!' This was the time Marianne had always dreaded, even when she thought she would be having the baby in hospital. She had assumed that, if the pain got too bad, they would give her an epidural. But now...

'We've got to find the doctor quickly,' she said. 'Where's the field?'

They pulled themselves slowly over a narrow stretch of grass, short and sparse after the winter, crossed a bank of small leafless trees and finally reached a fence. Beyond it they could see a road.

'This is the perimeter fence' Sofie said, then she hesitated, looking at the coil of rope. 'This won't be long enough,' she said. 'We'll have to go back and fetch the other end.'

Marianne groaned. *We've got to go back*, she thought. *I can't stand this for much longer.*

Sofie tied the end of the rope to the fence and they pull themselves back up the slope and across the car park to the SX1 building. She untied the rope from the beam and Marianne coiled it as Sofie pulled them back to the fence. Untying the rope, the firefighter led Marianne along the fence to the right, round a corner and down another straight stretch until she judged they were level with the middle of the field. She began tying the rope to the fence.

'You're sure he's in this field?' Marianne could hardly speak with pain and fear. 'I need the doctor as soon as possible.'

'Quite sure. George said he had just landed.' Sofie began to tie the other end round her own waist. 'Mind you, I suppose he might have left by now. It's taken us quite a while to get here.'

'No no no. If he landed just before time stopped then he must still be there. Everything outside a bubble is frozen somehow.'

They pulled themselves over the sparse clumps of spring grass and the dead remains of last year's weeds in the field, brown stalks snapping in their hands, Sofie uncoiling the rope and

Marianne expecting any moment to see a helicopter wheel or skid or a human foot. But five minutes and two contractions later they had still not found anything when they reached the wooden steps leading into the Globe on the other side of the field.

'We've missed it,' Marianne groaned.

'Never mind. I didn't expect to find it on the first pass. Let's go back and try again.'

They pulled themselves back to the fence, Sofie coiling up the rope so it remained manageable, and tried again in a slightly different direction, like a fisherman casting a line searching for a big catch. Each time they reached the far side of the field without seeing even the slightest sign of the helicopter or the doctor, Sofie tried to compensate for Marianne's disappointment by giving her a tiny sip of water, squeezing the plastic bottle to make it come out.

Every trip took longer; five contractions, six, eight. And with every failure, Marianne's desperation and her hatred of Karolyi grew stronger.

It's your fault I'm in this situation, Marianne thought. *Why didn't you bring the doctor? I wish I had found Danny instead of you. Where are you Danny mon chou? Catriona said he wasn't absorbed by the black hole so he must still be in the cavern. I wish you were here with me, chou. I'm sorry I trusted Karolyi. I know you can't stand him, chou, and you're right. He's no good. But I thought I had to do it. He said it would be best if I didn't move so I waited for him. I'm sorry.*

After five trips Marianne was too exhausted to continue. 'I can't do that again,' she groaned before a wave of agony overwhelmed her. 'Oh God!' She started grunting and straining, feeling the muscles of her lower abdomen tightening. 'It's coming,' she gasped between grunts. 'It's coming!' Still grunting, Marianne lifted her knees and tried to pull her trousers down.

Sofie didn't know where to look. *Calm down now girl*, she told herself. *You're in this situation and you're just going to have to cope with it. Look upon it as a part of your training.*

She helped Marianne slip her trousers off, then her pants. Marianne moaned and panted, waving her hand towards the firefighter, feeling as if she were sinking under the pain, needing something to hold on to. Sofie grasped her hand and squeezed, trying to communicate reassurance. Marianne puffed like a train at full steam then panted like a dog, squeezing Sofie's hand as if she was trying to break every bone. Sofie smoothed the hair out of her eyes. 'You're doing ever so well,' she said. 'Everything's going to be all right.'

'Of course it's not,' Marianne snapped. 'Have you ever helped with a birth before?'

'Well—'

'No you haven't and don't pretend you have.' She gave one last grunt and the pain abated a little. 'Oh, I'm sorry. What's your name?'

'I'm Sofie. Sofie Dialektaki.'

'Okay, Sofie. I know you haven't got any idea what to do. I can see it in your face.'

'No, I haven't,' Sofie said, 'but I learn fast.'

'But you haven't got time to learn! I need a doctor. This baby's breech. Please just get me to the doctor.'

Sofie was stunned. 'Get you...?'

'I can't stay here. Find him, Sofie. Take me to him. Quickly.'

'I'm going to have to carry you then,' Sofie said.

Marianne started moaning again.

After the panic died down, it took Sofie only a few moments to figure out how she was going to carry Marianne. She used Marianne's trousers to tie them together back to back, then she began crawling across the field as fast as she could, pulling the grass with one hand, uncoiling the rope with the other, Marianne moaning and screaming behind her. As her contractions grew stronger and faster, Marianne's screams grew louder. When the pain got really bad, Marianne reached down and pulled at Sofie's hair and her arms, demanding her hand to hold on to and Sofie had to stop and wait for the pain to pass, wondering if it was time to untie her and try to help with the delivery.

Sofie had made another five or six crossings of the field, still without any sign of the helicopter, and was at the fence preparing for another strike when Marianne gave an unbearable scream and started choking on her own vomit. Sofie quickly unstrapped her and turned the woman over. A tiny leg had appeared. Sofie didn't know much about childbirth, but she knew the head was supposed to come out first.

'That's it, Marianne!' she said. 'It's coming! Keep pushing. Good girl!'

Then Marianne began to push again. 'Mungh!' Another leg appeared. For a while she puffed, apparently exhausted, then she began to repeat over and over: 'It's breech. It's breech.'

Now Sofie knew exactly what that meant. 'Yes, Marianne. I know. It's all right. We'll cope. You're doing very well. Just keep pushing.'

And what am I supposed to do now? she thought. *Should I keep trying to reach the doctor? This is when she really needs him, and he's only twenty or thirty metres away. And why's the bubble moving? What did Marianne say? "Something's gone into my abdomen. That's what makes the bubble." But what the hell is it? She never told me that. But if the bubble's moving then this thing, this thing inside her must be moving. Moving with the baby. So what will happen if the bubble moves so far down that her head is outside? Marianne said everything outside the bubble is frozen. Blood doesn't flow. So what will happen? Will her brain die? I've got to do something. Urgently.*

Marianne began to scream. Sofie rubbed her back, feeling utterly useless. Marianne's jacket was soaked with sweat. Sofie thought she could see her melting away before her eyes. 'Would you like to take the jacket off, Marianne? You might be more comfortable.' She helped her out of it, easing away the large clot of blood which glued the jacket to her blouse, and saw for the first time the even bigger stain on her blouse. Sofie stared at it, shocked and frightened, thinking: *If she was in hospital there'd be a team of doctors clustered round her. But all she's got is me!* Sweat was still pouring off Marianne. Every few minutes she moaned and grunted and pushed and the baby's legs slowly emerged as far as the waist

And Sofie saw that the baby was a little boy. Suddenly and without warning Sofie was overwhelmed by a feeling of compassion. Here he was at last, this tiny little baby, this miracle of new life, who was relying on her to save his life. She felt that the whole cycle of creation was playing itself out before her eyes and she was a part of it. She hardly notice the blood smeared across the white waxy coating which covered his skin. All she saw was the lower half of a lovely little baby, hanging there, stuck, waiting to come out into the world and join the human race. She had never seen anything so dramatic or so beautiful. She felt as if she was in the presence of something almost holy.

When she looked at Marianne's body, it too seemed holy, almost as familiar as her own. There was no embarrassment in anything now. All she felt was fear for the baby's safety. She wanted to grab his legs and pull, but she dare not touch him. Her grass-stained, tarmac-damaged fingers hovered near the tiny legs, longing to pull them but afraid lest she pass on some terrible infection or damage him in some other way.

'It's a lovely little boy, Marianne,' was all she could say.

'I know,' Marianne groaned.

But his head seemed to get stuck. *And his legs aren't moving…*

That was when the struggle really started, the struggle between Sofie telling Marianne to push and Marianne telling Sofie she couldn't.

She can't stay like this. If she doesn't complete the delivery soon that baby's going to die, if he isn't dead already. And Marianne might die too. Even with proper medical attention childbirth is pretty dangerous. Under these circumstances her life is in real danger.

After half an hour Marianne finally gave up. The contractions seemed to be getting weaker instead of stronger. The baby wasn't moving and Marianne slept, utterly exhausted.

Sofie was desolate. *I've failed him.* She kept going over everything that had happened, trying to work out how she could have done something different, how she could have made sure the baby would survive. She tried the radio but just got the white noise. *We should have stayed near the engine.* In spite of what Marianne had said, Sofie still believed the doctor was probably in the SX building by now, if not down in the ATLAS cavern. And she couldn't stop thinking about all that water in the back of the engine. She examined the plastic bottle. Only a few little round balls floated about inside it. She shook the bottle and they spun down to the end. *Two mouthfuls at most.*

This was Sofie's worst time. Everything that could go wrong had gone wrong, and she felt she was to blame. Then, on the verge of tears, she remembered that briefing George Gabor had given his team a few weeks ago. He was standing before the white board in the training room, his white face calm, his blue eyes looking into each of theirs in turn. "Sometimes you will lose one or two," he had said. "Sometimes, no matter how much you try, you won't be able to save them. When that happens, you need to know that you've done your best. As long as you've done everything you could then it's not your fault. We are in the Fire and Rescue Service. We're not gods. We can't do miracles. We can only do our best. After that, after it's all over, then try to learn the lesson, tell your brother firefighters about it, then go home and get ready to do it all over again tomorrow."

The tears began to well up in Sofie's eyes and she didn't try to stop them. She let them gather in little puddles around her eyelids, feeling the tension flowing out of her, feeling George's strong supporting presence, proud to be a member of his team. *Even if I lose both of them, I'll still be a firefighter. And nothing will ever scare me again*, she thought, *not after this.*

An hour or so later, Marianne awoke and began pushing again with new vigour. Gradually the baby's head started to come out.

'That's it, Marianne! Fantastic! Keep going. Great! Oh that's good, very good!'

Sofie wiped her hands on her T-shirt and got ready to catch him. She worried what would happen if she dropped him, slimy and slithery and covered in white wax and Marianne moaned and screamed and then the head came out and Sofie saw that there was a piece of blue crystal buried deep in the poor little boy's skull. He must have been dead for hours.

Episode 18 The Palace, the Temple

Cjingha was fleeing from the rocks

While Cjingha was fleeing from the rocks falling on the University, swerving around its curving outer wall heading towards the city, Sam was slithering across the slippery floor of his little crystal cave. He bounced off the walls several times until he finally crashed into the sticky mound of Michael's regurgitated honey. He threw his arms over it, heedless of the mess it was making of his jacket, and lay panting and looking down onto the flowering forest passing quickly beneath the cosmic egg.

Joining hundreds of other fleeing Entroilians, Cjingha sped back along the river towards the city centre. A stream of red and black Entroilians was flying past her the other way, some clutching swords while others held bows and arrows in their front legs.

Soldiers! Sam thought. He turned to watch them follow the fast-flowing torrent up the mountainside. There were thousands of them, flying up the almost vertical cliff towards the towering peak overhanging the University.

As Cjingha descended the river, a ledge came into view just below the summit. It was not easy to see without his glasses and with the view partly obscured by cloud, but Sam thought he saw tiny white creatures scuttling on the ledge, and in their midst stood what looked like a huge beetle with enormous horns. As the swarm of Entroilians approached it, the beetle threw one last rock at them before the little white creatures led it into a cave at the back of the ledge.

Cjingha left the river and began to fly between taller brown structures. Sam lost sight of the mountain and rolled over to look forward, anxious yet curious about where she was taking him.

Nestled at the pyramid's foot was a white ovoid

She was flying towards the huge black pyramid standing in the city centre near the broad waterway, surrounded by an orderly collection of small brown domes. Nestled at the pyramid's foot was a horizontal white ovoid, the top section made of blue glass, making it look a little like a gigantic aeroplane fuselage without wings. An assembly of tall white towers, each topped with a transparent dome, separated the pyramid from the ovoid, around which stood huge horns and hexagonal structures burnished with some shiny yellow metal which looked like gold and, most impressive of all, at the ovoid's nearest end stood two huge red and black Entroilian soldiers holding golden spears. Sam only realised how huge they really were when Cjingha flew between them and he saw, with relief, that they were not alive but merely statues. Their colossal bulk dwarfed everything around them, silently proclaiming the power and importance of the ovoid structure they guarded.

Cjingha flew past the statues towards the ovoid. Sam could see it was clearly more than just a massive sculpture. Entroilian workers were flying in and out of a small opening in the ovoid's nearest end. A group of Entroilian soldiers was buzzing around a landing-platform near the entrance. Cjingha landed before the largest of them. 'Is this the right way into the Palace? Councillor Moshendiar asked me to bring this Cosmic Egg to the Council Chamber.'

The soldier touched antennae with her, ran his antennae over the Universe, nodded and waved her on.

Cjingha walked through the little opening and hesitated, apparently unsure which way to go. Inside the Palace was a huge light airy atrium, totally unlike any other space Sam had been inside so far. The curving walls were painted with images of Entroilians, some feeding larvae, others flying round flowers, more building hives. Gold and silver glittered everywhere. The floor was carpeted with a thick green sward of grass, real grass as far as Sam could tell, scattered with the most beautiful tiny flowers.

Hundreds of Entroilians filled the hall. Some stood on the grass in small groups talking excitedly. Others sat in chairs adapted to suit their enlarged back segments poring over charts and books resting before them on tables. More flew along the hall, some carrying equipment, groups of them sharing the load of heavy objects. The Palace was a veritable hive of activity.

And everywhere there were beautiful flowers. Sam's head swam from the scent of them. They grew up the walls, trained between and over the paintings, reaching up to the high-domed roof from which golden statues of flying Entroilians hung on long slender threads.

Through the blue glass roof, Sam could see the tops of the tallest white towers clustered around the far end of the Palace, and beyond them the summit of the black pyramid. Now, for the first time, he noticed a small white structure perched precariously on its peak. He was still squinting up at it, trying to work out what it was, when Cjingha stepped aside as a group of soldiers marched past. As the group past Cjingha, the soldiers drew back to reveal a huge Entroilian in their midst, so vast that it dwarfed all the other Entroilians around it. Its body was mostly purple. Its large rear section was purple with black stripes and its legs and antennae were black.

'Is that it?' the giant said in a resonant, authoritative voice. 'Is that the Cosmic Egg which produced this exciting new emergent?'

Cjingha bowed very low, almost hitting the Cosmic Egg on the grass. 'Yes, Your Majesty. Councillor Moshendiar asked me to bring it to the Council Chamber.'

Your Majesty? Sam thought. *This must be the Queen.* He looked at her closely. She was about ten times bigger than any of her soldiers, each of which was much bigger than Cjingha.

'Tell me about the emergent,' the queen said. 'Quickly!'

'This universe has produced two emergents, Your Majesty. One is highly developed both intellectually and physically. He deliberately broke the event network to suspend time so that the rest of his planet would not be absorbed. Councillor Moshendiar wanted this Egg to be safe when the University was attacked, if it please Your Majesty.'

As she spoke, Sam noticed that an endless stream of Entroilian workers was constantly flying down the atrium, landing close to the Queen's rear end, collecting small white objects and flying away with them. *Eggs,* he thought. *She's laying eggs all the time, like a machine.*

'And you are?' the Queen intoned.

'Cjingha Itoodoo, if it please Your Majesty. Professor of Comparative Cosmology at Sedtia University.'

'You work at the University? How interesting.' The Queen's purple head came close to the Universe and tilted so Sam could see the hundreds one hexagonal facets in one of her enormous blue eyes. 'And the other one?'

Cjingha hesitated then said 'Oh yes, Majesty, the second emergent. I hope it's still in there, Majesty. It's very tiny, not like the big one. I was just about to examine it when the attack started.'

'Very interesting, Professor Itoodoo. I think you had better follow us.' Her head moved away from Sam. 'Proceed,' she said to the soldiers and they marched on down the atrium towards the tall towers at the far end, Cjingha trailing in their wake, flying occasionally as she tried to keep up with the massive Queen.

When they reached the foot of the central tower they began to fly up through its many floors, each of which had a hole giving access to the level above. Here too, paintings covered the circular walls and furniture stood upon carpets of grass. The pictures in the lower floors were of eggs and larvae, but the higher they went the more dramatic the pictures became, the richer the upholstery and the thicker the carpets.

When they reached the Council Chamber at the top of the tower, the guards took up positions around the hole in the floor and Cjingha sat on one of the seats ranged around the Chamber's circular wall.

A semi-circular table stood in the middle of the round room, where a dozen Entroilians of various colours and sizes sat awaiting her presence. As the Queen approached, flanked by two small assistants, they stood and bowed.

'Sit,' she commanded and reclined her bulk upon a massive couch which towered over the table's straight edge, leaving her rear segment hanging over one end of the couch. Sam watched as, about once every ten seconds, after some waggling and winking from the orifice in her rearmost segment, a little white egg was ejected, to be carried away by the workers who ceaselessly flew in and out. The Queen seemed to take no interest in any of this, as if it was no business of hers. At the other end of the couch, a worker disgorged some food from its mouth and began to feed her. The Entroilians at the table sat and waited.

The wall which curved around them was covered in paintings depicting scenes of battles between Entroilians and various other types of creatures, some of which looked to Sam very much like giant ants, beetles, centipedes, dragon flies and spiders, while others had huge spines on their backs, some were shaped like balls, some had long tails they were swinging around as weapons. It was a menagerie of weird creatures. The same creatures were depicted in the golden statues which hung from the transparent domed roof, each being killed by a fierce-looking Entroilian.

When the Queen's appetite had been sated, she lifted her head and said in a tired voice 'Proceed'.

A yellow and black Entroilian sitting next to her rose to his feet. Sam immediately recognised him from the University as Moshendiar. 'This emergency meeting of the Privy Council is now in session. Marshal Gallrage, would you like to update us on the situation?'

A fat Entroilian struggled to his feet. The red eyes sticking out of his large green head gave him a sinister appearance, but Sam almost laughed out loud when he spoke, for his voice was as high-pitched as the squeak of a mouse.

'I received a report of a Strongarm hurling rocks down from Mount Deeva onto your University, Your Majesty,' Marshal Gallrage squeaked. 'Two platoons were immediately dispatched to the scene of the incident. They found ten Argolaths controlling the Strongarm.'

'Slaves I presume?' the Queen said.

'Yes Majesty, slave miners.'

'And their guards? What were they doing? Sleeping?'

'They had killed their guards, Majesty. We found their bodies at the bottom of the copper mine.'

'Obviously security in the mine is completely inadequate. Moshendiar, can you explain this?'

'No, Majesty.' He did not sound worried by her imperious tone. 'Security is Commander Bogmon's responsibility.'

'Well, Commander?' the Queen said to a thin Entroilian sitting next to Gallrage. He rose to his feet and stood beside Gallrage who was staring thunderously at Moshendiar. Bogmon seemed to be totally monochrome. The parts of his body Sam could see were either black or white, without any hint of colour.

'Yes, your Imperial Majesty need have no concerns about this matter.' Bogmon's silken voice floated in the air like gossamer. 'I have initiated an investigation into how this incident occurred. Be assured, Your Royal Majesty, that such an incident will never happen again.'

'You better make sure it doesn't. Otherwise you'll be skewered and thrown to the Argolaths. Is everything under control now?'

'Yes, Your Majesty,' Gallrage squeaked, 'completely under control. The Argolaths involved have been killed.'

'Including the one that escaped?' Moshendiar asked.

'One escaped?' The Queen sounded alarmed.

'We are searching the mine for him right now,' Bogmon's voice was silky smooth. 'I am confident he will be recaptured within the hour.'

'Make sure he is, Commander,' the Queen said. 'We cannot afford this type of security lapse, especially once we start work on the tunnel.'

'I believe Majesty,' Bogmon said, 'if I may make so bold as to say so, that this is the very root of the rebellion. My security officers questioned the Argolaths before we executed them, to find out why they made this attack. They said they were protesting about the tunnel.'

'Protesting! Slaves have no right to protest!'

'The miners are frightened, Majesty. They say it would be dangerous to dig the tunnel to the East which Your Majesty is proposing. No Argolath has ever tunnelled under the Malordon Mountains, Majesty. They believe it will require far more miners than we have enslaved so far. Also they say it could never be done in six months, the time Your Majesty has commanded.'

'It must be! I want it before the winter returns. I know it can be done, if you only have the will to do it. You will simply have to capture more Argolaths, Gallrage. Capture them and keep them secure. Is that clear?'

'Yes, Majesty.' Gallrage said.

'Enough of this. Sit!'

Gallrage and Bogmon sat whispering, their heads close together, their antennae hanging limply.

The Queen ignored them. 'Now, Moshendiar,' she said, 'tell me about this Cosmic Egg.' She nodded towards Cjingha.

Moshendiar followed her look and nodded too. 'Perhaps Professor Itoodoo would be the best person to report on that, Majesty.'

There was silence in the room. Cjingha hesitated and Sam could feel her tremble. Slowly she stood and lifted the Universe in her hand-like front claws. 'I collected this Cosmic Egg from the Nursery this morning, Your Royal Majesty,' she said in a quaking voice—'

'Yes yes, I know all about that. Tell me about the emergent.'

Cjingha described Michael in great detail. The Queen watched her attentively and, as she listened to the description of his private parts the hole in her tail began to quiver and pulsate so fast that a stream of eggs shot out, hurtled across the room and hit the opposite wall.

'Wonderful! Wonderful!' the Queen said when Cjingha had finished describing Michael. 'How long do you think before he will pupate?'

'I, I am not sure, Your Majesty. I assume it will be the normal ten to fourteen days.'

'And the second emergent? You say it is not equally well endowed?'

'No, Majesty, not that I have seen.'

'And where is it now?'

Cjingha lifted the Universe higher. 'In here, Royal Majesty.'

'Good. Clearly that Cosmic Egg is potentially of supreme importance. Moshendiar, you did well to have it brought here. I want it taken into the Temple and blessed by the High Priest, then taken back to the University and both the Egg and the emergent examined closely. Gallrage, you must ensure the University is completely secure.'

'I cannot do that before we recapture the escapee, Majesty. May I suggest that Professor Itoodoo remains in the Temple until I send word that all is secure?'

'Very well. Send two guards along with her. Any more business, Moshendiar? I'm tired.'

Her two assistants stepped forward and began feeding the Queen mouth to mouth as Moshendiar rose to his feet.

'Yes, Your Majesty, one thing I'm afraid. Actually it is connected with this incident. I have some bad news from my spies in the

East. King Flenkt is planning to free all the slaves from our mines, forges and workshops.'

The Queen stopped feeding and pushed her assistants away. 'All of them? But that would destroy our whole economy!' The Queen turned to Bogmon. 'Do you know anything about this plot, Commander?'

He looked astonished. 'No, Majesty.'

'I thought not. You and the Marshal have simply got to increase security up on those mountains and start working out how you are going to guard the new slaves you will need to dig the tunnel. I'm relying on you two. Don't let me down or it will be the last mistake you make. I trust I make myself clear.' She turned back to Moshendiar. 'It's been a very useful session. Let me know how the new emergent is developing. And let me know what the Professor finds out about that Cosmic Egg,' she said as she walked past Cjingha and flew down through the hole in the floor. The guard followed her and most of the Councillors followed the guard. Finally only Moshendiar, Gallrage, Bogmon and Cjingha were left in the Chamber.

'Why didn't you tell us about this so-called plot, Councillor?' Gallrage hissed.

'I was waiting for the Commander to report it, Marshal,' Moshendiar said. 'I assumed his spies would hear the same stories that mine did.'

'I am the Chief of Security,' Bogmon said. The softness of his voice had been replaced by a vicious anger. 'You have no right using spies in the East.'

'As the Chair of the Privy Council I have every right, Bogmon, as you well know. I think this tunnel is going to cause us tremendous problems in the coming year. I suggest we form a special team to ensure the whole project runs smoothly. I propose to call a—'

'The Queen has made the army responsible for subduing the

East,' Marshal Gallrage said, 'and digging the tunnel is just a part of the plan, as *you* well know, Mister Chairman. We have everything under control. There is no need for you or anyone else to get involved. In six months Karolinda will be Queen of all Entroilia, and the army will be totally victorious. I'm warning you, Moshendiar, keep out of military business. Otherwise it won't just be the Argolaths who'll be in trouble.'

The two Entroilians gave Moshendiar meaningful looks, their antennae waving rapidly up and down, then picked up their weapons and flew out of the Chamber.

'I'm sorry about that, Professor Itoodoo,' Moshendiar said, beckoning her over to the Council table. 'I'll write you a note of authority to enter the Temple.' He sat and began to write on a sheet of headed paper. 'This must be a bit of an education for you, Professor?'

'Yes, Councillor. I had no idea about any plan to invade the East.'

'No, of course not. It's top secret. You must not speak of it to anyone. Bogmon should have told you this himself. I'm afraid our army and security service are not headed by the brightest szemzions in the firmament. Here you are. This letter should get you anywhere inside the Temple complex. Take good care of that Cosmic Egg.'

Two soldiers were waiting for Cjingha at the bottom of the tower when she flew down. They offered to take the Cosmic Egg off her but she insisted on carrying it herself and followed them back along the atrium to the entrance. Once outside, they flew around the outer wall, past the towers and into a large group of brown, beehive-like structures at whose centre stood the black pyramid. The sheer scale of it took Sam's breath away.

This must be the temple complex, he thought.

Now he was close to it, Sam realised that the temple, although dark, was not completely opaque. Through the pyramid's wall,

Sam could see the Sun on the other side, gradually descending towards the distant horizon. He could still see the Sun's round shape through the darkening glass, its light dimmed sufficiently that he could stare straight at it without discomfort.

That's not my normal Sun, yet it looks just like it. Same size, same colour. Everything here seems the same, just grown to a different size. If I didn't know I'd left the Universe I'd say I was still on the Earth, on some weird island somewhere.

He watched it as Cjingha followed the guards around the pyramid, across a courtyard and was astonished that the Sun disappeared, hidden by something moving about inside the pyramid.

It's hollow!

There was a small hole cut into the bottom of one face and, as they approached, an Entroilian flew out. He was draped in a long black robe and he stood before the entrance and challenged Cjingha's guards. From the conversation Sam deduced that this was one of the priests. Cjingha showed him Moshendiar's letter.

'And that is the Cosmic Egg Her Majesty has commanded be blessed? Give it to me. I will take it to the High Priest.'

Cjingha politely refused to part with it.

'Then you will have to wait until the princesses have finished their initiation. You two stay here,' he said to the soldiers. 'Weapons are not allowed inside the Temple.'

Cjingha followed him through the entrance and they flew up into the vast echoing hollow pyramid. The sound of chanting filled the space. Hundreds of other priests in black gowns were flying round and round a long thin sliver of black glass which arose from the floor and broadened into a flat platform in the centre of the Temple. More black slivers arched from it up towards the huge sloping walls.

A small inner circle of Entroilians wearing long white gowns flew slowly around the platform. *They must be the princesses,*

Sam thought. The priest led Cjingha to join them and she too began flying round the central platform. One after another, the princesses flew down to the platform where a black-robed Entroilian was standing waiting to perform the initiation ceremony. Each one took about five minutes. Words were spoken in a language Sam could not understand. Food was passed from mouth to mouth. Arms, legs and antennae were waved about and touched. Small golden statues of Cosmic Eggs and larvae were lifted and kissed. More unintelligible words were spoken in solemn tones.

The mumbo-jumbo of religion, Sam thought. *If you believe in something then it works. If you don't then it just seems ridiculous.*

'You're not a princess,' a haughty voice said close beside him. One of the white-gowned princesses was flying close beside Cjingha.

'No,' she said. 'I'm a universe historian.'

'I am Princess Uskabellu,' the other said. 'I am going to be initiated.'

'I know.'

'What are you here for?'

'For this to be blessed.' Cjingha held up the Universe.

'Oh!' The Princess exclaimed, examining the Universe closely. 'Is that it? The Cosmic Egg the new emergent came from?'

'Yes. Queen Karolinda has asked for it to be blessed.'

'Strew! Is it true what they say about him, that he bears the marks of the Chosen One?'

'He is certainly well endowed,' Cjingha said.

'And do his turds carry the odour of kingship? And is his mind as bright as the Szemzion at midday?'

'Yes, the odour of kingship is very strong and he certainly seems very intelligent. He deliberately broke the event network to save his planet. But it is too soon yet to say whether—'

'I want him,' Princess Uskabellu said. 'I must be his Queen. Can you put in a good word for me? What did you say your name was?'

Episode 19 Crystal Airlines

Alex's glance shifted up from the two metal rings wrapped tightly round George's fists to the two cold eyes frozen into his stone-white face. 'So the idea is that you go down to the Earth while I carry on into space, yeah?'

George just stared at him.

'It's a good idea, György,' Alex said, nodding and forcing a grin. 'An excellent idea. And just how fast would you say we need to separate in order to achieve this fascinating manoeuvre you're planning?'

'Oh, I'd guess a damned good shove will probably do it.'

'Really? You're sure about this are you, György? You've done the calculations and everything?'

'Calculations? No, of course I haven't, Karolyi.'

'I'm only asking because I think you might find that even after the two parts of this so-called rocket separate, they're still both drifting out into space. Only one's going a bit faster than the other.'

George's eyebrows twitched.

'And which trajectory were you thinking of sending me along, Cosmonaut Gábor? Because you don't want us both travelling parallel to the ground, do you?'

Alex's hands moved together in front of his chest. As George watched warily he moved them away from each other towards the sides of the bubble.

'Because if you're not careful they could both end up going out into space but in opposite directions.'

George's eyebrows flickered again as his eyes returned to Alex's face.

'But I'm sure you've thought all this through very carefully haven't you, Cosmonaut Gábor?'

George sighed and Alex noticed, with some relief, that he slipped the two metal rings off his fists and back onto his belt.

A huge gobbet of saliva detached itself from the blue lips of the unconscious Alex Karolyi and drifted slowly towards George Gabor's face. George watched it getting closer, not caring whether it hit him or not. He was busy trying to stop his jaw vibrating.

All I want to do is sleep like you, Karolyi. You look so peaceful with that smirk on your stupidly handsome face.

Somewhere at the back of George's oxygen-starved mind he knew his brain cells were dying by the million, but it didn't matter. Nothing mattered.

I'm going to die. This is hopeless. It's impossible. We're doomed. This is just so utterly Hungarian! But if I die at least I'll stop shivering.

Then Alex's cold saliva hit George's face and outrage swept up his body and out into his arms. His hand took on a life of its own. It lifted and wiped the disgusting mess off his cheek then moved down to his radio and clicked it on. Harsh white noise echoed round the bubble.

There's got to be a message in there somewhere, if only I could figure it out.

He listened to the crackling hiss, focussing his mind, searching for meaning. But he found nothing.

How can I send a message back to Earth? Got to at least try to warn them.

Then a light seemed to go on somewhere at the back of his head. He pulled out his notebook. His frozen fingers could hardly hold the little pencil but he managed to scribble

STAY IN CONTACT WITH GROUND

He tore the page out and breathlessly pulled the rope that tied him to Alex, his head spinning from the effort. Alex moved towards him and George pushed his frozen fingers into the young man's shirt pocket, pulled out the blue crystal and stared at it. It looked blurred. Everything looked blurred.

Bloody little swine! You're the cause of all this trouble.

He wrapped the paper round the crystal and lifted it. The effort of moving his arm exhausted him.

Not sure I've got enough energy to throw it down fast enough. Feel as if I've been slipped a massive Mickey Finn.

He gave the paper one last squeeze and suddenly the crystal was flying towards Karolyi, pulling George after it. He crashed into the unconscious man and gripped the crystal tighter, unwilling to let go now this was happening. It pulled him harder, pushing Alex ahead of him. He was dimly aware that the flow of rings had changed direction. As his mind finally drifted into oblivion it occurred to him that this all seemed to be happening to somebody else.

When Alex regained consciousness, the first thing he thought was: *How come I'm still alive?* The last thing he remembered was feeling horribly cold and hardly able to breathe. But now, now he felt warm and could breathe easily. *We must have come back down towards the Earth! But how?*

His second thought was: *Wonder how Marianne is.* And his third: *Why is George pushing against me?*

Instinctively he felt in his own shirt pocket. *Crystal isn't there! Shit! What's happened to it?* In panic, he looked at George. He was unconscious, floating very close to him, one arm raised. Coloured rings were flowing through the bubble, coming from somewhere behind Alex's back. *We're still moving.*

Looking at the rings, he immediately saw the tell-tale ridge where two bubbles joined. *Definitely still got two crystals in here.*

So where's mine? It didn't take him long to work out that one bubble was centred on George's massive raised fist and the other came from a crystal in the firefighter's trouser pocket.

Alex reached up and grasped that fat fist with his two hands. Something was clenched inside. *Looks like a sheet of paper.* Even using all his force, he could not make the firefighter's fat fingers give up their prize. *Rigor mortis?* But the hand was not cold and George's chest was slowly rising and falling.

Abandoning that crystal, Alex reached down, pushed his hand into George's trouser pocket, pulled out the other crystal and pushed George away from him. He drifted away until the rope that tied them together was taut.

He held the crystal lightly between finger and thumb, considering it thoughtfully.

We've come back down so it must be something to do with the way you were holding this. He looked at George's fist, wrapped his own hand round the crystal and squeezed. The crystal tried to fly out of his grip! He held on tight as it pulled him to the right, despite the pain as one of its four sharp corners jammed into his palm. *That's it! This must be what happened with George.*

Then he felt the rope pulling on his waist. George had swung round on the end of the rope and was now following after him like a glider behind a tow-plane. The pattern of rings was now coming from Alex's right.

'Whoop!' he yelled, feeling euphoric. 'It works! It really freaking works! But how?'

He relaxed his grip but the rings continued to flow. *We're still moving. So how do I stop?*

It took him some experimentation to discover a way to control his flight.

Pressing on the fourth face with one finger

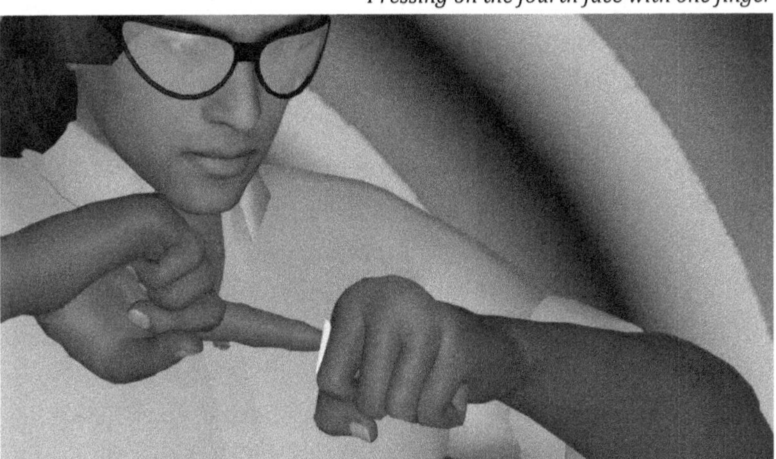

He finally succeeded by making one hand into a fist, pushing the crystal into the hole made by his thumb and first finger, then pressing on the fourth face with the finger of his other hand. The three edges of the crystal pushed against his fist, but not the sharp point. He could change direction by rotating his fist. By swapping the crystal to the other hand and pressing in the opposite direction, he was able to make the bubble's rings move slower and slower.

A moment later, George crashed into him and bounced away, still unconscious, pulling Alex after him in a different direction. By watching the pattern of the bubbles and carefully pressing his crystal, Alex was able to bring both men to rest, so both bubbles were entirely covered by the random pattern.

I've done it! We've stopped! So I can go straight, I can turn and I can stop. I can fly! I really can fly! 'Hey, wake up György,' he called, and pulled on the rope. When there was no response, he began flying in a circle, making George spin round on the end of the rope. He spun faster and faster, the rope pulling harder and harder against his waist, until the firefighter finally opened his eyes. Alex put on an American accent, saying 'Good morning passengers. This is Captain Karolyi speaking. On behalf of the crew and myself I'd like to thank you for flying with Crystal Airlines today on this short flight out of Geneva. We hope you enjoyed your trip and will want to fly with us again soon.'

'What shit are you spouting now, Karolyi?' George growled.

'As a special treat I will now demonstrate to passengers how to control this Crystal Bubble Flier. Please observe how the pattern on the bubble changes as I press the crystal.'

Alex was feeling a little dizzy by now and, only with some difficulty, he brought them both to rest once more. He stared at George, as elated as a child in a fairground.

'Okay, Karolyi, very clever. Now let me have a go at flying this freaking crate. You've obviously figured it out better than I did before I passed out.'

Alex couldn't help smiling as he watched George copying his way of flying using his own crystal. 'Guess these Hungarian brothers did pretty well, sticking together, eh György?'

'Don't count on being so lucky next time, Karolyi. We're from opposite sides of the river. Just remember that.'

Alex knew what he meant. George obviously assumed that Alex came from Buda, the affluent part of Budapest on the western bank of the Danube. Alex was still considering whether to put him right about that when the firefighter interrupted his thoughts with the simple question: 'Okay, Karolyi, so which way is down?'

Alex stared at him blankly. As usual, George had gone straight to the heart of the problem. Without gravity, there was no way of telling how to get back to the Earth.

'What's the matter, Captain Karolyi? Lost the bloody flight plan?'

'There must be a way to work this out,' Alex said slowly.

'You realise, of course, that if you'd only left the bloody bubble moving the way it was when you woke up we'd probably have hit the ground by now!'

'That's bullshit, Gábor György. That way I'd never have learned how to fly. I guess we'll just have to pick a direction at random. It's a 50-50 chance whether we're going the right way.'

'And we'll be able to tell we've gone the wrong way when tree black out again, I suppose Karolyi?'

'Something like that, yes.'

'Hmm. Great idea, Cap'n. Got any more?'

'Well, we could fly round in ever increasing circles, I guess. We might hit the Earth quicker that way. I wish I knew how high we are.'

'I'd say we're less than three thousand metres,' George said, sniffing. 'Much higher than that and you can tell. The air begins to get thin.'

'So you mean we might only be a hundred metres off the ground?'

'We could be, yes.'

'Listen György: ever increasing circles would be too difficult, but what about if we fly straight for ten minutes. Then, if we don't hit the Earth, we turn through ninety degrees. We do this four times and if we still don't meet the Earth, we turn through ninety degrees in a plane normal to the first and repeat the whole manoeuvre but flying twice as long each time.'

'Okay,' George shrugged. 'I guess you know what you're talking about.' He let him take control, trailing quietly behind him, keeping a check on the time, telling him when to turn. Every half-hour or so George would growl 'Your plan's not working, Karolyi.' But when Alex said 'So what do you suggest?' he never had an answer, just 'I'm still thinking.'

After two hours, and with enormous relief, Alex saw a large dark shape come into the bubble. The branch of a tree, green with needles and heavy with snow hit Alex's arm and almost knocked the crystal out of his fingers. He turned his fist and pressed it in a different direction, steering away from the tree then turned it round and pressed hard to slow down. George kept moving, swung round in an arc on the end of the rope and crashed into the branch. A little cloud of snow flew up and engulfed him. Alex dragged him clear of the branch but kept close to the tree as he brought them both to a stop.

'So I got us this far,' he said, feeling proud of his flying skills. 'You want to work out which way we go now? But one thing, György. Before you go shooting off into the air next time just make sure you untie me, okay? From now on I'm sticking close to the ground.'

'Okay,' George said. 'We're below the tree line so we must be under two thousand metres.' He used his crystal to fly around, trying to work out the lie of the land, pulling Alex behind him. The forest was a mixture of green spruce and brown needle-dropped larch. He soon discovered that it sloped away dramatically on two sides. 'We're on a ridge,' George said. He chose one of the slopes at random. 'We'll go down this side. We'll stay roped together for now.' He towed Alex over the ragged surface formed from the tops of trees, the short rope taught between them.

The trees thinned out and they flew down to a snow-scattered grassy bank. George had just passed between the trunks of a few more conifers when a tide of water suddenly swirled into his bubble, swept weightlessly over his head, splashed across the ridge between their bubbles and sprayed Alex with an icy shower. Both men stopped and the water sloshed around inside their bubbles in large wobbling icy free-floating globules. For a moment Alex had a glimpse of the rocky bed of a stream then George swore and flew a few metres higher.

Alex was relieved, but also astonished, to see the water pass out of the bubble wall as he followed George upwards. He reached out and touched the bubble. It still felt hard and still gave him an electric shock. *So how did the water pass through it?*

'Looks like we've reached the bottom of the valley,' George said. 'If we follow the stream down we'll get out of the mountains.'

Alex dismissed the puzzle of the water. There was something more serious on his mind. 'I wonder how Marianne is? How far do you think we are from Geneva?'

'How should I know? I'm not even sure if we're in the Alps or the Juras. Come on!'

They followed the flow of the little stream, skimming over green lichen-encrusted rocks and dodging overhanging branches. Alex wondered which of the two mountain ranges they were in. He thought of the map of Lac Léman. Geneva curves like a fingernail round the western edge of the lake, where it points down into the belly of France. The Juras lie to the north of the lake, the Alps to the south.

After a few hundred metres they almost crashed into a small wooden bridge carrying a road over the stream. George followed the tarmac and picked up speed. A few minutes later they reached a three-way fork in the road. It took him a few minutes to figure out which way was down. With no gravity to guide them it was not obvious. During the search they found a small shrine enclosing a statuette of the Virgin, a few scattered wooden chalets with rusty iron roofs and a blue truck parked on the edge of a precipitous roadside slope. 'French plate,' George said as he led them out of the hamlet. 'Looks like we're in France.'

Surprise surprise, Alex thought. *Drive ten kilometres out of Geneva in almost any direction and you'll cross the French border. That still doesn't tell us which mountain range we're in.*

Thinking about the lake and the fragile little figure of the Virgin Mary, Alex remembered once again his last night with Marianne. He had sailed his luxury yacht out into the middle of Lac Léman and after a slow dinner they had started making love. They were still at it when the Sun rose next morning. He remembered the pink light of dawn painting her face with roses as she lay beneath him on the deck, moaning in ecstasy, thrusting against him like a racehorse, then trembling and crying when she finally came. As he lovingly licked away the tears from those tender eyes, Alex decided that this was the face he wanted to look down on for the rest of his life. To prove how serious he was, later that morning he promised her he was going to get rid of all his other girlfriends.

But as he was breaking the news to the first of his current harem over lunch in the CERN Cafeteria, Marianne happened to walk past. She stopped, told him she never wanted to see him again and walked away. Alex had acted cool. He bided his time, knowing she would eventually change her mind and come back to him.

She loves me. After that night I know that for certain. Yes, it had been a shock when she started going out with Danny Schneider the following week, but I know why she did it. She was just trying to punish me. She couldn't possibly love a plate of porridge like Schneider. She's a girl who needs the spice of some real Hungarian goulash!

Alex had begun a campaign to win her back by kindness and patience. Even when she announced she was pregnant and that she and Danny were getting married, Alex had not given up hope. He had had many affairs with married women. He was still convinced that eventually she would leave Danny and come back to him.

Ten minutes later they crossed another bridge over the stream and, skirting around a tarmacked area, they reached a low metal fence bearing red, white and blue shields.

'War memorial,' George said. 'This should tell us where we are.'

They flew up the narrow stone spike and hovered near the top, reading the inscription.

1914 - 1918

ENTREMONT

À ses enfants morts pour la France

Alex stared at the words with a sick feeling in his stomach, translating them into Hungarian. *To her children dead for France.*

'Entremont?' George said. 'Never heard of it. Come on.'

Alex said nothing. All he could see was the naked body of Marianne floating before him, dead in childbirth. He hardly noticed George dragging him around the square looking for the way down to the plain.

Is she still alive? Alex thought. *I've got to get the doctor to her as soon as possible.*

George found a bridge and he flew down to where their little stream met a broader river flowing to the left. He flew up the far bank, discovered a road and flew along it, swerving over cars and round hairpin bends, dragging Alex behind him.

There was a small petrol-station in the next village, marked by a roadside sign, and George wanted to stop for food and drink. Alex was hungry and thirsty too, but very reluctant to stop. 'What time is it?' he said.

'A minute to three.'

'And it was eleven thirty-something when we left SX. So that excursion of yours has just wasted us three and a half hours! Jesus, György, Marianne could have had her baby in this time! Can't you hold on a bit longer?'

'Come on then Karolyi. At least we've learned how to fly.' George put on a burst of speed as they flew on down the winding mountain road. The central white line flickered beneath them as George sped around hairpin bends, apparently unworried about meeting vehicles and only narrowly missing a truck. But in spite of his apprehension at George's dangerous flying, Alex wanted him to go even faster. He kept feeling guilty about Marianne.

It doesn't matter that she's Schneider's wife. What the hell does marriage matter now? Time's stopped for god's sake. All that matters now is that I love her and she loves me. I know for certain she doesn't love Schneider. I want her and I'm going to get her back.

Finally the road ran beneath a robust bridge. George led them up and onto a motorway. There were no road signs in sight. He chose a direction at random and flew along the motorway, searching for a sign.

Alex let him take control, still deep in thought. *I always knew that one day she'd see the error of her ways and come back to me. What better time than this? With the world laying in ruins the most important thing now is to go for what you really want, and we are made for each other.*

It took them another half-hour to find their way back to the Pont du Mont-Blanc in the centre of Geneva, where the Rhone runs out of Lac Léman. They crossed the bridge, followed the Rue de la Servette up the hill, under the railway bridge and into the Route de Meyrin, heading straight towards CERN.

Episode 20 The Helicopter

Marianne had fallen asleep again, her head still in the bubble, but the baby was moving slowly away from her, turning in the air. The bubble's pattern turned too as it drifted towards Marianne's feet. *I've got to stop him moving too far and leaving parts of Marianne outside the bubble*, Sofie thought. *Otherwise she could die.* She looked at the umbilical cord that still joined the baby to Marianne. She didn't know what to do. She knew one was supposed to cut it, but had nothing to use and anyway she wasn't sure whether she ought to tie it up first. She decided to wait for the afterbirth and wondered how long it would take.

She looked at the tiny floating baby. The hole in his head was horrible. Marianne's trousers were lying against the wall of the bubble. She reached for them, opened one leg and slipped him carefully inside, holding him as if he was still alive and talking quietly to him. It made her feel better, let her forget that she was holding a dead baby. It was what Marianne would have wanted. Then she slipped him behind his mother's back, tying the trousers around her waist with a strap so Marianne wouldn't see him when she awoke. Then she tried to decide what to do next.

Marianne might easily have picked up some sort of infection. I tried not to touch her but I might have done. My fingers are filthy. If I did then it would be serious. She's got to see the doctor. He'll probably give her antibiotics. From what she said it sounds like she would be in some sort of limbo without this crystal. If I take it away from her, that might stop any bacteria from growing. But I can't take the baby while he's still joined to Marianne.

She waited and dozed a little. About half an hour later, Marianne woke up and began to push. The placenta came out quite easily and Marianne said something then fell asleep again.

She looked absolutely awful, a haggard half-naked zombie. Once more Sofie opened the leg of Marianne's trousers and pushed the afterbirth in with the baby, then she tied the ends of the trouser leg to her harness with two short straps. To protect the poor sleeping woman's modesty Sofie carefully pushed her jacket between her legs and tied it to hold it in place. Then she pulled herself along the ground, leaving Marianne behind, uncoiling the rope, breathing fresh air for the first time in hours.

After using the rope to traverse the field five more times Sofie was hot, angry and confused. She hovered above the middle of the field and tried to remember the exact wording of the last message she had heard on the radio, just before Marianne appeared like magic out of the shaft.

'Control to Oscar Three. Helicopter in field north of Globe. Doctor on board. Over.'

She was sure that's what they had said, but the helicopter wasn't here.

Surely they hadn't meant the big farm-field outside the fence? No, if the helicopter was going to land north of the Globe it would be in this piece of empty ground. Obviously the message was not right. He must be still hovering up there somewhere. She looked up, considering whether to launch herself into the air and try to find him, but rejected the idea as too dangerous. *So where can I get help? The nearest place is the CERN Medical Centre. They don't have doctors there full-time, but there are nurses and they'll certainly have antibiotics. That's my best bet.*

It's going to take ages to get over there using this rope. I've got to get across the Route de Meyrin first. Will the rope reach from the Globe to the Reception building? If it does then I'll have to go up the car park to Entrance B, down Route Pauli and up Route Einstein. How far's that? Must be at least a kilometre. That's ten rope-lengths!

With a sigh she continued to crawl across the field, uncoiling the rope, when a hole opened up in the bubble above her and she saw George Gabor flying head first down towards her. She was almost as shocked as she had been when she first saw Marianne. Something blue was shining between the meaty fingers of his outstretched fists. *It's the same as this thing in the baby's head!*

But most astonishing of all was that when he saw her he stopped. Just like that! Just stopped in mid-air! He was surrounded by a bubble and a rope trailed from his harness through a hole into another bubble. The rope slackened and the hole grew larger as another man came flying along, crashed into George's feet and stopped too. It was obviously a doctor. He was middle-aged, wearing a white coat and with a medical bag hooked over his shoulder. He looked dazed and bemused. She knew how he must have been feeling.

George's icy blue eyes scanned her bubble and homed rapidly in on the bag tied round her waist, then examined her face. 'Did Marianne Schneider give you her crystal?' he said with a frown.

Sofie shook her head. 'She's had the baby.' She could hear her own voice trembling with emotion.

The doctor moved closer, listening intently. He too seemed able to fly at will. They both watched in silence as she unclipped the tiny bundle from round her waist and held it out to the doctor with a feeling of relief. 'It's in here,' she said. 'He's dead, I'm afraid.'

But as the bundle moved so her bubble moved too and she realised she couldn't hand over her burden yet. *If I give it him I'm going to be left frozen.*

'Were you with her, when she had it?' George said.

Sofie nodded.

'Let me see,' the doctor said. He spoke with a French accent.

'He's got some blue stuff...' She unwrapped the strapping and held out the trousers to the doctor.

He put on some latex gloves, carefully opened the end of the trouser leg and peeled it back. The tiny feet flopped out.

'Oh God,' George said and turned his face away.

The doctor lifted the corpse out of the trousers and peered at the crystal embedded in the baby's skull. Sofie moved closer. 'Good gracious,' he said. 'This must have hit her before she delivered. What state is she in?'

'What is it?' George said, his ashen face turning to look. 'Oh, the poor little chap. I thought it might be bad. Is Marianne all right?'

'No, she's in a bad way,' Sofie said. 'I had nothing to help her, George. Not even water. It was horrible.' She felt the emotion welling up inside her and with a struggle just managed to keep it bottled up. She wanted to pretend it had not affected her, to make a joke of it like Ludovico would have done, but she could not. It was all she could do to stop herself bursting into tears.

'I'm sorry you had to go through this Sofie.'

'Where is the mother now?' the doctor said. 'I'd like to see her as soon as possible.'

'Hold on a minute, doc,' George said. 'That's her crystal isn't it, Sofie?' He nodded towards the baby. 'Or has she got another one?'

'No, that's the only one we had.'

'Then there's no urgency, doc. Can you get it out?'

'Get what out? This blue thing? Yes, but I think I should see the mother as soon as possible. She might have—'

'She hasn't got a bubble so she's all right,' George said.

The doctor looked confused. George tried to explain about time being frozen outside a bubble so Marianne wouldn't get any worse but the doctor couldn't believe what he was hearing. In the end George gave up. 'Look, doc. Sofie needs that crystal, just take my word for it, and I don't really want her carrying a dead baby around. Please just do me a favour and get the bloody thing out so you can get on with saving the patient.'

The doctor looked shocked and angry but he did what he was told, while Sofie huddled in George's bubble.

'Have you heard about Robert?' George said.

She shook her head. 'No. What's happened?'

'I'm sorry,' he said. 'I'm told that he's dead.'

Robert Moore's dead. That silly little funny little Englishman who couldn't speak French and who always seemed to be out of his depth is dead.

Firefighters aren't supposed to cry. They aren't supposed to show their emotions, especially not to their brother firefighters. Firefighters have to face death, both their own and that of others. It's part of the job. If you can't control your emotions then how will you control your actions in an emergency? But despite all her efforts a single tear escaped one eye. She blinked and it floated away and hit George's face.

George put his arms round her and gave her a huge bear-hug. For a long time he didn't say anything and didn't seem to want to let her go. Her cheek felt cold. She pulled her head back and looked into his face. There were tears in his eyes.

Sofie was totally bewildered. She had always thought of George Gabor as one of the coldest, most sober men she had ever met. This display of emotion was so utterly unprofessional she could hardly believe it. Sofie had always respected George. He had exactly the qualities a firefighter crew leader needs: courage, calmness, the ability to inspire confidence and trust, good judgement. She could never understand why he was only a crew leader and not a team leader or even the Chief of the Service. But now that she had seen how emotional he could be she felt even more respect for him. There was a warm heart in there somewhere. *He is human after all!*

'Where's Marianne now?' George asked as he pushed her away and floated beside her, quickly wiping his tears away.

'At the other end of this rope, near the fence.'

'Good God, you were only a few metres away from the doctor! I'm really sorry, Sofie. Look, once he's got that out we'll have three crystals. I'll take the doctor to Marianne and I want you to go—'

'I'll go with the doctor.'

'Sorry, Sofie, but you need a break. You've done your share, more than your share. I'll take him. I've left Karolyi in the helicopter. I want you to go up and—'

'Helicopter?' Sofie said. 'Where is it? I've been looking for it.'

George nodded upwards. 'About twenty metres up there. Yes, I heard the message that it had landed, but it was still hovering when the disaster happened. And now, it seems, it will stay up there for ever. I'll take the doctor to Marianne. I want you to go up and get Karolyi. He gave his crystal to the doctor on condition that I went back to collect him as soon as we got another crystal. It goes against my better judgement but a promise is a promise.'

Sofie didn't know who Karolyi was so she mentally repeated his name a few times. It seemed vaguely familiar. Then she remembered Marianne asking 'Have you seen Alex Karolyi? He's supposed to be fetching the doctor.'

'Oh, I'd like to see him,' Sofie said. 'Where is he?'

'Up in the helicopter. Go up and bring him down to Marianne and we'll take it from there.'

'Go up? Isn't it dangerous just drifting about in the air?'

'You're damned right it's dangerous. Karolyi and I nearly died up there, but that was before we learned how to fly. I take it you don't know how to do that?' She shook her head. 'I'll show you. How you getting on doc? Okay,' he said, seeing the doctor poking a long pair of tweezers into the baby's skull. 'You carry on. I'm just going to teach Sofie how to fly. Back in a second.'

George went behind Sofie, gave her his crystal, clipped his harness to hers and looked over her shoulder as he explained what to do. He made it sound easy enough. 'You hold three sides in one fist like this, point it the way you want to go, press the fourth side and you move. The harder you press, the faster you go. Turn it to steer. Point it back the other way to stop. It's easy.'

But it wasn't easy. It took her several minutes to even begin to get confident at it, but George was very calming and patient and eventually she got the hang of it. 'Obviously the most dangerous part is when you lose contact with the ground,' he said, 'and that's what you've got to do to get Karolyi. Once you get used to it you'll be able to fly without a rope, but for now I want you to stay tied on. Okay, well you've past the probationer's exam so let's go see how the doctor's doing.'

They zigzagged along the ground until they found the doctor. He was wrapping the baby in a plastic bag. 'Can you take these?' he said, the bag in one hand, the crystal in the other. She was grateful to see he had cleaned it.

'Put the baby in the helicopter Sofie,' George said. 'Can't think of anywhere else to put him for now. Bring Karolyi down and meet us where Marianne is in five minutes. Synchronise watches. Sixteen hours fifteen.' Sofie adjusted her watch, wondering why it had been half an hour slow.

When they had gone, Sofie tied the bag to her belt then practiced flying round in little circles to gain confidence. Finally she took her life in her hands and slowly flew straight up, watching the little green patch of Earth disappear from the bottom of her bubble. Looking up and letting the rope slip away from under her arm she finally saw the skid of a helicopter poke into her bubble. She was more confident of flying now.

She untied the rope from her harness, tied it to the skid and flew slowly round the red fuselage, keeping it always in sight, feeling like an astronaut flying around a space station and suddenly finding herself exhilarated and enjoying the experience of free flight. *This is like a dream. If only I could see outside the bubble I'd get a great view from up here.*

The helicopter door was open

She flew towards the helicopter's open door, proud of her first solo flight and slightly nervous of entering a machine that was not actually held up above the ground by any natural force. She recognised Alex Karolyi as soon as she saw him sitting inside, his feet up on a stretcher, and her heart sank. When George called him Karolyi she hadn't realised she was going to collect the notorious Alex. She had often seen this loud, showy young man around CERN, always with a different woman.

'Hello, Mr Karolyi,' she said, wishing she didn't have to speak to him at all. 'George Gabor has asked me to bring you down.'

He grinned at her with a sort of lop-sided smile. 'I'm sure you ain't gonna do that sweetheart. Call me Alex. But you have the advantage of me. What's your name, gorgeous?'

'Sofie Dialektaki,' she said and felt his eyes slither down her body like a snake.

'Come up here baby,' he said, holding out his hand to her.

She looked at him with a cold sneer. 'I know you expect all women to drop their knickers as soon as they meet you, Mr Karolyi, but not this one.' She had heard the rumours about him. About the affairs he had been having with several women on the staff, about the broken hearts he was supposed to have left bleeding around the place. *Can't for the life of me think why any woman would want him. He's so full of his own importance. Obviously thinks he's God's gift to women. Not my type at all.*

His grin widened. 'Didn't György tell you what happens if parts of your body are outside a bubble honey? There's a few bits here I'd rather like to keep.'

'From what I've heard it might be better if some of your bits froze and dropped off,' she said, but she thought *I suppose I've got no choice. Got to get close to this cheap womaniser. Don't want to kill him.* She flew into the doorway but kept a cold, distant look on her face.

'Don't you like boys then, young lady?'

'I like nice boys, Mr Karolyi. My boy-friend in Greece, for example. He's very nice.'

'Oh good. Well you won't have to put up with me for very long,' he said. 'Let's just fly down to György and I'll fly out of your life forever. I just hope the doctor wasn't too late.'

'Marianne told me you were supposed to be fetching the doctor,' Sofie said. 'What went wrong? Meet another woman on the way?'

His smile vanished. 'You've spoken to her?'

'Of course.'

'How is she?'

'She's not good. Is it true that she sent you for the doctor, Karolyi?'

'Yes, well actually I offered to go,' he said, 'but unfortunately I had to take a slight detour up to the top of the atmosphere thanks to your friend Gábor György.'

'So now you're trying to blame George for what's happened, you coward!'

'What do you mean?' The grin had gone from his face now. 'What has happened?'

'She's had the baby.'

'Oh God! Is it dead?'

'It's in here,' she said, unclipping the bag from her belt. She wanted to throw it at him. 'He was born dead and this was in his head,' she said, waving the crystal in his face. 'The doctor took it out.'

His eyes followed the crystal for a second then he looked at the bag and his expression changed. Pain and compassion replaced the brash arrogance that had shone in his eyes before.

So the man is human after all. Sofie was surprised. *He obviously has slightly more depth than I thought.*

'Poor Marianne!' he said, then looked at Sofie. 'Were you with her? When she had the baby?'

'Yes.'

'You poor thing. Was it very bad? Yes,' he said before she could answer, 'I can see it was. I can see you're upset. Was it just you? On your own?'

In spite of herself, Sofie felt all the emotions of the day begin to well up inside her: the shocks, the horrors, the grief, the pity. She nodded and looked away from him.

'Good God,' Alex said, 'how terrible. Come here.' He put his arms round her waist and pulled her close. She felt herself melt towards him. There was a strong animal magnetism about the man. He handled her body as if he owned it.

I can understand why women throw their knickers at him, she thought.

He gently lifted her face and looked into her eyes. 'Nobody should have to go through something like that alone,' he whispered. She could smell him, his breath, his aftershave, his sweat. Normally such smells would repel her but he smelt different from any man she had ever met and she sniffed in deeply. His head twisted to one side and his lips moved towards hers. She could feel her body yearning for comfort, for human contact after the nightmare of the day. *But not like this, not with him. Anyone but him.* And as his warm breath brushed her lips she slapped him across the face so hard it made her hand sting.

'George wants me to take you down to him,' she said moving out of his arms. 'Otherwise, Mr Karolyi, I'd have left you here.'

His head moved back and a big slow smile crossed his face as his cheek began to glow red.

'Then perhaps we'd better go,' he said. 'Don't want to keep Gábor György waiting.'

'George told me to leave this here,' she said, holding the bag and looking round, wondering what to do with it.

'Give it me and I'll put it on this seat.'

He slid off the seat and took the clear plastic bag off her. Then he hesitated, said 'Is it a boy or a girl?' and brought it close to his face. Sofie could see the reddening mark on his cheek. As his black eyes ran over the baby's body a look first of surprise, then of disbelief and finally of shock followed each other rapidly across his handsome features. Then to her utter astonishment he brought the bag up to his lips and kissed the tiny head through the plastic, a look of utter misery on his face.

Episode 21 Return to ATLAS

Alex gently laid the baby in his plastic shroud on the helicopter's seat, his eyes lingering lovingly on the tiny face. *I'll be back and give you a proper burial later*, he thought, then turned to the girl. He could still feel the sting of her hand on his cheek. *No girl ever did that to me before. She's got spirit anyway. Nice figure too. Is that why I tried it on with her? No, just force of habit. A habit I've got to get out of. I'm Marianne's man now. Marianne's and nobody else's.*

'I think you'd better fly,' she said, offering him the crystal, holding it out at arm's length as if she was afraid of getting too close to him. There was a quizzical expression on her face. *She's puzzled by me kissing the baby* Alex thought as he took the crystal.

'Okay,' he said, 'but I'm afraid you're going to have to put your arms round me, sweetie, and give me a big hug.'

Without a word she moved behind him, passed him the crystal and wrapped her arms round his chest. To keep her feet inside the bubble she lifted her legs and wrapped them round his. He tried not to notice her warm body pressing against his back as he flew out of the helicopter. *Old habits die hard*, he thought. 'Which way?' he said over his shoulder.

'There's a rope tied to one skid. Follow that.'

He found the rope and followed it down to the field, the girl swinging around on his back like a giant rucksack, then he traced the rope over the grass and in less than a minute they reached the fence. The doctor was helping George to strap Marianne into an orange stretcher which, Alex assumed, the firefighter had collected from the fire engine. Alex could only see her face. She looked terrible, pale and exhausted. When she saw

Alex she gasped 'Danny?' with a wild look in her eyes.

'No, Marianne, only me,' he said.

'Where's Danny?' she groaned.

'He's still in the cavern,' George said and turned to Sofie. 'We're taking her to the Medical Centre, Sofie. It's a waste of time going to the hospital. They won't have any facilities that work. I want you to go and find Danny Schneider. Don't revive anyone else. You know what Schneider looks like?'

'No, sorry I—' Sofie said.

'I know him, György,' Alex said.

'Okay you go and find him, Karolyi. When you find him give him your crystal and send him to the Medical Centre. Understand?' There was a fierceness in his voice that meant business.

'Okay György. Sure.'

'You know which way to go? Follow this fence round to the next straight stretch, then head over the car park into the SX building. You come with us, Sofie. You can help the doctor with Marianne. Be as quick as you can, Karolyi.'

'Alex!' Marianne moaned as he was turning to go. He flew back and she peered at him from under the orange stretcher cover. She was pitiful to see, her face grey and her eyes encircled by dark rings. She looked like a very old, very sick woman. All the words that Alex wanted to say to her bubbled up into his throat, almost choking him.

To see her in this state tore him apart. Not for one moment did his passion for her weaken. Seeing her helpless like this only made him feel more guilty for having failed to get the doctor to her, more determined to look after her, more convinced than ever that she was going to get well and be the only woman in his life.

'Don't tell him about the baby,' she whispered.

'What?' *Who's she talking about? Oh yeah, that jerk she married in a moment of insanity.* 'Okay Marianne,' he said cheerily. 'I won't.' Her eyes closed. 'I'm so sorry Marianne,' he said. There was no response, as if she hadn't heard him. He bent and kissed her nose. Sofie clipped herself to the stretcher, George and the doctor lifted it, George gave Alex another threatening look and the three of them flew awkwardly away across the field, carrying the stretcher between the two bubbles, as Alex turned and headed along the fence.

Once she was out of his sight, Alex felt glad to be getting away. Marianne was in good hands and he was eager to get back into the cavern and start looking for more crystal.

She needs a crystal of her own so she can get well again, and I've got to give one to Schneider so he can go and slobber all over her. I'd hate to have to give him my last crystal. That would really slay me. No, I've got to have a quick look round and try to find at least one more. And suppose I found two, or ten, or a hundred! What would I do with them? This stuff is obviously incredibly important, far more precious than gold, and here am I, Count Alex Karolyi, heading down into the crystal mine! I'm going to get rich and get the best girl in the world. Why not? Go for the best, that's Karolyi's motto.

As he left the fence and flew over the little bank of trees to the car park he blessed Marianne for asking for Danny and giving him this opportunity. He had no hesitation in flying now. He skated over the car park with no fear of losing contact with the ground. On the rare occasions when he did, he always knew where he could find it.

There was a big red fire engine parked inside SX1. Flying round it, he found a rope attached to a winch on the front. This was obviously what had been pulling Marianne up in the stretcher. He followed the rope, still wondering how many crystals there were down there, when the little Irish girl with the ginger hair loomed through his bubble wall. She was floating just above the winch rope staring towards the fire engine with a sad, wistful look on her oval face but that changed first into surprise and then into delight when she saw Alex.

'Oh Alex!' she gasped. 'Thank God!'

'Hello little Kata.' His heart sank when he saw her.

'Oh Alex, I've still got your watch!' She unstrapped it from her ankle and held it out to him, her open mouth smiling.

He flew to her, took the watch and politely kissed her cheek. It was the way he always greeted females he knew, but her response was completely unexpected.

'Oh Alex, I'm so glad to see you!' She flung her arms round his neck, her tears splashing onto his face. 'I had to help Marianne. It was awful. We waited such a long time for you. Where've you been? Have you brought the doctor?'

Alex's anger flared. 'Why is everybody blaming me?' he snapped. 'What right have you got to question me, little girl?' He eased her arms down from round his neck. 'I've got work to do, Kata. George Gabor has sent me on a job.'

It felt good to be able to blame György. After all it was his fault that Alex had failed to get the doctor.

'But what about Marianne? She needs the doctor urgently, Alex.'

He looked at her, wiping the tears away on the backs of her hands. *Your heart's in the right place at any rate,* he thought. *You're worried about Marianne not yourself.* 'Marianne's with the doctor now, so you can stop worrying. And she's asking for Danny, and George has sent me down into the ATLAS cavern to find him, so I haven't got time to stay here chatting with you, little girl. Just wait here and somebody will come and pick you up. Eventually.'

Catriona wasn't listening to his words. She was reading the look in his eyes and not liking what she saw there. She began to wring her hands together. 'Please don't leave me, Alex.' Her face crumpled like a used paper cup.

Alex felt like slapping her and telling her to snap out of it. 'This job's important, Kata,' he said, his voice betraying his exasperation. 'You know Danny? Marianne's husband? She's asking for him. I've got to—'

Immediately Catriona's look changed to one of surprise. 'You've seen her?' she whispered. 'You've seen Marianne? How is she?'

Okay, he thought. *I give up. I'm going to have to tell you. Let's get it over with.* 'She's had the baby. It's...'

He paused, Marianne's words echoing in his head: "Don't tell him about the baby".

If I tell Kata the truth, she might blurt it out in front of Danny. That's exactly the kind of stupid thing she would do. Can't take that chance. Wish I'd said Marianne was still in labour. Too late now.

'How is she?' Catriona whispered.

'She's fine,' he said.

'Thank God! And how's the baby?'

'It's fine too.'

'Oh thank God!' she yelped and hugged him, raining kisses on his face. Alex began to think it would have been quicker to tell her the truth. And when she began to cry again, he decided he'd had enough.

'Look, I've got to go now. You can come if you want or stay here. I don't—'

'I'll come. Please let me come, Alex,' she said, wiping the tears away and laughing. 'I'm so happy for her. This makes up for everything that's happened. Oh Alex, I'm so happy,' and she wrapped her arms and legs around him like a koala bear, and he pressed the crystal and followed the rope down into the ATLAS cavern, Catriona on his back, her face rubbing warm against his ear. She had flipped from deep depression to high elation in a matter of moments and now seemed to be on top of the world. Alex tried to put her out of his mind. *I'll get rid of her as soon as I can. For now there's a burning question I want to answer.*

When Robert Moore's head came into the bubble

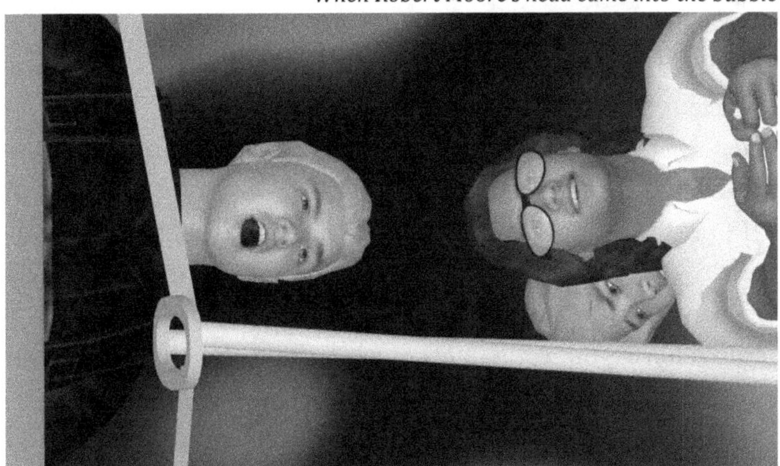

When Robert Moore's head came into the bubble, Alex stopped and studied him while Catriona turned her face away and began to whimper.

'Wonder what killed him?' Alex said. 'Marianne thinks it was because his head was outside the bubble, but I'm not so sure. Maybe…'

'Maybe what?'

'Maybe a piece of crystal hit him like…'

'Like what, Alex?'

Alex had to think fast. He couldn't say "Like Marianne's baby" which is what he was thinking, so he said 'Like a bullet, and killed him.'

Catriona thought about it. 'Could be, but so what?'

'So there would be a piece of crystal stuck inside him.'

He flew around the body and the stretcher hanging beside it, inspecting them from all angles. He saw a small hole in the stretcher's plastic base but could not see any injury on Moore's body.

'Can't we just leave him? I thought we were looking for Danny?'

'But if there was some crystal in him,' Alex said, talking to himself, 'then he would have a bubble, and he doesn't.'

'Like Marianne's baby did, you mean? No, he hasn't got a bubble. It's a miracle that baby's survived,' Catriona said. 'A real miracle.'

'Yes, isn't it? Okay, let's go and find Schneider. Last time I saw him he was coming out from under ATLAS.'

He pressed his crystal and flew back up the rope to where it passed the huge blue pipe which joined ATLAS to the cavern's end wall. He turned and followed it towards the wall.

'Why have you come back up? I thought you saw Danny underneath ATLAS?' Catriona said.

You're obviously not as silly as you look, honey, he thought, and said 'Yes, but while I'm here I want to search for more crystals. We're going to need as many as we can find. Keep your eyes open for more bubbles, Kata.'

'But I thought we were looking for Danny? Isn't Marianne waiting for him?'

'Listen, I haven't forgotten Marianne, believe me, but at the moment she is in the Medical Centre getting cleaned up and Schneider can't do anything to help her so there's no hurry. There could be hundreds of crystals down here just waiting to be found.'

As he flew across the big brown disk fixed to the cavern wall, Catriona asked 'What do you think about Marianne?'

Alex was surprised, not only at the question but at the strength of his reaction. He wanted to say "I love her" but managed to stop himself and say 'Why do you ask that, Kata?'

'Because I think she's the nicest and kindest person I've ever met. I think you were good friends with her once, weren't you?'

Why don't you mind your own freaking business? Alex thought as he began to search across the Big Wheel's brown plates, descending in wide sweeping curves towards the cavern floor. 'Yes, more than once,' Alex said trying to make a joke, but the girl didn't laugh. 'She was a good friend. Now will you just shut up about her?'

Catriona was quiet for a few seconds, then she said 'Danny's not so nice though, is he? I can't understand why she ever married him. Can you?'

Alex reached the cavern floor and stopped. 'She married him because she was pregnant and she's a Roman Catholic. Okay?'

He was disappointed at not finding any more bubbles and angry with Catriona's babble. He was determined to try to find at least one more crystal so he wouldn't have to give his final piece to the man who stole his love. He flew back up to the blue beam pipe shield, over to the other Big Wheel fixed to the ATLAS detector and again began to scan its surface.

'I'm so glad she's had that baby,' Catriona said. 'It will help to bring them together.'

Alex felt his stomach muscles tense and his temper start to fray. *And now that the baby's dead with a bit of luck it might help to tear them apart,* he thought.

'Babies do that, don't they, bring couples together?'

'I wouldn't know,' Alex said. 'I've never had one.' He flew all over the Big Wheel's surface, finding the damaged plates where the toroid tube had exploded as the black hole quenched the magnet, but did not find any more crystals. He flew down to the floor again and went into the cramped space under the ATLAS detector, deliberately avoiding the side where he knew Danny had been plugging in the toroid tube.

'Danny must be on the other side, isn't he?' Catriona said.

'For Christ sake shut...Look, Kata, just give it a rest. I'm searching for a piece of crystal to give him. Otherwise you and I are going to be frozen down here while he's up there flying around. Is that what you want?'

There was not enough room to fly so he began to pull himself under ATLAS's curving lower surface, Catriona pressing against him as he squeezed between the beams and cabinets and supports and cables.

'But surely that's what Marianne wants,' she said. 'I mean, does it matter if we're frozen if it means he can see his new baby? I'd be quite happy to give up my crystal for that, if I had one. How incredible that it's still alive. Did you get the doctor to her?'

Alex did not answer. He had gone all the way down one side and emerged into the open space between the Big Wheels at the other end of the cavern without finding any more crystals.

'Is it a boy or a girl?' Catriona asked as he flew across to the other curving side of the detector.

'It's a boy,' Alex said as he pulled himself into the narrow gap thinking *At least that bit's true.*

'I'm just so happy for her that the baby's alive. Was it an easy birth? Alex? Did you get the doctor to her?'

Alex could feel himself winding up to breaking point. His guilt at failing to fetch the doctor was coming back with bitter force and it was all this stupid Irish girl's fault. Why couldn't she just—

'Jesus, look at that!' He had almost reached the other end of the detector when he found himself looking through not just one bubble but a whole series of them. At least four crystals were resting against various pieces of equipment, their bubbles merging into a honeycomb of space. Alex stopped and gave a whoop of delight. 'There must be four, five crystals here.'

'Did you get the doctor to her, Alex?' Catriona said. She didn't seem to understand the implications of what they were seeing. She didn't seem to know that the whole situation had suddenly changed. She slipped off his back and pulled herself round so she was floating in one of the other bubbles, looking into his face. 'You didn't, did you?'

He smiled at her. Even Kata looked kind-of attractive at that moment. He was feeling really pleased with the world. 'Didn't what?' he murmured.

'Get the doctor to her?' He stared back at her and she must have seen the truth in his face. 'You didn't! Tell me what happened. Tell me the truth.'

'No God dammit, I didn't get the doctor to Marianne. You want the truth? Okay, Kata, the truth is that she has had the baby but it's dead. She nearly died herself having it. You want the truth? Okay. The truth is that I love Marianne from the bottom of my heart and I wish to hell that she had never married that arsehole Danny Schneider. You want the whole truth? Okay, here it is. That baby she just had? It was mine. Mine, do you hear? Mine. Not Danny Schneider's. Mine! He was my son. There. That's the truth. You feel better now you know?'

Catriona had gone pale. Now with a sob she pushed herself away from him and drifted off into the honeycomb of bubbles which lay ahead of them. Alex watched her go, glad to be rid of her, then pulled himself forward and began to collect the crystals.

Episode 22 Return to the University

It took a long time for all the princesses to go through the initiation ceremony. Sam longed to know what was happening to Marianne and everyone else on Earth but he dared not disentangle himself from the pool of sticky food to stand and look through the crystals. He found himself drifting off into a fitful sleep, rocked by Cjingha's constantly circling flight, dreaming of being slowly eaten alive by giant bees which crunched their way up his legs and were just beginning to feast on his genitals when he was awoken by the sudden descent of the Universe. Looking out he found himself leaving the Temple and emerging in the brightly lit courtyard. Sam blinked.

'...no word yet from Commander Bogmon,' one of the two guards was saying.

'Where can I take this universe to keep it safe?' Cjingha sounded worried.

'Why not take it up to the Holy Sanctum?' Princess Uskabellu said. 'It's the safest place here. I'll show you.'

She led Cjingha and the guards up the sloping outer wall of the Temple towards the small white building perched on its very summit. As they flew higher Sam looked down on the city spread out below him, surrounded on three sides by the curving waterway and on the fourth by the distant mountains. He had never been so high. The flower-filled forest surrounded the city, even spreading up into the lower reaches of the mountains.

The Holy Sanctum was not as small as it had looked from the ground. It seemed to Sam like a white box which had been jammed onto the pointed top of the Temple. Cjingha showed her letter to a black-robed priest guarding the little entrance and he accompanied the two females into the Sanctum, leaving the two soldiers waiting outside. It was so dark Sam saw only vague shadows but Cjingha gasped 'What's happened to the Beeing?'

As Sam's eyes accommodated to the darkness he saw a huge golden shape dominating one side of the Holy Sanctum. The priest scuttled around in an excited state, bowing before the statue, his antennae quivering and vibrating rapidly up and down. 'We have restored his face to its correct shape,' he said. 'Now that the Son of Beeing has come we finally know his real appearance.'

As the details of the statue became clearer, Sam felt a shiver of wonder. The statue was in the shape of a bee. It had a golden head and body. Between its pinky-red eyes, an extra layer of carving decorated its face. Its features were carefully painted and unmistakable. It looked exactly like Michael Zhang. Its two dangling antennae emerged from his forehead.

It looked exactly like Michael Zhang

'The university's safe now, Professor,' a soldier called through the Holy Sanctum's doorway. Cjingha emerged from its coolness into the heat of the afternoon with the Universe carefully held in her jaws. From his vantage point in the Universe's crystal network, Sam could see heat shimmering up the black face of the Temple which sloped down to the Palace far below. The broad brown Entroilian city stretched away to the distant mountains.

Princess Uskabellu flew after Cjingha with her long gown fluttering in the rising heat. 'Where are you going?' she called after her. 'Will you be seeing the Second Beeing?'

'Seeing the...? Oh, you mean the emergent. Yes, I'll probably need to talk to him at some stage about his Cosmic Egg. Why?'

'Can I come with you? I've got to have him, Professor. I've got to be his Queen. I'll die if I don't mate with him. I'll do anything, anything at all, whatever it takes. I've been through the induction now. It's no good staying in the Temple. Praying to the Beeing isn't going to achieve anything. I'd rather come with you and see his living Son.'

'Look, I don't think for a minute that he is the Son of Beeing. That's just a rumour, probably started by the Priests to gain public support for the Temple rebuilding programme. As far as we know at the moment he's just an emergent, nothing more.'

'But the signs! He bears all the signs!'

'Yes, yes, but...'

'You said yourself his mind is bright and his reproductive organs are well developed. Er, did you say his excrement bears the sweet smell of Kingship?'

'Yes, but—'

'And now we know his face is the same as the Beeing's.'

'But that's because the priests have changed the statue! That proves nothing.'

'It does. It proves the prediction has come true. Please let me come with you, Professor Itoodoo. Please.'

'Oh, come then. I suppose I can't stop you.'

Cjingha and Uskabellu flew across the city towards the distant structure at the foot of the mountains, which Sam now knew was the university.

'What's going to happen if there's only one emergent?' Uskabellu said.

'What do you mean?'

'Well, normally there are thousands of emergents coming out of a cosmic egg. In this case we've only got one.'

'Well, there are two actually. There's another one in here, at least I hope it's still in there.'

'Oh really? What's it like?'

'Don't get too excited. It's very tiny and puny looking.'

'Oh dear. Well anyway, if there's only one or two emergents, what's going to happen about the Swarming? Will Queen Karolinda want him?'

'I think she might,' Cjingha said. 'She sounded quite excited when I described him to her.'

'That's too bad. If she chooses him to mate with then none of us princesses will get a look in. Unless…Do you think the other prediction could be true, Professor?'

'What other prediction?'

'You know, the one in the Hidden Scriptures. The one that says the real Son of Beeing will survive the mating.'

'I haven't heard that one. Survive a mating? I doubt it. Drones always die during mating. Their reproductive organs explode; everyone knows that.'

'Yes, but suppose this one didn't. Then he might go on to choose one of the princesses for his Queen, and they would fly away and start a new colony on another island somewhere, like they do in other Entroilian cities. Don't you think that's possible? Just imagine it, a living God who could mate with you again and again! It would be heaven.'

'You're getting carried away, Princess. Actually I'd be perfectly happy just mating once, myself. I think our whole system is completely unfair. I'm a female too.' Sam could feel Cjingha's jaws shaking slightly. She obviously felt passionate about this. 'Why should I have been born sterile when females like you are able to reproduce, just because you've been fed different food? It isn't fair. There's no reason why all females shouldn't have eggs of their own, if we just fed our larvae right.'

'But that wouldn't work. There would be far too many children. We wouldn't be able to feed them all.'

'Yes we would. Our doctors could genetically engineer us so we would just lay one or two each. It would be much better than what we've got now. That's what I would call heaven.'

'That will never happen, Professor.'

Sam must have dozed off at this point because the next thing he knew was being awakened by the heat as Cjingha drew open a shutter and a strong beam of sunlight streamed through the outer wall of her laboratory, through the projector and into his crystal hiding place. He was still lying on his back, his jacket still held in the thick Entroilian honey which was rapidly melting in the heat. Overhead he saw an image of himself appear on the screen.

'Oh, is that it?' Uskabellu sounded terribly disappointed.

'Yes, I'm afraid so. Not much of a specimen, is it?'

'Is it still alive?'

'I'm not sure. When the Argolaths attacked I was just about to lower the probe and pull it out.'

Sam yanked his arm out of the warming pool of honey and struggled to his feet shouting 'No! I don't want to be probed!'

Both Entroilians stared at the screen, their antennae quivering.

'It can talk!' Uskabellu said.

'The other emergent must have given it some honey,' Cjingha said. 'Yes, there it is on the floor. What's your name?'

'Sam Fitzpatrick.'

'What kind of creature are you?'

'I'm a man.'

'Did the other emergent give you that food?'

'Yes.'

'What kind of creature is he?'

'He's a man too, or he was when we left Earth.'

'What's his name?'

'Michael Zhang.'

'Michaelzhang,' Uskabellu sighed. 'What a heavenly name.' She began to whisper it over to herself. 'Michaelzhang. Lord Michaelzhang. I love Lord Michaelzhang...'

'Are you sick?' Cjingha said, ignoring her. 'Your skin looks very loose.'

'This isn't my skin. It's a suit.'

'Clothing? But Michaelzhang wasn't wearing any clothing.'

'He was when we left Earth. He swelled up a lot when he swallowed the pink stuff. His clothes must have come off then. He was a bit smaller than me to start with.'

'Swallowed the pink...You mean he swallowed some of the event record from your Cosmic Egg?'

'That pink stuff down there,' Sam said, shrugging and pointing.

'So that explains how that deep hole was created...'

Uskabellu suddenly took an interest. 'So you and he are the same? Are you male or female?'

'I'm a man. I'm male!'

'By the blessed Beeing, Cjingha, do you see what this means? If Samfitzpatrick goes down and swallows some of the event record he too might be transformed, like Michaelzhang. Then we would have two Sons of Beeing so even if the Queen takes one, I could have the other! Can't we lower him down so he can eat some—'

'No,' Cjingha said firmly, much to Sam's relief. 'It's my job to try to work out what happened in the history of that Cosmic Egg. I'm doing a research project for Councillor Moshendiar, trying to discover why some universes produce better emergents than others. If we can figure that out then we can make all her Majesty's cosmic eggs as productive as this one. If I let Samfitzpatrick eat it and make more holes in it then I may never be able to figure out its history.'

'I suppose you're right,' Uskabellu said. 'Is there any chance that the Cosmic Egg can be fixed? If time could be restarted then more Sons of Beeing might come out and then I would get a permanent mate.'

'I've been wondering about that. It depends how much damage Michaelzhang did to the surface when he swallowed some of the event record. Let me have another look at that hole he made.'

The heat left Sam and the image on the screen went pink. He saw a bright spot of light move across the pink ocean far below.

'There it is,' Cjingha said. On the screen, Sam saw the hole which he had seen before, winding deep down into the pink surface as if a worm had burrowed into an apple. 'That's the hole Michaelzhang made. The viscosity of the event record must have kept it open while he floated up and broke the event network. Then the fragments must have fallen down into the hole.'

'So why didn't the hole just close up afterwards?'

'I suspect that it's being held open by some negative energy strings.'

'By what? I can't see anything.'

'No, you won't. Negative energy threads are microscopically narrow. They have a repulsive gravitational field which could hold open a tunnel like that.'

'So can you fix the event network and restart time?'

'I would need to retrieve all the fragments from the Cosmic Egg without causing any more damage. They're crysorganic so they would re-assemble themselves if I arrange them in the right way. I wonder how deep it is?' The bright light moved back up to Sam. 'Samfitzpatrick, did Michaelzhang say how far down he had gone?'

Sam thought about what Michael had said. 'He made out he was a God at first—'

'You see!' Uskabellu cried. 'I told you!'

'—and he said all the secrets scientists had been trying to work out had been revealed to him and he knew the whole history of the Universe up to the moment we left it.'

'So he must have gone right back to the beginning,' Cjingha said. 'So that hole must go right down to the middle of the cosmic egg. The fragments could be anywhere in that universe's history. This is going to be a big job. But you're right, Uskabellu. If we can recover all those fragments and fix the event network then time will restart in the cosmic egg and we could get more emergents out, hundreds, maybe thousands. What's the population of your planet, Samfitzpatrick?'

'Millions,' Sam said. 'No, billions!' He was happy to go along with all this. *They're talking about restarting time in the Universe. That's what I want more than anything.*

'The trouble is,' Cjingha said, 'I can't use the probe on the universe. That causes so much damage it would never function again.'

'Why don't we just send Samfitzpatrick down that hole to collect the fragments? He's small enough. He'd fit in there easily.'

Sam suddenly felt a good deal less happy. He still remembered the horror of almost drowning in that thick jelly-like pink stuff and never wanted to go back into it again. 'I think I would be more use to you up here,' Sam said. 'I can talk to people on Earth. They might be able to help.'

'Are you saying some people are still alive on your home world?' Cjingha said.

Sam nodded.

'That's very strange. I thought time had stopped there.'

'Yes it has but people who get a fragment of crystal can still move around. Each one seems to be surrounded by a sort of bubble of time.'

'How fascinating,' the Professor said. 'Presumably those fragments still contain some event quanta. Tell me, Samfitzpatrick, how do you talk to people on your home world?'

Sam began to describe what he did.

'Show me.'

He stood and began looking through the crystal ends surrounding him. 'I can see a blue cabinet in that one,' he said. 'And in that one I can see...Good God, it's George Gabor!' George was flying along a road pulling an orange stretcher behind him.

'And you can speak to them?' Cjingha said. 'And they can speak to you? So I was right. Those fragments of crystal must still be linked to the crystals surrounding you by negative energy strings. You are in the gap where the broken pipe originally stood. These communications are obviously carried by vibrations in the strings. What are the other people doing?'

Sam began to look through the other crystals, hoping desperately to see his beloved step-daughter.

And to his delight, after only a few seconds searching he saw her! She was talking to Alex Karolyi, who was holding the crystal Sam was looking out of. He heard her whisper 'You've seen Marianne? How is she?'

'I can see my step-daughter!' he gasped and waited breathlessly for Alex to answer. He too desperately wanted to know how Marianne was.

'Stepdaughter?' Uskabellu said. 'What does that mean?'

When Sam didn't answer, Uskabellu shook the projector and he fell over.

'I said "What does that mean?"' Uskabellu repeated.

Sam sighed, longing to listen to Catriona but powerless to exert his own will. 'I am not her father but I married her mother and I raised her as my daughter.'

'No, of course you can't be her father otherwise you would be dead,' she said.

'How did you know her father was dead?'

'Isn't it obvious? He must have taken part in a mating and all drones die after mating.'

'Drones? You mean men? No they don't die, at least not on my world.'

'You see!' Uskabellu shouted. 'These drones do survive the mating! Michaelzhang IS the Son of Beeing and I WILL marry him! I will, even if the Queen has him first!'

'Look,' Cjingha said. 'Forget about that for now. I think I see a way of fixing the event network. Samfitzpatrick, please tell Stepdaughter to collect all the crystals and bring them down the tunnel. Tell her that if she can do that we will be able to restart time in your universe.'

Sam didn't like the sound of this. 'Michael Zhang said this might happen. He said you might be able to fix the machine and restart time.'

'Yes, I should be able to,' Cjingha said, 'as long as she brings all the fragments down the tunnel.'

'And how will she find this tunnel?'

'It has to be somewhere near where they last saw the black hole. The negative energy strings start where you are, which is where the broken event pipe used to be. They go down into that hole we can see in the cosmic egg. From what you've told us, Samfitzpatrick, the strings must go right to the heart of the egg, where the history of your universe began. From there they must go up inside the egg to just below the surface of the event record, which corresponds to the time and place where the black hole absorbed you. And because they have negative energy, they hold open a tunnel through the history of your universe.'

'Would she have to bring all the fragments of crystal back?' Sam said.

'Of course. If any are missing I won't be able to fix the event network.'

'That might be a problem. I don't think Alex Karolyi would willingly give up his crystal. It would mean giving up his life. In fact I don't think anyone would give up their fragments. She's only a young girl. She can't force them to give them to her.'

'Sounds like she will need some help,' Uskabellu said. 'I think you're going to have to send Samfitzpatrick down to help her, Professor.'

'Oh no!' Sam cried. 'Please, no, look, oh, surely there's some other way of doing this?'

Episode 23 Plan to fix the Universe

'What a pathetic sort of drone you are, Samfitzpatrick!' Uskabellu said. 'Entroilian drones would rather die than refuse an adventure like this!'

Looking up from his crystal cave, Sam could still see her huge bee-like head staring at his image on the screen of Cjingha's projector. He felt ashamed of his outburst and utterly humiliated, but still terrified at the prospect of following those eggs down that dark winding hole deep into the pink ocean.

'Listen,' he shouted, 'I love Catriona! I would do anything to help her. But what use would I be if I was drowned?'

'Pathetic and useless,' Uskabellu said. 'Can I see the hole in the cosmic egg again, Cjingha?'

The light moved off Sam and he stood alone in the darkness feeling a complete failure, torn apart by guilt and misery.

'It's a pity that hole is so small,' Uskabellu said, looking up at the screen. 'Otherwise we could have sent some Entroilians down there to help stepdaughter to collect the crystals. They would be more use than Samfitzpatrick.'

'That's not a bad idea, Princess,' Cjingha said thoughtfully. 'It's true we can't use full-grown Entroilians but we might be able to get some eggs down there. They would be small enough to fit into the hole.'

'But how could we make sure they go all the way down?'

Cjingha considered this for a moment. 'If we put some food down the hole then it might wash them down. And even if it didn't, they'd have to crawl down to get it after they transform into larvae. Either way they'd certainly go down the hole. After that, we'd have to wait for a couple of weeks for them to pupate and become Entroilians. Then they could set about helping

Stepdaughter get all the fragments. They could fly up the tunnel to Samfitzpatrick's home planet and collect them all, then fly back down with them.'

I don't like the sound of this, Sam thought. *I'd rather keep aliens as far away from the Earth as possible.*

'But how would they know what to do?' Uskabellu said.

'Stepdaughter will have to tell them. She'll have two weeks to get all the way down the tunnel to the centre of the cosmic egg. If she swallows some of our food when she gets there, she will be able to speak Entroilian, the same as Samfitzpatrick.'

'Have you ever put Entroilian eggs into a Cosmic Egg before?' Uskabellu asked.

'No, but I see no reason why it wouldn't work.'

'Okay, I'll go and collect some new little eggs from the nursery,' the princess said. 'Back in a moment.' She flew out of the laboratory.

'Right, Samfitzpatrick,' Cjingha said. 'Tell Stepdaughter what to do. Tell her she's got two weeks to get all the way down the tunnel. Make sure she takes at least one crystal with her, so you can keep in touch with her.'

I suppose I have no choice, Sam thought as he stood once more and his eyes sought again the crystal where he had seen Catriona. *Cjingha has a plan that might revive the whole Universe so I have no option but to help her. But maybe I can find a way to do it without letting the Entroilians find Earth.*

It did not take him long to find Catriona, but now she was in a completely different situation, floating in a narrow gap between metal pipes and a bank of cables and a row of metal cabinets. The scene around her was lit by the pale blue glows from several crystals. In the background he saw the huge outer surface of the ATLAS detector curving down into the darkness near the floor.

'Catty!' he called.

She ignored him at first. She was obviously in one of her

moods. Sam kept calling.

'Go away Alex!' she snapped. 'Go back to Marianne.'

'Catriona, it's me!'

'Sam?' she whispered.

'Yes, Catty. Down here!'

She looked down, saw the crystal, pushed herself off a girder and floated directly towards Sam. His heart went out to her. He had only ever seen that look on her face once before, when Trackaway, her old St Bernard dog, had died. She reached out, took the crystal and held it close to her eye. Her long lashes hung heavy with tears. *What's upset her like this?* Sam wondered.

'Sam? Is it really you? Oh God! I can see you.' Her voice was small and faint.

'And I can see you too. Now listen, Kitty-Cat, we need your help—'

'Where are you, Sam?'

What can I tell her? Sam thought. *I don't want to frighten her. Best keep it simple.* 'We're at the bottom of the tunnel, Catty.'

'Michael's there too?'

'Well he was. He's not here at the moment. Now please listen, sweetie. This is very important. You've got to collect as many crystals as you can find and bring them down the tunnel and come down and help us. It's vital. Can you hear me, Catty?'

'Yes I hear you. What tunnel do you mean though, Sam?'

'There's a tunnel. It probably starts near where you last saw the black hole and it leads down here.'

'But where are you, Sam? Where are you?' She began to cry. Her hands closed round the crystal and he lost sight of her. All he could hear were her sobs.

'Don't cry, Kitten,' he called. 'Try to stay calm. Everything's going to be all right, if you just stay calm. I'm sorry, I can't tell you where I am. I don't really understand it myself. All I know is that there's a tunnel and you've got to find it. Then I want you to bring the crystals down.' *If she brings all the crystals down then there will be no need for the Entroilians to go up to the Earth*, he thought. 'Try to collect as many as you can, all of them if possible. Understand? Now I know that might be difficult. People won't want to let you take their crystal away. But do your best, Catty. Get as many as you can. Are you listening?'

'Yes,' she said in a tiny voice as if trying not to cry. Her fingers moved and he saw her again.

'You've got two weeks to get down the tunnel, so you'd better take some food and clean clothes. And a toothbrush.' But even as he said this Sam began to realise how ridiculous it sounded. *She's a young girl of fourteen. How can I ask her to do this? But what choice have I got?* 'It's going to be a wonderful adventure, Kitten,' he said, trying to sound enthusiastic and literally thinking on his feet. 'But, I think it might be dangerous too.' As soon as he said this he remembered helping Marianne on the balcony and a new plan popped into his head. 'Try to take one of the men with you. George Gabor would be best. In fact I don't want you to come down the tunnel yourself, Catty. I want you to give all the fragments to George Gabor and tell him to bring them down the tunnel. Tell him exactly what I've just told you. Okay?'

She frowned and nodded.

'This is a very important job, Catty,' Sam went on, feeling a lot happier now. 'If you can just do what I've told you and ask George to bring the crystal down the tunnel then we can restart time. Do you know what that means, Catriona? You can help to save the Earth. But we need all those crystal fragments. If we don't get them then the Universe will stay frozen for ever, Catty. For ever, so remember to tell—'

'I've got about a dozen eggs,' Uskabellu said, flying into the laboratory. 'That's all I could carry.'

'Right then,' Cjingha said. 'Put them onto that dish. Right. Here we go.'

Glancing up Sam saw a mechanical arm descending towards his crystal cave and he lay on the floor, afraid of being knocked out of his cell. He lost sight of his beloved step-daughter. Hanging from the arm was a tray upon which lay a dozen capsule-shaped white eggs and a syringe. The arm slipped easily between the gaps in the pipes of the crystal network and continued on its journey down, past Sam's cave and he watched it descend rapidly towards the pink ocean. It approached the hole in the surface, lifted each egg in turn and dropped it into the hole. Then it lifted the syringe and squirted something thick and gluey into the hole. It drained slowly away. Finally the arm rose back up past Sam and retracted into the projector.

'There, that should do it,' Cjingha said.

'Wonderful,' Uskabellu said. 'What are you going to do with this cosmic egg now?'

'I suppose it should go back to the Holy Sanctum for the next two weeks, until the eggs pupate,' Cjingha said. 'That will be the safest place. If those Argolaths attack again—'

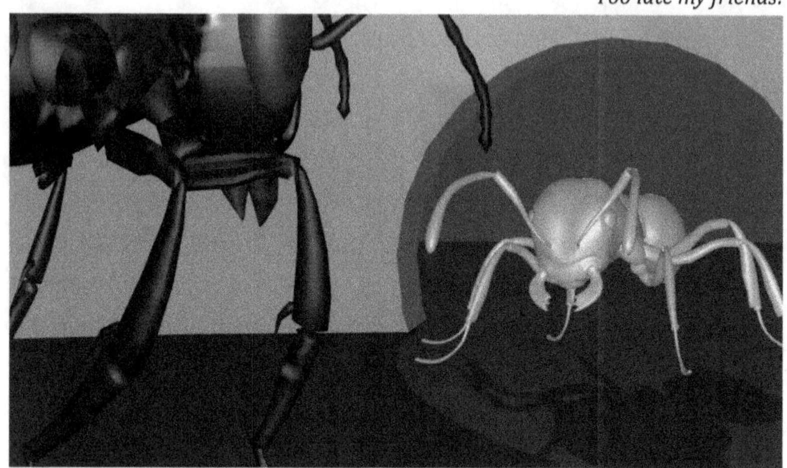

'Too late my friends! We already have,' said a voice, speaking Entroilian but, even to Sam's untutored ear, with a heavy accent, and with a tone different from any Entroilian's: harder, harsher and more aggressive. Sam turned to see the white head of an insect poking through the laboratory entrance. *I saw faces like that on some of the statues in the Palace.*

It was very different in appearance from the Entroilians. Its face bore almost no hair, its eyes were small and mean looking, its jaws were thick and strong, its antennae very long and bent in the middle. It bore a strong resemblance to an ant, Sam thought.

'Move aside ladies or you might get hurt,' the creature said and a moment later an acrid smell filled the little laboratory as a white mist sprayed into the faces of the two Entroilians. They flew up to the ceiling, wiping their heads with their front legs. The white creature darted forward, its jaws grabbed the Universe off the projector and, while the Entroilians were still recovering, slipped away through the entrance carrying the Universe with it.

Sam's crystal cavern shook as the creature crawled rapidly down the inner wall of the university. It was dark here and there were few Entroilians about. Moments later the thief reached the floor and ran into a tunnel that led down under the ground. There was a heavy thud as a door slammed shut behind. The ant stopped running. It glowed white in the gloom and Sam saw another insect waiting in a side-tunnel.

'Did you get it?' a voice said. It spoke perfect Entroilian.

The ant held up the Universe.

'Very good,' the Entroilian said. *I know that voice*, Sam thought. 'You know what to do with it.' The Entroilian's black hairy face was looming down at him. Its eyes were completely white.

'What are you doing down here?' Danny Schneider snapped as if Alex had just entered a forbidden zone. 'Go back you fool.' Danny's hard sharp features were still pinched with the tension of fighting the black hole, a tension which only deepened when he saw Alex flying towards him.

Okay, I get it, Alex thought. *For you no time has passed since the moment the hole hit the ground.* He stopped, giving the man time to adjust. *Why do I hate you so much Mr Schneider? It's not just because of Marianne. Of course I'm as jealous as hell, but I disliked you even before you married her. Look at you. You're not just afraid of that black hole. You're angry with it. You're angry because it's had the insolence to come and shit inside your beautiful ATLAS detector. I think you're more in love with that machine than you are with your beautiful wife.*

Danny's eyes widened as he caught sight of the bubbles moving around Alex. His head jerked about as he scanned them. There was no fear in his expression, just surprise, puzzlement and deepening anger. Then he frowned at Alex. 'What is that? What stupid game are you playing, Karolyi, you fool?'

Alex too felt his anger rise, and with it an overwhelming urge to move back just enough and leave Danny's withered black heart outside the bubbles. *I'd love to watch you die in agony you*

Austrian swine. That would really make my day. Nobody would know it wasn't an accident. With you gone and the baby dead, she'd be wide open for me to take her. But I can't do it. Marianne's had enough suffering for one day. I couldn't make her life worse. She wants you, Mr Perfect, not me, so I've got to play the messenger and deliver you to the clinic.

Alex pressed the crystal he was using to fly and moved closer, ensuring even Danny's feet were inside the bubble.

'You're floating!' Danny shouted and he too began to float, drifting up to the top of the bubble and bouncing off its roof with a cry of startled pain, then coming back down to Alex, his arms flailing, yelling in fury. One leg hit the bubble and he twisted and tried to cling onto Alex, knocking the crystal out of his hands. It went shooting away and disappeared in a closing window as its bubble separated from the others.

He's going to do some serious damage if I don't stop him.

Alex grabbed Danny's green jacket, twisted the man round and wrapped his arms round his waist but Danny kept struggling, his arms reaching up over his shoulders, trying to grab Alex's long hair. Alex jerked his head back and his hair flopped behind him. 'Stop that, you stupid bastard. I'm trying to help you!'

Although he had not had to fight since his days on the streets of Budapest, Alex had not forgotten how. He slid one arm up Danny's chest, wrapped it round one of Danny's arms and pushed on the back of his neck. Danny's head flopped down onto his chest, but he didn't give up easily. His free arm struggled even harder, but he was not a powerful man and was smaller and older than Alex.

Alex lifted his other hand and grasped Danny's throat. 'I'm gonna throttle you if you don't stop struggling, Schneider!' he hissed. 'Don't think I wouldn't like to, but Marianne wants to see you so I don't want to hurt you too much. Now for God's sake calm down.' He tightened his grip on Danny's windpipe, saying

'Stop struggling,' until Danny did as he was told.

'If I let go of your throat will you be a good boy?'

Danny nodded. Alex let him go and began to feel in his pocket for one of the other three crystals he had found. 'Good boy,' he said, speaking as calmly as he could. 'Now let me tell you what's happened. Gábor György has taken Marianne up to the Clinic. She wants to see you for some reason. You remember Marianne? Your wife?'

As he spoke Alex slowly released the pressure on Danny's head. Danny looked up as if he was searching for the stretcher, as if he didn't believe what Alex was saying.

Alex found a spare crystal, pulled it out of his pocket, brought it round in front of Danny's chest and held it up so he could see it. 'See this? It came out of the black hole. Did you see it explode?'

Danny looked at the crystal and frowned. 'Well, I saw a blue flash just after the black hole reached the cavern floor. That's the last thing I remember.'

'Yeah, there was a sort of pause. I was expecting the black hole to start absorbing the Earth, but luckily... Well, never mind that now. For now we have some other problems and the first one to sort out is to get you to the Clinic. I'm going to teach you to fly, but there's something I want you to see first.'

Alex began carrying Danny upwards. When they reached the beam pipe shield he flew round it until they met the corpse of the firefighter. Alex stopped so that Danny was staring straight into Robert Moore's agonised face.

'This is what happens to you if you let any part of your body outside this bubble. You get the picture, Mr Schneider? Okay, let's go.'

Alex followed the rope up the shaft into SX then hesitated, trying to work out the best way to get to the Clinic.

'Just stop here, Mr Karolyi. I'm not going any further until you explain to me exactly what's going on. ATLAS is my responsibility, or it was until half-past eight this morning when my shift ended. Technically it's Dr Soubise's responsibility but she isn't here, so I'm the next best thing and I want to know—I need to know—exactly what you think has happened.'

'It seems to me that time has stopped everywhere except inside one of these bubbles,' Alex said.

'That is complete nonsense Karolyi. Time cannot stop. Time and space form a four dimensional manifold. Have you never heard of Einstein's special theory of relativity? The universe isn't some sort of machine that you can turn part of it on and off.'

'Okay,' Alex said. 'Good point. Let's try an experiment. You got a watch?'

Danny showed him his watch.

'What time do you make it?'

'Eleven thirty-six.'

'By my watch it's five thirty.'

'So yours is a bit slow. So what?'

'No. Your watch is different because it was outside a bubble and it stopped. I've lived six hours more than you.'

Danny frowned. 'Let me see your watch. Take it off. Give it to me.'

Alex handed him his watch and Danny checked it. 'Okay, so both watches are working. Now, I will adjust the time on your watch so it is the same as mine. Okay?'

Alex shrugged. 'They're both wrong so it makes no difference.'

Danny adjusted Alex's watch and handed it back to him. 'Now leave that outside this thing you call a bubble.' Danny said.

They were hovering near the rope that led up from the shaft. Alex strapped his watch to it, then he led Danny along the rope to the fire engine where he pulled another piece of rope out of the back.

'We'd better stay roped together until you get used to flying.

Once you lose contact with the ground it can be hard to find your way back.'

He tied himself and Danny to the rope, then flew them both up into the middle of the SX building, gave Danny a piece of crystal and showed him how to fly. The engineer learned very quickly.

When he was proficient, Alex told him to keep the crystal and took another out of his pocket, thinking *Only one spare left now.*

It was tempting not to warn him about the danger of flying away into space, but after a moment's hesitation he told him about his experience with George. *There must be other ways to get rid of him which don't involve losing a precious crystal,* he told himself.

'Right,' Alex said. 'Now let's go and check my watch.'

They flew back down and Alex found his watch and gave it to Danny. 'They are different,' Danny said as he compared them. 'But they're both still working!'

'Surprise, surprise,' Alex said.

'Yours has only changed by a few seconds. I can't understand how this can be possible. This crystal and this bubble, none of it makes any sense. I think we need to ask Professor Romani about this. I'm only an engineer. This needs a top scientific brain.'

'Well that counts me out. Guess it's time for you to go see Marianne. Come on. I promised György I'd deliver you to the Clinic so that's what I'm gonna do.'

He escorted Danny as far as the Clinic Door. 'Marianne's in a pretty bad state,' Alex said, untying the rope that still held them together. 'Give her my love, won't you?'

'Do not be so insolent, young man. She does not want your love or anything else from you.'

'Maybe not, Mr Schneider, but she used to and I've got a feeling she will again, one day.'

'Why don't you come in and ask her?' Danny sneered. 'I'm sure she would be glad to tell you exactly what she thinks about you?'

'I'd love to, but I've got a little job to do first,' Alex said. He nodded, turned and flew back along the dotted line down the Route Einstein over the stationary cars and pedestrians frozen as they crossed the road. He began to think about his marketing plan.

It's not obvious what the strategy should be. There are plenty of disgustingly wealthy Genevans, even with the state of the Swiss economy, but will people really want to live in a frozen world? If time's frozen then there'll be no electricity, no heat, no shops, no TV, no radio. There might not even be any water in the taps. Looked at from the customer's point of view, maybe crystal isn't such a great buy after all. This needs a bit more thought.

Still, I might as well collect as many crystals as I can while I've got the chance, just in case I figure out a great way to sell them. I'll start with the one Schneider knocked out of my hand! If I don't get them somebody else will. Little Kata, maybe? No, she wouldn't know what to do with them. But Gábor György would. Oh yes, he will certainly want to claim them all for CERN.

Alex flew as fast as he could towards the cavern, trying to work out how long it would be before George arrived. *Only a matter of minutes I reckon. If Schneider tells him that I've flown away then György will know that I've found at least one more crystal. And even if Schneider doesn't tell him, György will figure it out for himself and go back to the ATLAS cavern sooner or later looking for more crystals. It's the obvious thing to do. I certainly don't want to be there when he arrives. So how long will it be before György follows me?*

Episode 24 Temptation of Alex

'Sam? Where are you, Sam? Where've you gone?'

There was no answer. Catriona turned the crystal round in her hands, looking at it from every angle, desperately searching for him.

The crystal was perfectly clear inside. She could see straight edges and corners where the faces met, misplaced and multiplied by reflections within the stone as if she was looking into a room full of mirrors. She could see reflected glimpses of the apparatus around her and distorted images of her own fingers holding the crystal but she could not see Sam.

She had seen him a second ago when she held the crystal close to her eye. He was in the middle of those strangely angled inner edges, very small and blurred, but it was him alright. She had seen his balding head, his silly little brown moustache, his blue Marks and Spencers suit stained with concrete dust, even the red handkerchief hanging out of his jacket pocket. But now she could not find him no matter where she pointed the gem. 'Where are you Sam?'

The stone was almost completely round

The crystal felt as hard and cold as glass as she turned it in her two hands. The stone was almost completely round, with many flat shiny faces all meeting in straight clean edges. It was as big as a tennis ball, much bigger than the little pyramid Alex had been using to fly with. As she turned it the inner faces rotated too, and sometimes there were little rainbow-coloured borders around reflected images of the things in the cavern, but Sam was nowhere to be seen. It was very frustrating.

Desperately she kept turning and calling but still Sam did not answer until finally, with a sob, she gave up. Her fingers closed tight around the crystal and her eyes closed tight against fate.

This isn't happening. It can't be! It can't be down to me to save the Earth. I'm not even fifteen! This isn't fair. I only wanted to come here to solve the mystery of daddy's death. I thought I was going to solve the mystery at last, after all these years. And then I met Alex and I thought I had found the man of my dreams. But then Michael was sucked up by that stupid black hole and Alex is in love with Marianne and doesn't care about me one jot and the whole world's disappeared and all I can see is this horrible bubble. It's just not fair! Why are all these bad things happening to me? What have I done wrong? Was there ever anyone so unhappy as me?

She gripped the big crystal tighter, wrapping her fingers round it is if it might somehow impart comfort through the palms of her hands.

And now Sam says I have to collect all these crystals and give them to George Gabor and tell him to take them down some stupid tunnel. What tunnel? There are millions of tunnels down here. Oh, I'm so confused. What's going on? I don't understand any of this and I don't want to. I don't want to be here. I wish I'd never persuaded Sam to come here. The whole idea was completely stupid. I don't want this to be happening. It's not happening, not really. It's a, it's a, a dream, a nightmare.

But she knew it wasn't. She peeped out of one eye and looked at the bubble surrounding her. It was horribly real, although somehow it looked bigger, much bigger than the other bubbles she had seen. Marianne's bubble had been tiny and cramped but this one reached far down the long narrow space beneath ATLAS.

Oh well, it's no good hanging around here. Suppose I'd better collect as many crystals as I can, like Sam told me. Why didn't Alex show me how to fly?

As soon as she said it she saw once more the blue light flying over the pond outside her father's laboratory on the night of her eighth birthday, and her eyes looked down at the crystal in her hands.

It's the same blue! It's exactly the same! That man was flying using a crystal! He must have been!

Catriona felt as if the whole world turned upside down at that moment and her heart began pumping so fast she thought it was going to burst out of her chest.

It was all true! The man shooting my father through the window. The bee flying down and catching the gunman and carrying his body off up into the sky. It was true, and Michael Zhang knows something. Everyone thought I was mad, and even I thought so sometimes, but I wasn't. The colour of this crystal and the fact that we can fly proves it. I wonder what Michael Zhang knows? I've got to ask him. Sam said he was at the bottom of the tunnel too. Maybe George Gabor will take me with him and I can go and ask him. Or maybe I'll be able to see him and talk to him through this crystal, the same way I did with Sam.

There was another bubble ahead of her. She put the big crystal into the pocket of her miniskirt, pulled herself into the second bubble and found another crystal jammed under a metal pipe. This one was small, like the one Alex had been using. She prised it out and just about managed to squeeze it into her pocket with the big one, then she began pulling herself through the tangle of equipment in the space beneath ATLAS, looking for more.

She found another small fragment and tried to put that into her pocket with the others but her skirt was too tight and the edges too sharp. She thought about putting it in her mouth but decided it wasn't clean. *And anyway it might be poisonous.* She ended up stuffing it into one side of her brassiere with the point sticking safely outwards into the padding. She now looked ridiculously lop-sided, one breast looking as if it had a huge pointed nipple, so she took the other small crystal out of her pocket and was just shoving that into the other side to balance herself up when Alex scared the life out of her by saying 'Have you found some of my crystals, little Kata, or are you just pleased to see me?' His long hair was boiling around his grinning face like a black halo.

She yanked her hand out of her bra, furious at him for laughing at her when she was only trying to do her best and when all this responsibility was driving her to distraction. The bitterness she had felt boiled back up inside her, but mixed with anger now. Somehow she felt that all of this was his fault.

After all, it was him who found the cosmic monopole StoreGate thing in the first place. It was him who pretended he liked me when really he was in love with Marianne. It was him who hid up on the balcony when Sam rushed down to help Danny fight the black hole. Maybe if he'd gone then he would have been taken away instead of my poor soft Sam. And that would have been good riddance to bad rubbish! He's nothing but a Don Juan.

'Go away, Alex Karolyi! Go and see if Marianne will have you back, but somehow I don't think she will. She told me you were seeing lots of other girls at the same time as you were going out with her. Is that true?'

A strange little half-smile twisted across his face. 'So you two had a nice girly chat about me, did you? And did you decide which one of you loves me most?'

'Don't be so sure of yourself!' she shouted. 'I can find better boys than you on the streets of Dublin any day of the week, thank you very much.' All the tension was coming out of her and she let rip. 'You haven't got any morals at all, have you? I can read you like a book, Alex Karolyi, and it's pure pornography. It's about time you realised that some boys love girls for what's inside them, not just for their looks or their bodies. You can't just trample on our emotions to suit yourself. I mean, some people love each other without ever even touching each other, but you wouldn't understand that, would you? Have you ever loved anyone, apart from yourself? Or are you just completely and utterly selfish?'

'I hear what you're saying, Kata,' Alex said, his smile gone. 'Look, it's none of your business, but for your information you are right. I used to just use women for my own evil ways until I met Marianne. I was hoping to marry her, except she went and made a stupid mistake and married Danny Schneider. That was the worst day of my life, I can tell you, and I've been trying to get her back ever since. If you can't accept that, then fine. I've got work to do. I want to collect as many crystals as I can before Gábor György arrives.'

'George is coming here? Good. I need his help. Sam said I had to collect all the crystals—'

'You've heard Sam again?'

She nodded. 'I saw him too. He said I have to give the crystals to George and tell him to take them all down the tunnel to Sam—'

'What tunnel?'

She shrugged. 'I don't know. So that Sam and Michael can restart time.'

There was complete seriousness on his face now. 'Did Sam say he could restart time?'

She nodded again. 'But only if I can collect all the crystals and get George to take them down the tunnel. Sam said it would be dangerous and I should take a man to help and George would be the best one.'

'You want György to help you? To do what?'

'I just told you. Are you deaf? I've got to collect all the crystals and give them to George and tell him to take them down the tunnel.'

'What tunnel?'

'I don't know,' she screamed. 'Sam said there's a tunnel.'

'Where?'

'I don't know,' she moaned. 'He thinks it's near where we last saw the black hole.'

'Where does this tunnel go?'

'To Sam.'

Alex thought about it. 'To be honest, Sweetie, I think you might have a problem persuading György to help you. He's a CERN man right down to the soles of his big black boots. As far as he's concerned, these crystals belong to CERN. I don't think he'll let you or Sam decide what will happen to them. That will be down to Francesco Romani. You remember him?'

She nodded. 'He's the fat Italian who brought us down here

this morning so Mother could meet Michael.'

'He's the Director General of CERN. He's the only person who can give you permission to take those crystals away.'

She thought about it. Francesco didn't look like he would easily part with the crystals either. She dare not ask him. 'I've got to get all the crystals down to Sam. Oh Alex, will you help me? Please?'

'Sure, I'll help you collect the crystals, Kata. No problem. Come on, let's get start—'

'No, I mean will you help me take them down the tunnel?'

'Now just hold on a minute, honey. You don't know anything about this tunnel. It could be dangerous. I mean, I'm all in favour of a calculated risk to make a profit, but I'm not too keen on jumping off cliffs—'

'Well then I'll have to save the Earth on my own.' When she heard herself say it she realised how ridiculous it sounded, ridiculous and impossible and horrible and stupid. *Everything is all horrible. Horrible. Horrible. Sam being sucked away and these crystals and this whole place and these bubbles and Alex Karolyi and everything. It's all just horrible. It's too much for any girl to take. Not on her own.* She started crying. *And I am on my own. Totally.* Once she started she couldn't stop.

Alex put his arms round her saying 'It's all right, little Kata'.

She tried to push him away but he was too strong and he stroked her hair making shushing noises. She lay in his arms, thinking wildly.

There isn't anyone else who can help me. It has to be Alex. I've got to get him on my side no matter what it costs. There are only two things he's interested in: crystals and girls. I've just got to help Sam and to do that I've got to get this foul man's help. I'm a girl, and I've got three crystals. They're the only things I have to offer. Well, if that's what it takes...

Choking back her sobs she reached up and laid her trembling hand on his. It was surprisingly soft and smooth.

'You feeling better now, little Kata?' he said.

Without a word she pulled his hand and laid it on her breast. She could feel the pressure as the crystal dug into his palm. She looked up into his face and forced herself to smile, thinking: *I'm sorry Sam, please forgive me for this. I'm trying to help you.* 'I've got two of these, Alex,' she said. 'Can you look after them for me?'

'Sure...' Alex said, but for once he sounded far from sure of himself.

Catriona lifted his hand away and pulled the brassiere cup down so he could get a good look at her breast with the crystal resting against the nipple. Alex's eyes widened then he frowned.

She pulled his hand, pressing his cold fingers around her breast. His fingertips stroked across her tingling skin as they closed around the crystal. 'If I...,' she whispered, hardly able to speak, her mouth was so dry. 'If I let you have me...would you...would you come and help me to find Sam and save the Earth?'

'I found some milk in the fridge,' George said as his bubble merged with Sofie's. She and the doctor were floating in the middle of the Medical Centre's reception area, huddling together inside one bubble. They had left Marianne without a crystal in the treatment room at the far end of the little Infirmary, and come back here because George had said they all needed a drink. Now he handed them each a plastic bottle filled with milk.

It felt cold as Sofie gently squeezed the bottle and began lapping the exquisitely delicious liquid from the top.

'It's just as I thought,' George said, a white moustache of milk curving over his upper lip. 'There's no electricity, no water, no gas, nothing. The toilet won't flush. It's a good job there's only a few people alive. It would be a disaster if everyone had survived.'

Sofie was wondering why the milk was still cold when she

heard an angry cry and a man in a green jacket flew into the reception area, his bubble merging with theirs.

'Ah Danny,' George said. 'Marianne's further down the corridor. Doctor, this is Marianne's—'

'Karolyi said there was a problem with Marianne,' Danny snapped. He sounded angry. 'Is the baby okay?'

'I have some bad news for you, I'm afraid Mr Schneider,' the doctor said. 'I'm sorry to tell you your son was stillborn.' A blank look descended onto Danny's face as if somebody had dropped an invisible bag over his head. Sofie felt as if she knew what he was going through. She had shared the agony with Marianne and wanted to give him a hug, so they could comfort each other, but there was something that held her back. She had never met Marianne's husband before, and she was surprised at what she saw. He was a fair bit older than Marianne, about thirty-five Sofie guessed. His face was careworn and his skin yellow. It wasn't surprising, after all that had happened to him. She knew he was one of the people who had been trying to fight the black hole. But there was something utterly cold about him. He didn't look like the kind of man that you would ever want to snuggle up to. Sofie wondered what Marianne saw in him. Marianne, even in the state she was in today, was a very beautiful girl. She could have got somebody much better than him.

'Are you happy to discuss this in front of these two people?' the doctor was saying.

'What? I'm sorry?' Danny seemed unable to understand him.

'I need to talk to you about your wife's treatment. I assume you're a scientist?'

'No, I'm an engineer,' Danny said, his voice dull and lifeless.

'Okay. So I had a bit of a problem when deciding on the handling of your wife's case, Mr Schneider, and I just want to check with you that you're happy with what I decided. Can we talk about it now?'

Danny gave him half a nod.

'Thank you,' the doctor said. 'Now, according to Mr Gabor, time is frozen outside a bubble. I'm not entirely convinced on that point but—'

'It's true, doctor,' Danny said, coming back to life a little. 'I did an experiment and proved it. It goes totally against the basic laws of relativity but it's true.'

'Well I'm not a scientist either, Mr Schneider, just a humble medic, but given that your wife delivered her baby in conditions of complete lack of asepsis which could obviously lead to serious infection—'

'I'd like to know what happened,' Danny said.

'Of course. Sofie was there,' the doctor nodded at her, 'and I'm sure she'll tell you about it in a minute, but as I was saying, conditions were not sterile. As you can imagine, this is the first time I have ever treated a patient under conditions where time doesn't function. I doubt if any doctor ever has. I have no experience to guide me so I have to rely on my judgement or, if you prefer, on my instinct. There's another complication which is that there's no electricity here, no running water, and the fireman thinks that this will apply even in the hospital.'

'Yes I do,' George Gabor said. 'Time has stopped. Everything's frozen.'

'When I first saw Mrs. Schneider,' the doctor said, 'I considered it prudent to administer a strong antibiotic as a precaution, and I'm sure that was the right decision. However that raises the question now of whether she should be left outside a time bubble or whether she would be better inside one. This is the point I need to consult with you over.'

The doctor paused. Sofie looked at Danny. His eyes had glazed over again. He's not listening to you doctor, Sofie thought.

'The two sides of the argument are this,' the doctor went on. 'If we put her inside a time bubble, then the antibiotic will begin to fight any infection she may have, whereas if we leave her outside a bubble, as she is now, then I assume the infection will be suspended and will not get any worse. However, there is a risk to this, the risk being that bacteria might not be suspended. I don't know anything about how this suspension works. So what I want is your opinion on whether we should leave her outside a bubble or put her inside one.'

A silence descended on the four people as they waited for Danny to answer.

'There's a practical issue too,' George Gabor said. 'If we give Marianne a piece of crystal then that would leave us only two fragments between the four of—'

'I'm sorry,' the doctor cut in, 'but I don't think that should be a consideration in this decision. The welfare of the patient must come first. As well as the infection,' he went on, turning again to Danny, 'there is also the abdominal injury to consider. I took the—'

'Injury?' Danny said. 'What injury?'

'Oh, you don't know? A piece of crystal hit her abdomen and passed into her uterus. But I'm much less concerned about the lesion than about infection. Postpartum uterine contraction has reduced and sealed the lesion but the infection, both from the wound and from the birth, is a much bigger issue.'

Danny looked at the doctor as if he was trying to understand a foreign language.

'You mean...Did it hurt the baby?

'Yes it did. It struck him, I'm afraid. This was the cause of his death.'

Danny was obviously stunned. 'You're telling me that Dragomir was killed by a piece of crystal?'

'Yes, Mr Schneider,' the doctor said.

'You mean it wasn't the breech?'

'Was he breech? I didn't know. No, even if he had not been

breech he would never have survived.'

'The crystal killed him,' Danny muttered. 'The crystal!' Then he looked around at the three of them. 'Where is it now?'

'He's in the helicopter—'

'No! The crystal. Where is it now?'

The doctor looked at Sofie. 'Well I'm trying to remember.'

It was this one, Sofie thought, glancing at the crystal she was holding with a feeling of disgust.

The doctor said 'Let me think. I took it out of his skull and—'

'Oh my God,' Danny moaned.

'—and I gave it to you, I think, didn't I?'

'Yes I think so,' Sofie said. 'There was so much going on—'

'So have you still got it?'

'No,' George said. 'Sofie gave it to Karolyi, Mr Schneider.'

'That's right,' Sofie said with sudden relief, 'I gave it to Karolyi—'

'Karolyi!' Danny said with a sort of snarl. 'Karolyi has Drago's crystal? That's too much. Why did you give it to him?'

'George told me to, so that he could come down to rescue you, Mr Schneider,' Sofie said.

'What's that?' Danny looked at her then slowly took his crystal out of his pocket. 'You mean it's this? The one Karolyi gave me?'

'I don't know, Mr Schneider. I suppose it must be.'

Danny stared at it in amazement then his fist closed around it. 'Unless it was the other one.'

'What other one?' George said.

Episode 25 George Returns to ATLAS

Sofie thought she could see an avalanche approaching behind George Gabor's eyes. His pale face had gone completely white as he stared at Danny Schneider. Finally the avalanche rumbled out of his mouth. 'Karolyi has another crystal? I don't believe this!'

'He has more than one, I believe,' the sombre Austrian replied. 'There seemed to be several bubbles surrounding him.'

'Good God,' George said spinning round to face Sofie and the doctor with the avalanche rising to a crescendo. 'There could be hundreds of these freaking fragments down there and we've been sitting up here huddling between just two! Okay, okay,' he said as he gained control over the avalanche but still looking at Sofie with a steely hard glint in his eye, 'I obviously need to go down and help the poor little chap look for more. I'm sure the greedy fat pig is only collecting them for the good of everyone else. Not!'

'But that doesn't answer my question,' the doctor said with a tone of impatience. 'Should we put Marianne into a bubble or leave her frozen? Do you have any thoughts about that, Mr Schneider?'

'If time really is frozen outside a bubble, which I think I must accept for the time being,' Danny said, 'then it must be frozen for everything, bacteria as well as people. I proved that Karolyi's watch stops when you leave it outside the bubble. There's not a lot of difference between a watch and a bacterium as far as I can see so I think they must stop growing too. I cannot imagine how the bubble might affect one and not the other. I think it's best to leave Marianne outside a bubble until we can get her to hospital.'

'Thank you,' the doctor said with relief. 'That accords precisely with my own appraisal of the situation.'

'Okay, so we've got three crystals here,' George Gabor said briskly. 'I suggest that you three stay here and share two of them while I fly down with the third and see if I can find my friend Karolyi and get a few more. Everybody agreeable?'

They all nodded.

'So,' Danny said, as George flew away towards the Infirmary door, 'can you please tell me what happened when the baby was born?'

Sofie did not want to relive that horrific time any more than she had to, but Danny had a right to know. Marianne was his wife, after all. She described the events as briefly as she could. It was painful for them both. As she spoke, the glazed look came back into Danny's eyes as if he was watching the scene playing out at the back of his mind. By the time she had finished, the invisible bag seemed to have fallen over his head once more.

Sofie handed him her half-empty bottle of milk and he squeezed it into his mouth absentmindedly, with his face a stony wall of sadness. A long silence fell upon the three of them. She wondered whether the doctor should offer him a tranquilliser but even seeing Danny in this state, Sofie still didn't feel she could comfort him any more than she could hug an injured tiger.

'Can I have a look at that crystal for a minute, Sofie?' the doctor said eventually.

She handed him her crystal, glad of anything to break this awful silence, and watched him compare the two crystals, one in each hand. 'They seem to be identical,' he said. 'Same size, same colour. Even their bubbles seem to be the same size.' Sofie saw a little ridge opening up between the two bubbles as he moved the crystals away from each other. Then he brought then back together and their bubbles merged into one, the colours brighter and—

'Good God!' the doctor said with a tone of alarm. Sofie looked at him. He looked surprised, frightened, and let go of the crystal as if it had bitten his hand.

'What's wrong?' Danny said, still sipping his milk.

The doctor didn't answer, just stared at the crystal floating in the air before him. Sofie looked at it too and her eyes widened. 'Oh!' she said.

'What?' Danny's angry glance flashed from the doctor to Sofie.

'Can't you see?' the doctor said.

'See what?' Danny exploded, milk spraying out of his mouth and drifting in a fine white mist towards the doctor. He seemed to be looking at the world from a long way away.

'Look Mr Schneider!' the doctor said reaching out and taking the crystal from where it was floating before him. 'Can't you see? We had two crystal fragments before. Now there's only one, but it's twice as big as before!'

It's twice as big as before!

Danny was frowning at the double-crystal but Sofie's eyes were wandering around the Infirmary. 'But doctor,' she said quietly. 'Where's the bubble gone?'

As soon as his hand touched Catriona's breast the frown vanished from Alex's face, instantly replaced by a look of hot anger. He yanked his hand away with the crystal in his fist and waved it before her face. 'How old are you Kata?'

She reached up and gently stroked his face, blowing kisses at him. 'I'm sixteen, darling,' she pouted.

'No you're not!' he shouted. 'You're thirteen at the most! Put that away,' he said with a nod at her breast.

Catriona let the brassiere cup slap back over her little breast with a hollow flop. *So that's why I failed. My boobs aren't big enough for him yet. Marianne has big ones. So does Mother.* Catriona remembered how Alex had stood gawping down into Ambassador O'Brien's cleavage during the journey down in the lift this morning. *He's a boob man. The world's going to be destroyed for want of a pair of big breasts! How pathetic is that?*

'Now I know you think I'm a totally selfish bastard Kata,' Alex was saying, 'and I guess most of the time you're right. There are reasons. I'll tell you about them sometime. And it's true, I like women, I like them very much, but I don't abuse little girls like you, Sweetie. I never have and I never will.'

His face was deathly white. *He's really angry with me. Oh God, I've blown it!* She could feel the tears of despair starting to well up from the pit of her stomach.

Alex breathed in deeply and checked his watch. 'I do realise how important this is, Kata. We're all in a critical situation. Time's stopped and if Sam says he can fix it then we've got to help him. I know that. We've got no choice have we? You don't need to sell your body to me, Catriona. I do have a few morals left, you know.'

The tears had reached her chest by now and as they passed her beating heart they seemed to change colour, from deep painful purple into tender pinky-blue. She stared at him as they bubbled up into her eyes so that Alex was swimming around in two little pools. One seemed to be made of sadness tears and one of joy tears, but she was totally unsure which emotion she ought to be feeling. It was agonising ignorance.

'You mean, you mean you'll, you'll come?' she whispered. It was the hardest sentence she had ever spoken in her life.

'Yes, I'll come. I'll come with you. Didn't you know that Hungarians are well known for their suicidal tendencies?'

'Thank you, Alex,' she said quietly, and gently kissed his cheek. She wanted him now, wanted to give herself to him now, in deepest gratitude. *I don't care what you've done with other girls,* she silently pledged herself to him. *You are a good man. I'm the only one who really understands you. I'm yours now Alex, yours whenever you want me, yours forever my darling.* His cheek felt fuzzy on her lips and when she smelt his musky aroma she felt the passion for him surging back, stronger than ever. *Everything's going to be all right now you're on my side.*

She knew this wasn't the same puppy love she had felt this morning. Now she was feeling like a woman feels. *I want to feel you inside me. I've never felt like that about any boy before.* 'Alex,' she said, stroking his forehead as he looked at his watch, 'I want you to—'

'Listen, Sweetie,' Alex said. 'György could come here any second. We've got to collect all the crystal we can find and then get the hell out of here and go somewhere safe and see if we can talk to Sam again and find out exactly what he wants us to do.'

'All right. Sounds like a good plan. We've got two weeks so it's not that urgent. I need to collect stuff for the journey anyway. Sam told me to take a toothbrush.'

'A toothbrush?' Alex laughed. 'What, no toilet paper? Okay, so let's see how many crystals we can find in the next five minutes. Where have you looked so far?'

'All along here. I was going that way.'

'Okay, let's carry on down there. Danny Schneider made me

drop a crystal on the other side, so we can look for that too.'

They pulled themselves along the narrow gap below ATLAS, the space lit by the faint blue glow coming from their crystals. After five minutes they had only found two more. Alex slipped them both into his pockets. Then they went round to the other side of ATLAS, but only found the one that Danny had knocked out of his hand.

'Okay,' he said. 'I can't see any more and anyway we're running out of time. György might come down here any second. Before we go, let's just see if we can find this mysterious freaking tunnel. You say it's near where we last saw the black hole?'

Catriona shrugged. 'Sam said he thought it might be.'

They pulled themselves past the Big Wheel into the space beyond the end of ATLAS and Alex took one of his crystals out of his pocket. 'Let me teach you how to fly first. Get your other one out, Sweetie.' He grinned at her. 'The crystal I mean, not your boob!'

She slipped the fragment out of her bra and he showed her how to use it. She found it very difficult to master the finer points of crystal control. 'That'll have to do for now,' Alex said after half a minute's practice. 'Let's get out of here before György shows up.'

'No, wait a minute. I thought you said we were going to look for the tunnel? Can't we try, just for one minute?'

'Shees... All right then, come on then. The last place I remember seeing the black hole was near the ground.'

Swervingly she followed him down to the floor and crossed the gap between the Big Wheels. They began to search, flying back and forth across the floor several times, widening their path each time until they reached the cavern's side.

'It's not here!' Catriona said feeling bitterly disappointed. 'Sam must have been wrong about the tunnel. What are we going to do now?'

'You're expecting it to be like a man-hole in the road are you Sweetie? I don't think it'll be like that Kata. If this tunnel exists then it won't be a normal physical tunnel like we're used to. I think it's some sort of hole in space-time. My guess is it'll be very, very small. Don't you remember what happened to Sam and Michael when they were absorbed by the black hole?'

She nodded. 'They shrank,' she said in a tiny voice. She remembered it all very clearly. It was forever burned into her memory: Danny shouting 'Okay, here goes,' as he switched on the electric current and the black hole suddenly lurching down past Marianne's stretcher towards the magnetic tube. Catriona remembered screaming 'Oh no!' and seeing the tube lift as if it was being sucked up by a vacuum cleaner with Sam and Michael stuck to it, spinning in mid-air and shrinking away to nothing. It had all happened in a moment but she could still see every tiny detail.

'Yes, and I think the tunnel might be very small too. See this?' They had flown back to the middle of the cavern floor and he was pointing at a small round depression in the concrete between the Big Wheels, a tiny dent getting narrower as it went down. It was white and clean on the inside as if something had recently chipped it out.

'That little thing? What about it?'

'Maybe that's it. I told you I didn't think it would be very big. It's the only—'

'Now come on, Alex. We're looking for a tunnel, not one of Marianne's dimples.'

'But think about how Sam and Michael shrank, Kata! The black hole was very small.'

'But the black hole isn't there anymore, Alex! If that's the start of the tunnel then we're never going to get into it. We've failed before we've even started! Sam will never get this,' she said, looking at the crystal in her hand. This was too much to bear.

She felt as if her heart were breaking.

'Of course we haven't failed, Sweetie. Don't give up so easily. Do you want me to look after that for you? Is it your last one?'

'No, I've still got this one.' She gave him the little crystal and took the big round one out of her pocket.

'Jeepers!' he said, taking the small crystal but with wide eyes drinking in the extraordinary majesty of the large one. 'What a whopper! So that's where this big bubble's coming from.'

His eyes moved upwards, admiring the large bubble that spanned the space between the two Big Wheels. 'I was wondering—'

His smile suddenly vanished. Catriona looked up too and saw a pair of large black boots sticking through a hole in the top of their big bubble. She gasped but Alex put his hand over her mouth. 'It's Gábor,' he hissed.

She watched the boots move across the top of their bubble. They were hanging through a little round window where the firefighter's bubble intersected theirs. She could see his grey overalls foreshortened as she looked up along the length of his body, but she could not see his face. He stopped and her heart seemed to stop too. He hung in the air for a few seconds, then flew on rapidly towards ATLAS and she lost sight of him as his bubble moved away from theirs.

'Quick,' Catriona said as soon as he was gone, her heart pounding. 'We've got to find that tunnel.'

'I don't think we can find it, not now Sweetie. Let's get out of here and come back to look for the tunnel when Gábor's gone.'

'Which tunnel would that be, Mr Karolyi?' George's voice boomed as he flew across the floor towards them.

'Hang on Kata!' Alex said as he flew his crystal with one hand and grabbed her arm with the other, pulling her after him. Inertia carried her round to his back. She jammed her crystal in her pocket and wrapped her arms round his waist. Alex let go and used both hands to accelerate away from George. When he reached the Big Wheel at the end of the cavern, Alex swerved upwards, the brown plates flashing past him like a muddy field. Glancing down, Catriona could see George in hot pursuit, his bubble overlapping hers, his face contorted with rage, his hands outstretched before him controlling his crystal. 'He's gaining on us!' she screamed. 'Faster Alex!'

A moment later, Alex reached the huge blue pipe that ran across the gap between the two Big Wheels. He swerved around it, sending Catriona flapping from side to side like a cloak, then continued heading up towards the ceiling. She glanced back and was horrified to see George's grasping fingers. He was holding his crystal in one hand and the other was groping for her feet. She could see from the vicious look on George's face that Alex had been right about him. *He's never going to let me take the crystals down to Sam.*

She snapped her legs up, lifting her heels as high as she could, but that still left George's hand almost touching Alex's shoes. At that moment Alex must have reached the cavern ceiling because he swerved sharply. George seemed to anticipate his next move and began swerving too. *He's going to catch us if I don't do something.* There was only one thing she could think of. Forcing herself to imagine George as the enemy, she closed her eyes and wildly kicked both feet. One heel made contact with something hard and she heard a howl. Nervously she looked down to see blood running across George's eyes before he vanished from sight as the window between their bubbles closed.

'We've lost him!' she yelled as Alex flew across the white curving ceiling, following one of the huge shiny metal ducts which hung below it. She remembered seeing these before, when she had been standing on the balcony looking up at the winch rope hanging from the wide shaft in the cavern roof. *This pipe leads up to the surface. We're going to escape!*

Rioting around inside her was a painful mixture of triumphal exhilaration and awful guilt. *I just kicked a man in the face, a man who had saved my life on the stairs. I hope he's all right.*

She had never before felt such an exquisite confusion of anticipation and grief, of hope and fear, and this feeling was redoubled a moment later as a hole opened in the bottom of her bubble and George came hurtling up towards them once more, blood still spurting from a cut in one eyebrow and splashing starkly red across his white face, every feature of which revealed his rage.

I've got to stop him. Without even thinking about it she pushed herself off Alex's back directly into George's path. *At least Alex might get away.* Released from her weight, Alex shot away up the huge shaft as George crashed into her, knocking the breath out of her body. With a horrible curse he grabbed her and hurtled her downward with all his strength, then flew past her up the shaft.

For several seconds she floated free, struggling to get her breath back as coloured patterns flowed around the large bubble which surrounded her big crystal. Finally she managed to force herself to breathe in just as she crashed into one of the Big Wheels. She clung to a flat brown segment, her stomach muscles aching, trembling from the shock of what had just happened, feeling utterly alone and terrified that George would come down and catch her and take her last crystal off her but hoping all the while that it would be Alex who would fly down and carry her away to safety.

She waited for what seemed like hours. *Has George caught Alex? Which of them can fly the fastest? Well I can't just stay here. If George comes back I'm done for. He's going to be really angry with me. Oh, I hope I haven't hurt him too much. I didn't mean to hurt you, George, I really didn't. I suppose I've got to try to find this stupid tunnel on my own before he comes.*

She put her hand in her pocket and pulled the big crystal out. As soon as she saw it an idea came into her mind. 'Sam!' she called, 'Sam!' looking into the crystal. 'Can you hear me?' There was no answer. Inside she could only see the shimmering multitude of glittering edges. 'Sam please answer.' A conviction began to grow in her that if Sam didn't help her now she would never find the tunnel, never save the Earth, and her heart began to break. She had failed. 'Sam! Please Sam! Please please answer me darling.'

She had never called Sam "darling" before. She had never realised before this very moment how much she loved him. He was more than a father to her. He was a friend. He alone had listened to her story about the bee when everyone else said she was making it up. He had always been there for her when Mother was off making TV programmes and going to fancy balls and receptions. Last year he had even given up the chance of becoming a headmaster. He pretended he didn't want the job, but really she knew it was because he wanted to be there for her. He was the best man in the whole world and she was trying her best to help him now, as he had helped her, but he wasn't there. 'For God's sake Sam!' she called, but there was no answer, only the deafening sound of her own voice echoing off the brown plate and then there was a roar and a rush and a movement above her and she looked up to see a bloody face flying down the Big Wheel towards her.

She grabbed the crystal in her two trembling hands and pressed it, trying to fly away from him. She still hadn't learned to fly properly and George swooped down on her like an eagle, his face a fierce mask of anger and then she heard Alex say 'Press the top Kata,' and she pressed the top of her crystal and she was suddenly shooting downwards and Alex's voice said 'Point it to the left' and she turned it how she thought he meant and she was flying along just centimetres from the floor and the dimple they had seen in the concrete was dead ahead of her.

'That's it Kata. Fly into it!'

Time seemed to stand still for a second. She held the big crystal between her two hands as tightly as she could, pressing one face with both thumbs until she was pointing straight at the shallow depression in the ground and then she jammed her thumbs into the back of the crystal like Alex had showed her before and she shot forward and the depression was coming towards her fast but in slow motion and she knew that if she missed the entrance to the tunnel and hit the concrete then she would break her neck and she knew that this might not even be the tunnel but it was her only hope. She had to try because if she didn't get away from George into that damned tunnel then he would get this crystal and nobody would ever take it down because people are so stupid and selfish and short-sighted and childish and Sam and Michael would die down there without it and the Earth and the Universe would stay frozen like this for ever.

So Catriona O'Brien, fourteen and a half years old, flew at one hundred and sixty-seven kilometres per hour head-first into a tiny dip in the concrete floor of the ATLAS cavern.

Michael's Diary: Cosmic Egg 2

I desire to record my knowledge for the benefit of all Entroilia. I have to complete this task during my development because, once I am mature, I anticipate having far more important tasks to fulfil. Hence, over the past few days, I have dictated a summary of the history of the Cosmic Egg to the Princess Uskabellu, a record which she has deposited in the Sedtia Library.

That task is now complete, and I have begun to record this, your intimate history, Oh marvellous Monopole, dictated in secret and kept strictly hidden. It will contain my private reflections and speculation upon what has transpired since time stopped. For although I know everything which happened inside the Cosmic Egg prior to breaking the event network, and I know that Sam Fitzpatrick was able to communicate with humans in the time-frozen Universe, but I have little idea what has happened since I was removed from the Cosmic Egg. All I know is what Uskabellu tells me, and although she tries hard to obtain information on my behalf, she certainly does not have direct access to all the relevant information, nor is her memory infallible.

My dearest wish now is that the event network can be repaired and time restarted in the Universe. I regard this as absolutely essential in order for me to achieve my goals. Uskabellu has reported that Fitzpatrick did indeed follow my instructions and told his step-daughter Catriona to bring all the fragments of the broken pipe down the Time Tunnel. So allow me to explain, Oh Monopole Supreme, the configuration of this tunnel as I understand it.

   Here is the remainder of the diagram drawn for you with loving care by the Princess Uskabellu.

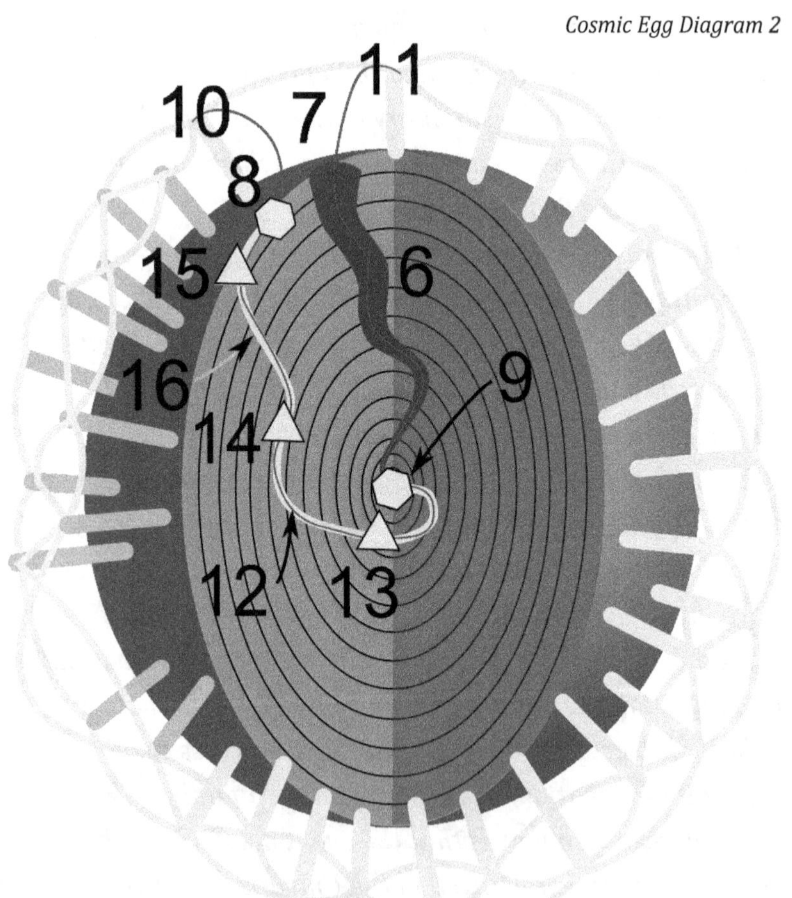

Cosmic Egg Diagram 2

   When I broke one of the pipes in the event network (which Uskabellu has shown as a gap 7), this had several consequences. One was that events stopped flowing throughout the network and the rain stopped. As a direct result, time stopped everywhere within the Cosmic Egg, and hence also within my universe which forms part of it. This was my intention. My home planet would not now be absorbed by the black hole and, what is more, Entroilia was now safe from more emergents.

For I should explain that, although I have never admitted this to anyone, my motive for breaking the crystal network was not just to protect the Earth, but also to prevent other humans from being absorbed by the black hole and arriving here in Entroilia.

You know nothing of the human race, Oh Monopole, so I have to inform you that mankind is not inherently suited to wield such knowledge, for with knowledge comes power. Men achieved a great deal during the last ten thousand years of their history, using the power bestowed upon them by increasingly sophisticated technology, and latterly by science, but their minds have not evolved at anything like the same rate as their knowledge. They still have a tribal mentality and find it almost impossible not to compete with each other. Competition is in their genes. They have built it into their educational, social, judicial, economic and political systems. Aggressors are always more successful in competitive environments.

In their rush to follow the leading university, the winning team, the best lawyer, the biggest company or the party with the most power, other men will readily trample underfoot the visionary, the individual, the weak, the gentle or the pacifist. Such a species is not capable of responsibly exercising the enormous power bestowed by complete knowledge. I resolved therefore to prevent others from following me out of the Cosmic Egg. It was the only way to save both the Earth and Entroilia from destruction by these aggressive creatures. I had to arrest the functioning of the event mechanism.

Thus, for what seemed to me two very good reasons, I broke the event network and consequently stopped time in the Cosmic Egg. But there were other, unintended consequences which I admit I had not foreseen.

Unknown to me at that time, the event network had been designed to cope with exactly this circumstance. When I broke the pipe, it sent out a signal to alert the Entroilians that an emergent had appeared. A worker soon arrived to feed me and thereafter I received the food and care I needed. From that moment to this I have been here in the Entroilian nursery, gradually growing through the larval stages of development which all Entroilians follow.

Soon afterwards, Professor Cjingha Itoodoo collected the Egg itself and took it away for microscopic examination. I had not anticipated this either, and it has subsequently led to the theft of the Egg by the Argolaths.

Other consequences followed when the fragments of the crystal pipe which I had broken fell down to the surface of the Cosmic Egg.

Two of these fragments (which Uskabellu has shown by the blue hexagons 8 and 9), were larger than the others. These had originally been sitting on top of the two tall crystals at the point where the broken pipe met many others (10 and 11). I will call these large crystals "End Fragments".

When the two End Fragments reached the pink event record, they floated at first. But one of them (9) must have fallen into the burrow which I had created (6). It slid down the burrow, going back in time to the very beginning of history at the centre of the Egg.

Now you need to be aware, Oh Wonderful Monopole, of an important additional fact about the crystalline network which constitutes the outer shell of all cosmic eggs.

The pipes not only conduct event particles and allow them to rain down upon the pink surface, so allowing time to flow. Each pipe also has, embedded within it, a bundle of exotic, microscopically thin strings made of matter consisting of negative energy. They are fundamental to the physics which enable cosmic eggs to function. Different eggs contain different numbers and arrangements of these negative energy strings. This is one of the major differences between eggs.

Unlike the crystals which form an egg's outer shell, negative energy strings are elastic. Even after I broke the crystal pipe, the negative energy strings remained intact, still joining together all of the fragments. Even as they fell down towards the surface of the event record, the fragments were still strung out along the negative energy bundle, like beads on a necklace.

Uskabellu has shown the bundle of negative energy strings as a thin blue line which starts and ends where the two End Fragments used to be (10 and 11). Here it joins the negative energy strings in the rest of the crystal network.

Sam Fitzpatrick soon found his way into the gap (10) created when End Fragment 8 fell down to the pink event record. It was these invisible strings which would later allow him to see and hear out of the crystal fragments far below him. And this proves that the negative energy strings remain intact.

As End Fragment 9 slipped down my burrow (6), it carried with it the rope of negative energy strings. One half of the rope was left winding up the burrow until it joined with the other crystals in the shell (11). These strings within my burrow had a very important effect, which arose from the fact that negative energy is gravitationally repulsive. I do not have time now to explain how this repulsive gravitational force is caused, but it had the effect of holding my burrow open. I am hoping that this will prove extremely useful later.

The other End Fragment (8) still floated on the surface of the pink event record, which corresponded to the very moment in history when time stopped. Thus the two End Fragments found themselves separated in time, one at the start of time, the other at the end.

As End Fragment 9 sank down the burrow, the rope of strings between the two End Fragments (12) was dragged down into the event record, and it carried with it most of the smaller fragments which had originally formed the long body of the pipe. Uskabellu has shown two of these as blue triangles 13 and 14. They sliced down through the pink event record, penetrating into deeper layers and hence going back in time. Eventually almost all the small fragments were submerged within the layers of the pink event record, each one at a different point in the historical record.

Not all the small fragments were dragged down, however. It seems that some of them remained floating on the surface *near the upper End Fragment. Uskabellu has shown one of them at 15. It appears that there was a small cluster of them within the ATLAS cavern.*

As I have explained, the most important consequence of my breaking the crystal pipe is that the whole Universe is frozen in time. However there is one exception. Because the crystals are still linked to the negative energy strings, they are still in contact with time. Each fragment is therefore surrounded by a bubble of time. Any object which happens to lie in close proximity to one of these fragments also retains time. That is why some people, such a Sam's stepdaughter Catriona, are still alive.

Because the bundle of negative energy strings (12) have gravitational repulsion, a new tunnel must have opened up around it once the bundle was inside the Cosmic Egg. Uskabellu has shown this new tunnel in green (16). I will call it the "Time Tunnel". I assume this links together all the crystal fragments which originally formed the pipe which I broke. It is this Time Tunnel upon which all my hopes are pinned.

I am convinced that, if Catriona is able to collect all the fragments of crystal on the frozen Earth (such as 8 and 15) and then go down this tunnel and collect all the other fragments scattered along its length (such as 14 and 13) along the way, and bring them down to the centre of the Cosmic Egg, then collect the End Fragment she will find there (9), she should then be able to leave the universe and ascend up my burrow (6) to emerge entirely from the Cosmic Egg.

Professor Itoodoo should then easily be able to reassemble the fragments to re-create the broken pipe. Indeed, because these fragments are crysorganic, they should even reassemble themselves once placed together in the correct sequence. If she replaces this pipe where it had originally stood (7) then I see no reason why time should not restart within the egg. I have discussed this plan with Itoodoo and she agrees it should work.

And yet I have severe doubts that this young girl Catriona is capable of completing this task on her own. Yet if she fails, or if she does not bring all the pipe fragments with her, then the Universe will stay frozen forever. That would be a tragedy with the most catastrophic consequences not just for the people of Earth, not just for the Universe, but for Entroilia itself.

The fate of all this hangs by the feeblest of threads, namely the life and spirit of a young girl called Catriona. May the Beeing protect her during her enterprise, perhaps the greatest ever embarked upon by any human.

Appendices

For the reader's convenience, I have added in the following pages some information which might prove useful when trying to follow the events and ideas described in Time Crystal.

The appendices consist of the following sections:

Principal Participants

This is far from a complete list of the people involved in this story, but I include it to help the reader become more familiar with the main participants.

Glossary

A list of some of the technical terms used within this book.

Bibliography

A list of the references to books, websites and other sources of information to which I have referred in this book, mainly in the footnotes.

Principal Participants

Alex Karolyi

Alex Karolyi was born in Hungary on 3 January 1986, making him a 26 year old Capricorn on **Crystal Day**. He claims to descend from Count Mihály Ádám György Miklós Károlyi de Nagykároly (1875 – 1955) who was briefly Hungary's Prime Minister and then President in 1918-19 during a short rare spell of democracy. Many people question whether this story is true, however.

Alex was the eldest child of a small import/export wine merchant in Budapest and his mother was a flighty woman of Austrian descent who was too busy chasing men to look after Alex.

As a child, Alex remembers constantly crying for his mother. When he realised that she was not going to look after him, at about the age of eight, he decided he must take care of himself. This determination was sealed when his father's business collapsed, his father turned to drink and his mother committed suicide.

From that moment, he had to take care of himself, and devoted his time to making money. Initially he sold newspapers on the streets of Budapest, rarely going to school. His life on the streets soon led him into petty crime and eventually into buying and selling drugs.

He was rescued from this decline on one of his rare trips to school where an inspiring teacher, recognising his natural talent and intelligence, taught him how to program a computer one afternoon. From that moment Alex was inspired with the idea of starting a programming business. He soon wrote a successful program, gave up the drugs business and started a software company.

He now runs more than ten companies, all based in Eastern Europe. His ambition is to be a millionaire within the next year. His software company not only wrote Atlantis (the programme the **ATLAS** scientists use to visualise particle events) but also all the simulations in the ATLAS Observation room, the Globe of Science and Innovation and the Microcosm beneath the **CERN** Reception.

Until he met Marianne, Alex had a butterfly personality, flitting from woman to woman, from one new scheme to another, never spending much time or energy on anything. Like most extroverts, he seemed unable to commit himself to any one thing, incapable of devoting his attention to anything for very long. He was fun-loving and did not hesitate to indulge himself in the pleasures of life, and for this he needed as much money has he could get.

All this changed when he fell in love with Marianne. He seemed to have found the stability which he had always lacked in his life.

Nevertheless he is still a risk-taker, but he always tries to calculate the risk first. He is still charming, especially with women, but his laid-back appearance is deceptive. He is now capable of extremely hard work, especially when a deadline is looming, and his businesses have boomed with his new-found stability, which is one more reason why he is convinced he needs to have Marianne as a permanent part of his life.

Alex Karolyi

He has thick long black hair above a sun-tanned face in which nestle two beautiful dark-chocolate eyes. He is fully aware of their power on women. His lips are thick and sensuous, his nose not too large, and his body is tall and muscular, although his hands are surprisingly small and beautiful. He always dresses for summer, even in the middle of winter, and almost always wears sunglasses except when he wants to unleash those eyes on a new victim.

His voice is deep, languid and as sensuous as a water-snake. He wears musk-based aftershave.

Brigit O'Brien

Brigit was born on 12 August 1977 making her a 34 Leo on Crystal Day. She was the only child of Declan MacMaster, a wealthy landowner and farmer in Wicklow, south of Dublin. He was a weak personality and the family was dominated by Kathleen, his wife.

Brigit was educated in a private school, had a large garden and her own horses, and was an only child. She was rather isolated from other children during her childhood but was deeply attached to her mother.

Brigit matured into a beautiful young woman and her mother Kathleen felt threatened and jealous. She began to shut her daughter out of her life, taking more interest in social activities and spending less time with her precocious offspring. Brigit felt abandoned and rejected, and tried to put on an act to become the person her mother would admire and love, but without success.

Brigit went to Trinity College, Dublin to study media and politics in October 1996. While at Trinity she began to work as a volunteer in RTE, the Irish national broadcaster, and was soon offered a job as a trainee.

During the first term at Trinity, she had a short torrid affair with a physics lecturer, Dr John O'Brien who was 28 at the time. Unluckily she fell pregnant and her father forced John to marry her, threatening to have him sacked if he did not.

Brigit had never wanted children, but when she found she was pregnant she had hoped for a boy, so a female child for her was worst possible outcome. She was never close to her daughter, almost exactly repeating the bad relationship she had had with her own mother.

Brigit's primary concern is to present a successful image. She cares deeply about her appearance. She uses her clothes, hairstyle, movements and her voice to exhibit her desirability and importance. She is a great actor and performer, able to charm any man to get what she wants.

She is driven by ambition and sexual desire, which for her is a way of gaining power and attention. She is especially drawn to men whom other women find attractive. Her laughter and exuberant behaviour make her the focus of almost any group, especially when there are men whom she can attract.

When she found herself saddled with John O'Brien, a man of mediocre attraction and low sexual libido, she began to search for other lovers who will satisfy her desires.

Brigit O'Brien

She is not tall but gives the appearance of being taller by wearing high heels and growing her blonde hair long. She wears it piled up on top of her head in curls and cascading around her shoulders in torrents. She loves wearing reds, vermillion, maroon, lime green, any pure vibrant colour that will make her stand out. She spends a fortune on clothes and shoes.

She likes to drink and fights to keep her weight down. She has a good figure which she delights in showing off to its best advantage, with large breasts (of which she is very proud), a narrow waist, smallish buttocks and fairly slim legs.

Catriona O'Brien

Catriona was born in her parent's home on Sunday 11 November 1997 making her a 14 year old Scorpio on Crystal Day. Her father was John O'Brien, a young lecturer at Trinity College, Dublin, where her mother Brigit was a student. After the birth, Brigit took the rest of the year off, living mostly with her parents. She returned to Trinity the following year, taking Catriona with her but leaving her with child minders most days, paid for by her rich father.

Catriona grew up very isolated and lonely. Her mother gave her very little attention or affection, obviously resenting the year that she had already 'wasted' on Catriona. Catriona's father was also a distant figure, intellectual and busy with his research, but he tried his best to give her the love he knew she needed. She felt closer to him than anyone else.

It was a total shock to Catriona when her father left home in the summer of 2005. This followed months of arguments between her parents over who should look after Catriona. Brigit was by now a busy TV personality and John was deeply involved in a research project which often required him to visit CERN.

Trying to bring her father back into the family, Catriona took the family dog Trackaway and walked to his laboratory on her eighth birthday. While waiting for him to come out of the laboratory she witnessed a frightening and incomprehensible sequence of events which led to his murder. From that moment her life was devastated. She felt guilty that she had been unable to prevent his death.

As a result of her father's death and her mother's cold and unsympathetic response, Catriona's relationship with her teacher, Sam Fitzpatrick, deepened and Sam began to visit the family home, eventually marrying Brigit. He transformed Catriona's life, giving her the love and stability she had so far lacked.

Her strongest characteristic is her sense of insecurity. She is always looking for something, always hoping to find something or somebody that will give her a solid rock upon which she can build her life. She feels like she lives on quicksand, always threatened with going under. Her love for Trackaway, the family St Bernard dog, was a manifestation of this search for security.

When she learns that her mother, who is now the Irish Ambassador to the United Nations in Geneva, has been invited to CERN, she persuades Sam that it would be a good idea to visit her for the Easter holiday. She knows her father used to work there much of the time, and is hoping that she can solve the mystery surrounding his sudden death.

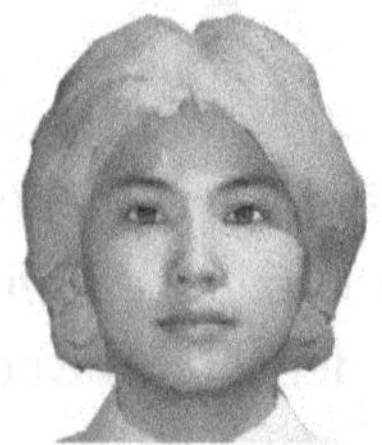

When she goes to Geneva, she is a petite fourteen, wiry, tough yet gentle. She is pretty with emerald green eyes, a neat, snub nose, full lips and medium-length ginger hair which is typically wild and ungovernable. She loves the colour green, and many of her clothes reflect this. Her figure is underdeveloped for her age and she has the smallest breasts of any girl in her class, something of which she is acutely conscious.

Danny Schneider

Danny Schneider was born in Graz, Austria, on 4 November 1976, making him a 35 year old Scorpio on Crystal Day. His father was a Bulgarian immigrant who worked in a menial position in a car factory, preferring to spend his time drinking rather than use his intelligence to get a better job. Danny's mother was loving but passive and was subject to physical abuse by her husband.

Danny had an extremely unstable childhood. His father was cruel and abusive, especially when drunk. He sometimes beat Danny with a stick. Danny was more intelligent than both his parents and felt he did not really belong to them. He soon took on the task of making things better. He wanted to fight his father and take care of his mother, but was too weak to do either.

In a reaction against his father's abuse, Danny became committed always to doing the 'right thing'. Laws and rules dominated his thinking. He loved maths and science because they were logical and based on clear rules. He did well at school.

Danny went to Heidelberg University in Germany and studied engineering, then began to work within the physics department of the university as a technician, finally moving to CERN.

On Crystal Day he is the shift leader who restarts the ATLAS detector after the winter shut-down.

Danny is a control freak. He always wants to control or repress his anger and instinctual energy, terrified lest he act like his father, but his anger is very easily roused.

He directs all this emotional energy into his work, often working 80 hours a week. He believes he is motivated by a desire to do what is right for the world, to help to make the world a better place.

Danny Schneider

IIe almost always wears the same green jacket no matter what the weather. His face is usually ashen grey as it sees very little of the Sun. He sweats a great deal, his palms feel sticky when you shake his hand. When he is angry the tip of his nose turns white. His hair is mousy brown, thin and dull.

Danny married Marianne after she became pregnant in the late summer of 2011. She had not been working in CERN very long and her tempestuous affair with Alex Karolyi had just finished. She started going out with Danny on the rebound. They married in February 2012.

Francesco Romani

Francesco Romani was born in Milan on 28 August 1960 making him a 51 year old Leo on Crystal Day. His father was a professor of chemistry at the University of Milan and his mother was a lecturer in history.

Francesco was raised to study, surrounded by the intellectual elite of Milan. He was always overweight from the prolonged dinner parties his parents gave; he was never going to be an athlete or football player. Nevertheless he was very popular at school and never happier than when he was organising an activity for a group of his friends.

He progressed naturally into the academic world, first studying chemistry but soon moving to physics, which he felt gave him the deepest possible understanding of the world.

He served in the Italian army as a conscript from age 19-21 which gave him experience of and a taste for leadership.

After his PhD, he quickly rose to the top of the Italian Institute for the Physics of Matter and moved abroad, spending time in France and the USA before being offered the Directorship of CERN, one of the most prestigious and important jobs in all physics.

One of the reasons he has been so successful is the strength and subtlety of his personality. He is utterly charming and able to make friends with anybody, being extremely sociable and jovial, especially over dinner. But at the same time he has an extremely clear vision of what he wants to achieve from relationships and knows exactly how to get there.

He has steered CERN safely through some dangerous waters during the past four years, when funding was tight and the LHC project was going through some difficult times.

Francesco Romani

Clinically he would be described as "obese". He wears expensive Italian suits cut to make him look slim, a task which is not always achieved. He has a head of thick dark hair, dyed to hide the streaks of grey, a full Roman nose, a broad smile and heavy features. His hands are large and the fat makes his handshake soft and squishy.

George Gabor

Named in accordance with Hungarian tradition, where the given name comes after the family name, Gabor György was born in Budapest on 15 December 1968, making him a Sagittarian. He is 43 on Crystal Day.

His father was Gabor Ignác, the origin of whose given name is obscure but is perhaps related to ignis meaning "fire". Ignác was a staunch Communist, one of the few in Hungary when George was young. He was fiercely opposed to the economic reforms being introduced by the government, and therefore gave his new son very little attention. Ignác killed himself while preparing a home-made bomb when George was four.

George's mother was a factory worker who worked hard to raise her seven children, having little time for George.

He could see that his father wanted to create a world that was fair to all people, including the poor, and the young George agreed with this, but he did not think that Communism was the answer. To him it seemed that reform was required. George also saw that protesting against reform was not only absorbing his father's time and energy but stopping him from advancing and helping his family.

George turned away from politics and decided he wanted to help people in some direct, practical way.

George was conscripted into the Hungarian army for three years and found he enjoyed the discipline and camaraderie but didn't like the idea of killing people. When he came out he joined the Budapest Fire Department and quickly rose through the ranks to be the Chief of a small station. He had two children in early 1990.

In 2009, seven of his men were killed in a huge fire in Budapest. At the time, George's marriage was also going through a difficult period and, blaming himself for the loss of life, he suffering a mild mental breakdown.

His children had left home, so to escape from the guilt, he volunteered to work in CERN, where he has been ever since.

While working in CERN, his main aim in life is to help others, both through his work as a firefighter and as a volunteer mountain rescue worker. He nurtures and nourishes his crew, and is widely acknowledged as a superb team leader. However, following his experience in Budapest, he has no wish to progress up the career structure in CERN, even though he has the ability.

George is a huge man, over 190 cm (six feet three inches) tall, physically powerful and rugged. He is completely bald and he seldom smiles. His craggy face and white skin give his head the appearance of a weathered cliff.

Marianne Schneider

Marianne Peeters was born in Lille, France on 12 February 1988 making her a 24 year old Aquarian on Crystal Day. Her father was Belgian and her mother French. She has a sister 4 years younger.

She was raised as a Catholic, going to a private Catholic College in Lille, and both girls were sent to church regularly although they both stopped going when Marianne was ten.

As a child she did not easily identify with either her mother or father, feeling different from them and from her school-fellows. She felt there was something special about her, and turned to introspection to try to understand what it was. She therefore had very few friends.

The older she got, the more convinced she became that she was not like other girls. In fact she became sure that she was not. She went through periods of serious depression in her teens, contemplating suicide more than once, until she went to University and finally began to mix with people who, she felt, were more like herself. She realised that perhaps she was not unique, and developed some close and lasting friendships.

She studied French, English and art, then spent a period of unemployment until she stumbled across a job as a guide at CERN in 2011.

She had only been at CERN for a few weeks when Alex Karolyi asked her out for a date. She found him attractive, but she had heard of his reputation so she refused. However he was persistent and eventually he persuaded her to go to a nightclub with him. It was not long before she was sleeping with him and they saw a lot of each other during the summer of 2011.

It was towards the end of the summer that Danny asked her out. Danny was totally unappealing to her and she refused without a second thought, telling him she was going out with Alex. The next day he told her that Alex was going out with at least two other girls as well. When she challenged Alex about this he did not deny it.

Marianne finished the affair soon after, although she felt utterly distraught, and started going out with Danny. In a moment of drunken madness she slept with him and fell pregnant.

They were married in February 2012. The baby is due about four weeks after Crystal Day.

She is a dark, brooding, self-absorbed introvert. She longs to develop her creative, artistic side and dreams of writing poetry or acting or singing, but never does anything about it. This failure makes her feel ashamed of neglecting her own talents.

Marianne Schneider

She is widely regarded as one of the most beautiful girls in CERN, although she has no idea why. She has long dark hair, dark eyes which can sparkle with life when she is amused and smoulder with inner passion when she is frustrated. She often dresses in dark clothes and there is an aura of mystery about her which frightens some people.

Michael Zhang

Michael Hamilton Zhang was born in Dublin on 3 January 1984 making him a 28 year-old Sagittarian on Crystal Day. His Chinese parents had moved from Hong Kong the year before when they realised that the British Colony would soon return to Chinese ownership. They passed through Britain and moved to Ireland to open a Chinese takeaway restaurant.

Michael's origins made him feel different from other children in Ireland and he was considerably more intelligent than any of the others around him. He began to search for his own understanding of the world and soon settled on science, and in particular on particle physics, to provide the knowledge he sought. But he was also intensely interested in his Chinese origins and studied as much as he could. He had few friends and none of them were close.

His adolescence was dominated by academic study. When he was 18, he had a single attempt at intercourse with a fellow student at Trinity College, Dublin. When that failed, he was too afraid to try again, considering himself impotent and he became convinced that he is not interested in girls. He gradually withdrew from society and became almost a monk, devoted to the worship of science.

After he achieved a brilliant joint first-class honours degree in physics and maths and Trinity he moved to the Dublin Institute of Advanced Studies (the youngest person ever to work there) and began his PhD under the leadership of John O'Brien. He moved to CERN in 2010.

He is driven by the hunger for knowledge. It is an obsession with him. He wants to prove that Chinese brains are better than Irish brains, with the possible exception of 19th century Irish mathematician William Rowan Hamilton, after whom he was named. He is convinced that he is going to discover something Earth-shattering soon and be recognised as a genius. He will stop at nothing to achieve this. It is the complete focus of his life.

Michael Zhang

He takes absolutely no care of his physical appearance. He wears the same stained pink T-shirt and blue jeans for weeks on end and seldom takes a bath, but since he does not sweat much this is not noticable. He lives alone in a caravan in a wood near CERN, from where he cycles to work early every morning.

Sam Fitzpatrick

Sam was born on 7 July 1959 near Cork, Ireland, under the sign of Cancer, making him 52 years old on Crystal Day. It was a rural, Catholic family. His father James was a low-paid farm labourer. His mother suffered from depression. Sam was her second child. She had six more children after him.

Sam's father had no time for the family and his mother was often totally withdrawn and left the family to get on as best it could. In his attempts to win the love of his father, Sam took on the role of mother of the household, looking after his younger brothers and sisters. But the harder he tried, the more his father seemed to hate him, and the harder Sam worked to show he was good.

His childhood experience led him into teaching. He loved primary school, loved helping the teacher. On his first day, he resolved teaching was what he would do when he grew up. This resolve grew when he found, aged about five, that boys cannot give birth to babies, which had seemed to him the only thing in life worth doing. So instead he resolved to nurture children in school.

As a young teacher, Sam caught mumps from one of his pupils and this developed into orchitis accompanied by high fever, severe pain, and swelling of both testes, nausea, vomiting, and abdominal pain. Fever and gonadal swelling stopped in a week but tenderness persisted for months.

He was told by a consultant he could never have children. He decided at that moment he would never marry, since it would not be fair on any woman. His commitment to teaching became total.

Sam's childhood had a profound effect upon him. As an adult he always tries to win the love of everyone he meets by being kind to them. Yet winning their love is only part of his ambition. He really loves being able to control people without their realising it.

Sam Fitzpatrick

Sam is a balding, middle-aged man who tries to always look smart in order to set his pupils a good example. He is short-sighted and usually wears glasses.

Sam was Catriona's teacher when she witnessed her father's strange death on her eighth birthday. When she returned to school he knew she was not ready and drove her home to talk to her mother after school. Brigit realised he cared for her daughter and recognised an opportunity to have somebody who would look after the child she did not care for. He was flattered by Brigit's attention and longed for a child of his own. Consequently he married Brigit, whom he loved emotionally but without physical passion, so that he could be near to Catriona.

Glossary

ATLAS

ATLAS (A Toroidal LHC Apparatus) is one of seven detectors receiving high-energy particles from the LHC (Large Hadron Collider) in CERN, Geneva.

ATLAS image copyright CERN

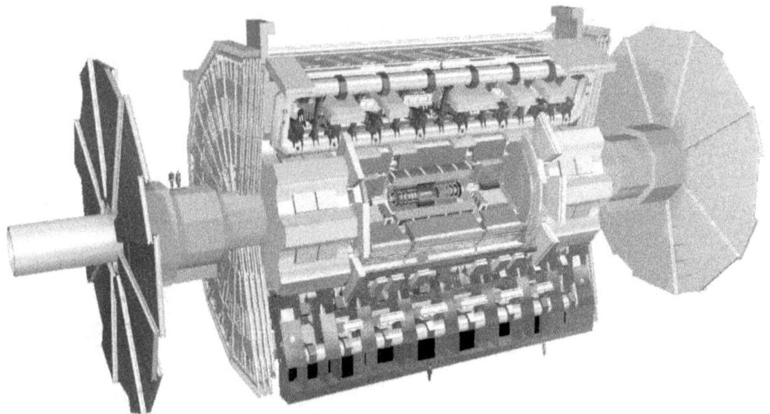

ATLAS is shaped like a barrel lying on its side in a cavern about 100 metres below the ground in the main CERN site near Meyrin, Geneva. It is the size of a cathedral, about 46 metres long and 25 metres in diameter, and in total weighs about 7,000 tonnes. Its scale can be judged by the two tiny people on the left of the diagram, and two more at the bottom.

Note the two circular discs shown at each end of the diagram, and two more attached to the ends of the detector; these are the so-called "Big Wheels" which are referred to in the story. Also note that this diagram is cut-away to reveal the inside of ATLAS; in reality these are not visible from the outside.

About 3,000 physicists from over 175 institutions in 38 countries are involved with experiments using ATLAS. It was one of the two experiments which discovered the Higgs boson in July 2012 (see bibliography entry (1)).

The main ATLAS website is given in the bibliography entry (2). The main parts of the detector, some of which are mentioned in the "Into ATLAS" chapter of Michael Zhang's Diary, are described in links found on the web page shown in the bibliography entry (3).

CERN

CERN (the European Organisation for Nuclear Research) is an international collaboration of scientists and engineers seeking to understand the fundamental nature of matter. One way it does this is by using the world's largest accelerator (the Large Hadron Collider or LHC) to create beams of high-energy particles travelling at close to the speed of light. These particles are then collided together and gigantic detectors (such as ATLAS) are used to examine the results.

According to the convention which founded CERN just after the Second World War, its purpose is to conduct "nuclear research of a pure scientific and fundamental character... the Organization shall have no concern with work for military requirements."

About 11000 scientists from 645 universities around the world use CERN's facilities. In addition, CERN employs about 2500 physicists, engineers, programmers, technicians, craftsmen, firefighters and administrators.

Many technologies have been developed at CERN including the World Wide Web, cancer therapy, medical and industrial imaging, radiation processing, electronics, measuring instruments, new manufacturing processes and materials.

When it was founded in 1952, its name was originally "Conseil Européen pour la Recherche Nucléaire". It soon changed "Conseil" to "Organisation", but retained the acronym CERN because it was easy to pronounce.

Map of CERN's Meyrin Site. Copyright Open Street Maps

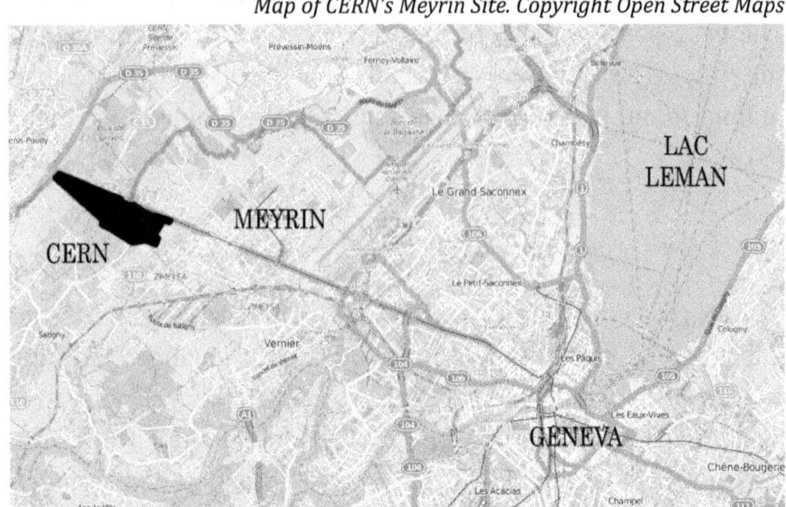

The main site (outlined on the left of this map) spans the border between France and Switzerland. It lies close to the Swiss commune Meyrin and the city of Geneva.

For more information about CERN, see the link in the bibliography item (4).

Cosmic Egg

The expression "Cosmic Egg" was first used on Earth by people thousands of years ago, who imagined that the Earth, and everything it contains, hatched from some sort of primeval egg.

In 1927, the Belgian physicist and catholic priest Georges Lemaitre suggested that the universe originated from what he called the "primeval atom" and that it expanded rapidly to form the universe we know today. He was thus the first person to propose both the Big Bang theory and the expansion of the universe.

On **Entroilia**, cosmic eggs are part of the life-cycle of both Entroilians and Argolaths. Entroilians call them all "cosmic eggs", but reserve the name "The Cosmic Egg" for the egg from which Sam and Michael emerged. Some information about how they work is contained in the "Cosmic Egg" chapters of Michael Zhang's Diary.

Cosmic Monopole

In the world around us, we always find magnetic poles in pairs: north and south. The Earth, for example, has two poles, and so does every fridge magnet.

On the other hand, a "magnetic monopole", such as that featured in this history, is a particle which carries just one magnetic pole.

Their existence was first suggested on theoretical grounds by Paul Dirac. See entry (5) in the bibliography for details of his original paper and entry (6) for a link to download a PDF of that paper, in which Dirac showed that, if at least one monopole exists somewhere in the universe, then he could explain why particles such as electrons have a fixed amount of electric charge.

Until **Crystal Day**, there was no evidence that any monopoles existed. Dirac had not *proved* their existence, but his theory *strongly suggested* that at least one might. To quote Dirac:

[T]he present formalism of quantum mechanics...leads inevitably to wave equations whose only physical interpretation is the motion of an electron in the field of a [magnetic] pole...[O]ne would be surprised if Nature had made no use of it.

However before Crystal Day, despite many searches, no evidence had ever been found for their existence. Dirac postulated the reason could be that:

[T]he attractive force between two [monopoles] of opposite sign is...4692.25 times that between electron and

proton. This very large force may perhaps account for why poles of opposite sign have never yet been separated.

A "cosmic monopole" is a magnetic monopole which is found outside the Earth. But all that changed on Crystal Day when a cosmic monopole was trapped by the magnetic field of **ATLAS**. It is interesting to note that, up that date, no scientist had ever assessed the risks, the feasibility or the possible consequences of such an event. You cannot blame them. The existence of monopoles had not even been established, and they took all reasonable precautions to assess the safety of their experiments, and published reviews of their assessments. You can find links to these reviews on the web pages cited in bibliography entries (7) and (8).

Nevertheless, on 5 April, 2012, a cosmic monopole was indeed trapped inside the **LHC** beam pipe where it began to absorb particles from the beams and was transformed into a black hole. The rest, as somebody might have said, is this history.

Crystal Day

The events described in this narrative began at 11:22:50 on April 5, 2012, the day which would later become known by the survivors either as "Crystal Day" or "Disaster Day".

Because time had stopped, the rest of the Earth continued at this date and time until the moment when time was restarted. How, when and why this happened will be recounted in this history.

Small Time Crystal and Bubble

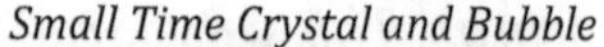

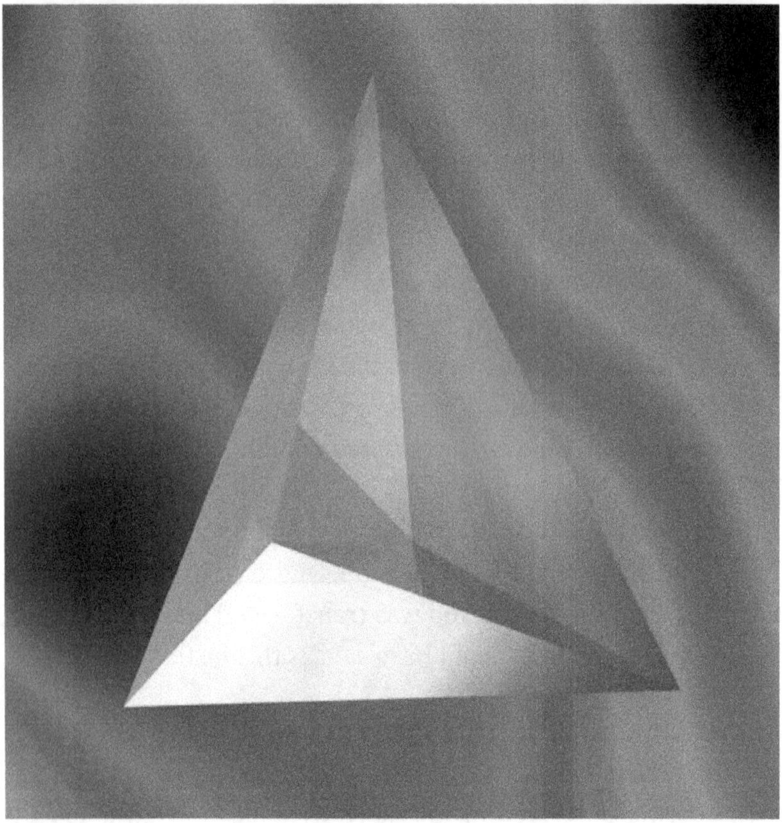

However, even after time stopped in the universe, time continued in small spheres surrounding fragments of blue crystals, Time Crystals, from which this narrative derives its name.

Entroilia

Until **Crystal Day**, nobody had any idea what existed outside the universe, or even if the expression "outside the universe" had any meaning. The problem was that scientists did not understand how or why the universe had been created. This was perhaps the greatest mystery facing mankind, and it was in the hope of finding some clues to resolve it that the **LHC** and **ATLAS** were constructed.

The mystery was indeed resolved, but in a totally unexpected and disturbing fashion, as related in this narrative.

It turns out that this universe is only one of many. Before Crystal Day, there had been several serious scientific theories which supported this idea, often called the "multiverse" hypothesis. But no scientist had ever suggested (nor would ever dream of suggesting) that our universe was part of the life cycle of extra-universal beings, which is the astounding discovery made on Crystal Day. See **Cosmic Egg** above for more on this subject.

Large Hadron Collider

Map of LHC copyright Open Street Map

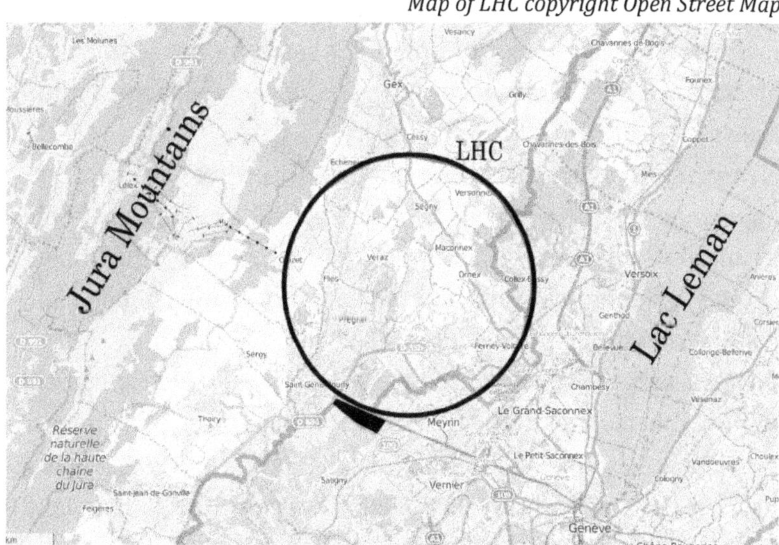

The Large Hadron Collider (LHC) is currently the world's largest and most powerful particle accelerator. It is the main accelerator at **CERN**, and consists of an underground circular tunnel 27 kilometres long (marked on the map) stretching from Geneva airport to the foothills of the Jura Mountains. It contains superconducting magnets, cooling systems and other infrastructure surrounding two beam pipes. These receive particles from a chain of lower-energy accelerators within CERN (shown as a black area at the bottom of the LHC).

The particles' energy is boosted by accelerating structures until they are travelling at near the speed of light. They travel in opposite directions around each of the beam pipes.

They are then forced to collide inside underground detectors, one of which is ATLAS. For more information about the LHC see entry (9) in the bibliography.

Quench

Within **ATLAS** (and many other pieces of scientific equipment in CERN and around the world) there is a need for very strong magnetic fields. These can only be created by using very large electric currents. Normal copper wires have resistance, limiting the amount of current they can carry.

To make the current strong enough, the wires which carry it have to be very cold. This is achieved by using helium gas cooled to almost absolute zero temperature. If part of the magnet should accidentally heat up for any reason, it stops being a good conductor. This is called a quench.

The resistance of the wires which carry the electric currents within the magnet increases with temperature. This releases more heat, so increasing the resistance even more. A runaway process begins. If left uncontrolled, a huge amount of heat could be released which would seriously damage the detector, costing millions of Swiss Francs to repair. This is what happened on 19 September 2008, the day when a quench in the magnets of the **Large Hadron Collider** led to an explosive release of helium, causing huge damage which took over a year to repair.

To avoid this, when a quench occurs, the electricity is automatically diverted away from the delicate equipment into special electrical circuits which absorb the energy by heating up lumps of metal called "quench heaters". Sadly, there was a faulty connection between two of the LHC magnets, as described in Bibliography entry (10).

Layout of Point 1, CERN

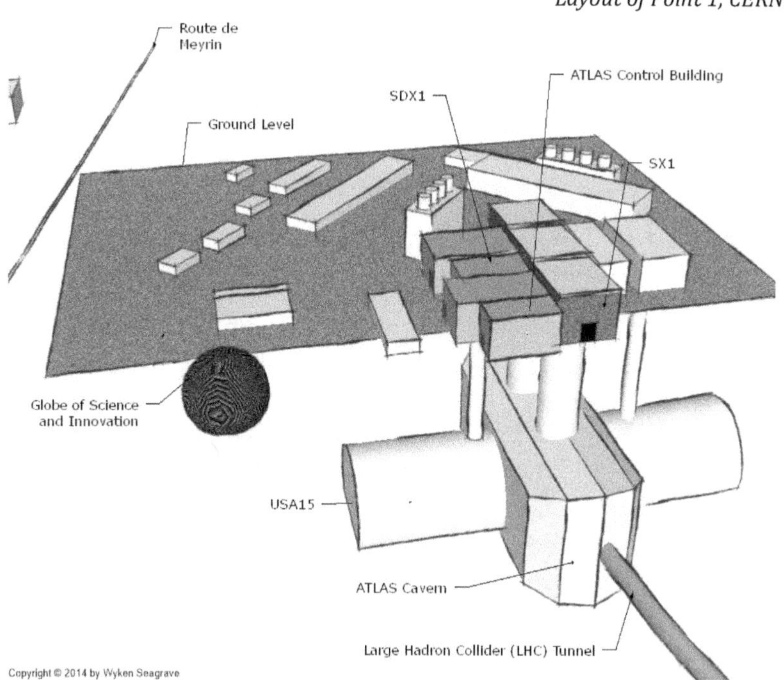

Copyright © 2014 by Wyken Seagrave

Episode 6 of this history describes how the black hole which had formed around the **Cosmic Monopole** burned its way out of ATLAS and causing a quench. The Monopole grew as it went, causing increasing amounts of damage until it led to a helium leak.

Initially much of this helium evaporated, then began to accumulate on the floor of the ATLAS cavern. Eventually it rose to the level of the quench resistor which was hot from absorbing the energy of the quench. The liquid helium was then rapidly heated and this led to the massive explosion which rose up the shaft above it and blew off part of the roof of the SX1 building. The roof landed on the lift tower in the SDX1 building, causing it to collapse, so trapping underground those people in the USA15 cavern.

Bibliography

References within this book to items in this bibliography are shown thus: (3)

1. **CERN.** Higgs Boson discovery at CERN. [Online] http://home.web.cern.ch/topics/higgs-boson.

2. **ATLAS Experiment.** ATLAS Home Page. *ATLAS Experiment Website.* [Online] http://www.atlas.ch/.

3. **ATLAS Experiment.** Major components of ATLAS. *ATLAS Experiment.* [Online] http://www.atlas.ch/detector.html.

4. **CERN .** CERN Home Page. [Online] http://home.web.cern.ch/.

5. **Dirac, Paul Adrien Maurice.** Quantised Singularities in the Electromagnetic Field. *Proceedings of the Royal Society Series A.* 1 September 1931, pp. 60-72.

6. **Dirac, P.A.M.** Download PDF of Quantised Singularities in the Electromagnetic Field. [Online] http://timecrystal.co.uk/pdf/QuantisedSingularities.pdf.

7. **CERN Press Office.** The safety of the LHC. *CERN Press Office.* [Online] http://press.web.cern.ch/backgrounders/safety-lhc.

8. **Ellis, John , et al., et al.** *Review of the Safety of LHC Collisions.* Geneva : CERN, 2008.

9. **CERN.** Website for Large Hadron Collider. [Online] http://home.web.cern.ch/topics/large-hadron-collider.

10. **CERN Press Office.** CERN releases analysis of LHC incident. *CERN.* [Online] 16 October 2008. [Cited: 30 September 2015.] http://bit.ly/1O7sNO3.

11. **Seagrave, Wyken.** Radiation Levels in Time Bubbles. [Online] Penny Press Ltd, 5 9 2015. http://timecrystal.co.uk/?p=445.

Now Read On!

Thank you for reading The Cosmic Monopole. I hope you want to follow Catriona and Sam as they travel through the entire history of the universe. The second volume in the series is
The Time Tunnel
  http://timetunnel.org.uk
Find out much more about the Time Crystal series at
  http://timecrystal.co.uk/

Please write a review

Let other readers (and me!) know what you thought about this book by writing a short review. You can find links to this and my other books at the following sites:
My page on Amazon
  http://amzn.to/1M7oBNF
My page on Goodreads
  http://bit.ly/1JVKuNm
My page on Shelfari
  http://bit.ly/1JVKGMJ

My Newsletter

Subscribe to my newsletter
  http://bit.ly/1r2KbXq

History of the Universe

  For my factual account of the history of the universe, visit www.historyoftheuniverse.com

Wyken Seagrave

www.wykenseagrave.co.uk

www.ingramcontent.com/pod-product-compliance
Lightning Source LLC
Chambersburg PA
CBHW051005180726

48291CB00006B/1978